THE FOOT
ON THE CROWN

THE FOOT ON THE CROWN

Christopher Fowler

bantam

TRANSWORLD PUBLISHERS
Penguin Random House, One Embassy Gardens,
8 Viaduct Gardens, London SW11 7BW
www.penguin.co.uk

Transworld is part of the Penguin Random House group of companies
whose addresses can be found at global.penguinrandomhouse.com

Penguin
Random House
UK

First published in Great Britain in 2024 by Bantam
an imprint of Transworld Publishers

A CIP catalogue record for this book
is available from the British Library.

ISBN 9781787637443

Typeset in 10/12pt Sabon LT Std by Jouve (UK), Milton Keynes
Printed and bound in Great Britain by Clays Ltd, Elcograf S.p.A.

The authorized representative in the EEA is Penguin Random House Ireland,
Morrison Chambers, 32 Nassau Street, Dublin D02 YH68.

For those I loved most, and who loved me.

Gemme of all joy, jasper of jocunditie,
Most myghty carbuncle of vertue and valour;
Strong Troy in vigour and in strenuytie;
Of royall cities rose and geraflour;
Empresse of townes, exalt in honour;
In beawtie beryng the crone imperiall;
Swete paradise precelling in pleasure;
London, thou art the floure of Cities all!

– William Dunbar

Gentle Reader,

The bridges into Londinium were constructed so far back in prehistory that by the time Julius Caesar arrived on these shores they were ancient ruins. When the Romans left, cold and miserable, their flourishing settlement ceased to thrive. Londinium filled with ghosts and faded from sight.

The Dark Ages lasted for five hundred years. Nobody knows what happened during those lost centuries. Few written documents have ever been found. Perhaps other dynasties rose and fell, other monarchs ruled and other wars were fought before the Norman invasion. Even if we know nothing of them now, they left their marks on the way we live today.

Which of history's memories are true, and which are false? We may be certain of only one thing: that almost everything we know about the past is wrong.

– Rev. Charles L. Chancery, 1856

PART ONE:
History

1

The Boy and the Cow

The target is sighted.
Breath fills the chest.
The bowstring creaks.
The smooth wood slides.
The tension increases.
A moment of silence.
A soft outward breath.
And a release.
The arrow arcs, its aim true.

Archery was cancelled because Watborn had accidentally shot the cow.

His father was furious. The arrow had only sunk two inches into her flank but she was far from happy and Ivor was sure that her milk would be soured.

The cow was everything.

Without her milk the family would starve because nothing grew on their allocated land. It was just two poles long and was so badly waterlogged that only frogs lived on it.

The cow grunted but seemed unfazed. As blackflies settled and resettled on her withers, Ivor teased the arrow out of her rump and treated the cut with a sprig of goldenrod.

He refused to forgive his twelve-year-old son for such clumsiness. In the golden evening the shamed boy led the cow home and tethered her, and worked at his chores until the sun became a crimson sliver and his father returned.

As Watborn loaded a trug with kindling, the yellow-eyed girl watched him.

He knew she was looking at him. She was a strange one. She was nameless, and lived alone at the end of the village, talking to herself in the dusk-light.

She secretly watched him from morning to night, careful to keep her distance, especially if Watborn's parents were near by. It was as if she was bewitched by him. If he touched a tree, she tore off a twig and kept it safe. If he caught a bird, she stole a feather. She collected pebbles and grasses from the spots where he had sat, and wove them into necklaces. Sometimes she arranged the little totems he had touched in circles and triangles, and sang strange, high-noted songs over them.

When Ivor taught his son to fish in the brook that flowed beyond the last house in Breornsey, the girl was waiting. She hid herself behind a hawthorn bush and watched Watborn's every action intently, never moving. The boy pretended he could not see her. He tolerated her presence because she was touched and needed no more troubles, but he was angry that this witch-child should intrude upon their peace.

One afternoon she leaped out of her hiding place and tried to take a minnow from his hands. Shocked, he pushed her aside and she fell into the stream. After that she kept her distance.

When the elders met to allocate provisions to the village families, she appeared in the doorway and shrieked at them, warning all that she had cursed Watborn's family cow so that anyone drinking from it would endure blackening of the extremities and quickly die.

Soon Watborn's parents found that they could sell no milk, and their household began to suffer greatly.

The girl watched from the hedgerows and took pleasure in their plight. She was not mad, as some thought, but angry and desperate for a change in her circumstances.

A few nights later there was a tremendous, earth-shaking thunderstorm that set fire to a rowan. It was taken as a sign that the cow had been cured, so everyone happily bought her milk again and the balance of life briefly returned. Watborn studied the witch-girl through the trees and relished her defeat.

The village of Breornsey was not much. Thirteen mildewed

houses, a defunct pagan chapel and a stone hall constructed around a crossroads. Once it had been larger but the Kingsmen had managed to reduce the population through thoughtlessness. Breornsey traded in skins and ironware and, when times were good, in a particular type of blue glass jar. But when battles were fought, charters were signed and matters of historical importance took place, they always happened somewhere else. Despite this, the village was a thorn lodged deep in Watborn's heart that could never be removed.

One morning he was sitting in a patulous pear tree trying to catch a tiny chirruping blue-wing when four Kingsmen rode into the village dressed in crimson and silver. They came once a month to bargain for sheep and wildfowl, but this time they left with just a few sickly ducks and the witch-girl, who ran beside their horses and persuaded them to take her away from Breornsey. One of the men swung her up and on to his saddle and then they were gone.

Several moons passed and she failed to return, so her mother went to the crossroads, knelt down and cut her own throat.

Watborn knew there were things afoot that were beyond his understanding, but he did not care to explore them. Life was a mystery he had no time to unravel. He barely had time for his learning after the daily chores were done.

His best friend, Finmoor, was always there to warn him. 'The less you know, the safer you'll be,' he cautioned. 'Don't ask questions. Just keep your head down and get on with your work.'

When the four riders returned, they did not head for the village hall to bargain for livestock. Instead they cantered through each of the fields in turn, checking the barns. They said good morning and politely asked to enter, but were clearly looking for something.

When they reached the Watborn cowshed, they disappeared inside and quietly closed the door behind them. Watborn waited outside with his father until, twenty minutes later, the men reappeared with a mackerel-skin bag. One of them counted out several silver pieces and pressed them into Ivor's hand without saying a word.

A creeping coldness passed over Watborn as he walked towards the shed. His father called him back but he would not be stopped. In the dimness of shit and straw he could see the hulk of the cow's steaming body lying on its side. Her heart had been cut out, leaving a gaping hole beneath her sawn-through ribs.

Watborn ran outside and looked for the riders, but they had

already gone. On the furthest ridge of land, where the horizon became blue and hazy, the castle-city waited for them all. In the terrible months that followed, Watborn could only look upon it with rage in his soul.

The boy could not comprehend why his father had allowed the Kingsmen to slaughter their cow in return for a few silver coins, but he had misunderstood what had passed between them. Ivor had no idea why this strange and terrible thing had happened, and was just as surprised to be paid a recompense.

Life takes without giving and offers no answers. As the years fled by, Watborn survived to grow strong and reach manhood. He said nothing, and heard much. His head became filled with beliefs. That nothing was chance. That life had a plan. That the yellow-eyed girl had sealed all their fates when she somehow guided his arrow to the flank of their cow. There were days when he felt bewitched. He had strange visions, but could never quite recall them.

He became the finest birdcatcher in the Marshlands and spent his days inside cleverly constructed hides, waiting for unsuspecting creatures to strut into his traps.

Is Watborn to be the hero of this tapestry? Perhaps not in the traditional sense, for we'll often find him off to one side of history's terrible events. Yet without him, none of this could ever have occurred.

2

The Family Tree

Giniva clutched her golden heart as she ran.

On the spiral staircase to the East Tower there were brass scorpions whose tails tugged at her gown, snagging the sapphire hem and snatching her back. Finally she was forced to run with the material gathered at her knees, and run she did because she had committed the crime of being late for dinner.

She knew every corridor, staircase, turret and spandrel in her vicinity. They all conspired against her. The corridors were lined with the body parts of enemies. Their heads had been threaded with gold and silver wire and hung in blue glass jars full of pickling vinegar.

Far below, on the bitter stone landings where the commoners worked and lived, life was austere and windswept. Freezing in winter, goosepimpling in summer. Autumn was arriving, soon brown, then grey, the time when all the beetles fell out of the roof timbers, dead. The time of the Princess's age-coming, the testing of her courage.

Giniva knew no other home than this. She dreamed of living in a great open space free from clutter and dust, mildew and gloom, where nothing was more than a few decades old and she could breathe without drawing the dirt of ages into her lungs. She imagined stretching out her arms to bathe in warm shafts of sunlight. But there was no escape from her home, her heritage, her albatross.

She tripped on the bottom step and nearly overturned one of the immense amphoras that stood on blood-red pedestals beside the staircase. Catching sight of herself in a scabrous mirror, she readjusted the violet clematis petals in her hair. She liked clematis flowers because they had no smell. Her home held too many odours:

herb-soap, stagnant pools, cold stone, damp latrines, warm meat, hot iron, burnt flesh.

'I will show fortitude,' she called loudly to no one. 'I am about to come of age. I will no longer need to obey.'

Ahead was the passage that led to the Seven Sepulchres of Shame, lined with the dessicated corpses of disgraced horses. Giniva darted past the strange chapel known as the Heart of All Counted Sorrows, where no woman, not even the Queen, was allowed to set foot for fear of spreading impurity. The men were squeamish about females. Not understanding them, they cast their eyes aside and angrily pointed at rules.

As she crossed the servants' corridor, heading in the direction of the Tainted Hall, a slender figure stopped before her. Leperdandy pulled a lilac silk handkerchief from his purple quilted jacket and flicked it under his quivering nostrils, enveloping them both in the scent of bitter lavender.

'You're as late as I for dinner,' he sniffed. 'Father went in before the sun sank. There is to be an announcement of great importance. The Great Wound will be most displeased.'

She fell into step beside her brother. 'Have you ever seen him pleased about anything?'

'Not since they burned all the ginger cats,' said Leperdandy. 'Let's not go down that passageway. The air is too cold. I'm sure it gives me wrinkles, and I pride myself on looking lovelier than you.'

As they crossed the flooded stones the damp air clung to their clothes. Shadows drifted across the gargoyle-filled sepulchres which had given Giniva such nightmares as a child. Opening the great studded iron doors of the hall where the family took its meals, one of the servants tugged a chain that rang a distant bell, a warning to the kitchen staff to be on their toes.

The great table, arranged in cruciform and draped in holly-green linen, was occupied along its far side. The waiting diners swivelled their eyes disapprovingly to the latecomers.

Timekeeping was a family obsession. The monstrosity set in the wall above them had a finely painted face depicting the Devouring of St Bartholomew by Crows Driven Insane by the Sound of Bells. It was a unique and ancient timepiece, one of many ancient water-clocks, sundials, hourglasses and clepsydras, none of which worked properly.

The family members seldom spoke over dinner. All that could be heard was the steady slurping of stew and the clonking of the clock's movement, which sounded like pebbles being dropped into a tin funnel.

'Is it too much to ask that we might share a meal together on the eve of your age-coming?'

The King's good eye glared wetly beneath a bushy brow. He jutted from the table, an emerald cloth splayed at his throat. His fire-hued hair was shaved up to his ears and swept over so that it still fell to his broad shoulders. Now it was tinged with grey.

He was, by any account, the embodiment of a warrior-king. There was a ruined grandeur about him, even with globules of soup hanging in his densely forested beard. A dripping spoon poked out of his meaty fist. His vast shoulders rose and fell with the wheezing passage of his angry breath, like an old steam engine labouring up an incline.

King Archim Scarabold III, the Great Wound himself, doer of dark deeds, rectifier of wrongs, monarch, warrior, father to Giniva and Leperdandy, had watched the severed heads of his enemies bounce down the steps of the Imperial Museum during the Great Siege of '28 with less passion than he now displayed at the lateness of his offspring.

Only the Grandmater, his wizened mother, who took wars and weddings equally in her stride, did not seem to mind their delayed arrival. She never minded anything. Food drew her attention more than children.

Behind her head, on the wall above the dining table, was a vast parchment displaying the royal family tree. Half the names had been painted over and replaced, entire branches had been erased and new offshoots had been grafted on, so that it appeared less like a spreading oak and more like a diseased parasite.

Brother, sister, mother, son, next in succession, third in line – these titles were never entirely correct owing to the confusing system of royal governance that had developed over the last three centuries. For every rule there was an exception, printed down the side of the tree in a barely legible hand:

Only male heirs recognized **except** *for the eldest daughter of the eldest son.*

Princes to inherit **except** *when born under the Law of Damage.*

The King's wife to be his Queen **except** *when he takes a second spouse.*

There was rumoured to be a Fourth Exception, but no one had ever found it.

The family tree had dark roots. There were kings who might or might not have been related to the present monarch: Engelfrith, Aethelweard, Omblewig, Imar the Boneless and various other disastrous rulers. Then there were the black sheep, the ne'er-do-wells, the murderers, miscreants and defilers, the relatives-you-must-never-speak-of who had earned the right to representation even if it was only below ground.

Sometimes a branch became a root, and the family tree had to be pruned once more. No root ever returned to being a branch, for the tree was unforgiving. Fortunes went down, never up.

Nothing here was straightforward and no one could keep track of it all. It was said that in the entire kingdom there were just two people who knew how the royal bloodlines worked. One was the Decrepend, the chancellor and record-keeper, and the other was the ancient tutor Ambrosius.

The servants had their dinners at tables of one hundred each, and did not dine from the royal cold-stores. As for the commoners beyond the walls, little was known about them. Their taxes were not unduly extortionate, their children were not too frequently stolen, their tortures and executions were not too protracted, and the turbulent green river that passed around their land only occasionally washed their homes away. In this harsh world, it was enough.

'The mosaic courtyard is half flooded,' Giniva told her father. 'I had to go all the way around and through the under-chancery.' She had, in fact, spent too long at her toilette and failed to register the lateness of the hour.

'Do not lie to me, greenling,' warned Scarabold. 'We cannot put the matter off any longer.'

'Your father has something to tell you, Giniva,' called her mother, ignoring the steaming monarch at her side, 'just as soon as you are settled. You are to listen only, and obey.'

This, thought Giniva, *sounds ominous indeed.*

3

The Connubial Decision

Few were brave enough to withstand Mater Moribund's scorching gaze. She was a woman who knew how to hold the reins of power.

She was the keeper of secrets, the family's true source of strength. Usually she was stone-faced and regal but today she fidgeted, re-arranging the folds of her gown with impatience. Her skeletal form, so thin that her ribs could be counted through the violet bombazine of her gown, was bedecked with ropes of jewellery that glistered like the lights of river jetties. No item of clothing was ever donned without a purpose.

Her first name was Meldred, but no one had ever dared even to whisper it except the King when he was drunk. She frowned at the only other women allowed to dine at the head table.

'Come and sit near me, both of you,' said Lady Dwinoline with a kindly smile. She was Scarabold's demoted First Wife. She had been wed to the Great Wound first and discarded for being barren. Now she occupied an inferior role in the household, forgotten but not gone. Plump and lumpen and draped in various feathered shades of pheasant brown, Lady Dwinoline was resigned to the sidelines of the royal menagerie. She tended to the children (children! Giniva was hours from her sixteenth year and Leperdandy was barely a twelve-month older) and provided the maternal warmth they did not receive from Moribund.

Dwinoline looked along the table, smiling blandly at the sunken Aunt Asphyxia, who sulked behind her goblet, nodding to the bibulous Quaff so that he might commence the evening toast, even though he had already drained his own cup.

'O cruel, cruel gods, please hear the lowly call of this great family,' bellowed the Quaff, who had no faith in the power of prayer and planned to be heard through the expedient of shouting. 'We give most humble thanks . . .'

Humble, thought Giniva. *The word has long since been excised from the rulebooks. We have no faith. The chapels are defunct. The toast is given instead of grace, offered up to no one but ourselves.* She caught her brother's gaze and held it. Their aptitude for passing private messages was so finely honed that the merest twitch signified histories. They were, some felt, too close, as if their secretive alliance was a mark of family disloyalty.

They had grown up side by side behind the moss-green walls, hiding from their ranting, stamping father. They had rescued each other from the freezing grip of the moat's shattered crust and fought secret battles behind the dust-filled curtains of the crimson theatre in Leperdandy's apartment. Childhood confederates, they stood together on the cusp of adulthood.

The Decrepend prepared to deliver the blessing. He was so old and craggy that nobody could recall him as a young man. Dressed in a flame-coloured blouse and breeches, he resembled a meteorite with eyeballs. He droned on, his narcotic tone pitched just above the sound of falling rain. Somewhere near by, water began to drip into a tin bucket. Giniva noted with amusement that every seventh drip coincided with the clonk of the clock.

Scarabold's thick forefinger traced the ridges of the scar that bisected his face, the result of a sword blow that had granted him the title of the Great Wound. He well remembered his encounter on the Rushing River during the Battle of the Seven Hundred, when he had stood between his one-year-old daughter and the barbarian's blade, absorbing the blow which he thought would split his skull. Giniva knew nothing of her escape that night and would never know, for Scarabold had no desire to alarm her.

Beyond the windows of the Tainted Hall the sky was filled with green-grey bruises. Within, the family was safe and secure. Outside, the turmoil roiled around them, lightning bolts striking sheep dead. Not that Scarabold knew anything about his peasants. They were simply somewhere in the distant view, doing peasanty things. They provided horses and carried supplies from the old treaty port of Cedd, and took their furtive pleasures in the reed-beds, and were mostly either young and fit, or dead.

The Decrepend ended his prayers with a sudden thud, smiting

the table with a fist that drove home his message, making mortals jump. The soup was now crusted and curdled, and Mater Moribund snapped her fingers at the servants, who scurried to remove the bowls.

Scarabold seized the moment to address his daughter. The clearing of his throat was like someone shovelling coal.

'Giniva, the arrival of your sixteenth birthday demands the surrender of childish ways.'

'But I am still young!' She all but stamped her foot.

'Hardly,' said the King. 'In bygone times you would have been wed at twelve. It is my duty as your father to appoint a suitor. In short, it is time for your deforestation.'

'Your nuptials,' suggested the Mater.

Giniva stared furiously at Scarabold. She respected him as a warrior but considered him an odious beast as a relative. In her early years he had thundered about on his hands and knees, a bearded giant willing to let her ride him around the playroom. He would take her to the armoury and let her try to lift the axes. But as she grew, his attention withdrew. She studied his broad back hunched over maps in the strategy chamber, listened to the whispered schemes not meant for her ears, and knew she had lost him.

Lately she had also come to imagine him as Moribund's seducer. The thought of his agitated entrances into her mother's bedchamber had multiplied her distaste tenfold. She wished Dwinoline could have been her mother.

'I suppose I have no say in this matter.'

'Certainly not,' bellowed Scarabold. 'You have no knowledge of alliances and allegiances. You could not possibly know who is politically suited for connubial union. The decision has been made, the bargain struck. Your opinion counts little against the bounty of estate. Your suitor will shortly arrive to meet you privately in the Ceremony of Introduction.'

'What does that involve?' asked the Princess. 'How will he be assured of my suitability?'

'One would not buy a horse without first taking it for a canter,' said Scarabold. 'At the end of this time, he will decide your worth and we will discuss terms. If he rejects you, there can be only two further candidates.'

'And if I reject them all?'

'Let's not consider that possibility. Your mother will attend the preparations, and Dr Fangle will be on hand to confirm your maidenhood.'

'Dando,' hissed Giniva beneath her breath, 'you have to set me free from this disgusting humiliation. Fangle's bound to be drunk and I am to be left alone with some hideous old lecher who'll paw me and bargain me away for land. Who knows what might happen?'

'I thought we agreed you'd go through with it,' her brother whispered back. 'If he accepts you, you'll only have to stay with him long enough to provide a legitimate heir. That could be, oh, ten minutes or so. Perhaps not even that.'

'I know I said I'd do it, but I can't. It's a stupid, revolting law. All our laws are stupid and revolting. Most of them don't even make any sense.'

'You can't say that!' hissed Leperdandy.

'The women of the family have always had their suitors chosen for them,' snapped the Quaff, slopping his claret. 'After you're married it's just a matter of keeping your legs open and your eyes shut.'

Giniva felt sure that somewhere beyond the walls was another way of living, where clans were not knotted together like rat kings . . .

'Drifting! Drifting!' screamed Aunt Asphyxia in a voice that could scratch patterns on a windowpane. 'See, she barely attends to your words, the minx. While we wait to be reborn, she sits and counts the clouds instead of studying that.'

Here she pointed to the great painting of the family tree and touched on a truth: if Giniva failed to produce an heir, and very soon, there would be no one to replace the Great Wound when he passed. A gap would be created and, as everyone knew, when a wall was breached the barbarians came through. They were waiting below in the marshes with the taste of blood upon their lips.

'Surely you wish to know the identity of your future husband?' asked the Decrepend, not unkindly.

'I wish to know nothing!' cried Giniva, shoving herself back from the table and grabbing her brother's hand. Her chair tipped over and hit the flagstones with a crash. The sound jolted the Grandmater awake. She looked around for cake.

'Leperdandy,' the Princess instructed, 'come to my suite.'

The boy pushed himself awkwardly away from the table and joined her, grimacing apologetically to his parents. Dwinoline pouted in sympathy and returned to the embroidery she kept beneath the tablecloth.

'See she is ready at the appointed hour!' called Moribund, already losing interest. She twisted in her chair to berate the servants for the delay between courses. Behind her, the head cook bore a tureen of bloody meat and knobs of bone, his gore-streaked apron a testament to his labours. Asphyxia licked her fingers in anticipation.

Giniva ran. Leperdandy raised his knees in pursuit, the scarlet side-ribbons on his striped leggings flapping and snapping. 'Giniva, please wait, you know I can't run as fast as you! Not in these shoes!'

She flew ahead, vanishing around each stone corner with her sapphire gown rucked up around her knees. One corner then the next, silver bells tinkling, hem vanishing and reappearing. As she ran through the Vault of Echoes she yelled to hear her voice thrown back at her.

She will have to calm herself, her brother thought, *or accept sedation before she discovers the identity of her suitor. There are horrors ahead.* Abandoning the effort to keep up, he watched her fleeing figure fold into the misted gloom.

4

Londinium

Consider the world, thought Watborn, pulling a flea from his armpit as he looked down. Chalk cliffs and lush valleys, undulating fields and peaks, floodplains and reed marshes. Each feature named by those who lived there: the Underlands, the Uphills, the Marshlands, Flint Ridge, Lion Tor, Wolf Rock, the crossroads where Brendell the Beloved had his head torn clean from his shoulders. This much he had learned by talking to those who passed through Breornsey.

Just beyond the crossroads was a patch of crimson earth where nothing grew. When Old Mother Rams-Tail had stopped giving the villagers extra eggs because her hens had beak-rot, they had dragged her there and pushed holly leaves up her nose with a caulking stick until she expired in great pain.

It seemed that the only thing spoiling this world was people. And the only thing that kept the villagers from burning each other's houses down was the understanding that it would change nothing, because their lives were short and pointless. So they resolved their differences and got on with their planting.

Watborn always thought that if they ventured beyond the end of their barley fields, they might become more generous of spirit. He wanted to push back the walls of his own world and see if there was more to life than being a birdcatcher.

Enough cloud-dreaming, he thought, returning his attention to the bird.

It had no idea it was in danger.

Red of face and yellow of wing, it ratcheted its head and hopped further out along the branch of the dead oak. The rest of its flock had already risen in readiness for the long flight south. It was alone and oblivious.

Watborn reached forward and released the cord, so that the trap came down about it. The two halves of the reed dome swung over the finch, locking it within a woven globe.

'Not worth trapping, is that,' said Finmoor. 'No meat on those bones.'

'It's not for eating,' said Watborn. 'It has a nice song. I'll keep it caged.'

'A nice song?' Finmoor gave a bitter laugh. 'A song won't get you through times of an empty belly.'

'We've enough fat wood pigeons to last a two-week.' A pair of doves took fright and hurtled upwards, sounding like books thrown into the air.

'You're a good catcher,' Finmoor conceded, 'despite your size. You can't hide in a bush.'

The twelve-year-old Watborn would not have recognized himself at eight and twenty years. He had become broad-featured and long-limbed, taller than anyone else in the village, bone and sinew and muscle. His veins stood out like worm casts. His face was open and friendly. He listened and watched but spoke little.

Unhooking the reed globe, he thrust a stick through it and swung it over his shoulder. The finch hopped about, twittering lightly.

Finmoor slapped blackflies from his face. 'I don't call that singing.'

'She'll sing once she's settled.'

'I don't see why we should always turn over our catch to the village elders.'

'Because there's them who can't hunt, as well you know.' Watborn whistled at the finch.

'Then let them die, and let those who can provide for themselves survive.'

'Life can't just be about survival, my friend.' He gave Finmoor a friendly pat on the back. 'Ants survive.'

The fields were noisy in the autumn sunshine and the reek of animals was everywhere. Goats, chickens, cows and birds squawked and burbled. The air was black with skittering insects. Watborn could smell hay, gardenias, wet grass and manure. The golden butterflies on the thistledown bushes were so densely clustered that he could have put in his hand and grabbed a gilded fistful of them. The skylarks and swifts would be followed by bats. After sunset there would be badgers, snakes and wolves. They were too far south for bears.

Watborn breathed deep. The rolling greenery looked like paradise until your eye came to rest upon Londinium. The coming change in the weather would drive most life away. They needed more stock for winter, but if they hunted too close to the castle, men would ride down and take their haul.

They called it Londinium because it was the old name, from when the Italians had been here. It extended one mile in each direction, a great grey square of clifftop land above the Tamesis, also known as the Rushing River, upon which had been builded the most extraordinary edifice.

The wind in the marshes sounded like the distant roar of a crowd. Watborn and Finmoor took the next path back to the village. At the crossroads, four men rode past in black and green, the burly man on either flank guarding the pair at the centre. They had been riding hard, for their coats were spattered and their matted horses steamed and stank.

Finmoor stopped sharp and cast his gaze down.

'Men in costumes,' he warned. 'Never a good sign. Best not to look at them. There's only one place they can be making for and it's not for our likes.'

As the riders passed, one of them twisted in his saddle. 'Swamp people,' he said, indicating the hunters. 'They'll stand like corpses all night, star-gazing. They're riddled with diseases. Cover your mouth.'

Watborn had overheard. There was no way of hiding his height, so he stayed as still as a tree. Allowing his ebony hair to fall across his face, he listened with interest as they talked among themselves. The high-born assumed they could not be understood by others.

'This is as far as we can go, Your Lordship.' One guard gestured to the other and they reined in their horses.

The tall, thin man in the middle sat back in his saddle. He studied the castle-city while his horse champed and pawed. 'They say it has ten thousand rooms. So many that no one has visited them all.'

'There is no admittance after nightfall,' said one of the outriders. 'You'd best be on your way, Lord Carapace. It's not far now. When you require an escort back, send word.'

'Tell the General he has my gratitude for sparing his men in these difficult times.' The Earl turned to his valet. 'We must press on with all possible despatch.'

'You heard him.' Watborn watched them go before moving on. 'That was Lord Carapace, the Earl of the Sheathwing at Warenne.'

Finmoor soured his face. 'How would a barn-door of a bird-catcher know that?'

'I seen him ride by here before. You have, too, if you did but remember. His men always spit after he passes them, and curse the ground.'

'I take it he is not much liked.'

'He said "difficult times". You know what that means.'

'What?' Finmoor asked.

'What it always means. War.' Watborn swung the caged bird back on to his great shoulder.

Finmoor regarded him. 'Who are you? Sometimes I look at you and see a changeling.' He gave a scoff of amusement. 'Anyway, when did you ever see any fighting around here?'

'Not in my years, but wait a while,' Watborn said. 'First the treaties get torn up. Then the food supplies stop. Then the soldiers appear. Then the people are taken.'

'Where have you ever been?' Finmoor kicked a stone from his path. 'You know nothing but the village.'

'The village has been my life,' Watborn agreed, 'but I keep my ears to the wind. I know what goes on beyond the end of the field.'

'You don't know what goes on behind those walls.'

'I know more now than I did, for this time I have heard something I should not. Words can hide grains of gold.'

'I heard nothing,' said Finmoor gratefully. 'My right ear is dead since I stuck an arrow in it.' He dug his finger in deep and pulled out an impressive peel of brown wax.

Watborn said no more but looked beyond the brow of the next low hill. As they passed between the hedgerows the chaffinch began to sing.

The villages of the Marshlands were surrounded by slate and flint thick enough to defeat any plough. Planting was always too wet or too dry. On the only plain of arable land within twelve leagues was Watborn's home, Breornsey, upriver from the Old Port Cedd.

He tried not to think of the black stones that filled the sky behind him, yet they haunted his every waking hour.

Many legends were told of Londinium, the castle-city that stood on the horizon, each tale grown around a single seed of truth. He and Finmoor regarded it as they would a mountain. It was simply there. It had probably been there since the dawn of time, but as none of the commoners lived longer than five and thirty years and nothing was written down, the phrase was meaningless. Occasionally someone ventured close to the walls and was never seen again. More fool them, said everyone else, casting a brief glance back before returning to their turnips.

Londinium had other names, like Castle No-Land, for it owned no other territory but that upon which it stood. Mostly it was just called Londinium because it was between invaders, and new arrivals liked to name things after themselves in ceremonies. It had been constructed upon the tines of an ancient encampment, then spread like barnacles on a whalebone, less an edifice than an accumulation. The oldest part was called CaerLlud of the Seven Gates – Old-Gate, New-Gate, Bishops-Gate, Cripple-Gate and so on – on the banks of the Tamesis in the Kingdom of Albion, with who-knew-what lying beyond in the marshes. Everybody said the Italians had builded everything but they had not, although they may have added parts.

Watborn had listened to all the stories and kept his counsel. Londinium had offered protection to those who sought an escape from the savagery of the River People. It attracted only the keenest survivors, and had achieved status as a royal palace the second they had kicked out all the commoners. Its residents had begun trading with a vengeance. In this way it had made itself powerful.

But that had all been a long time ago. A royal family was supposed to live deep inside, though no one he knew had ever seen them. They were said to eat children, crunching their bones like biscuits. They were said to marry their sisters and dance in devil-rings. They were said to do something with piebald goats that would make your eyeballs stand up in their sockets.

Londinium, a place damned by every lord who wished to see Scarabold dead, and that was almost all of them. Its base was measured at three hundred and twenty poles square, although its walls had since tumbled outwards. As tall as it was wide, it ran to seventeen floors, seven wooden roof-halls and four basements, not counting the sub-basements, storage chambers, barrel vaults and charnel houses.

It had been added to so often that it looked more like a kingdom, and certainly ran as one, with the richest on high and the least advantaged far below. It survived not because it did good works or ruled with a fair hand, but because no one could challenge it. No tribe from the Uphills or the Marshlands would combine its might with another. Each lord was too fearful and suspicious of his neighbour to join forces.

The great blackened edifice was scarred with vertical streaks of red and blue and brown: red from the corpses beheaded at its windows, blue from the dye-tubs the washerwomen emptied from its balconies, brown from the shit that cascaded from its emptied jakes.

Its lanthorns were rarely lit at night, for few dared to venture out after sunset, but funeral pyres burned low and long when servants died, there being only one cemetery at its core and that reserved for royal blood.

A hard, harsh place, then, but for those blessed with the accident of high birth, a world of illicit pleasures. A nest that had always to be sat upon for fear of being usurped. For those who lived within, it was the entire world; nothing outside existed. The residents scurried from chapel to hall, kitchen to bedchamber, armed with gossip, robed in the importance of their lives, unaware that there was anything beyond other than filth and idiocy.

The rulers were vastly outnumbered by servants and had an army strong of thigh from daily marching. Their clerics were weak-minded from a confusion of half-recalled idolatry, and their royal family was full of terrible secrets. It was in this time, the late summer, in the last grand period of the House's life, that the legend was forged and then forgotten.

A legend is just a beautiful lie.

5

The Ebony Earl

King Scarabold was breaking wind in the armoury.

'Godspawn, that's more like it!'

His efforts dislodged some startled crows nesting in the filigreed gilt portcullis of the chamber and resonated away through the trellis like dying pummels on a tambourine.

A luckless valet named Ratchet shared the room, and was attempting to attach a pair of golden anklets to the braced monarch's ceremonial battle-boots. The Great Wound raised a cheek of his ample rear and forced out an alarming fusillade, then fell back against the ambergris velvet cushions on his dressing bench.

With the anklets in place, the valet winced and began thrusting needles into the monarch's doublet. Scarabold was forever splitting his clothes.

'She has never shown any bloody respect for the traditions of her family,' the King complained. 'She should be pleased to mark her passage into womanhood in so regal a fashion.'

'If it please Your Grace,' coughed Ratchet cautiously, 'perhaps the Lady Giniva has deduced the identity of her suitor, and is less than overjoyed at the thought of the match.'

Scarabold's face crumpled as completely as if it had been drawn on parchment and crushed into a ball. Valets had no opinions, and if they did, they should never be allowed to voice them; and if they did voice them, they should never mention subjects of indelicacy. Ratchet had been there so long that he was treated as part of the furniture, which is to say that everyone sat on him.

'I mean,' he stammered, sensing the heat of the royal glower upon his vulnerably thin neck, 'how fiercely she cast her glance aside when introduced to Lord Carapace in the Cathedral of Pons Minor.'

'I do not give a maggot's egg what you think of my choice, you oafish seamster,' Scarabold blasted. 'The land is much changed since they last met. The Earl's armies are now the finest warriors in the Marshlands, and we are in urgent need of allies. He has long shown an interest in the youthful glory of the Princess.'

The withered valet remembered only too well. They last time he had attended court, Carapace had barely been able to tear his gaze from the pale flesh of Giniva's bare shoulders. Ratchet gave an involuntary shudder as he recalled the eerie clicking sound the Earl made with his throat when considering matters of a carnal nature.

Even now he was beetling towards Londinium in his iridescent ebony armour to claim the Princess. What would follow? A brief participation in the Ceremony of Introduction, then the betrothment, a nod from the Bishop, two names scratched on to a parchment scroll, and off to bed for a seeding.

Scarabold's bodily eruptions continued unabated, causing garlands to drop their petals. Ratchet returned to his work, mourning the fate of females born into nobility. Many years ago he had been employed by the gracious Lady Dwinoline, and look what had happened to her, poor thing, forced to become the King's under-wife because she had failed to secure him a son. She had been retained in the hope of producing heirs, but her pipes were not so inclined.

As for Mater Moribund, it was whispered that three girl babies had been secretly drowned in the moat before she had finally given birth, but who knew the truth of it?

Once a month the Great Wound dropped upon her like a wardrobe and pounded away as if driving a nail into a floorboard, but there had been no further issue carried to full term, and now she feared he would root elsewhere for an heir. One dark night, she felt sure, she would be weighted with lead, bundled into a silken sack and follow her babies down into the dark waters. This was such a familiar feeling to the women of Londinium that it even had its own word: trothicide.

As the silver needle slithered through his gnarled fingers, Ratchet considered the night that now lay ahead for the Princess and her suitor. It was well known that Carapace never travelled without his skittering 'courtiers'. He prayed that Giniva would somehow find the strength to survive her ordeal.

The great lunar clock of Fascinus would have been easier to interpret if it had still sported hands. Unfortunately, a slow-turning central spindle and a racing quarter-second arm were all that remained, although it still showed the phases of the moon. Giniva kept it mounted above her bed because its mother-of-pearl case shifted like a starlit sea. But now the remembrance that Fascinus was a fertility god brought fresh qualms.

'I don't understand why you won't help me escape,' she sighed, staring up at the shimmering disc.

Leperdandy moved the Princess's lolling leg and perched himself on a corner of the crimson cretonne coverlet. 'I don't want you to incur our father's wrath. You know how slow he is to forgive. The marriage carries political weight.'

'And the intrusion upon my own desires does not?'

'Royal families have to withstand much worse. Duty must always precede personal preference.'

'Now you sound like him.' She sat up sharply and narrowed her opal eyes. 'Do you know the identity of my suitor?'

'I have my suspicions.' He coughed delicately into a pale fist.

'Dando, you must tell me the truth. Is it someone I abhor?'

Her brother's cough turned into a suspicious hacking fit.

'That awful man who smelled like a pond and was covered in mud. Ethelplum-somebody . . .'

Leperdandy, crimson-cheeked, shook his head and spluttered.

'Not that fat little king from the north-east who paid court to the Mater, the one with the leaky eye . . .' She froze with a sudden thought. 'Not Carapace.'

There was a horrible, confirming silence.

'No, Dando, not the Beetle Earl . . .'

The Ebony Earl owned a swathe of land that started 240 furlongs to the east of the great House and ran almost to the sea. It had little width and was barely arable but was of enormous strategic importance. To call Carapace the Beetle Earl was somewhat demeaning; he was a clever strategist and cut a fine figure on a horse. He demanded great loyalty from his men and rewarded them well. He was also very clean. His beetles removed anything objectionable or dirty from his presence, but they tended to bother the squeamish.

'Carapace campaigned long and hard for you,' said the boy. 'If you fail to abide by Father's decision, he'll treat it as a matter of treason.'

'Traitors must be entombed alive. He wouldn't do that to his own—'

'The law is the law, blood or no blood.'

Leperdandy had once visited the grim, stinking dungeons beneath the castle to see for himself the pitiful creatures captured as prisoners of war by the King. These emaciated albinos with flaking skin and wheedling, whispery voices had been forgotten by all except Fumblegut the jailer, who was rumoured to play elaborate carnal games with his charges in return for mildewed bread and brown water.

'Then you must find a way to save me,' cried Giniva desperately.

He fidgeted with the quilt, running the fronds of a puce tassel between his fingers. 'There is a way, but it would leave you on your own beyond the walls. I could not come with you.'

'I wouldn't ask you to,' she said, her face softening. 'Oh, Dando, don't you see? I'm not like you. I have to leave whatever the cost. Just take me to the broad night sky and I will do the rest.'

6

The Bear in the Fireplace

At nine o'clock Lady Dwinoline knocked at the bedroom door and asked to sit for a while, but her offer was curtly refused. She hovered outside, undecided about what to do, then went away. Giniva hated to offend her but feared that sharing the plan of her escape would place those she loved at risk. Besides, she was not entirely sure that her secret would be safe.

At a quarter past eleven she rose from her dressing table in a high-necked robe of fluted jade silk that whispered across the flagstone floor. She raised the hook of a slim lead-glass lanthorn containing three lit candles and left her apartment, locking her bedroom door behind her. She did not dare glance back at her lifelong home for fear of losing her composure.

Tonight the corridors of the West Quadrant seemed alien and friendless. Fewer lamps were lit than usual, and the shadows were of a deeper hue. The entire edifice was sealed in darkness and cold air; servants waged an eternal battle against rising damp, falling soot and leaking ramparts. Yet there were a few pockets of warmth within the castle, and the Princess knew them as well as the kitchen rats did.

She measured her tread to the funereal drumbeat that sounded within the Chapel of Introduction.

The six-sided stone room was severe and barren. Two long chaise longues faced one another on either side of a latticework window, each with a single gold-embroidered cushion set upon it. To one side was a basin of spring-water in a white china bowl on an iron stand. Mater Moribund had slept here on those nights when her husband had returned drunk, reeking and muck-encrusted from his skirmishes in the rookeries.

As Giniva approached, her heart sank. The Mater was already in attendance, talking softly with Dr Fangle as he wiped his pudgy hands on a strip of linen. What if Leperdandy had fallen asleep? Consciousness slipped from the sickly youth as easily as an oilskin cloak. She was forever nudging him awake during the weekly Cursing of the Poor. What if he failed to keep their appointment?

'Come, child,' beckoned Moribund, her amethyst wristlets chattering. 'Let Dr Fangle examine you.'

The short, pustular physician, Scarabold's dropsical and permanently inebriated family doctor, revealed a disarray of hard yellow teeth. He strummed his hand across his housecoat before offering it to shake. 'An auspicious occasion, Your Highness.'

He stepped aside to reveal an oddly shaped wooden chair that had been designed with but a single purpose.

Seated, Giniva shuddered as the physician's frozen fingers brushed the insides of her thighs. She was frightened that her mother, peering over Fangle's shoulder, would spot the heavy woollen travelling clothes hitched up beneath her gown.

'You understand this is necessary because there can be no infection,' said Fangle with an air of obsequious apology. 'The country is teeming with leprosy, plague, spotted fever and the pox. We must ensure that no harm befalls you. Your vital humours must be held in balance. The Earl is also undergoing examination, for the royal bloodline must remain pure and unsullied.'

'But I am chaste,' said Giniva, horrified.

'Of course.' Fangle grinned into her face, breathing rum and raw garlic. '*Intacta*, veritably,' he whispered. 'Most encouraging.' He removed his digit with some reluctance.

'That's enough, Fangle. Take the chair and get out. Your job here is finished.' Moribund pushed him aside as Giniva hastily dropped her gown.

'But surely the Princess must be taught the facts of life,' Fangle pleaded, still looming over his royal patient.

'They will shortly become clear enough to her,' snapped Moribund. 'On your feet, child. You have little time to spare. If all is well and the Earl approves, we can have you married off before the moon wanes.'

Sweating from her layers of clothes, Giniva clambered into an upright position and adjusted herself. 'What will happen during our meeting? Will he ask to see my teeth, as if buying a horse?'

'What happens between you is not my concern.'

They took their leave of the physician and Giniva fell in behind her mother. 'I know the facts of life, and I know that I do not wish to have the Earl within a day's horse-ride of me,' stated the Princess. She longed to run off into the torch-lit corridor but forced deliberation into her movements. In a few minutes she would be on her way to freedom.

'Of course you're nervous, just as I was long ago,' intoned the Mater, rattling her beads. 'Before my wedding night I presumed all kinds of painful wonders lay in store. Imagine my disappointment when the great sweating brute landed upon me like a felled tree and tore at my flowerpot of femininity with a fleshy little twig that discharged its sap and promptly vanished back into its shrubbery. No danger of that happening to you, though, as I understand from Carapace's physician that the Earl's maleness could put knots on a galley if raised as a mast.'

Giniva was too appalled to pass comment.

The fireplace was fast approaching.

The chimney breasts of all the fireplaces in the West Quadrant were linked to a central passage lined with ceramic bricks. The original plan had been for one huge boiler to provide gusts of warm air on every floor, but it had been abandoned after the mother of the Squeam, the House's general factotum, fell into a grate with a belly full of damson liqueur. The resulting explosion had ruined a sacred mural.

Leperdandy was pushing through the cobwebbed passage that ran parallel to the hallway. Separated by three feet of stone, he strained to catch the sound of their progress, but could discern nothing.

'Bumscuttle!' he cursed. 'I was sure I'd be able to hear them.'

A whiskery nest of spiders spread webbing across his eyelids. He could hardly see a thing. How would he be able to time his emergence from the fireplace in order to snatch his sister? Bursting the bulbous black arachnids, he watched as they spread hundreds of babies across the stones.

Leperdandy was not suited to heroics. He possessed a finely honed sense of the theatrical, but tonight it did not help matters that he had elected to wear the skin of a brown bear in order to disguise himself. His reasoning was sound: there were those who believed that such a creature roamed the servants' passages, and he reckoned that the moth-eaten fur might provide him with anonymity and the advantage of surprise. But if it came to fisticuffs, there was likely to be a display of tearful hysteria that would instantly reveal his identity.

On the other side of the wall Giniva slowed her pace, gradually dropping behind. She needed to put as much distance as possible between herself and Moribund before reaching the great carved fireplace.

'Don't dawdle, girl!' The Queen looked back. 'Carapace is not a man to be kept waiting.'

'I'm sorry, Mother. My hem is caught.'

She stopped and affected a study of her ankle. Leperdandy, hearing the exchange through a crevice like Pyramus awaiting Thisbe's whisper, drew a great breath, burst from beneath the marble mantelpiece in a shower of soot, gave a rather unmenacing growl and grabbed his mother.

Moribund screamed and stabbed him through the shoulder with the silver pin she kept concealed on her person for the purpose of dealing with Scarabold.

'You've killed me!' gasped Leperdandy through the bear's maw, clutching at the protruding pin, his white eyes bulging out of his sooted face like night-time sea beacons.

The bear costume failed to hoodwink the Queen for a mite's breath. 'You idiot whiskerless boy,' she cried, whipping the pin from his stinging flesh and tossing it aside. 'This is no time for your imbecile japes!' With that, she seized Giniva by a pale wrist and thrust her into the bedchamber ahead.

'Dando!' Giniva flung back the plaintive cry as she was swept inside and the door boomed shut behind her.

Mortified by his failure, the boy limped into the shadows to nurse his burning shoulder. He relied upon his sister to make life bearable, and would do anything for her. He would now be forced to embark on a course of action that would lead to the eventual destruction of everything he knew.

Nobody enters the history books by being cautious.

7

In the Eye of the Mind

'I seen this before, but I have forgot what it was called.'

Finmoor pulled his tanned hands from the damp clay earth and raised the object, which left the brown muck with a soft sucking sound. He never minded the mire and would kneel in it for hours.

'Take it to the pump,' Watborn suggested. 'Clean it up.'

They loped across the heath to their village, which lay in a bracken-filled dell below them, beside a twisted plait of shallow streams. The dogs ran out to snap at their heels as they walked through the main street. It was rutted and flooded. The houses on either side looked as if they would dissolve in a strong rain.

When they reached the well, Finmoor placed the thing he had found beneath the pump's spout and pushed the handle. Wiping off the last remaining clods of mud, he held the object up.

The iron disc was set in a half-bowl within a ring. He tipped it this way and that, noting that the centre always stayed level. The pointer held within it spun and settled in one direction, remaining constant whichever way it was turned.

'It is a device for divination,' said Watborn. 'It holds a lodestone and always points to the North Star. I seen one of these when we were small. My grandfather had one.'

'Garn!' Finmoor punched his shoulder. 'What use would your old grandfather have for such a thing?'

'He was a clever man.'

'He wasn't from around here, then.'

'No, he was not. Nor were my parents.'

'That explains your colouring. You're from further south, where the sun burns. I always thought the fields had darkened you.'

They studied the device in wonder. It had such smooth curves and finely bevelled edges that it could not have come from around there. The only metalwork carried out in the village was by the blacksmith, and he was rarely sober enough to do more than shoe a mare.

'I know of other things like this. I found something that I never seen before,' Watborn said. 'I have it at home. I have had it since the poor cow was killed.'

'Don't start on about the cow again,' warned his companion. 'You cannot say one thing led to another in that case. I know what you got, Watborn, and it don't amount to a bag of nothing.'

'Then I shall show you, if you don't believe me.'

Minutes later, Watborn met Finmoor at his house with a hemp sack in his fist.

Gwenor came out to greet her husband, wiping her floury hands on her shift. 'I don't want you bringing your layabout friends in with you, Finmoor,' she warned. 'The pig's got itself by the fire. I'm still waiting for you to kill it.'

'This is man's business, woman. Leave us be.' Finmoor pushed his way inside the smoke-filled den. A grimy boy sat playing with the pig. 'What ho, jolly Andrew.' He patted the child on the head, then wiped his hand clean. 'He still don't speak. We think either his tongue is cleaved to his mouth or he's simple. Seems happy enough, though.'

'I thought his name was Fleetbone.'

'That is his birthname, yes, but we call him Andrew at home in case he never learns to run. We tried the burning sticks on his legs but he was happy to let them scorch him.'

Watborn dragged his hemp sack across the earthen floor, squatting over it. Opening its mouth, he withdrew a ragged piece of crystal and held it on the broad bridge of his nose. He looked across at his friend and blinked.

Finmoor burst out laughing. 'You look like a mole.'

'You can make fun of me all you like, but with the crystal against my face, everything in the distance can be seen close by,' Watborn explained. 'It's magnifying glass, dug from the land and ground fine with sand until a curve is created. My grandfather made it.'

'Your grandfather worshipped the Devil,' said Finmoor gravely. 'I saw him drawing in the earth with a stick and talking to foxes.'

'You think everyone who has something to say for themselves worships the Devil.' Hauling himself to his feet, he headed outside and turned to face the green hills beyond the village, beckoning Finmoor.

The storm rains that had washed the divination device to the surface of their field had now cleared, and a carmine sun was staining the sky.

'Look up there and tell me what you see,' he said.

Finmoor took the lens and squinted at the great black block. Its mass was irregular, time-pocked and cloaked by a ring of raw, iron-grey clouds, as though it generated its own weather. It was backed by a long hilly ridge notched with gullies, through which a dozen narrow rivers flowed on their way to the great winding river that led to the sea.

'I see what I always see,' Finmoor said, handing back the lens.

'And what is that?'

'A thing deep-rooted and damned, to be looked away from.'

'It is Londinium.'

'I've no desire to go to Lombledumdum. I don't know who lives there and I don't give a pismire's turd for any that do.'

'That's because you never seen them up close and they never seen you,' said Watborn, adjusting the lens on his face.

'I never want to see them neither,' said Finmoor with a disapproving pout.

'Shall I tell you what I can see?' Watborn craned his thick neck forward. 'I see as clearly as if I was a hawk sweeping over the rooftops, peering into every one of their private chambers. I see soldiers in fine uniforms armed with long silver spears, marching along the battlements. I see courtiers in a great hall, and a fat king in thick furs shouting at his guards, and a beautiful young woman in a turret.'

'Then you must imagine dancing girls in a bonfire's flames,' said Finmoor, 'for you cannot see them. They would never come down here.'

'Of course they would not,' said Watborn, as if it were obvious. 'They are too far ahead of us. There's a gap, see, between us and them, far too big to jump. I been watching them a long time.'

'Keeping secrets from your kin now. That's a sign of devils. What is the point of watching them?'

'I think something will happen and I want to be a part of it.'

'And what if you go to them?' Finmoor prodded his friend in the chest. 'What if you tell them what happened to you when you was twelve? What if you say our children are starving, our cattle are sick and our crops are blighted, and when the villages of the lowlands flood every spring the babies die? What if you say that our neighbours wage war on us and the Kingsmen take half of all we grow?'

'I don't know.' Watborn refitted the crystal on his face.

'Then let me tell you,' Finmoor said with vehemence. 'I think they would listen to us with patience and politeness, then knock our bloody heads off.'

Watborn gave up on the lens and rubbed his eyes. 'Perhaps I could not see everything quite as clearly as I said, but it is all there in the eye of my mind. They are there and we are here, and that is how it has always been. But that doesn't mean it is how it will always be.'

Finmoor nodded sagely. 'You're right. Things could change. The sky could turn green and rain broomsticks. But you and me, we will always be in the wrong bloody place when it happens.'

'Then I shall have to go up there and see for myself.'

'Up there?' Finmoor spat. 'One look at you and they'll throw you into the river.'

'I suppose you're right,' Watborn agreed with reluctance.

Instead of wondering further what treasures might be found within Londinium, he slapped Finmoor on the back and gave him a hand killing the pig.

8

The Touch of the Beetle Earl

Mater Moribund was nowhere to be seen.

Her role as procuress fulfilled, she had slipped through one of the six chamber walls, leaving her daughter alone with the Earl. She did not wish to witness the meeting. Carapace stood motionless between a pair of flickering lanthorns, barely discernible in his oiled black armour. His breaths were punctuated with tiny clicks, like insects scissoring their mandibles.

Giniva felt the splinters of the door at her back. She looked about at the guttering beeswax candles, a melancholy oil portrait entitled *The Rape of the Sultana* whose eyes were removable for spying purposes (mercifully no one occupied them tonight) and the bowl of water on the stand, beside which was a halved lemon studded with lavender seeds to 'ensure your freshness', as Moribund had put it.

As her eyes adjusted to the gloom, Giniva registered a shimmering movement behind Carapace, as though the black leather bag at his back was attempting to escape. The Earl removed his gloves with slow deliberation, cracking his knuckles. He had yet to glance up at her.

'Come closer to the light, my little one.'

Giniva took a small step forward and stared at her suitor. Carapace wore a segmented leather corset above his ebony codpiece. His facial features were gaunt and severe. A black shovel of a goatee framed his bone-white face. Six silver rings adorned the rim of each ear.

'They say the potters have created a ceramic that replicates the smoothness of human skin.' The Earl's glistening tunic made a series of little crackling sounds as he began to unbutton it. 'No

34

porcelain could ever be as fine as you.' He studied her face now, and smiled. His teeth were white and perfectly arranged.

The Earl's bag was shifting about as if pulled by strings. As Carapace seated himself in order to remove his leggings and boots, it all but dragged itself over the flagstones.

'Come, let me touch you. You have nothing to be afraid of. I have a gentility born from noble extraction.' He raised his arms to receive her.

'If I must be sold off for the sake of my family,' she stated, 'I will receive no overtures of affection from you.'

'Sold off!' cried the Earl. 'Who taught you to think in such a fashion? Betrothment unites great houses and makes everyone stronger.'

Giniva was incensed. 'Except for the female who has no say in the matter. This is the very mockery of love.'

'But do you not understand? I loved you from the first moment I saw you.'

'Upon my fourteenth birthday.'

'No, my dear, I spied upon you when you were ten. You were very pretty in those days.'

He stopped the shocked oval of her mouth with a searing perfumed kiss. One icy hand slipped into her bodice with practised ease and cupped her breast. As he tilted back into her cushion, she tried to pull herself free.

'I was not warned and I will not be touched—' Her voice was muffled.

'Stay your fears,' he whispered. 'The night is young and I am enormous.'

'The night!' Giniva squirmed. 'I was told that the introduction ceremony would last but the length of a prayer!'

His laughter followed her down as he cantilevered her on to the chaise longue. With his free hand he released the catch on his leather bag. There came a sound like a hundred pins being scratched across stone. From the corner of her eye she saw movement. Pushing the Earl from her, she looked under the chaise longue.

A chittering, wriggling morass of black legs and polished wing-cases. Hard-shelled creatures the shape of small gravy boats were roiling towards her. Recoiling, the Princess pushed herself away from the segmented bodies.

'My little courtiers are here to ensure cleanliness. They eat everything that's dead and rotted.' He dipped his hand into the iridescent insects and allowed them to run across his arm. They dropped and scattered to the corners of the room.

'Repugnant barbarian!'

She punched at his chest. Her gown tore in his grasp, and the woollen travelling dress slipped from its silken shell. Her pattens came off as she fought free of the makeshift bed. Her bare feet popped and crunched on the living floor. Reaching the far wall, she searched for the hidden handle.

'Listen to Lady High-a-Mighty.' Carapace sat back on the cushion as the beetles milled about the golden coverlet. 'As if you could afford to choose a suitor for yourself.'

'I will give myself to whomever I please and deny all others,' Giniva cried, close to tears, scrabbling around the inset brass ring, which refused to turn.

'You might try, but who would have you? Who would want someone from here? The door is locked, so calm yourself.'

She turned to face him, sliding her body along the wall. The exit through which her mother had vanished – if she could find it, she could locate the catch. All the secret passages opened similarly.

She bought herself time. 'What are you talking about?'

Carapace looked astounded. 'Do you honestly have no idea who you are?'

'My family rules this land. We ascend from generations of warriors brave and fair who builded here a mighty golden kingdom—'

Carapace snorted. 'Is that really what they told you? There were warriors here, my loveling, but you did not descend from them. They created everything one could require for the improvement of life, but it was all forgot. Tell me, what does this home of yours look like from outside?'

She caught her breath. 'They speak of silvered spires and colonnades so delicately traced that—'

Carapace crept closer. 'They speak? *They speak?* Who are they? Surely not the lowlanders, who have seen only mud and death? You have never seen the building from beyond, and do you know why? Because it is not safe for you to leave. You must be imprisoned here or you would be slaughtered in the winking of an eye.'

Giniva found it hard to breathe. No one had ever spoken to her with such disrespect before.

'You may have held power once but you are now captive to your own foul history. Believe me, I take no pleasure in telling you this.

You are lower than outcasts, lepers, half-bloods left to breed inwards and die. Londinium is a watchword for villainy. Even to converse with you is taboo. To touch you is punishable by death. Do you know what I risked to be with you tonight? To even consider taking your hand in marriage?'

After having had to think no further than what to wear at the next meal, Giniva's mind was suddenly a-whirl. 'You're lying!' she cried. 'I will stop my ears against such poison!'

Carapace leaped from the counterpane in a shower of bugs and pinched her face so hard that she squealed.

'Then learn for yourself. Ask your father about the so-called noble family from which you are descended. You will find nothing noble beyond the ridiculous escutcheon that bears your arms.'

'But we are good and wise, just and kind.' She knew this to be true, for it was the foundation of all she believed. But she spoke for another purpose. To hold the Earl in conversation was to hold him at bay.

'Answer me something.' His blackened lips were no more than a moth-wing from hers. 'If none of the serving maids dares to enter or leave, how do you survive here?'

'The servants? They are free to come and go as they please, as are we all.'

'Then why have you never left?'

'Circumstances have not been propitious, and I am only now of an age—' she began lamely.

'Tell me, what do you live on? What feeds and fattens you?'

'The livestock beyond the Rushing River—'

'—died of brain rot and were burned in pyres builded by your father's men. You cannot beg the question so easily. It is time for you to discover the truth for yourself. Remove the lids of the kitchen cauldrons and look inside if you dare. Or listen to me.'

And he proceeded to tell her what he knew.

'I will not hear it!' The Princess buried her fingers in her ears. She could not understand what this vile creature hoped to gain from such cruelties.

Carapace reached for her but she evaded him. 'Good lady, please believe that I have no desire to hurt you.'

Warily, anxiously, she lowered her hands. 'Do not lie to me in this matter, my lord, I entreat you. This is the only world I know. It extends as far as the outer walls and not a hair's width further.'

'I seek to open your eyes, my lady, and to show you what your family will not – or cannot. You are blind and I am offering you the gift of sight.' The Earl sighed. The coals of his lust had faded to embers, just as sap withdraws from a winter birch. 'Perhaps I am not destined to train you in courtly preparation for your betrothment.'

'No, sir, you are not. I do not know if I will ever be prepared for such an occurrence.'

'Then open your eyes, blind little Giniva. Open them wide and once you have seen, look in a mirror, for you will see such black and grainèd spots as will not leave their tinct.' His cold clear eyes stared into hers.

Giniva had a fearful thought. 'What will you say to my father?'

The Earl shrugged. 'That I no longer find you appealing. We must both save face. Goodnight to you, my Princess.'

'Goodnight to you, Lord Carapace.'

With the door catch between her fingers she fell thankfully into the tunnel, shoving the wall shut and running away through the mildewed passage.

Behind, she heard him call her name. 'Open your eyes, Giniva! Go to the kitchens and see for yourself!'

When Carapace's entreaties could no longer be heard, Giniva slowed her pace and drew breath, her heart still thumping. The only light in the tunnel leaked from the cracks between the bricks. Steep wet steps spilled down to a curving corridor.

Nobody knew how big Londinium was. Four years earlier the royal surveyor had been sent off to map its passageways and had never been seen again. It did not seem unduly vast at first, but it was high and deep and more treacherous than any maze. After setting out from the northern end your knees soon cracked and your muscles ached, and you walked for an age along tilting passageways, passing through all manner of courtyards and chambers and vaults, only to discover that you had covered no distance at all.

Giniva gathered the woollen dress about her, longing for the comforting arms of her brother and the yielding warmth of her own bed. First, she had to ascertain the truth. Peace would only come with the knowledge that the Beetle Earl had lied.

The best way to proceed would be to continue downwards and trust her sense of smell. The far end of the corridor thickened with the spicy scent of cloves, revealing the proximity of the kitchens. A rectangle of buttery light marked the passage's egress. Locating one of the wooden peg-catches that held shut a skivvy-door, she stepped through and felt the warm moist air envelop her.

The vermilion-tiled scullery was deserted at this late hour.

There was no sign of the head cook. The gigantic butcher's-block table, around which utensils stood in earthenware pots like bunches of steel flowers, was valleyed by chopping and had been scrubbed clean.

Pulpers, splitters, colanders, cleavers and dough-trimmers dangled from S-shaped hooks. Ninety knives, from poultry shears to bull-choppers, hung in glinting rows, ready for battle. Light was thrown from the flickering burners of the iron stove, as large as an ox-cart, that dominated the immense room. Beneath the dull roar of the flames, the Princess could hear logs shifting. By day, the kitchen boys riddled them into orange fireflies.

She approached the stove. Four spill-stained saucepans, each of them over two feet deep, simmered on the hob. Their handles were too hot to be clasped, so she plucked up a muslin dishcloth, wet it and wound it around her fingers. The roaring ring of flame beneath the cauldron illuminated her flushed cheeks as she raised the lid.

At once she smelled a dizzying aroma of cumin, coriander, spackwort, sorrel, samphire, marjoram, onions and, headiest of all, muttony meat. She waved a path through the steam and peered inside.

The bubbling brown liquid revealed nothing but chunks of turnip and fennel. She found a wooden spoon, a yard long and slotted at the bowl, and carefully lowered it into the boiling stock. The joint within was heavy and hard to raise without slopping juice everywhere, so she was forced to use both hands to balance the utensil.

The meat slowly surfaced and stared back at her.

It was a human head, probably male.

Its hair had been shaved away, and the lenses of its bulging eyes had boiled into orbs as hard and white as peppermints. The grey skin was loose and ready to separate from the skull. There were no teeth in the mouth, and the lower lip had come away from flayed purple gums. Giniva screamed and dropped the boulder of meat and bone back into the fragrant depths of the pot, sending its juices fizzing and splashing in waves across the burners.

Carapace's words came humming back into her ears. 'Your

family feeds on human flesh,' he had hissed. 'Your family, so proud and regal, are the eaters of corpses, devourers of unfortunate humanity. And you dare to think me barbarian!'

Bile had risen in her pale gullet. 'You tell me lies, all damnable lies!'

'Go to the dungeons and see what your father breeds before you damn me treasonous; see what happens to the brave war-prisoners you take. See how their souls reside in the overstuffed colons of your family. And consider how you yourself have been nourished upon the bones of your enemies!'

With a painful howl she ran from the infernal kitchen, leaving the boiling vats behind her.

9

The Picture in the Ditch

Watborn had a stick. His special cloven beech stick, for holding up branches.

He had a pot. A pan. A spoon and cup. A straw mattress. Two chairs: one wood, one horsehair. He had snares and cages. A washing bucket. A spare jerkin. His dry boots. His drawers, a comb, several good knives. He had a rash.

That was just about everything.

In truth he had more than many. He had once had a cow, and parents. There was very little to make him stay, but not much to make him leave, either. The laburnum at the end of the field was tall now, but he remembered when his grandfather had sat against it each afternoon, eating pears and getting drunk.

'Don't stay here, lad,' he had warned. 'The people are a bunch of stubborn bastards who all hate us. It's not their fault that they're so stupid. If you thought you'd raise a family with enough to eat, put a flock on your land and a roof over your head, you'd be disappointed to find yourself shitting under a bush and fighting a pig for a place near the fire. Get out of here while you've still got your wits and energy.'

'I got nowhere to go,' Watborn had reminded him.

The old man had raised a finger and pointed at Londinium in the distance. 'Go up there and prove yourself useful. They'll look after you. Ent nothing they can do for themselves no more. They need people like us, else they would fade right away into nothing.'

But his grandfather had died from a windy infection of the tripes and Watborn soon forgot what he had been told. Until now, when he looked at his meagre possessions and passed the neighbours who refused to talk to him.

He had asked the elders about the Earl but was told to go about his business. He knew that when men refused to come clean it was because they were involved in something dirty. They acted high-a-mighty but knew nothing, and covered it up by rubbing their chins and looking serious. Watborn the birdcatcher was not someone they took seriously.

It was their mistake. Watborn caught wildfowl and handed them to the elders, who sold them to the traders. They thought he didn't know that they kept most of the profits for themselves.

He knew where the money went and what the elders did with it. But he also knew to keep his counsel and wait until the time was right before taking action. The time was not yet right. His eye wandered again to Londinium. He sat back beneath the laburnum, bit into a nice juicy pear and waited for the last field-workers to return to their homes.

Once he was sure that no one could see him, he went to his special place, in a dip of yellow gorse just beyond the crossroads. At the set of the sun he sat on his heels in the dry dirt and reached down with his knife.

Carefully he scraped more soil from the little flat stones. Each one was a different colour: amber, azure and rose-petal red. Some had flecks of gold and silver in them. They had been cut and flattened so that each fitted perfectly to the next, so tightly that he could not get a fingernail between them. He had found them on his twenty-first name-day after falling on his face in the ditch, dead drunk. Since then he had worked to clean and preserve them, dragging branches across them to keep them hidden, for he felt sure that the others would smash the picture to pieces simply because they could.

It had been buried a long time, and was very hard to clean. He thought that perhaps a burst riverbank had flooded the ditch at some point and washed away a little of its topsoil. When he rose and straightened his long back he saw how the stone pieces formed the picture. There were parts missing, but he could make some sense of what was left. It must have dated back to when the Italians had been here.

In a great shining hall, several men in red and blue cloaks were waiting before a laurel-wreathed man seated on a golden throne. Next to him, a white bull was pulling a cart. Several girls danced with posies of pink flowers. Their long, draped clothing was unfamiliar. He had a feeling the picture extended many more feet on either side. A depiction of life inside Londinium. How long had it been here in the ground awaiting rediscovery?

He wondered if the residents kept watch upon the villages of the Marshlands, and whether they sent down spies. Finmoor and the others never showed any curiosity about them, if they noticed anything at all. Their world was hemmed in by hedges and straw and meals and babies.

Watborn saw. Every time a company of men rode down to the Marshlands for any reason other than to trade, it was with a single-minded purpose and rarely turned out well. There was always some activity between the castle-city and its surroundings, because men came to buy barley, wheat and spelt from them.

They arrived in carts that took away cabbages, turnips and parsnips. Sometimes they brought pottery, bronze and amber glass, although none of the villagers knew what to do with those things. Only the elders were allowed to speak to them, and they never imparted what they knew. Londinium was a kingdom to itself, and the sharing of secrets always came at a price. The yellow-eyed girl had not been the only one spirited away. Sometimes another of the village girls would go with them and not return.

He knelt down once more. Gold-flecked tiles gleamed between the clumps of mud. He did not know why it was so important that nobody else saw the great picture hidden in the ground. Shovelling dirt and dragging bracken over the excavation, he placed a few rocks on top for good measure.

If Finmoor was here, he'd call it the Devil's work, he thought. *He would make me go to the crossroads, turn around three times and put a toad in my mouth.*

Still squatting on his haunches, he looked back at the track and wondered about the man he had seen riding there. He was curious; someone else's life was more interesting than his own. He should have followed the Earl, just to see what would happen.

Screams of laughter came from the crossroads. Two small, filthy children were beating a puppy with sticks.

Squinting against the light, he studied the mist-wreathed castle-city with envy. *An auspicious sign*, he thought, *that's what I need*. He could not know that one was coming his way, or that it would be terrible indeed.

10

No Other World

Dwinoline rocked back and forth in her chair, rhythmically passing her needle through the tapestry. The boy was slumped before her fireplace and had barely moved in an hour. Now the apartment was lit only by sinking coals. Damp wood popped and spat in the grate. Soon it would be time to keep the fires lit every day.

'You cannot blame yourself,' she cooed, reaching forward to run her fingers lightly over his black hair, as elegantly curled as wood shavings. 'None of us can be protected beyond a certain age, and I'm afraid your sister's time has come.'

'It's so unfair.' Leperdandy's voice was muffled by her lace tabard. 'Why can't we remain like this for ever?'

'The young must be taught the ways of the world. Innocence never lasts long.'

Leperdandy raised his head and glared at her. 'Why are we not allowed to walk free?'

'For you there is no world beyond the walls. The family must endure, and that means staying together.' The needle lifted and dropped. 'Once we sought to rule the land, but now we seek only survival. Until Scarabold has found success in his endeavours, there can be no freedom for any of us.'

'It might help if he didn't cut the heads from all those who refuse his terms.' Stretching his wasted muscles, the princeling rose slowly and painfully to his feet. 'I must await my sister's return. If Lord Carapace has decided to marry her, she'll need comforting. Thank you for the advice, but it's clear you have no more of a solution to our predicament than I.'

She sighed. 'The young are impatient.'

'And the old are complacent.'

Lady Dwinoline watched him take his leave with anguish fevering her breast. The boy was not strong enough to lead an army of mice. 'So many secrets,' she muttered as she took up her embroidery once more. 'So many plots. The women must plan, the men must fight and all must hold to their strategies.'

She fell to stitching the head of a soldier's steed. Telling a story in loops of coloured thread was a woman's way of chronicling the truth.

For the remaining hours of the night, Londinium was filled with tortured bruits: the bitter tears of the mortified Princess echoing behind the reinforced door of her bedchamber, the enraged laughter of the Beetle Earl as he caroused with his men upon the ramparts, the mumbled confusions of Leperdandy twisting within soft bedlinen, and the comfortable, well-fed farts of the slumbering King.

But for all those who lived below and served them, there would be no easy sleep tonight; for the weathercocks were turning, the wind was in the east, and danger was riding towards them on billows of storm-crackling cloud.

11

Better Than This

Gwenor put the last of the pig – its ears – into the brine barrel and sealed the lid. The smell of the sty hung in the hut and the fire made her cough. When she looked down at her hands she found them spattered with scarlet droplets, but they were not from the animal. It felt as if there was a rash on her lungs. Drawing breath was like inhaling embers.

Her son sat on the floor, folding rushes into shapes that pleased him. Fleetbone was a surprisingly healthy child considering he spent much of the time moving things from the ground to his mouth. He would never be bright but might prove himself useful to the village by digging or lifting heavy objects.

She started at a noise behind her.

'Oh, you're back at last.' Gwenor wiped her hands on her shift. 'Now that you're here, you can take out the barrel.' The brined meat was stored for collective use in the stone hall, which was always cold inside.

'I'll do it in a minute,' Finmoor promised, waddling towards her with a fumble of his britches. Flipping up her shift, he bent her over with a muddy hand and thudded away at her for a minute before setting her free. 'Right,' he said, tucking himself away, 'now I'll deal with the pig.'

As Finmoor rolled the barrel towards the hall, his friend approached. Watborn fell in beside him and gave him a hand. As the tallest man in the village, the birdcatcher was used to heavy work.

'I been thinking,' Watborn began.

'Oh, *thinking*.'

'If we could get the elders to talk, they might tell us why those people up there never come down to the lowlands except to take tithes and buy vegetables.'

'You may as well ask why the wind from the Stew-Fens is always so bloody cold,' Finmoor replied wearily. 'We are here and they are there, and the two do not meet.'

'But that is not true,' Watborn argued, putting his shoulder to the barrel. 'Some come here and rob us blind in their dealings, and some go there and don't come back. The cow . . .'

'You must learn to let these things go, Watborn, or else ill humours will infect your brain.'

'What if they're living fine lives up there? What if they have beautiful girls who dance with posies while we work in the fields? Would you not like to see, just once?'

'I would not thank you for a chance to do so,' said Finmoor with a grunt. 'It's where the Devil lives. If you go there, he'll turn you into a goat.'

'Why would he do that?'

'For the sin of envy and for not minding your own business, that's why.'

Finmoor had no problem believing that souls rose to the clouds above and goats walked on their hind legs. The village did not prac- tise any form of worship, but there were some who were keen to recognize higher beings. One god or many, old ones or new? In the absence of any established doctrine they were free to pick and choose. For now, they believed whatever they wanted. The desire for a better life after death was the only principle common to all. Bloody recriminations would come later, once everyone had chosen faiths and felt the need to try to convert everyone else.

'I know where I belong, Watborn, and it's here with my family. It is different for you. You have neither wife nor child.'

It was a sore subject. The villagers found Watborn dissatisfied and difficult, as if he was too good for them. He shared their meals and dandled their babies but spent most of his time off alone. They were suspicious that he had not taken a wife. In these parts it was unheard of. People got married because they needed a woman to warm the bed and clean the pickle barrel.

'You mean you would not take a chance in order to improve yourself?'

'I ent interested in "improving",' Finmoor answered. 'We're here, then someone else is here. Naught else to say.'

'But what if we could make our time here count for something more?'

'We have always been provided for—' Finmoor began.

'You can say with no certainty that we have *always* done anything,' said Watborn, 'for we keep no records.' He stabbed his forefinger at the horizon. 'Up there, they are educated. They can read and write.'

'You know how to read and write. You're about the only one around here who can.' Finmoor made it sound like an accusation.

'They make us mark their order books. It means they know who they are and what they have been. It means they have history on their side.' *And I for one am keen to know their history*, he thought, *the better to know who I am.*

'You think that knowing what happens up there will improve your life?' asked Finmoor as a breeze lifted the ends of his hair. The reeds that formed a shifting plateau before the Rushing River were arguing with the wind. 'Would it make you happier than you are now?'

'I don't know if I would be happier,' Watborn answered as they cajoled the barrel to the steps of the hall, 'but I would rid myself of this feeling.' He rubbed his fist against his chest.

'Perhaps you think you will find a bride up there, seeing as our girls are not good enough for you. Or you could go north beyond the hills, where the women are like oxen.' With one final heave, Finmoor deposited the barrel under the eaves. 'My Gwenor is no beauty, it's true, but she can dance a jig and boil a pig, and she knows what she wants from life.'

'Which is what?' the birdcatcher asked.

'Why, nothing much at all,' replied Finmoor, as if the answer were obvious.

Watborn gave the barrel a final nudge into place with his shoulder. 'The village is growing old. Hardly any of the children survive. Harvest time is coming and there are not enough of us to bring in the sheaves. The elders voted against allowing outsiders. It was a long hot summer. The thatches are dry and our water is low.'

'It's all doom and gloom with you, isn't it?' said Finmoor, slapping him on the arm. 'You think too much. You should be like the grasshopper and enjoy the sunshine while it lasts.'

'The grasshopper starved,' Watborn replied, walking away.

12

The Floating Child

Finmoor had never cried before. It was not something he knew how to do. The idea of happiness or misery held little meaning for him. His mother, who had been born exhausted, had told him that life was a painful trek with a single reward: release to a better place.

It was over sooner for Gwenor, who died in the early hours of the morning and now lay on a wicker pallet in the assembly hall. While Finmoor built a pyre for her the villagers stood back, only paying their respects from the doorway, for they knew that she had died of wet-lung disease and felt sure that if they breathed in the hall's mal humours, they would also succumb.

Watborn felt shame for his friend. He had known that their house was too sodden to inhabit and should have tried draining it for them. Finmoor did not have what he needed to get through life, and now had even less.

With water-soaked cloths tied around their faces, the pair worked to send Gwenor to the gods. It was an unusually warm and clear autumn morning. Song-thrushes balanced on the thorn bushes.

Finmoor's son, Fleetbone, grew bored and killed a viper near the crossroads. The other villagers said it was a bad omen and that always meant one thing: banishment. The boy and his father would soon be made to leave the village. Everyone was afraid of becoming infected. There was always something to be scared of.

The pair finished strewing herbs over Gwenor's wrapped body and placed her upon the pyre.

Angus, one of the young tillers, timidly approached. 'You must move the bone-fire further to the end of the fallow field,' he called.

'Otherwise the mal airs will pour from it back into our homes. Whatever she did to attract this thing, we don't want it here with us.'

'She didn't do anything to attract it.' Finmoor placed some final sprigs of rosemary across his wife's chest.

'It's drawn to sin, and we know she lost a child before she met you. We don't want your Gwenor's miasma anywhere near our children.'

'This is my wife, the mother of my son!' Finmoor shouted. 'She did no harm to anyone. The disease takes who it pleases. She was kind and innocent and you, Angus, are a whoreson to deny her her final rites.'

'Finmoor, calm yourself,' begged Watborn, staying his arm. 'We don't need the pyre. I can move her.'

'He knows if we take her there she will be beyond the ground sanctified for burial, and her soul will not be able to rise up. She will remain imprisoned here in the stinking earth.'

Watborn did not believe in gods of any kind. He was suspicious of anyone who needed to be worshipped on pain of death. But he felt sorry for Finmoor, who only wanted what was right for Gwenor.

'Your wife will not fly up anyway,' said Angus with a bitter laugh. 'She's carrying too much arse-weight. The only reason she stayed faithful to you was because nobody else here wanted to swive her.'

'Blind your eyes, you'll pay for that.' Finmoor leaped forward and punched the tiller so hard in the throat that he spat blood. Angus fell heavily and lay sprawled on the ground, gasping for air.

Watborn had to pull his friend from the boy before there was murder. 'Angus, you had better stay away until we've finished here,' he advised. 'Else I cannot take responsibility for Finmoor.'

The tiller tried to speak but only managed an oily gurgle. As his friends helped him away, Finmoor looked down at his dead wife and began to unwind the wet cloth from his face.

'What is the point in pretending this life has anything for us?' he cried. 'She is dead and my son and I will be left to wander the Marshlands, feeding on weeds and elvers until the cold days come again. We will join all the others who are found in the reeds. Look what happened to your own kind.'

Watborn raised a broad hand. 'Fin, we must move the pyre, if only to keep the peace.'

'I want no peace with them. Let them come for me. When you needed help they turned their backs on you.'

Taking up one of the torches that burned at the village boundaries day and night, Finmoor returned to the pyre and quickly lit it. A cry rose from the other villagers, who shuffled back. No one came forth to stop him.

The fire caught fast, but Finmoor was not done. He ran to the nearest hut and thrust his torch under the roof. Somebody screamed. Two lads tried to stop him but he held them at bay. Darting from one home to the next, he swung fire at anyone who dared to approach. Considering much of the straw was damp, it caught light with shocking ease. Orange shadows flickered and lengthened.

Watborn felt the flames scorch his cheek. 'Finmoor, put it down,' he cried, but his friend was beyond reason now.

As Gwenor's fat began to liquefy, the smoke from her body billowed black and drifted over the village. A rising wail of terror filled the air.

Watborn grabbed his friend's torch-arm and stilled it. 'Think of your son,' he said, but could barely be heard above the crackle of burning branches.

The pair found themselves on the other side of a barrier of flame and smoke. The wind had picked up, carrying sparks from one roof to the next. In just a few moments the village was all aflame. Women ran into their burning homes to salvage their belongings.

'We have your child, Finmoor,' called broken-voiced Angus. 'If you want to see him again, give yourself up.'

Through the choking clouds they saw the boy pinned and struggling. Watborn grabbed at Finmoor's arm. 'If you go to them, they will kill you.'

'And if I don't, they will kill my son.' Finmoor pulled himself free.

'They will end his life anyway. They think he is infected. When did Gwenor first become sick?'

'She had the blood-cough for over a moon's length,' Finmoor said. 'She thought I didn't know.'

'Then there is a good chance we shall all die,' Watborn warned. 'Didn't she prepare food for the whole village?'

'What has that to do with it?'

'The miasma travels from one to the next.'

'So you won't come to us,' called one of the villagers. 'Then it is time for little Fleetbone to come to you.'

Watborn saw the boy's shimmering, bloodied shape appear in

the crimson smoke-haze. There was an explosion of cinders, as if someone had trampled a path in the flames, and an apparition floated before them. Fleetbone was drifting high through the fire, unharmed. His mouth hung open, his thin limbs rising and falling in the air.

'My son!' cried Finmoor, collapsing on to his knees.

The birdcatcher was not so easily swayed by the vision in the red smoke. Shielding his eyes, he looked again. Fleetbone's body had been skewered from the back by a long-spear, and was being held aloft through the barrier of fire by Angus.

'Don't!' Watborn shouted as Finmoor launched himself into the flames. He embraced the smouldering boy, then discovered the spear. With a cry of rage he pushed forward through the crashing branches and fell in a hail of arrows, flame and stones.

Fleetbone's thin body crumpled and vanished. Watborn could only stare in horror. If he moved, he knew he would be killed by the others.

Finmoor lay face down, thrashing in the fire, his skin already blackening, his hair burning off like wheat stubble. Part of Gwenor's funeral pyre had collapsed on him. Moments later the smoke grew so dense that there was hardly anything to be seen of the village or its inhabitants.

Stumbling away from the conflagration, Watborn watched for attackers, but no one was interested in him. Their fury had burned itself out, leaving only a devastating, shame-faced misery. As the heat abated he searched for Finmoor's remains, but found nothing to be saved. His friend's charred bones lay in the embers with his wife's and son's.

'Go, Watborn,' called one of the others. 'We have no fight with you, but you must leave.'

His own house was burning down, lit by his neighbour's flaming eaves. The little finch he had trapped lay unmarked but dead inside its reed cage. He salvaged what he could and left before the smoke made it appear that he was crying.

The village had existed for just a few decades, and had only begun when a riverbank had fallen in and rerouted the waters, draining a marsh. It was said there were hundreds of villages like it, most so small that they were nameless. Their inhabitants had forgotten everything they had once known about crops and animal husbandry, about health and wealth. There had been too many breaks in the line of history.

The villagers were spread across the lowlands and the southern plains, tending their mangy horses and cattle, handing over tithes in the form of vegetables, livestock and labour. The lands they owned were barely more than a few perches long, and fear of losing them stopped them from straying far. Watborn knew he could walk to another village just like this one and offer his services. Perhaps he could reach one of the larger towns and find work as a labourer.

But above him was Londinium, and even without his crystal lens he could see that its lanthorns were all ablaze with life and light.

The smoke of Breornsey was in his clothes. There was nothing left for him down here. He had little to lose by making his way there and attempting to gain entry. He cared not for his life; at eight and twenty he was very nearly an old man. It would be better to die trying for something than to sit in the marshes bemoaning his lot.

He added his sharpest knife to his bag and slung it over his shoulder. Pulling his jerkin tight around himself, he set off, ready to enter a new life, one filled with great feasts and dancing girls.

He looked back only once at the burning village. He would not turn around again.

13

Giniva Sets Her Mind

Far, far below the Princess's window, one of the villages appeared to be having a celebration. There was some sort of bonfire at its centre and lots of sparkling lights were set upon its houses. The Princess smiled upon the burning village, trying to imagine what it must be like down there, to be so joyful that one could light one's home prettily and dance about it.

The habits of peasants never failed to lift her spirits. She had never met any, but she could imagine how happy and carefree their lives were.

'You must try to eat something.'

Dwinoline raised the steaming ladle of bone broth. Giniva recoiled and knocked it aside, spattering an arras with ruby droplets and shreds of tendon. She dropped back on to the bed, sinking into its dull-gold pillows once more.

'How can I eat, knowing what I know now?' she asked. 'I shall never eat again. I'll let my skeleton rise through my pale skin until I look like Aunt Asphyxia. To think we are descended from the eaters of the dead.'

'Not descended,' Dwinoline insisted. 'We must try to think of it as an ascension only.' She knotted her dimpled hands in her lap and sighed, her breath clouding the bedchamber. The wind moaning through the arrow slits of the turret sounded like a distant mad organist. 'It began many generations ago, born of necessity.'

'Decency should have told you to desist.'

'Decency! We were the rightful owners of the land, all the way to the coast, until others stole it from us. The barbarians forced us back on to this mile of rock and clay amid slaughter and starvation.'

Dwinoline examined the tapestry's surface at eye level for stray threads. 'You can know nothing of decency until you have seen the heads of your subjects uprooted from their shoulders for the spoils of property.'

'Nobody can own the land,' said Giniva with vehemence. 'Why should men kill each other over it? I despise the entire dynasty.'

'Then you must despise yourself, my dear,' said Dwinoline gently, taking up the needle once more. 'For you too were fattened on the braised flesh of traitors.'

Giniva's opal eyes turned to her. 'Did you never think it was wrong?'

'I thought it the way of our world.' Dwinoline tucked in a stray brown cord poking from her dirndl.

'Then I shall adapt as well.' She reached down beside the bed and pulled out a raffia parcel of carrots and radishes that the head cook had thoughtfully delivered. 'From now on I shall eat only vegetables.'

'Your father will be most displeased. It can only lead to other forms of rebellion.'

The Princess dug a carrot from the parcel and disconsolately bit into it. The sound was like snapping wood but the taste was oddly familiar. Perhaps she had eaten them in a stew. 'My father will wage war until he is killed in the most foolish of all foolish wars, so Calmora says.'

'You should know better than to listen to women who make predictions. The seer says what you want to hear.'

'She warns that my life is in danger. She says there are enemies all around us who would see me dead to prevent the survival of our line.'

'Enough with your foolish notions, child. Scarabold is too angry to countenance your presence at table. He has allowed Carapace to take any of the ladies-in-waiting as recompense while he decides the best course for you. He must placate the Earl, whose alliance he desperately needs. The ceremony of suitors must continue.'

Giniva rose from her supine position in a chime of bedsprings. 'Not while my body has a breath left in it.'

Dwinoline felt she should deliver an admonition. 'The Great Wound will not wait for your agreement in this matter. Even as I try to placate him, Mater Moribund goads him on.'

'I can fight my own battles.' She studied poor Lady Dwinoline with some returning affection. 'Don't fret. I'll meet with my father and disarm his argument.'

'That, my little dovecot, is something the warrior-kings have failed to do,' said Dwinoline, reaching up to stroke Giniva's hair. 'Once our world was safe and sure but now it is adrift. The Great Wound listens to no one and will not be swayed from his path.'

Outside, the wailing wind rose even higher, as if in a panic to warn that change was coming.

Giniva ran along the corridor and hammered on her brother's door, storming inside when he cracked it open.

'Did you know?' She raged across her brother's bedroom, turning and turning. 'Have you seen inside the kitchen cauldrons?'

'How . . . do you mean?' asked Leperdandy carefully.

'You know everything that goes on. Have you seen the food being prepared?'

'Of course. I was taken as a treat on Paupers' Day when I was five. Only the most royal personages are cursed to eat this way. But you—' He sighed as if the weight of life had suddenly condensed about his thin shoulders. 'Giniva, I have something to confess.'

She'd had quite enough surprises lately, but bade her brother speak.

'After you left your mother's dry teat, the nurse was asked to feed you. Mater Moribund could not bear the touch of children. She feared they would sweat upon her skin and make her old. But the nurse could not make you eat, either, and couldn't bear to see you cry when she placed the meat-spoon in your dainty maw – so she threw away your meals and replaced them with her own preparations. It was a matter of trial and error, but she finally discovered what delighted you.'

Giniva's eyes widened. 'And what was I served that I accepted so easily?'

Leperdandy looked ashamed. He uncrossed his skinny legs and rose from the marble dais, pacing to the window. Through the smeared green glass he saw weatherbeaten hedgerows of ash and thorn lining the moat, and a palisade of wind-blasted cypresses beyond. His face was as pale as lightning.

'Vegetables, my lady, secretly dug from the gardens of the poor. You never tasted flesh as a child, and therefore had no craving for it. After Nurse Mentle succumbed to dropsical fits she left the secret recipe of your meals with the kitchen staff, and they continued their work until the rosters were reorganized. Since then I have done my best to keep people from your pot without drawing attention.'

'Therefore I am doubly unsullied,' she cried. 'Don't you see? You must take me to the source of this horror.'

'Having once descended deep into the heart of the prison chambers,' the princeling murmured, 'I can tell you it is not a sight for the eyes of a lady – nor for any who value their sanity.'

His ears pricked, and he yanked open his bedroom door before the knock. Aunt Asphyxia, all velveteen and liver spots, stood with her knotty fist still raised.

'Conspiring!' she cried, the word emerging from her frayed vocal cords as a muzzled scream. 'Always tucked away, the two of you. Too close, too intimate. Unhealthy! Unseemly! Always whispering and plotting!'

'How could we be, Aunt Asphyxia, with you or your children lurking behind every lectern and tapestry spying on us?' Leperdandy asked. 'Giniva wishes to visit the dungeons. I think we should let her.'

'Germs!' shrieked the old lady. 'Disease, deformity and diarrhoea! No high-born woman is allowed to take such risks!'

'Did you want something specific?' The princeling crossed his ankles and balanced a hand on his hip so that he prevented her entry.

'Tell the girl she must acquiesce!' Asphyxia suddenly screwed up her eyes and scratched her mottled nose as if to prevent a sneeze. It gave her a face like a diseased parsnip. 'She must apologize to Carapace and beg the Beetle Earl for his carnal attentions!'

'I don't think there's going to be much chance of that, Auntie. The wedding's off.' He started to shut the door, but she thrust at him in an angry cloud of musk.

'You have no inkling of the consequences, you spoutless young fop! We cannot afford to make an enemy of the Earl! Loyalties must be forged! Obeisance will purchase honour! Genuflection! Prostration!'

'Then the Great Wound will have to exercise some diplomacy of his own for once.'

With that, he slammed the door shut, but his heart was shaking. He raised a slim shushing finger to his lips, halting his sister's laughter. 'She's fidgeting about beyond the keyhole. She'll be out there for ages yet with her wrinkled old head glued to the woodwork. She's not as harmless as you might think. From her ears, straight to the war room.'

'Will you take me down to the prison cells or must I go alone?' asked Giniva.

'Fumblegut will never admit you, and you should be glad of that. The jailer's tastes are more exotic than the fevered excesses of your imagination. They say he keeps a terrifying creature in his cells that does his bidding.'

'Who are these "they"?' demanded the Princess. '"They" say this and "they" say that – "they" are always seeking to make us jump at shadows.'

Leperdandy sighed. 'This place is filled with whispering shades. But show some patience. Better by far to begin with Scarabold.'

'Do you really think so, brother?' Her headstrong ideas were usually mitigated by Leperdandy's guidance. 'Then I should go to him now. I will have my wishes observed. At midnight tonight I come of age. He can't stop me after that.'

She rose from the bed with a creak and headed purposefully for the door. Leperdandy worried a cuticle. At moments like this she showed a familial determination, even though she was frustrated in her desires.

'Giniva, if Scarabold forces another confrontation upon you, you will try to be ...' – he searched for a word that would not annoy her – '... reasonable, won't you?'

'I am quite reasonable. When my bathwater is tepid I hardly ever scold the maids.' She clasped the golden heart at her breastbone, the edge of which was set with six flawless rubies. She decided she would become her father's favourite little girl once more and get her way, just as she had always done. She could twist him about her finger when she had to.

'I need to find my dressmaker. Lady Vermilia will be sure to think of a finishing touch for my ensemble. I must appear serious in dark colours if I am to confront the King.'

Leperdandy furrowed his alabaster brow. The Princess was unversed in the art of discretion, and their father would not take kindly to accusations.

He began to regret suggesting a meeting so clearly fraught with dangers.

Nobody could recall much about St Stanivar except that he hacked out his wife's tongue because she would not stay quiet during a memorial service for those who died in the Great Fall of Mud. He kept it beside him in a golden casket for the rest of his life, and his name was taken up by a league of embittered zealots under the banner of the Devil's Tongue of St Stanivar.

The league had taken part of the north-west by force and periodically made sorties to the Rushing River. Whenever they did so, they attempted to infiltrate Londinium and inflict as much damage as possible before being slaughtered.

Word had lately reached them that the Princess was now the key to securing Scarabold's dynasty, so they circulated a suprisingly accurate sketch copied from her portrait and told their warriors to return with her severed head.

One of their most surefooted targeteers, Ormond the Steady, was even now creeping across the open-sided corridor that led to Leperdandy's apartment with a loaded twin-crossbow, the goose-feather flights of his arrows bearing the imprint of the Devil's Tongue, a black-and-crimson chevron. Ormond had short strong legs and large flat feet that held him rock-like to his task. His coney-skin coat allowed him to blend in with his surroundings. Having reached this hallowed ground by climbing a series of aquaducts that had twice nearly robbed him of his life, he had been waiting five days for a sighting of the Princess. Now he saw her hurrying before him like an ecstatic vision, and silently swung his weapon to his eye.

The arrow sang straight and true, cleaving the air and missing her by less than a barleycorn only because the hem of her dress was caught again and she ducked to free it.

Ormond was shamed; he never missed.

During the Siege of Bayne he had removed one enemy for every shaft he had fired in a hailstorm that had left half of his own men dead. A silly little sprite of a girl should have presented no problem. She stepped across the fallen arrow without even noticing it.

The elders of the Devil's Tongue thought of themselves as agents of chaos but preferred to hire others to do their dirty work. They had promised to pay Ormond in gold pieces for proof of the Princess's death. If Giniva Scarabold was gone, there could be no royal heir and the dynasty would fall.

Ormond the Steady had been given one order only: to kill and return. He could afford to bide his time. He stepped back into the shadows and closed his eyes, ever patient.

14

The Sealing of the Embrasure

The Great Wound had wondered how long it would take his daughter to come creeping back in a state of apology. It gave him satisfaction to see her humbly seated upon the edge of the burgundy recamier just outside the door to the Reading Room.

Checking the stopped clock which stood over the mantel (this timepiece at least had hands, which was more than could be said of its maker, who had been deprived of his so that he would never make anything finer), he noted that Giniva would still be fifteen years old for a further hour. It was the last time she would be legally under his control.

He strode across to the vast granite fireplace and stuck a lit taper into his briar, filling the room with an odour like burning sweetmeat wrappers.

Now Giniva made her grand entrance. She had woven tiny gold-stemmed violets into her hair and laced them through her bodice, an image of innocence that would sway Scarabold to her argument.

'Blud's teeth, you're a headstrong hussy and no mistake,' he complained, 'but I'm prepared to bygonify your quarrelsome attitude if you are willing to renounce your vestal status. Obviously if you give birth to a girl she'll have to be drowned, but a son will reinvigorate our blood.' He tamped his stinking pipe-bowl with a fat sepia-tipped thumb, clearly expecting no refusal.

'I came to speak of a more serious matter,' the Princess replied coolly.

'What could be more serious than the perpetuation of our sovereignty?' The Great Wound hissed and sucked at his pipe as if clearing a drain, peering at her with his good eye through a cloud

of cinders as though conducting a discourse through a raked bonfire. 'If we fail Carapace now, he'll deny us the alliance that secures
our future. Our fate is entwined with his.'

'You hated him once,' answered Giniva. 'You told me that the
iron rule of the dynasty was obeyed throughout the land, that it
held the valleys and coasts in its grip.'

The old King's good eye moistened in remembrance. 'The world
is changing. We are driven to befriend our former enemies. Londinium once thought itself to be the centre of all things, but we are
not as trusted as we were. We can no longer thrive alone.'

Giniva had no wish to hurt her family; her life knew nothing
else. She was beginning to appreciate her role and understand the
bargaining power it afforded her.

'I shall attempt to do as you wish, Father – on one condition.'

'Condition?' repeated Scarabold suspiciously. 'We don't do
conditions.'

'I must visit the dungeon cells wherein you keep our prisoners of
war. If you deny me this, I will never surrender myself to the Beetle
Earl in a thousand years.'

'But why would you wish to enter such a place?' For once Scarabold was genuinely nonplussed.

"I wish to see the men we herd like cattle and slaughter to fill our
bellies.' She included herself in this category, for her dietary secret
was the only unturned card she had left to play.

Within the vastness of his beardy undergrowth, Scarabold's lips
were pursed in anger. Who had informed the child, and for what
purpose if not to upset her? She would not be fit to sire a son for
him in this soured state. When a woman's innards curdled she
delivered enfeebled stock.

'So you know,' he said simply.

'We are the butchers of humanity and that is all you can say?'
cried Giniva, ending her determination to remain calm.

Before Scarabold could formulate an appropriate attitude, Giniva
felt her temper rise. Now she burst into a furious fit. She accused
her father of treason and murder and much worse besides, of lying
and hiding, of cowardice and bestial acts, of inciting blasphemy and
incurring damnation. She said so many things she had no intention
of saying that she wrecked any chance of reconciliation between
herself and the King.

More harmful still, she renounced her name and title, something

THE FOOT ON THE CROWN

she later realized no member of the family had ever dared to do. When her anger was finally spent, the clock stood at seven minutes to midnight.

Scarabold was so apoplectic that his head had turned puce. In a fiery cloud of briar embers he banished her from his limited sight and ordered that she should remain confined to her quarters for the rest of her days. Until she was sixteen, any law he passed against her would remain in place for ever. He exercised the right of the sovereign with just seven minutes to go.

Giniva ran from the room in a tide of tears and ransacked most of the West Quadrant seeking the comfort of her brother, but he was nowhere to be found. Returning to her bedchamber, she dropped on to her eiderdown and drifted into bitter, miserable slumber.

A short time later she was awoken by the sound of hammering.

Rising, she saw that nails were being driven into her bedroom door. One by one their sharpened ends popped out in ragged rows. She counted forty of them, long iron shards that protruded through the oaken piers of the door's arch. She tried the handle but it would not budge even a twentieth of an inch.

She was sealed up, and there she would remain. Had the Princess but withheld her wrath by seven more revolutions of the minute hand, her father would have been powerless to stop her.

Forced to reply to her bellowed questions, two servants shifted from spandrel to keyhole and admitted that they were merely carrying out Scarabold's wishes. From now on, they explained, her meals (meat and only meat) would be delivered through the fireplace grate.

She was to remain incarcerated until she repented and saw the error of her ways, when she was perhaps thirty-five or older. If she wanted something to read, they would be happy to slide a philosophical tract or two from the library beneath her door. The speaking-tube to her bedroom had been blocked up. She was to knock five times if she needed something. That was how it would be from now on.

She begged for them to summon Leperdandy, but there came no reply.

Giniva was finally, truly alone.

15

At the Oubliette

Spackle and Peut were running through the corridors playing Dead Man's Sting, a game requiring an intimate comprehension of its convoluted rules and an attitude of predatory spite.

The twin progeny of Aunt Asphyxia looked like a pair of shaved fruitbats stuffed into velveteen breeches. They were spoiled brats with not a single original thought to share between them, and were consequently used by their mother to spy on the rest of the family.

Asphyxia was not a genuine aunt but a sour-hearted widow inherited by Scarabold after he had made a promise to her dying husband on a gore-soaked battlement. In the emotional turmoil of the moment, the Great Wound had forgotten that his old friend's wife was heavy with child, and had found himself providing for one of the only noble families he'd never met before their first uncomfortable breakfast.

He did not know that she harboured a deep and abiding hatred of his children because of the way they fitted so smoothly into their privileged world. Giniva and her brother were so comfortable in the order of royal preference that they had no need to be ambitious.

Asphyxia's twins were only accorded places in the household out of respect for their father. She knew they would never earn any deeper approval, and therefore engaged them in the only way they could be useful: as an early warning system for trouble. Since it was obvious that their brains functioned poorly, she had long ago decided to employ their eyes and ears.

The Great Wound did not approve of the twelve-year-old brothers; their sly, underhand meddling offended his warrior sensibilities. They were spotty of face, slick of hair and knocked of knee. He would have approved of them even less now, for they had been sent at their mother's command on a spying mission.

Spackle stood at Carapace's door with his ear against the oak, and Peut stood on his brother's shoulders, peering through the engraved transom of indigo crystal. The cut and thickness of the glass gave him only the vaguest of refracted views, but magnified the voice of the Beetle Earl into reedy sharpness.

'There must be a way to make her see reason,' Carapace insisted, unaware that Giniva had already glimpsed the reverse when unsealing the kitchen's cooking pots. 'She's no longer a girl but a mature woman, luscious, full, fecund, bursting, bulging, a fragrant moist plum ripe for plucking and peeling and devouring.'

'Your trousers, sir.' That was the valet's voice. 'The buttons are undone.'

'Is it any wonder,' sighed the Earl, attending to his groin.

'He's smitten with the Lady Giniva,' Peut whispered downwards, always prepared to state the obvious. He resettled his boots on either side of his brother's spine. 'I don't know why he doesn't force himself upon her and have done with it.'

'Not everyone is like you,' hissed Spackle, arching his sore back.

'And now that Scarabold has sealed her up inside her bedchamber like an errant nun, how am I supposed to plight my troth?' There was a rip of silk as Carapace put his elbow through his shirt. The exasperated valet was attempting to dress his master as he paced. 'The Great Wound's loyalty to me is touching. Presumably he hopes to curry my favour by punishing the child. His actions have left us all without a choice.'

'Do we have to stay here much longer?' croaked Spackle. 'My shoulder blades are cracking.'

Beyond the door, Carapace's valet offered a solution. 'If I might be so very bold as to make the tiniest of most minuscule suggestions,' he began, the servant deferring to nobility with the acquiescence of a whore sinking into a mattress, 'why not perform a service for the Princess and endear yourself to her by fulfilling her desires? She's locked away; there must be something she needs, and such an act will confirm your allegiance to her.'

'Now I remember why I keep you on!' cried Carapace. 'For someone who lives in a world of socks and silver-polish, you occasionally produce a superlative idea. I'll venture to her rooms at once. This was my plan all along, of course.'

'He'll never be able to get the door open,' sniggered Peut, hopping down, to Spackle's relief. 'Come on, let's get there before him.'

As silent as a sunset, they made their way through a labyrinth of dribbling brickwork. It was within these walls that Suppurus, the disgraced Knave of Chaucery, had avoided his scheduled beheading by remaining hidden for six days and surviving on mice and his own regurgitated vomit. Although that had been nearly eighty years ago, his person, mummified by the crosswinds of the rumbling latrine flues, could still be seen in the passageway.

The twins arrived minutes before the Earl and secreted themselves in an alcove opposite Giniva's room, behind a weevil-chewed tapestry celebrating one of Scarabold's most senseless massacres. Giniva's door looked as if it would not be opened without the aid of a battering ram.

Shortly Carapace strode up, ran his tapering fingers across the pounded nailheads and brought his lips to the edge of the keyhole.

'My Lady Giniva,' he called gently, 'even though you refused me, I feel responsible for what has happened. Listen to me. I am mortified to find you imprisoned like this. Perhaps there is something I can do to secure your release.'

The twins failed to discern the Princess's reply as the draughts blowing along the corridor rattled and banged the tapestries, making parades of chivalrous knights dance about.

Peut peered out through a tangle of rotted stitches. Carapace was pressed intently at the mortise and nodding to himself. A small sheet of folded paper was pushed to him beneath the door. Gingerly, he unfolded the violet slip and studied it with rising consternation.

'What you are asking is utterly impossible,' he cried aloud, refolding the sheet. 'If the King found out, he would have me killed in some brutal, lingering fashion, and my people would declare war upon you all.'

He hunched against the door again, listening. 'Of course I desire it, with all my heart, but how can I—? Yes, most certainly I wish to prove myself to you, but is there really no other way that I can help—'

A foot kicked at the door from within, showering Carapace with rust and sending him back on his heels. It was clear that whether Giniva's terms were met or not, she meant business. The Earl deposited the slip of paper within his jerkin, shook out his hair and set off at a lick.

Spackle and Peut were stumped. As spies they had failed miserably. All they knew was that Carapace might or might not have agreed to aid the Princess in some treasonable enterprise of her devising. Asphyxia would be far from pleased by this incomplete bulletin.

Spackle scraped a curtain of greasy hair from his kohl-lined eyes and stared stupidly at his brother. Whatever Giniva had requested of the Beetle Earl, it was sure to cause upset in the household.

'We'll have to follow him everywhere,' said Peut. 'Use our initiative. If he does as she requests, he will antagonize the Crown. If he rats to the Great Wound, he will lose her for ever.'

'What about the Princess?' asked Spackle.

'Forget about her,' said Peut. 'She's a mere peg in a board to be moved about. She's not going anywhere. She will brood in her bedchamber, and rely on the servants to slide fillets of forest-cake under the door. Few would help her, for they dare not risk the rage of the King.'

'What about Leperdandy?'

'Pouting milksop!' Peut snorted derisively.

'Wheedling bilgebottom!' snittered his twin. 'He could not liberate a fart from his own bony backside!'

How they laughed as they crept back to Carapace's quarters.

16

House Like a Ladder

Watborn was about to cast the rainwater from his horn, thinking there would be wells inside the castle. Then it occurred to him that he might be denied entry or set upon, so he fixed the filled vessel at his waist. From what he had heard there was no reason to assume that the inhabitants were well disposed towards strangers. At the very least, they would think him stupid and try to trick him.

He made a fresh inventory of his possessions: one small bow, two arrows, his hunting knife, some cord, the guiding device, the lens and a badly whittled owl from poor Finmoor. He had nothing else but his wits and his strength.

The path broke apart every half-mile or so and was often lost beneath gorse. He removed the instrument of guidance from his jerkin and held it aloft. Londinium was due north-west, but the view of it was an illusion; it was much further than he had reckoned. The ridged green hills before it would have to be scaled first.

He made a bed of bracken on the most gentle slope of the ridge and lay looking up at the densely starred sky. He thought of Finmoor and his home, and how some unspoken need to leave had gnawed at him for so long.

At twenty-eight years Watborn was middle-aged but strong from his labours in the village, where he had worked to pay for his keep from the age of twelve, having lost most of his relatives to the dropsy. He had not been educated but possessed a fine curiosity, and by asking endless questions had learned more than the other children, who were still drawing with sticks in the dust. Even so, it was hard to know what was true and what was false.

The village elders joked that he knew a pie from a portcullis, but

Watborn's fascination with Londinium had made him appear touched. He had long ago decided that life was a matter of keeping your ears open and your mouth shut, and not doing anything stupid. Yet he had failed to save his family, or Finmoor and his child. He could not go home. There was something waiting for him in the shadows. Part of him knew what it was and he grew afraid, for he could not always control what was inside of him.

He thought of his mother and father scything their share of the barley, keeping watch on their baby boy. Leading the cow to pasture, letting him ride on her haunches. How they had sacrificed all for him.

Watborn had always known he was different. The villagers barely managed to survive from one day to the next. They died a few paces from where they were born. They had never questioned what lay over the next hill. What went on elsewhere had nothing to do with them.

As he stared up, three comets chased each other across the velvet blue. *Born and bred in one small village*, he thought, *but I know there are towns beyond my home, and a place where the land falls into the sea called the Old Port Cedd, and even though I have never visited it I have heard of the laden craft that come into the Rushing River. So it stands to reason that they come from places at the other end of the water, full of people just like me. And it won't stop there. Who's to say that when we look up, we might not be seeing others looking down at us?*

It was enough to make his head hurt, so he concentrated on more practical matters, such as planning to trap a pigeon for his breakfast and wondering how to make himself presentable for admittance. So that he did not look like a peasant.

But before he could reach any decisions he felt the waking world fade, and burrowed deeper into his bracken bed as it began to patter with rain.

He dreamed of a place where long-limbed dancing girls entertained youths reclining in robes, where white bulls were fed grapes and the sun shone in ways that it never could upon the marshlands of blackened Breornsey.

He awoke to the sound of yelping.

The boy had his shirt rucked up and was bathing his back in a stream, crying with each splash. The birdcatcher thought he called out because the water was icy, but then he saw the crimson stripes across the lad's back. Cupping his hands, he was dropping stream-water on to his wounds. Hearing Watborn approach, the boy turned in fear and anger.

'Who did this?' Watborn asked.

'The Kingsman who took my pony, the bastard.' The boy spat in the stream.

Watborn dug at a dry hummock of camomile flowers and rubbed some of its leaves to shreds in the heels of his hands. 'You've been up there?'

'I should never have gone. Dag's blood, I was warned enough. They take what they want from you and give you naught for it.'

'What is it like in there? Hold still.' He smeared the macerated leaves across the cuts. The boy cried out and tried to pull away. 'Leave it on.'

'It's a hellish place of turning spits and sharpening spears, but it is where all the people are.' The boy looked over his shoulder at the mess of greenery being stuck to his back. 'If you're born there, you may be treated well, but outsiders are shat upon. Still, if you want to get anywhere, it's where you must go.'

'They know you're not from there, then.'

'Know? Of course they know. It's in our darker skin, our eyes, our blood. They look at you and judge how much they can make from you.'

'Then why go at all?' Watborn rinsed his hands in the stream.

'If I stay here, I will starve. And starve I will now, without my livelihood.'

'How much further is it from here?'

'Three or four hours, no longer, but there's the river to ford. It's wide and fast, but someone will take you across for a rabbit. You'd best go in the morning when the light is high. The honest tradesmen start early. Later their places are taken by thieves and cut-throats. If you are inside when they shut the gates, you will not be seen again, of that I'm sure.'

'Did you see their ruler?'

He was unprepared for the boy's laughter. 'Course not – if such a creature exists. Londinium is like a ladder with the workers at the bottom, all being shat on by the ones above. You will get no further than the lowest rung. But you have a skill, for you've eased my wounds, and that will get you somewhere. Are you an apothecary?'

Watborn smiled. 'No, I just know plants.'

'You won't last long if you've nothing to trade. I must go home now without my pony, with only these wounds as a reward for speaking out about the price of my kindling.'

'How did you get in?'

'I waited outside the gates with all the others and pushed my way to the front, even though they threw stones at me. I've heard there are other more dangerous ways to get inside.'

'Thank you for your advice.' Watborn handed him a bundle of leaves. 'Look for the yellow and white flowers when you are in pain. You can chew them, but too many will make you sick.'

Taking his leave from the puzzled boy, he turned once more in the direction of Londinium.

Watborn knew he was approaching the river; he could smell fish and water-weeds. The wind rose and all birdsong died away. He passed through a dense stand of silver birches and there it was, a glistening ribbon beyond the reed marshes, wide and sluggish, set so low that it could not be seen from Breornsey. The water was surprisingly blue and clear with a pebbly bottom, and ripe with all kinds of rainbow-scaled fish. A number of barques and flatboats drifted downstream. Voices carried in the still morning air.

He climbed a birch as swiftly as a monkey and looked out with the crystal held to his nose. A plain wooden bridge with a third of its stanchions missing stood in the distance. It was overloaded with caravans of delivery carts. Beyond it a winding road led up to the main gate.

'You won't get in,' said a cracked voice below him, making him start. 'You're not early. You need to be early. It's still a long walk from here.'

Watborn looked down to find a hunched, scarred woman crouching on a rock, pulling a stringy length of moss from her teeth.

'Can I go in a cart?' he asked.

'They take vegetables and woven things and they like the coloured glass, but they won't take people. And the gatekeepers won't let you in, not unless you're one of them or you have a skill. Do you have a skill?'

'I am a fine birdcatcher.'

The woman spat green. 'You won't get in. And if you do, you'll never be allowed to leave. If you make a nuisance of yourself, they'll cut off your nose to be rid of you. Sometimes they just slit one nostril to let you off with a warning.'

'Is there another entrance?'

'Yes, where the shit comes out twice a day. I wouldn't be any-where near there if I was you. The smell can strip the feathers from a hawk.'

'Have you ever been inside?'

'Me?' She gave a squawk. 'Once, a long time ago, I was taken as a brothel-maiden. You wouldn't think to look at me now. It fair wore me out. I was fourteen then. My hair was yellow as wheat. I'm twenty-two. I've got the private parts of a seventy-year-old.' She tilted her head and listened. 'Sometimes, when the wind is from the west, you hear melodious sounds. Instruments made of gourds and catgut. Makes you think it might be nice to visit.' She raised what was left of her arm. 'Trust me, it's not.'

'I've heard a man may make his fortune there.'

'Yes, if he is willing to forfeit everything else.' She regarded the raggedly stitched stump of her wrist dispassionately. 'I used to have beautiful hands.'

Watborn took his leave of the brothel-maiden and headed off in the direction of the bridge.

17

A Crosshatch of Plots

Giniva paced the floor, wringing a yard of olivine dimity in her pallid hands, rage and disbelief battling in her heart. She watched as rain sprayed from the buttresses and leaked through the broken tracery of the stained-glass windows, discolouring the herringbone parquet.

To be rendered so completely powerless by the family! Well, she would show them all. Carapace would prove his love by visiting the dungeon chambers and arranging for the immediate release of the prisoners. Was that too much to ask?

She considered the consequences of her request. The family would be forced to curtail its practices and she would act as the voice of reason, leading them out of their squalor into a bright new dawn. She saw herself as a saint, her head aglow with a halo of golden rays, her samite garments rising and falling in the crossbreezes.

Think not too harshly of Giniva, those of you who find this account. You were young once too, and filled with golden ideals.

In truth, Scarabold was not prepared to heed his wayward daughter, even if the direst of circumstances demanded it. One contrary girl was not about to disturb the family's destiny.

Giniva's gown cleared a trail of dust upon the floor. It looked like the path of her fate. 'Do this one thing for me, Carapace,' she murmured to herself. 'Set the prisoners free, I beg of you.'

Fumblegut was pounding a mouse flat with a mallet.

Two more and he would have enough for a hat. He was too lazy to bother skinning them and simply smashed away at the pinioned rodents until their guts departed their hides. Flicking the mouse innards from his pudgy fingers, he buried his hand down the back of his breeches and gave the sweating cleavage of his rump a good scratch.

As he rose and tossed the mallet aside, his belly told him that it was time to eat again. Below ground there was no discerning night from day. The only source of illumination came from the reeking tallow torches. Nobody bothered him down here. Nobody wanted to know what went on, and that suited the jailer down to the gore-soaked ground.

He wondered about the stable-girl in Cell 46, a spirited young filly who had followed her mother into the pokey by admitting a minor act of theft. She was forever paddling her food plate against the bars, but had a tender appeal. Fumblegut fancied burying his teeth into her plump buttocks, but was forced to content himself with a cold tongue sandwich and a pot of porter.

Although some dank recess of his mind had registered an increase in the number of cockroaches and stag beetles scuttling over the dungeon floors, Fumblegut failed to spot Carapace approaching.

The chitinous Earl was sliding from shadow to shadow as he unlocked the prisoners' cells with the iron hoop of keys he had found tossed on a nearby desk by the careless jailer. Well versed in the ways of darkness, he slithered through the rows of stinking cubicles like a passing eclipse. When the gloom lifted from each holding pen, its inmate could discern a door standing ajar and offering freedom.

Many of the prisoners did not take this chance, so resigned were they to their fate. Others ventured to the light like spectres seeking the company of the living.

Fumblegut had no idea that he was being robbed of the monthly menu. Ensconced in his private chamber, seated beneath his rack of precious hand-carved dildos, he was focused on the bottom of his drained pint-pot.

Carapace stopped and sniffed the air.

He smelled something animal, a foetid, flyblown stench he had experienced once before in a private menagerie. He could see that many of the dungeon's denizens would be unable to leave unaided. Scarlet sores on their legs forced them to remain in strange static poses. Others had been fattened up so much that they could barely raise themselves on pustulant haunches from their rotted bamboo beds.

Here were diseases and tortures beyond imagining. Flesh had withered and spoiled on arms too long chained together. The degraded creatures lay moaning in their own filth until the time came for their purification in the kitchen's scalding pots.

One particular cell had been set aside for the prettiest prisoners, slender girls and golden boys curled up with nothing but their humiliation. They hugged the walls long after their door swung wide, such was their shame.

Carapace cast an anxious glance at the closed door of the jailer's office, if such a scrofulous den could be dignified with the title. He was convinced that at any minute all hell would break loose. The dazed prisoners were starting to emerge, stumbling against the walls. The sound of their shuffling was bound to reach the jailer's ears.

At the end of the muck-plastered corridor one further chamber stood alone. Cell 27 was separated from the rest. Carapace approached it with key hoop cocked.

Curiosity had bettered him; he was determined that his act of liberation would be completed. Reaching the single jail room, he lifted a torch from the wall and read the notice pinned to the lock.

FEED BUT DO NOT TOUCH
by Royal Decree

Carapace tipped his ear and listened to a laboured wheezing, then squinted inside. For a moment the cell refused to yield the figure within. He ran his torchlight over the poor inmate's features and was none the wiser. Lowering the light, he shone it at the prisoner's body and gasped.

What little colour there was in his face drained as he took a step back. Someone clearly knew about this; someone would pay, and someone else would have to be told.

Carapace knew far more of Londinium's history than his tender Princess. His familiarity with its inhabitants came from years of studying its form.

He reached out a hand to unlock the door but the keys jumbled themselves together. Fumblegut was emerging from his office to find himself jostled within a crazed cotillion of inmates.

It was clearly time to leave.

He searched for the entrance to the passageway that Giniva had so carefully described. She possessed hand-drawn maps of almost every known area (even though she had ventured into fewer than a tenth of them herself) and had passed one to him beneath her bedroom door. He prayed that he could decipher it fast enough to make good his escape.

As he hunted out the secret alcove, he forced himself to remember that any risk was worth taking for the warming glow of the Princess's approval.

As Carapace was making his way back through the castle, armed with his nugget of hitherto hidden knowledge, Leperdandy was plotting his own revenge for Giniva's sake.

Following a secret plan of his own devising, the princeling first visited Dr Fangle's medicarium beneath the eaves, then crept unseen into the kitchens to fiddle about in the scullery. Finally he made his way to the Tainted Hall, where fissures of steam wreathed the ceiling and draped the gargoyles in scarves of pale fat. There, he made a last-minute addition to the dining table.

Satisfied with his new role as an agent of disruption, he repaired to his toilette before attending the evening meal. His sister meant the world to him; without her laughter, life would be too grim to bear. And yet here he was, helping her to abandon the ancestral home. It would be his sacrifice and sadness, but how could he deny her anything?

For the past two hours, Spackle and Peut had been annoyed and confused in equal measure. After trailing the Beetle Earl from Giniva's apartment, they had managed to lose him somewhere in the stone corridors.

'Gone! But how?' cried Spackle. 'He turned, we turned, footsteps here, footsteps there – then nothing but urns and statues.'

'Naked ladies with no arms,' sniggered Peut. 'Can't stop you if you touch their breasties.'

'Where is the Earl?' Spackle shrugged. 'Vanished into smoke.'

It was as if Carapace had transformed himself into one of his beetles and disappeared down a crack in the floor, or had been provided with some secret knowledge neither of them possessed.

It was almost as though he had been given a map.

Peut slapped himself on the forehead: what about the paper that had passed beneath Giniva's bedroom door?

'What paper? You saw a paper? How?' Spackle was apoplectic. 'You piddling polyp!'

'You saw it too, brother. You share my brain and yet you failed to act.'

It meant that Carapace was doing the Princess's bidding, which spelled trouble for them both.

'We must find him, then!' cried Spackle.

'But how?' asked Peut.

And as they argued, even now the Beetle Earl was back outside his beloved's apartment, angrily removing each of the forty imprisoning iron nails with a claw hammer.

18

In Digestion

The dining hall was illuminated by two hundred and fifty-eight tall candles, the number of days into the year. The candle boy dreaded December, for should a wick lapse he would have a toenail removed to improve his future efficiency.

Picture the scene, if you fancy.

Scarabold, always the first to table, wedged between Mater Moribund and Dwinoline.

The Quaff sequestered in a poorly lit corner, the better to conceal his bibulous stupor.

Aunt Asphyxia with the twins at her side, framing her to the left and right, slouching like a pair of badly potted ferns.

Leperdandy, resplendent in a silk-starred waistcoat of midnight blue, touching his coiffure nervously.

The Decrepend droning on through the blessing of meats, even though two place settings had yet to be filled.

He stopped so abruptly that everyone at the table looked up.

Giniva entered the hall on Carapace's arm.

Scarabold's mouth fell open.

His daughter was wearing a floor-length cream lace gown woven through with honeysuckle buds. Their scent quickly filled the room, overpowering the stench of stewed flesh, banishing the reek of candle tallow, even muffling the musk of the Quaff's armpit dew.

The Beetle Earl was at her side, bound into a leather military corset knotted with polished darts that had been removed from the bodies of his enemies.

The Grandmater was so amazed that food actually fell out of her mouth. As the couple took their seats, no one could think of a single thing to say.

Giniva knew very well what she was about. Just one day into her new independence she felt something fresh within her grasp: the power to defy. It ran down her spine and tingled in her fingertips. The thrill of it lit her from within. She studied the assembly and steadied her breath.

Scarabold's immediate reaction – to blaspheme foully and throw his fists about – was stifled by the couple's calmness. Mater Moribund's eyes settled on them and narrowed imperceptibly before she turned her attention to the pouring of the soup. Leperdandy was shocked into another century. He had expected – counted on – Carapace to appear, but could not imagine what his sister thought she was doing. How had she been unbarred from her apartment?

After he had removed the last of the nails, Carapace had informed the Princess of his descent into the dungeons. As he described his freeing of the prisoners, she felt sure that the mission she had given him had transformed his nature, although she was a little surprised by the success of her pleas. To spur him on, she even consented to marry him, although she had no intention of doing so.

She considered the stratagems. Carapace would announce that he was still willing to form an alliance with the family. The King fancied he would have a strong new ally. Giniva would end their dependence on human livestock. And the Beetle Earl imagined that he would have somewhere to inter his aching fencepost. In this fashion, everyone would achieve a degree of happiness.

If there is one thing history teaches us, it is that nothing works out as planned.

As nobody wished to speak before the King and he was too surprised to issue an opinion, the assembly stayed silent. At first the only sound in the dining hall was the clicking of spoons in bowls. The soup appeared to be cream of turnip, but Giniva pushed hers to one side in case there was something of a more human nature eyeing her from its bottom.

Carapace ate heartily, ignoring the fascinated stares of Asphyxia and Leperdandy. He dabbed his napkin across his shovel beard and cracked his knuckles in a series of tiny pistol-shots. Setting aside his spoon, he sharply requested everyone's attention. A stag beetle fell out of his tunic and was hastily flicked aside.

It was the moment upon which the future of the family hung.

Carapace was about to reveal the one encounter he had so far with-held from the Princess, a discovery that would, he felt, reshape everyone's destiny.

Giniva's darkling doubts were aroused as the soup plates were swiftly replaced by steaming platters of stew. Nausea cupped her belly as she recalled the uncaulking of the billowing kitchen pots. As Scarabold sat with a lump of grey gristle already pendant on his fork, Carapace spoke out.

'Your Royal Highnesses, my lords and ladies, Your Graces, you may well be wondering how I come to be seated here at table with my future bride.'

In the ensuing uncomfortable silence, he balanced his fork between thumb and forefinger and stared at each of them in turn.

'The Princess Giniva agreed to my marital terms on the fulfil-ment of a certain stipulation. Namely, that I should enter a private area beneath us and free the prisoners held therein.'

He looked around the table, confronting a set of stony glares. Nobody uttered a word. 'You all know the purpose of penning up those poor dregs of humanity, even if you prefer to turn a blind eye to their misfortune.'

He paused for dramatic effect before preparing to deliver his bombshell. How long could he let them think that, even now, those prisoners might be burrowing up towards the dining hall to burst through the doors in insurrection?

Carapace held the sweetness of the moment. 'However,' he con-tinued, 'I did not set all of those poor unfortunates free. There was one prisoner kept in a solitary cell whose flesh is not for the delect-ation of his betters.'

At the furthest end of the dungeon he had discovered a secret that could undermine everything. Having toyed with the meat-laden fork, Carapace slid it into his mouth, savouring the taste of victory a moment more.

'You know who is there, but you may not know his real name.'

The Earl was an ambitious man who preferred to play a complex hand. He had affected to enjoy Scarabold's company so that he might receive the attentions of his daughter, but his discovery had opened up another possibility. By revealing that the Great Wound had lied to his family, he would earn Giniva's unreserved gratitude and isolate Scarabold.

'It is Tinfoot,' said Carapace, chewing slowly. Unfortunately, his mouth was so full of meat that hardly anyone could decipher his words. He took a sip of cloudy water, enjoying the looks of puzzlement that surrounded him. Revenge was a dish best served cold.

But not served as stew.

Suddenly he began to cough, then to choke, and then to scream out. Dark ribbons of blood streamed from his ears and nostrils.

Everyone watched in horror except Leperdandy, who stared down into his plate. The powder he had removed from Fangle's poison cabinet had been mixed with finely ground glass and liberally shaken over Carapace's dinner. Poison dusted his cutlery and glittered at the rim of his water goblet. And what an awful poison it was, capable upon entry of causing epilepsy in a month-old corpse as it inflamed and split each internal organ.

Now there could be no sham marriage and no dynastic alliance. Scarabold would no longer see him as an ineffectual fop but as a powerful political force. He would never be underestimated again. It felt good to be an agent of change.

He smiled to himself as the Earl sprayed spouts of gore about the table, staining the white damask burgundy before his chair shot backwards and he smashed on to the flagstones with a final flinch.

A single golden goblet rolled around the floor. There was a last belch of blood, then shocked silence fell. Giniva gingerly raised the tablecloth corner and stared at the shuddering shape that had been the Beetle Earl.

No prisoners assailed the dining hall. Carapace could not have known that Fumblegut had successfully halted the escape. In a moment of rare inspiration he had opened the sewage valves and flooded a section of the dungeon passage, forcing his inmates back into their cells.

Leperdandy had prepared a short speech to explain Carapace's alarming demise. He caught Scarabold's good eye and was momentarily shaken by the Great Wound's odd reaction.

The King was smiling.

Then he lowered his fork once more, dug into a whirlpool of streaky crimson meat and shovelled the lot into his mouth. 'Well,' he burbled through fat and tendons, 'it's a bloody shame the Earl got took sick. I wouldn't touch his portion if I were you. I suppose we'll never know what he was going to talk to us about. Better get Goldhawk to give his crockery a bloody good rinse.'

Leperdandy sat back, appalled. What had he missed? Where had

he gone wrong? Slowly the suspicion dawned on him that somebody else's plot had interfered with his own.

The Great Wound chewed happily. His kingdom was safe and
sound once more. Carapace might have unearthed a buried truth
but Fate had lowered her ebony wings across his path, bearing him
away into the land of eternal night.

The King's good eye roamed the diners, wondering which of
them had done the mortal deed. What did it matter so long as the
dynasty continued without change? *Let secrets stay secret*, he
decided, *that's what secrets are for*.

'Cheers.' He raised his goblet and sluiced down a particularly
stubborn piece of gristle as the servants discreetly dragged the
Beetle Earl away. 'Good health to all.'

19

Low Finance

Londinium had a management system of surprising sophistication. Its bankers were chosen for their mendacity and meanness. They were hutched in a warren of latticed iron cubicles on the fourth floor, where Mr Thredneedle could keep a watchful eye on them.

Thredneedle had been the manager of the Royal Counting Chamber for over thirty years, and retained his powerful position by treating each penny in the coffers as if brigands were trying to lift it from his own pocket. He would betray his oldest ally if it improved his balance of payments, and would monetize the drippings from his clerks' noses if he could find a way to do so. In this manner he retained his position as the most powerful commoner in the castle.

'You should try this, Canterby,' he told his chief accountant, thrusting his pipe into a crackling candle-flame. 'The peasants steep it in herbs and dry it on the banks of the Tamesis. It greatly aids cogitation.' He did not mention that most of the peasants had been drowned as the Devil's cohorts for doing so. His chief accountant waited while the manager sucked at the weeds in the pipe's bowl. 'Let me pose a question for you. Who do you think holds the most power here?'

It was not the kind of question one cared to consider, let alone hear asked aloud. Canterby stroked the crimson boil at the end of his nose and fidgeted uncomfortably. 'Well, that would be in the divine gift of the monarch, sir,' he decided finally. 'He keeps the kingdom from falling.'

'And under what circumstance would it fall?'

'Only before the might of an invading force.'

'Why could that not happen?'

'Our army remains the strongest in the land.'

'Because?'

Canterby was stumped. He searched about himself, as if hoping to find the right answer woven into the threadbare strands of the ancient rug at his feet.

'Because we feed it gold from the coffers,' Thredneedle replied softly, as if luring a child into a rat-pit. 'And the coffers remain full because we manage the money. If it were left to the King, we'd have nothing but moths and maggots in the treasury. We run everything. We compose the contracts that no one understands. We balance the profit and loss, and keep the leaky vessel of state afloat.'

The grand manager decided to omit his only misgiving: that the financing of the Counting Chamber remained a theoretical process. No one had been down to the treasury for generations. Whether there was actually any gold left or whether it consisted entirely of promissory notes and rodent droppings, nobody knew. The system only needed to work on paper.

Thredneedle was not alarmed; he knew that kingdoms thrived by being in debt. It ensured that everyone who was owed money paid close attention.

For almost two centuries Londinium had managed to be entirely self-sufficient, but these days, as the nurserymen could grow little in the acidulous soils of its terraces, they had come to rely on stocks from farmers in the Marshlands.

At the port on the Rushing River, ships regularly arrived from the north-east, but none of the dockers had been paid in an age, and the complaints from suppliers were becoming too hard to ignore. One could only have so many of them drowned or accidentally trampled by bullocks before tongues began to wag.

'So, we have a problem,' Thredneedle told his chief counter. 'I understand that Carapace's valet is nowhere to be found, which means that news of the Beetle Earl's sudden passing will spread fast. The Sheathwing army is strong, but not so strong that it can vanquish us alone. While he seeks alliances, we must prepare for the worst.'

Canterby was confused. 'You know of this, yet the King does not?'

'The King is not a strategist. We have to enlist new recruits and pay them. To do that, I need to know the state of the coffers.'

'Then we must arrange for a visit from an auditor,' Canterby suggested.

Thredneedle drew on his pipe. 'Precisely my conclusion. I have decided it must be someone from outside, someone who has nothing to gain from lying to us.'

The accountant looked as if he could not imagine such a thing.

'To that end, I sent a message to a fellow who comes highly recommended,' Thredneedle said through a haze of calming vapour. 'I want you to look after him well. See that he has everything he needs during the day and everyone he wants during the night. Show him the counting-books and the calculation bibles, bury anything that might be blameful and make sure he explains how we may increase our profits threefold. Better make that fourfold.'

Satisfied that everything would soon be under control so that the bedraggled army could kit itself out in shining new armour, the manager of the Royal Counting Chamber poured himself some wine. Like many men of vision in the world of capital, he sat back and polished his nails as death and disaster approached.

20

The Hunter

Watborn walked all day, but after his encounters with the kindling boy and the brothel-maiden he decided to keep himself hidden from the cart track.

The going was slow and exhausting. He fell asleep beneath a gorse bush and awoke to find a chaffinch on his boot, which he took as a good omen. Very slowly he raised his right hand towards it, but the bird flew away. It was used to people and too fast for him.

Evening dew drooped the ferns, a reminder that autumn had arrived. His stomach rumbled. He needed a wash. Rising from the bracken, he made his way to a tumbling stream and disrobed. He had just finished his ablutions when someone called to him.

'Hail, fellow!'

The man was roughly his age, dressed in a hooded jerkin of green rushes, with marvellous teeth; that is to say, a full set of them. He stepped forward through the ferns with a hand raised in greeting. 'Who are you?'

Watborn said nothing while he decided if this was friend or foe.

'A word of advice, friend. It will take a time for those clothes to dry. The sun won't reach this side of the hill until noon tomorrow.'

Watborn realized he shouldn't have washed them all at once. The man in green pulled a sack from his shoulders and opened it. 'We don't get many from the Marshlands up here.'

'How do you know I'm from the Marshlands?'

'That's marsh-lamb wool you've just chucked in the stream, right? And your accent.'

'I ent got an accent,' said Watborn indignantly.

'Oi arven't gort an aaccent,' mimicked the man good-naturedly. 'Don't worry, it took years to get rid of mine.'

'Why would you need to?'

'You're going to Londinium, aren't you? Must be. There's nothing else around here but goat turds.' He squinted towards the fortress at his back. 'The more you sound like a peasant up there, the more they will cheat you. Here.'

He threw Watborn a bundle.

'Dry clothes. Not as fine quality as your marsh-lamb but good enough for now. Your first time away from your village?'

Watborn nodded grudgingly as he pushed his wet legs into warm dry trousers.

'I've just been up there, taken them four brace of fine pheasants. I have a deal with Goldhawk, the head chef. At least he doesn't cheat me.' He studied the birdcatcher's clumsy attempt to dress with amusement. 'Won't you tell me your name?'

'Watborn.' He held out a broad hand, and it was clasped.

'And I'm Herne. Why are you going?'

'I never been before. My village burned. There's nothing to go back to. I thought to make my fortune.'

'Then you're greener than my jerkin.' Herne laughed. 'What do you know about the folk there?'

Watborn thought for a minute. 'They keep to themselves, except when it's time to buy our goods, or to collect taxes and tithes. They live different to us.'

'And that's the sum total of your knowledge, is it?'

Herne seated himself on a tussock. He dug in his bag once more and handed Watborn a piece of dried coney to chew. 'The men are much as you would expect, but it's the women you must watch for. They're a sharp-eyed bunch. Scarabold's family is as ancient as moss. The King believes he is still important, but he has no power any more. There are no male heirs left. His need is urgent and that makes him dangerous. The royal family will take everything from you and give nothing back.'

Watborn fastened his buttons. 'What makes them so different?'

'They live in ways far advanced from us. But they have bred themselves too fine to survive. One day their walls will tumble and they will be forced out into the lands below. Then we will have some merriment.'

'You know how to deal with them.'

Herne tapped the side of his long nose. 'I know what they're looking for and how to provide it – strictly business. I never go inside, for if I did I would not be allowed to leave until I'd been cheated. A word of advice.' He beckoned Watborn closer. 'Don't call at the gates asking for work, or they will slave you like a mule and throw your corpse over the ramparts.'

'Then what should I do?'

Herne clapped a hand on Watborn's shoulder. 'You and I are strangers, but trust me about this. Do not under any circumstances try to enter by the gates. The guards make a game of drowning unwanted callers. Are you sure you really want to get inside?'

'I must do so.'

'May I ask why?'

'That is my business.'

'Very well. There is a culvert.' He saw the look of incomprehension on Watborn's face. 'A pipe, if you will. I can show you the exact location. Somebody opens the sluices to the latrines and leaves them to drain for a while after. If you enter that way and you are fast, you will soon be inside.'

'Is it safe to do so?'

Herne laughed again. 'No, of course not.'

'And once I am within?'

'You will need to wash because they'll find you from the stench. You should observe the inhabitants unseen. Get knowledge of them first, friend, before they have a chance to gain knowledge of you.'

Taking Watborn's hand, he led him to a cleft in the trees. 'See those brown streaks upon the wall?' Herne asked. 'When the servants have full guts they stick their arses out of the windows. Beneath them is the cloaca trough leading to the big iron hopper and the pipes. If you can see light through the grille, it means the drain is open. If it's shut, you'll have to wait. That's the only other way in.'

'What if they open a sluice while I'm inside?'

'Then, my friend, you will be drowned in shit. But there is a way to survive if you think fast. An air-pipe rises above to prevent the detonation of foul odours. If a flood comes, make sure you are standing beneath it, but hold on to the wall behind or you'll be swept away.' The hunter clasped his arm. 'I know this only from what others have told me. Do you have to go there?'

Watborn held his gaze.

'Very well. It would sit uneasy with me if I sent someone to their death. This is where I must leave you.'

'You have been kind to me, Herne.'

'That I have not,' replied Herne. 'For I have gained a suit of wool and left you with hemp.'

Watborn was dumbfounded by the hunter's considerate nature. Producing the compass from his jerkin, he handed it over in cupped hands. 'Keep this,' he said. 'It will always guide you northwards. I have no more use for it now.'

Herne studied the guiding device in wonder, twisting it this way and that. 'Why, this is something I thought I'd never see again. Perhaps the Marshlands have more to teach than I thought.'

'I will find a way to repay your counsel,' Watborn promised.

'Just make sure you keep yourself alive,' warned Herne, placing the device in his sack. 'And be mindful of the time that passes. Those who stay too long never return.'

21

The Rules of Departure

The King received his daughter in the Morning Room, a tiled chamber from every nook of which dangled drooping lilies, due to the fact that it had once been used for family wakes before the letter 'U' was dropped from its title.

Scarabold was accompanied by the Decrepend, who held before him a wide roll of parchment yellower than his horse-teeth.

'I obtained this from our lawyers, Snear, Muzzle & Crouch,' Scarabold began, strolling with his hands behind his back. 'It sets out the terms of your coming of age. As the document has lain in the undercrypt unchallenged for over two hundred years, I think we can safely assume it remains in effect and applies to you.'

'Why is it needed at all?' asked Giniva with a defiant jut of the jaw.

'My little petal-pudding, you don't have to worry your pretty curls about it. As the grand judge Arnelthus Pandergreen is so fond of reminding us, if we ignore the law we have nothing.'

'Nothing,' agreed the Decrepend.

'We make our laws and they make us. I think you'll find this quite progressive. Obviously, females can't hold property, opinions and so on, but this document was formulated to ensure that the female line understands what is expected of it.'

Giniva was suddenly apprehensive. 'What does it decree?'

'That until your sixteenth birthday you were to remain within the care and consent of your legal guardians, but now that this date has passed you are free to take leave of the family home whenever you wish to do so, and roam wheresoever you care to roam, and so on and so forth.'

'So forth,' repeated the Decrepend.

'But Father, that is wonderful—'

Scarabold held up a pair of stained digits. His gesture was instantly copied by the Decrepend. 'The Rule of Departure comes with two exceptions.'

'Exceptions!' coughed the Decrepend, as if preparing a mime. 'Two parts.'

'First, you may leave the castle and its grounds on the condition that you return before the hour of darkness. This is, of course, for your own safety. Wolves, brigands and suchlike. Second, to make sure that you obey this rule, any sibling, half-sibling or quarter-sibling will be held in our custody until your return. A precautionary measure, nothing more. In the event of your failure to appear, the aforementioned sibling, half-sibling or quarter-sibling will be walled up alive in the Great Well. Apart from that, you may stay away for as long as you like.'

'But how can I? Darkness falls at the end of every day.'

Scarabold scratched at something in his beard. 'Well, that certainly puts a time limit into effect, I admit.'

'A limit,' repeated the Decrepend, making a noise like a donkey eating turnips.

'What if I return just a little late?' Giniva asked, threading the weighted hem of her satin gown through fretful fingers.

'Then the aforementioned sibling—'

'—half-sibling or quarter-sibling,' the Decrepend added.

'—who remains behind is placed in the dungeons at the disposal of Fumblegut, to do with as he wishes for as long as he wishes until your return or until said sibling ceases to be, and so on and so forth. The rest is just small print. So you see, my little thistle, there are no shackles binding you. You are entirely released.'

The Decrepend handed him a worn leather case, from which he pulled a huge dry scroll of paper. 'Simply fill in these application-to-travel forms and return them to Snear, Muzzle & Crouch three weeks before your planned date of departure, and I have no doubt that the Department of Voyages will pass them. Do we still have a Department of Voyages?' The old monarch's eye softened. 'You understand that to preserve the purity of the kingdom it is necessary to restrict the passage of its citizens. We don't want you going out there for weeks and coming back dropsical, covered in running sores. I don't know where the commoners get them, but they all do.

Something about the mal humours from the marshes. We could have types of every shade passing through here, and then what? As a member of the royal family, you are expected to place duty ahead of selfish desires. Rebelliousness is not a sought-after quality in a princess.'

'But Father—'

'Enough! There are matters of more pressing urgency to which I must attend.' Scarabold slapped his broad hand on the table, signifying an end. 'News of the Beetle Earl's demise will escape these walls and hop to the east faster than lice on the heads of paupers, and when it does we must face the possibility of dreadful repercussions. Therefore, other allegiances must be forged as soon as possible, and that means finding another royal son susceptible to your unsullied charms before the moon wanes.' He pawed his whiskers, thinking. 'I may have to offer a dowry and throw in the last of the good furniture.'

Giniva gave a cry of frustration and stormed from the room, not quite realizing that war had been declared between them.

22

The Arrival of the Auditor

Just before nightfall, Claude Silvercannon appeared on the commoners' causeway and was admitted to the vestibule of the Royal Counting Chamber, where he rattled the rain out of his greatcoat and stamped the storm from his boots.

The auditor was a slight, semi-transparent sort of man, with a lick of vaporous blond hair that stuck up like a squirrel-tail and wide, inquisitive eyes that lent him a look of perpetual alarm, as if he had just discovered that he had shat himself. He was used to being the bearer of bad tidings, but this was the first time he had been asked to appear before someone who had the power to order his death. Usually he worked from his office in the Old Port Cedd and was deferred to, for he could bankrupt a fleet with a swipe of his pen.

'Ah, yes, thank you . . . ah, no, I'll keep that if you don't . . . yes, that's mine too.' Silvercannon allowed himself to be spun about by a squadron of servants who yanked his wet woollen jerkin and ermine-collared jacket from him, fighting to free him from recalcitrant sleeves.

Herb-tea appeared, and marzipan biscuits and a salver of persimmons, and a book of instructions was stuck in his fist, and quills, and a pot of ink and a map, and bristling with these accoutrements, his arms still partially pinioned by a half-removed cardigan, his valise, hat and notebag, he allowed himself to be led to the Counting Chamber floor.

Leperdandy's rooms were more than merely theatrical; they were the very essence of theatre itself. At one end of his bedchamber was a proscenium arch fitted with dusty scarlet velvet curtains and a tasselled gold rope that could be untwisted to reveal a stage. On it were props of every shape and size, columns, cannons and cutlasses, paper masks, silk ruffs and beaded jerkins stacked in tiers against the walls.

'It is my world,' he explained, rearranging a clay mannequin in the flamboyant costume of a corsair. 'Here I can create any scene and make it more vivid than life out there. I can't leave with you, for where would I go?'

'Anywhere that unbuds a flower and draws a smile,' cried Giniva. 'Anywhere the wind takes us. Anywhere that brings us pleasure!'

'That's all very well, but how should we live, you and I?' Leperdandy studied a vase of unruly lavender, found it displeased him and set about regimenting it. 'The diet of vegetables that has freed you to enter the world outside is not one that can sustain me. If I stay within these walls, I am fed. If I leave, I will starve.'

'But Leperdandy, can you not learn to love the taste of turnips?'

'They can't provide me with the nourishment I need.'

'Surely animal meat—'

'It has to be human. It was forced upon me until my body craved it. No, that's not quite true. I liked the taste, for I knew nothing else. Don't you understand? I have no choice. I must stay here. I cannot provide for myself in any way.'

'It is a paradox,' she said, turning over the problem. 'If I apply to go, they will hold you hostage. And if I return a minute late, they will remove your ears. Yet we cannot be parted, for I would die without you.'

'You will forget me in time,' said Leperdandy, flapping lavender dust from his slender hands.

Giniva tidied the end of Leperdandy's coverlet. 'Our father will see Carapace's death as a minor inconvenience.'

'My only thought was for your salvation,' said Leperdandy disconsolately. 'I see now that his removal achieved nothing.'

'What was it he said before he erupted?' she wondered. 'One prisoner who was not to be touched? What was his name? Foot-Rot?'

'Tinfoot,' Leperdandy remembered. 'I have never heard of such a person. Perhaps I can find out who he is.'

'If the Beetle Earl's discovery is truly so important, perhaps I can use the knowledge to escape.' She rose from the bed and walked to the window, pushing it open to feel the breeze. 'I have to go,

Leperdandy – you can see that, can't you? If I stay, I will join the ranks of the royal brood-mares.'

'There is only one solution,' said Leperdandy. 'Someone must smuggle you out.'

'But who and how?' Giniva spun on her heel vexedly. 'The only people who come and go are salesmen and seamstresses from the mid-towns, and farmers from the Marshlands. How am I able to meet such commoners? A princess may not mingle.'

'If you are to truly abandon your birthright, you must remove all notions of holding high station,' Leperdandy warned. 'I could not pass among beggars because my nostrils are too sensitive and I would quickly sicken, but there is a strength in you that will set you free. You could plot your own course in the world.'

'Do you think I should go to the scullery herb-beds and talk to gardening folk? They must make trips to the fruiting fields. Perhaps I could be hidden in a barrow.'

'And have a farmboy pass a pitchfork through you? I have a better idea.'

Arrivals here were rare and news of visitors travelled as fast as the mice that pattered the corridors. The princeling had heard from Cradleigh the under-footman, who had heard from Fetlock the ostler, who had stabled Claude Silvercannon's carriage-horses.

'There is a visitor, an auditor who has made a great name for himself. He is here to examine the war coffers for old Thredneedle.'

Giniva looked doubtful. 'How does someone like you know that?'

'When I'm not allowed to speak, which is most of the time, I listen. If you can persuade him to take you, I will take care of the rest.' He raised a meaningful eyebrow.

'But if he is found to be smuggling a royal personage, his neck will be pressed to the executioner's block,' said Giniva. 'Why would he agree to undertake such a foolhardy mission?'

'You might offer him royal patronage or appeal to his sense of justice. He is here to balance the accounts, so the notion of fairness may entice him. The alternative is to remain here until our father finds you a new suitor.'

With the thought of Leperdandy prepared to suffer in order to secure her freedom, Giniva set off to find the auditor.

As she danced down the stairs she caught glimpses of the world from the turret's passing arrow-slits. A squadron of geese honked past, their white wings in frozen poses. The perpetual mist that hung around the ramparts was suffused with amethyst hues after the storm, blooming hope in her breast.

She could not see the pretty village fires now, nor discern the figure of a man making his way from the still-smoking ruin of his home to the foothills.

Thredneedle, the manager of the Royal Counting Chamber, unpopped the top buttons of his waistcoat, rubbed his palms together and took a deep breath.

He pushed at the iron spar until it finally began to turn, shrieking in protest. Flecks of rust fell away as he unscrewed it. He had not been to the gold vault on the first floor in a very long time.

It took the combined strength of Canterby and two cashiers to pull open the two-foot-thick iron door. The air that roiled out was stale and unbreathed. Lanthorns were lit and passed inside.

The chief accountant ushered their guest into the chamber. 'I'm sure you will find everything you need in here, Master Silvercannon.' He undulated out of the way to allow the auditor's ingress.

In construction the vault was like a hammam, with arched coves arranged around a striped alabaster courtyard containing, of all things, a fountain. Silvercannon's look of surprise was noted by Thredneedle.

'It amused the sixth king to keep his gold here in liquid form,' Canterby explained. 'He would sit and smoke his pipe, watching the kingdom's wealth flow all about him.' He decided not to mention that the sixth king had occasionally melted his coinage into ore so that he could add baser elements to it and stretch it further. 'Beneath the fountain was a furnace that turned the ingots to molten gold. But that was long ago.'

'And where is the gold now?' asked Silvercannon, not unreasonably.

'It was returned to solid form and was gradually replaced with its equivalent value in paper. More modern. It foxes the coin-cutters.' Thredneedle pointed to the racks of cobwebbed boxes in the alcoves.

'You.' Silvercannon pointed at the chief accountant. 'When was the last time you totalled the amounts remaining in the coffers?'

'Oh, there was no need to do that,' Canterby simpered. 'After each transmutation from gold to paper the value was amortized; that is to say, a distribution of payment was divided into multiple cash-flow instalments so that each consisted of both principal and interest, then realized into assets offset by receipts drawn against the original value of the gold.'

'You realize that makes absolutely no sense?' asked Silvercannon, advancing on the nearest box and throwing back its lid, releasing hundreds of tiny black spiders. A second box set free a phalanx of brown moths. 'I would like your books delivered here immediately, and have my calculating machine brought forthwith.'

'With all due respect, sir,' said Canterby, 'I fear it will be difficult to transport your machine into the vault itself.'

'You have servants, don't you? And donkeys, and rope? Kindly set about it at once. I would like herb-tea served regularly every other hour with an arrowroot biscuit. I will take a light luncheon at noon – a cheese or a chicken, something recognizable, and fresh-baked bread. I will work until seven each evening, remaining until the last of the balanced books has been duly noted and accounted for. Then I will require a more substantial supper, with a cup of claret.'

'Perhaps I may be of some small service by remaining here?' asked Canterby.

'No, sir, you may not, for I fear your presence will inhibit my impartiality,' Silvercannon replied. 'I must have distance to identify your problems, although from the most cursory glance I fear that even I may find them insurmountable. If the fortunes of this kingdom were to be weighed in moths and termites, I imagine it would be very rich indeed.'

With that, he waved away the courtiers of the kingdom's finance, cracked his knuckles and set to work.

23

Jumblejoy

As the shadows lengthened, the great calculating machine was bumped and buffeted into the chamber beyond the vault, necessitating the hospitalization of a servant with crushed ankles and the execution of a donkey.

Claude Silvercannon began inputting his immaculate entries. By lunchtime on the next day his spirits had tumbled so far that he found himself sinking into a state of despairing shock. As soon as he felt sheets of rust crunch beneath his shoes from the vault's disintegrating floor, he feared the worst. A level of neglect existed far beneath his direst expectations.

The paper currency, promissory notes, IOUs, deferred bills and unrecalled debts were not worth their weight in gold, bronze or even pewter. The paper was, in fact, not worth the paper it was stamped upon. Oh, the bookkeeping had been cleverly handled, that much was clear, but it amounted to the mere shifting around of inconceivably huge debts. This was how empires fell: in banks, not on battlefields.

He was pondering the problem and realized that he had been sitting for four hours. Rising, he strode to the door of the vault and stretched. There before him, drifting down the spiral staircase into the antechamber of the Counting Chamber, was a vision of what he could only liken to that of a swan in sapphire silk.

Garlanded in tiny blue flowers, her plaited blonde hair fell about her shoulders like the molten gold that had once tumbled from the sixth king's fountain. Her angel-cupped breast, her slender-laced waist, her thighs . . . he coughed and halted his thoughts from travelling further.

He knelt for fear that his knees might give way, bowing his head low. For the first time he sensed he was in the presence of royal lineage.

Giniva always dressed as befitted her status. If she appealed to someone who might be persuaded to help her, so much the better. She smiled graciously in the direction of the auditor and raised the back of her pale hand for him.

'I am the Princess Giniva,' she explained, 'daughter to the Great Wound.'

'And I am—'

'I know who you are. I have a question that has long been vexing me. May I ask you?'

'I will endeavour to answer, Your Royal Highness,' replied Silver-cannon, bowing low.

'What is it like? I mean, outside?'

The question flummoxed the auditor. Surely she already knew?

'There are towns and villages, and lowlands and marshes, and places where no one may safely travel at any time.'

Giniva's puzzlement was matched only by her curiosity. 'You are an educated gentleman, yet you are not from here.'

'I descend from peoples trained in fiscal law.'

'So there are others like you?'

'Only a few now, Your Highness. Education does not survive if it is not nurtured. There are only chieftains and peasants in these dark days. They lack information but are rich in beliefs.'

'What kind of beliefs?'

'They worship magick, Your Highness, an irrational system that values instinct over evidence.'

The Princess tilted her pretty head, trying to understand. 'Give me an example.'

The auditor thought for a moment. 'They believe that sickness may be cured by urinating on a loaf and feeding it to a dog. That tying a bell on an ox stops it from being struck by lightning. That diseases of the heart may be cured by pressing a heart-shaped leaf upon the ribs. They leave their babies in the mud and eat poisonous weeds from the hedgerows. In a word, my lady, they are mightily ignorant.'

'And do you think us ignorant?'

'This is my adopted country, Your Highness.'

'I meant here, in the House.'

'No, Your Highness. You are enlightened. You had the Religions once.'

'Ah yes, the Italian gods and some others. I forget. Something with white bulls. We threw them out and beat the Abbot with hot iron sticks. Monarchs do not like to be told there are higher powers.'

'I think you are isolated by privilege.'

'And is that so bad?'

'Isolation leads to indifference and . . . a turning inwards.' The auditor spoke carefully, for he valued his head.

'And although the people outside are ignorant, they are not isolated.'

Silvercannon was loath to give a direct answer. 'Sadly, there has been a withdrawing of civilization in this country, Your Highness. The outside is now governed by violence and stupidity.'

'We are just as violent and stupid in here.' It was not what Giniva wished to hear at all, so she forced herself to change the subject. 'I understand that the King has summoned you to help him raise money for a war.'

Silvercannon felt the first tingle of alarm. 'Hardly, for I am here to appraise, not to raise.'

'And when will you present your findings to Scarabold?' She walked towards the calculating machine and ran a dainty fore-finger along its side.

'I suspect it will take me until the end of the week to reach a full understanding of the accounts, Your Highness.'

The calculating engine was square and iron and painted stove-black, with polished brass trims. Giniva peered into its mechanical intestines and saw gleaming levers, spindles, cogs and counters. It could not have been manufactured here. 'Tell me, how does this curious engine work?'

Silvercannon's eyes brightened. He loved discussing the mechanics of finance. 'It was developed in Ellada and uses a system that has not changed in six hundred years. I numerically input the monthly account balances, income and outgoings, finances, wages and bills outstanding, interest to be paid, interest accruing, debts and loans. To this must be added the movement of the planets. Then I manipulate the levers and receive back-readings. If you would please come around this side.'

He pointed at a black metal slot containing a long row of stamped symbols arranged like teeth in a mouth. Above it sat a life-sized male figure pressed from two iron halves. It had tortoiseshell pupils set in mother-of-pearl eyeballs, and half-raised arms with upturned thumbs and unseparated fingers. Its limbs and torso were stove-black, like the machine. It wore a gilt pinstriped jerkin and sat half buried in the casing with a brass bar across its knees, so that there appeared to be no separation between the statue and its surrounding mechanism.

'If it is a machine, what is this figure for?' asked Giniva, fascinated.

'To personify its actions, Your Highness,' said the auditor with the enthusiasm that all accountants have for hard cash. 'A calculating engine has no human face. It is easier to deny.

'I call him Jumblejoy,' continued Silvercannon proudly. 'This particular model was designed and builded in a far-off land where the sun rises as ours sets.'

'This is the land of Old Jiutu, yes? The portsmen bring us silks from there.'

'The engine was brought overland to the Middle Kingdom and thence here, Your Highness, in a journey that took many years.'

'What powers his calculations?'

'A great metal spring that must be greased and wound to function.'

'And how do you think we will fare when Jumblejoy has resolved our finances? Can we afford to win a war?'

'I do not have all the figures yet—'

'Please, Mr Silvercannon, you have no reason to conceal the truth from me. I am not my father's daughter in that respect, and have no influence in his affairs of state. What does the engine say?'

The auditor eyed the Princess warily, but she was a creature of such obvious purity and grace that he felt himself unable to lie. 'I have never seen such an astronomical figure,' he said. 'Its true number may be almost impossible for a mortal to conceive.'

'Then our ill-gotten plunder and punitive taxes have made us wealthy?' she asked.

'No, Your Highness, they have created a debt so perfect that it is almost without end. To view the true state of your finances would be like peering into a well with no bottom. There is only obscurity and blackness and infinite unknowing. The problem arose in the transition from gold to paper. The system only works if the gold is retained and stored somewhere, but I can find no account of what happened to it.'

'You mean we are fraudulent?' The Princess looked shocked.

'Your Highness, nothing is left. Or, to put it another way, there is such a negativity of wealth that it turns the concept of nothing inside out.'

'Then how is it that we survive?' asked Giniva, bristling a little.

'By borrowing on something that is not there,' said the auditor simply. 'And by having your last auditor disembowelled.'

Giniva examined the nail on her little finger. 'You do realize that if you tell Scarabold this, you will be putting yourself in the gravest danger? He will have your guts draped across the portcullis. Your head will be placed in a basket and carried to a pole above the moat where the crows will peck it apart before the next sunset.'

Silvercannon was aghast. His right eye began to tic. 'How can I lie? Integrity is all an auditor has to offer. Without it he is nothing.'

'Such is the peril of your profession. But there is a way,' said Giniva slyly. 'I can show you how to keep your head upon your shoulders. But you must do something for me.'

'Anything, Your Highness,' said the auditor, thinking of his tender neck. 'You have only to ask it.'

'You must take me with you when you leave.'

Silvercannon had been as pale as whalebone to begin with, but now he had the complexion of a codfish. 'If I am caught, I will be blamed—'

'You will not be blamed because the matter will not involve you. You will not be party to my escape.'

'But if I tell your father about the debt, he will kill me.'

'And if you lie, he will surely know. I agree, it is a conundrum. But there is a way that Scarabold can be told the truth without the court executioner coming after you.'

'Then please, I entreat you, tell me what I must do.'

'The matter is simply solved.' Giniva beckoned reassuringly. 'We must find someone else to blame. Someone who has no human life to lose. Jumblejoy, perhaps.'

Silvercannon felt cold fingers of fear grasp the back of his neck. He had no desire to become a part of someone else's stratagem. 'I don't understand,' he said.

'The answer is right before you.' The Princess gave him a secretive smile. 'But in order to slaughter two prey with a single shot, I will need the talents of my brother,' she whispered. 'Continue with your work and say nothing about your findings for now.'

'But what if I'm questioned?'

'If you are asked for figures, wave pages of numbers about. I'm sure you know how to do that. My father is happier with a sword than a pen. He has no patience for listening to expert advice. If he insists on seeing your calculations, give him too much information and his attention will quickly wander.'

The auditor looked far from reassured. She bestowed upon him a benign smile. 'Trust me, all will soon be made clear.'

'I really don't think I should be involved—' Silvercannon began.

'Oh, but you are now,' Giniva replied softly.

24

Lively Corpses

Crossing the bridge proved easy enough. The jam of carts prevented Watborn from being noticed. One laden with shiny blue bottles had broken an axle and slewed across the carriageway, causing tempers to rise and traffic to pile up.

The birdcatcher kept his head lowered as he stepped off the far side of the bridge. Pressing himself into the bushes, he became so still that sparrows alighted on him. He watched as the bottle cart was moved and dragged to the main gate.

After a minute an inset door creaked open and the quartermaster's arm appeared, beckoning. The carter stepped forward with a basket and removed its cloth, revealing a great bouquet of cabbages. The basket was taken in and the quartermaster extended his fist, releasing a few coins. The bottles were held to the light and examined before the cargo was accepted.

This was repeated a dozen times until one of the farmers, unhappy with his remuneration, demanded his basket back. He was pulled inside the door, which slammed shut behind him. Minutes passed. Eventually the door opened and he was expelled without his trousers, clutching a bloody nose with both hands.

Watborn shielded his eyes and looked up through the gap.

He saw a stone incline stitched with narrow windows. Steep staircases. A high blackstone archway. Ramshackle wooden structures. And at the centre, an immense statue of a rampant white lion wearing a golden crown, its great paws clawing at the sky. The inside of its mouth was painted crimson. A fearful symbol of Londinium's strength and dominance.

However, scratched in three-foot-high letters across the outer-most side of the lion's pedestal, the only part that faced away from the residents, were the words: *CASTLE NO-LAND*. Such was the disrespect of those who lived below.

Watborn shielded his eyes and tried to glimpse the rooftops against the setting sun. The main buildings were connected by battlements, bridges, tunnels and staircases, some in good repair, some lethal. The buttresses between them had crumbled and were propped up by thickets of wooden poles.

While marsh gases kept the surrounding villages bright-skied, the castle-city was fogged in obscurity. Mists, frets and frosts swept up from the river and concealed so much at different times that it was impossible to see more than a bow-shot's distance.

But now, at least, he was here.

Watborn was within fifty paces of the great stone conduit. He made his way over for a closer look. His boots sank into a puddle of grey-green sludge beset by dragonflies. The outpour from the pipe was fresh and deep. Its smell was astonishing, and brought up his stomach. The conduit's spatterings reached all the way to where he waited. It had just finished draining.

He peered between the stinking weeds that hung down from its brickwork. A family of tiny blue marsh-tits flew into his face. Light from the pipe glinted on stalactites of ordure. If the sluice gate was opened once he was inside, it seemed likely he would drown, but there was no other way to enter from the hill.

Now was the time to move.

You're a fool, Watborn, he told himself. *But if you're smarter than a cat, a little curiosity may not kill you.* Climbing on to the rocks, he hauled himself inside the outlet. The floor was as slippery as ice. The conduit was square and stepped at one side, so he could climb. If another flood rushed down, he would be swept away; there were no footholds or bars to cling on to.

There were rats, of course. He could hear them pattering about in the muck. There was something else snuffling, longer-bodied and sinewy. It looked like a cross between an otter and a weasel. Experience had taught him that such creatures had sharp teeth. It was best to stay away from the business-end of that.

The reek was a living thing. He forced himself to breathe through his nose and not take the miasma into his belly. He could see no more than a few yards ahead. It was important not to stop because then he would think, and thinking brought fear. As the pipe's incline increased he found it harder to keep his balance.

A rumbling sounded in the distance, and he made the mistake of halting. What did a sluice gate sound like? The grating, gurgling noise brought the stink of bowels and a change of air pressure.

The pipe was above him, but it was too high to reach.

When the sluice gate opened up ahead, a great blast of lumpen sludge roiled through the outlet on its way to the outside world, where it would no doubt kill all the fish in the streams. He backed against the wall as Herne had instructed and found an iron bar around which he could wrap his arm.

An inflated corpse rolled past him and became lodged against an outcrop. It was joined by a gape-mouthed second and a third the colour of ashes. The bodies were livelier in death than they had been in life. He grabbed at a tangle of coarse twine that had caught on the wall, thinking that it might be strong enough to lash the limbs of the corpses together. They were soft and slippery, but once they were tied he was able to clamber on to their backs and reach up above.

Moments after he managed to stand upright, the cadavers slid south from under him and he was left dangling from the ridged lip of the stench pipe.

25

A Life Anew

'Leperdandy, I need your talents.'

The Princess examined theatrical props and discarded them one by one. 'Scarabold does not know you were behind the demise of the Beetle Earl. If Spackle and Peut inform him, he will be loath to believe them. This places you in the perfect position of a double agent. You are versed in the manner of the stage and its effects. I need your help to save the auditor and effect my escape. What do you know about creating likenesses?'

'Ah, you have not met Copernia.'

Grabbing his sister's hand, he led her to the velvet-draped arch behind his bed and revealed his figurine with a flourish of musty cloth.

Copernia was stitched and stuffed, a little moth-eaten but the very image of Giniva, with a couple of differences: she stood at a height of just five feet, four inches shorter than the Princess, and had a cheerful smile. Some of her stuffing had fallen out and there were death's-head moths in her hair.

'I was going to fashion you a gown for your birthday but I couldn't find the right shade of jade silk.'

'We will need theatre paint, but if you are to save us both, you must teach me to be still. I must be like Moribund and show no emotion at all. I will replace Jumblejoy and make my escape.'

'Remember the last time you posed for your portrait? If I didn't know you were flesh and bone I would have had you for a statue then,' he laughed.

'So long as I don't need to scratch my nose.' The Princess loosened her stance and lowered her arms with relief. 'I pray the auditor has managed to unscrew the iron accountant from its perch, leaving its place for me. He finishes his work tomorrow morning and must present his case to Father. Only I can save us both now. If I fail, the Great Wound will nail me up again until a new defiler appears.'

The boy began throwing open drawers and cupboards, looking for his brushes. With his theatre paints he could duplicate any hue. 'My hands are far from steady, but Scarabold's remaining eye is weak and will not register imperfections,' he said. 'You realize there must be no one else present for the subterfuge to work. Not Thredneedle, nor any of his accountants. There can be only the three of you, and in poor lighting. You must ensure the servants remove at least half of all the lanthorns. And if you should twitch or sneeze—'

'You don't need to remind me of what's at stake.' Giniva raised a slender hand. 'No one must know of this. Not a word goes beyond these walls.'

But just outside, others were plotting.

'They're up to something,' said Aunt Asphyxia, lifting a bony finger to the air and listening. One could be forgiven for imagining that her ear had stretched itself upwards in the shape of a lily. 'The corridors are altogether too silent. Scarabold's children are growing up and becoming dangerous. I miss them running in the halls, flustering the tapestries, tipping over flowerpots. Now they are like adults, secretive and conspiring. They are planning rank mischief. I can smell the insurrection.'

She patted the greasy heads of the twins, who dropped obediently at her feet. 'Go out there, good Spackle, and see with my eyes. Fly, tender Peut, and listen with my ears. Report to me everything this night, and if you find nothing, stay until there's scandal to be found.'

Spackle and Peut kissed their mother's hand and rose as one, jaunting away into the corridors.

Archim Scarabold III was up on the battlements, smiting a bear.

The great creature had been captured in the vast forest that grew to the north-east, and was strung up by its paws so that the King could practise his punches on something other than a pauper. The poor were weak opponents and tended to come apart after a few blows. It was the job of the valet, Ratchet, to poke the bear with a stick to keep him attentive.

The rain began to fall hard, matting the poor creature's brown fur and robbing him of grandeur. Nothing but greyness could be seen beyond the battlements.

'First Carapace Sheathwing exploding himself at our meal table, now an auditor sniffing around the coffers, and still no suitor in sight for my daughter,' boomed Scarabold. 'Carapace's family must not discover how he died. We cannot afford a war with the people of the Marshlands. Our soldiers haven't been paid since the old quartermaster expired after his public flogging, and our cannons are so ill-fitted that we daren't risk firing them for fear of blowing ourselves to bits. This is a sorry state of affairs indeed.'

He ran at the bear and punched it hard in the solar plexus. The creature roared, whimpered and released a steaming stream of ursine urine. Scarabold drew off his steel gauntlet in disgust and hurled it to the flagstones. 'Even this isn't helping. Haven't you got any ideas?'

'War can raise fortunes,' ventured the sodden Ratchet, plucking at wet nether-garments through the gap in his doublet. Thunder cracked in the distance. 'But waging it is too costly unless someone else pays.'

Scarabold pinioned his valet with the gaze of his good eye. 'And who do you suggest for that?'

'If Carapace's family seek revenge and you were to suggest that Londinium might fall—'

'Which it very well might.'

'Then those who need the support of your army will surely suffer. Of course, I'm only a valet, but—'

'You are not just a valet,' said Scarabold kindly. 'You're also the Head of Endpapers and Captain of Scalding.'

'—but it occurs to me there are others who would be more than willing to donate gold for protection.'

'Les Sœurs aux Cadeaux Étranges,' said Scarabold, ignoring the bear and marching back towards the changing room to remove his tabard. 'The gods may blind me, but you're right. They rely solely upon our security, even though they regard us as heathens.'

Once, the province of Cadeaux Étranges had been the home of powerful knight-mages who roamed the land stealing treasures for their arcane rituals. Seeking revenge against them, it was said that the River People – a thick-necked crowd who worked as stevedores on the Rushing River – had raised an army and slaughtered them all, but failed to find the town's plunder. The Sisters had locked themselves away in a convent with their treasures, but before the situation could be resolved, the military regiments from the river towns had fallen upon one another in dispute and departed in disarray.

Lady Lavinia Travernum and les Sœurs aux Cadeaux Étranges remained behind to guard the looted hoard. The centrepiece of this was the Vessel of All Counted Sorrows, which was used in their rituals every consecration night. Into this vessel was decanted the Spirit of the Archangel, said to have been extracted from the intestines of Gabriel himself. On top of the Spirit, which was supposed to look like mead with bits of bed-fluff in it, was a small papyrus, tightly rolled and sealed in red wax, containing instructions for the End of Days. It could never be opened.

'If Carapace's men mobilize against us, the Sisters will be in their path,' said Scarabold. 'They'll cough up when they realize we're all that stands between them and the armies of the Marshlands. By the Devil's yard, that's a fine strategy. I should have thought of it earlier.'

The Great Wound donned his green leather jerkin and set off to hold a meeting with his envoys, leaving Ratchet to pick up his soaked garments. It seemed likely the bear would remain tied up, forgotten and unfought.

Giniva and Leperdandy stood holding hands on the battlements, looking out over the land.

The rain had eased to a light drizzle, the equivalent in the valley of a fine summer's day. A few indistinct moss-green hills appeared through a lifted veil and vanished again. It was a view that could be enjoyed by the partially sighted.

'Out there,' said Leperdandy, gesturing vaguely, 'beyond the safety of the great stone lion, you will be a mere commoner. There will be no privileges accorded to you. Your life will be a struggle, full of work and woe. If what the Beetle Earl told you is true, you will have to hide your real identity. You will not be able to survive by making royal visits to other tribes. Those people out there are not like you. Even their rulers are different. It's said that the Lord of Essender ate his own wife. Are you sure this is what you want?'

'What, not to be pampered and suffocated and waited upon day and night inside this musty old trinket casket? Who would not yearn to be free?'

Leperdandy leaned upon the crenellations and rested his chin on his hands. 'I bet that's what they always say, the royal children. Yet when they are set loose without the skills to fend for themselves, they are as babies tossed into the wild woods, their soft pale flesh torn by the thorns of nature. How long do you honestly think you can survive?'

'I'll never know until I try,' Giniva replied. 'Whether with cords of silk or iron, it is unnatural and unhealthy to be chained to family.'

Although her sentiments were fine, Giniva felt tremors of doubt. She wanted to commit an act of virtuous nobility, but what if it put her at risk? What if she was ridiculed or, worse still, hurt? It was hard to force such thoughts aside.

'Lady Dwinoline has been kind to you. I have tried my very best . . .' Leperdandy looked as if he might cry.

'I have no quarrel with you or Dwinoline.' She threw herself at him and hugged until he wheezed. 'You and I have a bond deeper than any brother and sister. We read each other's thoughts. There are such mysteries in here that their truths will never be revealed. Out there, I'm sure the world will prove to be a simpler, more honest place, less filled with foul intrigues.'

The princeling stuck out his lower lip. 'Probably not. By all accounts, the peasants are disgusting.' He switched his thoughts to a different path. 'I've been wondering about the secret Carapace was going to reveal before he detonated. I had not expected the poison to act so fast, or so violently. He had been to the dungeons, had he not?'

Giniva was not listening. For once, the siblings were not in tune. 'Out there,' she said again, 'the sun shines down on a race so noble and so different from us that we cannot begin to conceive of their world.'

Leperdandy peered into the mist and saw no nobility. No difference. No sun.

'I do not expect special treatment,' she said. 'I will no longer be a princess but an ordinary humble maid. I shall have Peticia lay out my peasant clothes, simple drab linens and practical footwear, for I imagine it can be muddy. Tomorrow, my life will begin anew.'

26

The Cost of the Kingdom

The calculating engine was wheeled before Scarabold III to reckon the treasury of war.

Thredneedle, Canterby and the clerks of the Royal Counting Chamber had been warned to stay away. Auditor and King met in the Chamber of Received Commoners. A commoner Claude Silvercannon might have been, but he held the fortune of the kingdom in his palm, and knew that the knowledge could end his life as swiftly as a lamp wick might be snuffed.

His discovery of the treasury debt placed him in a position of lethal risk, for once the King was apprised of the facts there was only one plan of action left open to him. As his accountants would not be able to solve the problem, he could only hide the truth and rid himself of the evidence.

But Silvercannon had come up with a cunning answer to the problem.

Now a dance of false camaraderie began, the King smiling with bared yellow teeth, the auditor papering light remarks across dark premonitions. Between them in the least lit part of the chamber stood the calculating engine. The facsimile of the human accountant at its core was seated immobile, not daring to breathe.

The King's impatience was starting to show. 'Well, tell me, then,' he cried, 'how stand our finances?'

'That is not for me to know, Your Majesty,' said Silvercannon with a deferential bow.

'Damn it all to smithereens, man. If you don't know, who does?' Scarabold's bellow was enough to ruffle the auditor's hair.

Sensing that her father's attention had now turned to her, Giniva held her breath and did not bat an eyelash. Lacquered into the space where the metal accountant had sat, the exposed parts of her skin painted in black, silver and gold, she remained perfectly still. The whalebone at her back helped to hold her in place and prevented her from breathing to any noticeable degree.

She stared straight ahead, knowing that even if she played her part to perfection, one thing could still give her away: the automaton's eyes had been carved from tortoiseshell, while hers were an opalescent blue.

Lurking behind the breastly marble mounds of the statue of Elizabeld the Slayer, in the furthest corner of the chamber, Spackle and Peut watched the proceedings with breath held as tightly as Giniva's. They had arrived late, after the princeling had fixed his sister into place, but could sense that something strange was about to happen.

'The calculating engine has no vested interest in the condition of your treasury, Your Majesty,' said Silvercannon. 'It has been analysing the receipts of your coffers, and when Your Majesty depresses this' – here he pointed to the long brass lever at the front of the calculator – 'it will reveal its final answer. That document will be the only evidence of its findings, which will remain unknown to me and anyone else outside this chamber. The matter is between you and the machine alone.'

'Just me and the machine, eh?' said Scarabold, lifting a leg and breaking wind. 'Porridge.' Silvercannon tried his best not to look horrified, and Giniva held her breath. Spackle almost choked with laughter until Peut pinched his nose and bade him be still.

'After it has performed its task, I will then take my leave,' the auditor explained, 'and you may decide for yourself which course of action to pursue.'

Which was not the best thing to have said, because it set Scarabold roaring. 'This is my kingdom and any courtier wishing to speak to me must assume a cringing attitude. Who are you to tell me what to do?' he boomed. 'I own you, underling, I own your company, your equipment, your wife, your children, your hens, your property, your land and everything on, in, over, under and around it! I will indeed decide which course to pursue, and it may be one that requires your eyes to be put out and your bare sockets to be filled with hot peppers. If you fail me, your guts will make my garters.'

The auditor quailed and appeared close to stumbling. Locked into her rigid pose, Giniva could not provide him with any consolation or encouragement.

Silvercannon found his equilibrium and stepped back as Scarabold sighed. 'Go on, then, bestraddle yourself and let me operate this damnable device. Wait outside until you are summoned.'

The Great Wound rubbed his calloused palms and stepped towards the machine. Giniva stared ahead. Scarabold raised his hairy nostrils and sniffed the air. A residue of perfume lurked, the faintest violet trace lingering at head height. Had the auditor been near his daughter? If he had, he would watch as his gonads were chopped with a chisel and pan-fried before him like sizzling scallops.

This momentary flash of fury was replaced by the burning need to know just how terrible was the situation in the Royal Counting Chamber. Scarabold approached the lever, flexed his fingers and gave it a downward wrench.

The engine's cylinders vibrated as cogs spun and springs unwound. A roll of parchment unfurled from the delivery slot beneath Giniva. Scarabold snatched up the accounts, tore them free and examined them.

They showed, in essence, barring a handful of owings and goings, that the kingdom had not a pot to piss in. Every last perch of scrub, stone, gravel and mire had been sold and sold again until not a grain of soil was left.

As comprehension blossomed like some poisonous orchid, the Great Wound released a roar that would have dislodged droppings from a doge. He had expected a row of noughts but had not anticipated figures stretching to the infinite, all of them preceded by a minus sign.

Peering over the page, he noted the toes of the auditor's pointed velvet boots protruding beyond the door. *Don't disembowel the messenger*, he thought almost charitably. *If you do, the reason why will become obvious, and if the news gets out . . .*

But the engine had to go.

Usually he kept a double-headed axe within swinging distance. He felt as if the statue was staring at him mockingly, and looked around for a sword. At least he could have the satisfaction of hacking off its head. He had need of a lackey, or preferably two. Where was everybody?

Just as he thought this, his good eye alighted upon two pairs of raven-black orbs squinting out from either side of Elizabeld the Slayer's formidable chest.

'Spackle, Peut, spying again! Come out from behind there if you value your miserable pustulant skins!' he roared. The twins had no fear of anyone except their King, and approached quaking in their tights. 'If you want to avoid a red-raw whipping, you'll get me a sword, fast – and make sure it's sharp!'

But Jumblejoy's eyes caught his own and touched a nerve. They reminded him of someone dear and close. His choler cooled. 'Never mind,' he said, 'just move this contraption. Get it into the vault.'

Under Giniva's instruction the auditor had greased the engine's iron wheels, but the device still weighed more than a percheron. No matter how hard Spackle and Peut pushed, they were only able to shift it half an inch.

Scarabold was turning crimson with the day's frustration. 'Get away from the damnable thing, you pusillanimous weasels! Bring ropes! Fetch reinforcements! I want it taken outside and tipped over the battlements before I return!'

He stormed outside to find the quivering auditor. 'As for you, wretched coin-counter, tell the others I harbour no feelings of ill will towards you. I want them all to know that. We are a fair-minded bunch here. Now, you'd best be gone before I set the bear on you.'

'Certainly, Your Majesty,' said Silvercannon, 'although there is the minuscule matter of my bill. And I need my calculating engine, so if you'll allow me to arrange for its removal— What bear?'

'Don't worry, I'll make sure you're paid in full,' said the King with sinister calculation in his voice. 'If you'll just wait for me in the vault, I'll have Thredneedle join you for the formal presentation of your charges.'

Sensing that all was not entirely under his control and fearing for the safe passage of the Princess, Silvercannon returned to the vault to await payment and make his escape.

27

Irreplaceable

It was not to be so simple.

The moment the auditor seated himself on the edge of the fountain, the great iron door of the vault swung shut on him and its spar spun, sealing him inside. He had thought himself safe; after all, the kingdom's paperwork was stored in the stone alcoves all around him and was irreplaceable.

And then he thought: *Irreplaceable.*

With no record of the debts, there were no debts to be repaid. He ran a finger under his stiff white collar and mopped the sweat from his brow. The vault was becoming unbearably hot. He tried to think clearly.

The debts stretching back into prehistory were incurred against those who could not return with an army. If their record simply vanished, someone like the Great Wound could be forgiven for imagining they did not exist.

When Silvercannon lowered his boot to the ceramic floor it stuck fast. He realized with a sinking heart that although the mechanism for turning ingots into a fountain of molten gold had been disabled years before, it had not been dismantled.

As the furnace beneath him was stoked, the temperature rose to one hundred, then two hundred and thirty degrees.

The paper bills that surrounded him lifted themselves in the hot dry air and spontaneously burst into flame. The floor became a hotplate, a baking tray for the cooking of the books. Soon the entire vault was a-roar with incinerating bills. The auditor's hair caught fire. He hammered on the searing door with blistering fists, but nobody heard the cries that dried in his burning mouth.

Outside, the Princess Giniva felt the ground rumble beneath her and ventured to swivel her eyes. A dozen men were pushing the calculating engine towards the drawbridge where stood the auditor's cart. She tipped her head slightly, just enough to glimpse the world beyond and feel its chill zephyrs against her stove-black cheek.

While seated immobile, she had dared to make plans; after being released by the auditor and reaching a secluded spot, she would divest herself of her disguise. Unblackening her skin, she would change into the travelling clothes Peticia had folded and hidden in the valise that sat between the machine's wheels. Leperdandy had packed some gold coins, a flannel and an egg-and-cress pudding. Then she would be on her own, and her life would start over.

There was another tilt, more alarming this time. She tried to observe but the whalebone at her back prohibited movement. From the corner of her eye she caught something, and though it gave her neck a painful twist she could not help turning to see. Sky. Wooden boards. Water. Pond-skaters. A frog. Father Sesquinatius.

The elderly abbot was directing two teams of varlets linked with hawsers. What on earth were they doing?

When the reek of stagnant water reached her nostrils, she realized she was over its unperturbed emerald surface.

The moat, wherein the giant black pike that feasted on the bones of executed men undulated silently through forest-green waters, rarely seen but for the flick of its tail. They were going to sink the calculating engine where no one would ever be able to reach it.

She needed to escape the whalebone, but knew that nothing could break it open. Why hadn't the auditor stepped up to release her? There was another lurch and she found herself pitched at a sharp angle that grew steeper by the second.

A moment later there was a great shifting of weight as she felt herself and the machine turn over and tip into the moat.

28

The Girl in Gold and Green

As the birdcatcher struggled to pull himself up through the pipe, he grew wary of what might wait at the top. Would he surface in the middle of a tourney court or an execution square? It seemed unlikely that an outlet for foul humours would be situated near the quarters of refined folk. More probably he would emerge near stables or dunnies, or in the underservants' quarters.

The rough iron seams at the pipe's sides gave him some leverage. When, with quivering muscles, he finally raised his head above the parapet, he exhaled and spat.

He was inside the barbican but outside the Squire's Wall, the main fortification. Directly ahead was a drawbridge, down, and the olivine moat.

Before the drawbridge was a bare flagstone field. It had begun to rain, coin-sized droplets darkening the ground. A lone guard leaned on a pikestaff, idly checking the contents of his nose. Watborn could creep up on a stork and noose it before it had a chance to move, but sentries expected to be attacked.

He slipped behind a hawthorn hedge and made his way towards the drawbridge. When the wind changed he heard a commotion coming from a spot just beyond his sight. Waiting until the guard followed the shouts, he ran low and fast, but what he saw drew him up short.

There came the sound of splintering wood.

'Put your backs into it.' Father Sesquinatius lashed out at one of his choirboys with a knotted leather scourge. 'I've seen more life in you before matins.'

'Yes, and the less said about that the better,' one chorister said to the next. 'There's nothing like a sly finger up the buttocks for making you jump while you're trying to slip into your cassock.'

Father Sesquinatius held no official position. The cult of the new gods had never taken hold here, but some rituals were performed out of sentiment and tradition, like folk dancing. The war between kings and gods had not been fought, with the result that neither were much attended.

The old abbot tutted. The calculating engine was halfway over and stuck. One of its wheels had punctured the rotten boards of the drawbridge. Jammed at a forty-five-degree angle, its levers and fly-wheels jangled and clanged like a collision of grandfather clocks.

The iron accountant was looking odd, too. The black paint on its face was starting to run in the light rain, and was that a strand of blonde hair coming loose from beneath its skullcap?

'Heave, my lads, and there'll be treats for you at vespers,' called the abbot, unable to resist squeezing a plump lad who was putting his shoulder to the machine.

Giniva could not draw breath. As the engine tipped, the whale-bone pressed so hard on her ribs that she feared she might burst. She crushed her eyes shut and prayed for the auditor to appear. With a sickening lurch, the engine came free of the rotten boards and for a brief moment hung motionless. Then it cantilevered into the moat with a hollow boom of parting water.

Father Sesquinatius stared down at the black hole that had been created in the emerald algae. A string of bubbles wavered and burst upon the surface. He was puzzled. Why had Scarabold commanded them to get rid of such a wonderful device?

As the engine sank, Giniva's breath was snatched away. The water was icily rancorous and the green murk revealed nothing but drifting tendrils. The device fell with its heaviest part leading, so that she was on its uppermost side. Stiffened with black varnish, her clothes had been hemmed into the space from which Silvercan-non had removed the iron accountant.

She could not detach herself from the whalebone. Leperdandy would have made a fine seamster. The stitches he'd made were small and tightly sewn. She twisted angrily at the threads, trying to tear them apart.

The great black pike lay in the brown mud of the moat.

It hardly ever stirred and never broke the surface. It was fifty years old and fourteen feet long. It had never spawned, and was embittered. It had nearly seven hundred teeth, some of which pointed backwards to stop its prey from escaping once it had clamped its jaws shut. Now that its sterile mate was gone (eaten for her failure to provide progeny) it lived on a diet of tinned food, dragging the rancid flesh of dead soldiers out of their armour, crunching their bones and discarding the plating, which lay in heaps on the moat-bed.

But now, a disturbance. Something large and metallic had thumped into its domain and was sinking down on to the clutter of tempered steel helmets and shields that sat in the ooze.

The pike bestirred itself and swam in for a closer look.

The engine had settled at an angle on top of the remains of the 4th Regiment of Archers, who had lost their lives in a lightning storm while drunkenly picking mushrooms from the underside of the drawbridge for the annual banquet of the lords' concubines.

The water was so freezing that it burned, spurring Giniva to frantic movement. She tore at the stitching along one arm of her tunic and pulled her right hand free, but was still held in place by the whalebone. She thought of the indignity of drowning in the moat, her wild dream of escape extending no more than a few yards from the portcullis, and struggled harder than ever.

From the ferny gloom a wavering shape appeared.

The snout of the great pike came into focus. Its broad pointed head was a mottled olive green, scarred and scratched pink in places. Shreds of chainmail trailed from the spines of its side-teeth. Its iridescent brown-green eyes had seen nothing but death and decay. It was as bad-tempered as only the old can be. A steely-scaled submarine of a creature, aggressive and territorial, it would have eaten its young had they been born. Capable of terrifying bursts of energy, it scented flesh once more.

Giniva tore at the stitches with her free hand and separated herself from her costume, but her legs remained trapped in place. She tried hard not to exhale but could not help but release a few silver bubbles.

The great pike undulated in an S, and now its full form could be discerned in all its prehistoric grandeur. It coiled back in the murky moat-water, preparing to strike.

Watborn became aware that some kind of calamity had occurred.

A number of choristers, a priest, some soldiers and several donkeys were ineffectually milling about a wheeled iron box that had partially fallen through the drawbridge's planks. As he watched he saw two things. First, that this piece of equipment would undoubtedly be lost. Second, that there was someone trapped inside it.

When the wood splintered and the machine splashed into the moat, he dropped below the water's edge without a further thought.

The sinking engine had disturbed any number of warrior corpses on the moat's floor, and now Giniva saw that a dented shield lay cradled in the mud behind her. Her fingers closed around the edge of the shield.

The pike loomed from the disturbed silt, springing forward with astonishing speed to punch the shield from her hands. It nudged around, clouding the water and snapping in frustration, then recoiled to prepare for a more formal attack.

Twisting about herself, Giniva saw the broken haft of a spear. It would never penetrate the pike's dense hide, but as the creature flashed forward again she hoisted it, using the tip to scratch at the gleaming jade plate of an eye as it passed her, forcing the beast to one side. The creature's jaw slammed shut just behind her, taking some of her hair.

It circled again, charging towards her left leg, and bit down.

She expelled the last of her air in shock. Hardly daring to look, expecting to see the water blossom black with her blood, Giniva realized that the pike had bitten clean through the tip of the bone that imprisoned her. As its great jaw opened, spiny teeth drifted and fell from its mouth.

Watborn swam through plumes of mud, down to the spot where the engine had fallen, and was presented with a vision.

Among the long green weeds and clouds of amber silt, a maiden drifted, her golden hair in a ragged halo, her arms waving above her head.

Kicking upwards, he returned to the surface of the moat, took a great gulp of air and dove down once more. Seizing the maiden's face in both hands, he placed his mouth over hers, releasing his unbreathed air into her lungs. She was only startled until she realized what he was doing.

She pointed at the whalebone. Together they lifted the damaged end. Giniva drove herself up to the surface of the moat.

The shattered edge of the drawbridge was directly above her. As she reached for the wooden boards, the great pike spurred itself upwards again, seizing the waist-chain she wore beneath her disguise and slamming back into the water as it tried to drag her down into its realm.

Watborn helplessly watched the great pike slide past him. The chain it had seized snapped at its weakest link, releasing its prey. The Princess grabbed at the boards and pulled as hard as she could, while the pike circled and prepared to spring again.

She rolled on to the planks of the rain-drenched drawbridge just as the great pike broke free of the water and rose twisting in the air, its jaws wide, taking a bite out of the bridge. The oaken splinters seared its damaged maw and it punched back below the surface in agony, slinking to the depths, deprived of its victory.

Watborn was directly beneath it. The steely scales slammed against his unprotected pate, knocking him out.

Sailing beyond the canned corpses of the archers, the pike burrowed away to nurse its wounds until another dining opportunity could present itself. But it had seen the pickings to be had above its dark domain, up where the light made the water thinner. It would never be content to slumber lazily on the moat-bed again.

Watborn drifted downwards, breathing in silt-water.

His last conscious thought was of the girl in gold and green, and the life-giving kiss they had shared.

Giniva struggled to be free of her wet clothes. She twisted and pulled at them until she was left lying on the boards in her white samite undergarments. Rough hands hauled her to her feet and led her back to safety.

'You had a lucky call, my lady,' said Manticore, the luxuriantly moustachioed Yeoman of the Guard, who had been changing the cavalry when the commotion started. He averted his eyes from her sodden undergarments.

Lucky me, thought Giniva, coughing out a foot of green weed as she squelched back inside. *Lucky to still be here in the bosom of my cursèd family.* She had no recollection of the man who had breathed life into her.

Giniva had been luckier than she realized. Manticore was stoutly loyal and would never mention that he had just seen the Princess emerging from the moat in most peculiar circumstances, stove-black still smeared on her neck and ears. He helped her out and went about his business.

It was not his job to wonder what the royals got up to in their spare time.

29

In Defiance of the King

'How is it possible you are alive?' Leperdandy cried, helping his sister into his rooms. 'I saw the machine tip over on the drawbridge. There was nothing I could do. You smell disgusting, by the way. I have rose-soap and many tinctures of cologne.'

She had already forgiven Leperdandy for not coming to her rescue; the distance between his suite and the moat was not far as falcons flew, but even the most fleet of wing could not have negotiated all those corridors and passageways in under ten minutes.

Settling the Princess in his dressing room, he turned his back while she disrobed. 'Did my eyes deceive me or did some kind of gigantic spiny fish nearly swallow you?'

'I thought I was going to be eaten.' Giniva looked over a bone-china shoulder as she dried her hair. 'It feels as if I have just supped a dozen bad oysters. Why did I never suspect such a thing before?'

'You mean the fish?'

'No, the *gold*. We are destitute. I have been lied to, Dando.'

'No, not lied to – shielded,' Leperdandy replied judiciously. 'Like everything else. It is in our character.'

She rubbed the prickles from her arms. 'It is more dangerous to stay here than to leave. I'm shaking. I thought I was stronger. I have more to learn. Do you have something warm to drink?'

'There is a kettle of nutmeg tea to your right.'

'Pour some liquor in it,' she instructed.

Her brother did as he was told. 'How did you escape?'

'I don't know.' She turned to her mind's eye. 'Oh.'

'What is the matter?'

'There was a man.'

'What man?'

'Under the water. A man brought me air and helped to set me free.'

'I don't see how that is possible.' Leperdandy passed her a hot bowl.

'It was hazy and hard to see. The mud was all churned up. I didn't imagine it. He swam down to me. Without his help I would have died.' She sipped the tea and coughed. 'What were you going to do if I had managed to escape?'

'I would have been found reading on my chaise longue, of course. Something classical and improving.' He indicated mock surprise, raising his palms to his cheeks. 'Giniva? Gone? Why, what on earth do you mean?'

She pulled on one of her brother's green woollen jerkins and tugged her hair out from its collar. 'But surely when they found my rooms empty the alarm would have been raised.'

'No, because I substituted Copernia . . . Copernia!'

'What?' She turned, dragging the garment straight. 'What is it?'

'She's standing in for you. I dressed her in your clothes. Right now she appears to be playing croquet in the Covered Court. We must get her back before Mater Moribund discovers her!'

Together they set off for the courtyard, a green rhombus surrounded by stilted sandstone arches. Leperdandy slid to a stop outside the main gates, out of breath, and peered around a column.

'Too late – she's already in there!' He pointed behind his palm. 'I swear she has a sixth sense about these things.'

'I said, why are you up here without your retinue, girl, when you should be at your studies?' called Mater Moribund crossly.

On the other side of the court, the doll Copernia was garbed, with far too many layers, as the Princess. She was awkwardly posed against a wall, fooling no one but the very short-sighted.

'Did you not hear me, wretched child?'

As the siblings watched, Moribund strode across the court and up to the dummy. A tussle ensued – quite how or what it involved they could not see – but when the Mater stepped back her hands were raised in horror. Copernia had fallen over and her head had come off, rolling away, leaving a trail of kapok like spilled innards.

'I only meant to cover your tracks for an hour,' Leperdandy whispered.

'Get out there and tell her something,' Giniva shot back, 'before she suspects the truth.'

Leperdandy swallowed, drew breath and strode towards his mother. 'A jest, Mater!' he cried. 'A merry jape to amuse!'

'You stupid witherling!' She smacked him loudly around the head. 'How will you ever take up your duties in the kingdom when all you do is play the fool? Why are you not studying the rules of engagement and learning how to terrorize your opponents? By now you should know how to slit a man's belly with a scimitar and hang his steaming guts around his neck.'

'I meant no harm,' he said quietly, cowed.

'And that is your curse. You are *meant* to mean harm – you are the son of the Great Wound! Now, forget this play-acting and go to the armoury. Get Vitrolio to teach you combat tactics until the supper-bell is rung. Wait – where is the Princess Giniva?'

'A-dream in her bed-suite, I imagine,' he replied, thinking fast. 'Shall I fetch her?'

'No, just make sure that she arrives at dinner on time for once.'

Leperdandy did not head for the armoury. Wanting to uncover the secret that Carapace had been about to impart before he died, he went to the Cistern Library to bury himself in books. He had little knowledge of the world – it had never been a subject of interest – but now he needed to know more.

Everything was turning upside down.

The royals were vile, not pure. Hated, not loved. Outcasts, not heroes. They did not seek to invade but to secure the little they had left. Their treasures were gone, their reserves spent. And he had made the situation worse by poisoning the Beetle Earl.

Biblius, the head librarian, refused to give him the keys to the rotunda at the sealed rear section of the Cistern Library, so he was forced to make do with censored volumes. He had once thought of breaking in, until the librarian vouchsafed that it was guarded day and night by Orobus, and as he did not know who (or indeed what) that might be, he decided not to take the risk.

Leather-mites scattered as he cracked open tome after tome, searching for histories of war and succession, but every chapter concerning the family tree and its place in the world had been excised with a sharp blade. As his thumb riffled the trims, his suspicions grew.

He found one sentence that began, 'When the noble knights sought to extend their power, their masters poisoned them under instructions from the Royal—' But from there the ink had been scrubbed out.

Outcasts are we, thought Leperdandy, *and no wonder*. Scarabold knew that if he allowed his children to roam, they would be vilified and spurned by all decent peoples of the plains and hills alike. High-born or no, the eaters of the dead existed at the base, beside those who made children with their own kin.

Searching for a complete volume on the family tree proved hopeless. There was only one thing for it: he would have to venture into the dungeons and undertake the same journey of discovery for himself.

30

A Diet of Lies

He would go after supper tonight, he decided, when Fumblegut was bloated and floating in the fug of his home-made rot-gut liquorice wine. Wondering if she might have information he could use, he went to call upon Dwinoline.

The former First Wife was in the Tapestry Room, where all the royal ladies went to work on their embroidery. Her fingers nimbly darted back and forth, weaving golden thread through the design: a depiction of the Eleventh Plague Striking the Paupers Blind.

'What was all the fuss?' she asked, setting aside the tapestry. 'I looked out of the archery window and saw soldiers milling on the bridge.'

'I think they were fishing,' said Leperdandy, trying to sound off-hand. 'I was just wondering, have you ever been to the dungeons?' As a change of subject, it was less than seamless.

'No, and why ever should I?' Dwinoline asked in surprise. 'Fumblegut's domain is not for royal visitation, and of course there is the health risk.'

Leperdandy toyed with a chased silver thimble. 'What health risk?'

'From his pet, M'Lin. That dreadful man owns one of the pleading apes of Sumavera-Sum. The wretched thing is not to be trusted, for M'Lin repays kindness by biting its releasers to the bone.' She picked up a dropped stitch. 'Its saliva contains an incurable form of the black pansy death. The Decrepend tried to have it put down last year, and the year before that, but M'Lin survives every attempt. Its breed is highly manipulative and seeks to involve humans in its games, which always end badly.'

'I've never heard of such a creature before. Surely they are not native to our land?'

'No, I think a foreigner brought it in as a gift. All sorts of oddities turn up from faraway places. Have you had a banana? I thought it was a table decoration but I ate one and they're delicious. Unfortunately nobody can remember where they came from now, otherwise we'd have sent a boat for them. There's much more you will not have heard of, my stripling, for you are delicate and need protecting from life's harsh realities.'

'Why does Fumblegut keep such a beast?'

'We won't pay him for an assistant, and he says he needs something to threaten the prisoners with.'

An ape? thought Leperdandy. It didn't sound like a reason for Carapace to rise and make an announcement at the King's feasting table. Hadn't there been something about a special prisoner?

'If you're thinking of going exploring, may I suggest you avoid the lower regions,' said Dwinoline, returning to her tapestry.

'Oh, I once went all the way to the ground floor,' said Leperdandy, seeking to impress but unwilling to reveal that he himself had once ventured into Fumblegut's domain.

'But there are four more floors below that at least, and many other unvisited places across the bridges,' said Dwinoline, pausing. 'Did you not know?'

'No one ever told me.'

'Perhaps you never sought to ask. You've always been an incurious boy. A word of advice, then. Stay away from them. You are our only inheritor and we need to keep you in one piece.'

The princeling was puzzled. 'But I cannot inherit.'

'Think, boy! Giniva may marry into another royal family and choose you to share her power in some minor capacity, but we frown upon the idea of endogamy, which is—'

'Marriage within one's own tribe. I know.'

'We don't say "tribe", dear. Tribes are down there in the marshes and lowlands. We are a dynasty.'

'So my sister must remain here to marry and rule, as I must stay and inherit.' Leperdandy had gradually come to realize the binding limit of his options. 'And we are to be controlled in turn by the senior members of the family.'

'Of course, but you will have almost anything your heart desires.

Why, what else would you want to do?' Dwinoline tutted in good humour and shook the very idea from her curl-capped head.

'Have you never longed to see what lies beyond Londinium?'

'I know what is out there, silly boy.'

'How? Have you been there?'

'Why no, bless you. But I have seen scenes painted from life in lanthorn shows, in tapestries and in our history books. There's land, then coast, then water – nothing very interesting. There's something else after that – sand, I think – and mountains, where the people cannot talk properly and wear the most ridiculous clothes. It is not safe to travel so far away. There are sea-dragons and people with their faces in their chests, and angry things with many arms that breathe flame and hop about on a single leg.'

'And dragons?'

'No, they are mythical.'

'How do you know all this?'

'Scarabold told me, and I have seen pictures in books, so it must be true.'

'I have been to the Cistern Library,' said Leperdandy, 'and there are few texts from outside. Most of the history books are by learned men who never left here. They have painted scenes from their minds. They are fantasies. We have been fed on a diet of lies.'

'Would you say my stitchwork depicts naught but fantasies?' asked Dwinoline, picking up her tapestry once more and peering at it. 'They are stories told from long ago passed down by many mouths and hands. Stories are flowers that spring from the seeds of truth.'

'But surely they are written down somewhere? So that those who come later will understand?'

'What they understand will have little to do with what happened,' said Dwinoline, pulling at her thread and biting it off. 'Our deeds are swiftly washed away. Imagine if this great House was gone and all that was found was my tapestry. Why, our story would only be told by what lies here beneath my fingers.'

She tapped the brightly sewn pictures with a nail. 'You cannot stay innocent for ever, my child. There is such pain ahead that you and your sister will look back on these times as golden. Without offspring the dynasty will collapse upon itself. Have you never seen the squirrels on the tourney court? They have malformed bones and piebald fur because they cannot escape and may only breed with each other. It makes their eyes grow close together and they become mad.'

'Can that be true?' Leperdandy was aghast.

'I have seen it.' Dwinoline gave a shrug. 'The same with people. The flesh will be outlived by these stitches. We are what we leave behind, nothing more. You must stay and perform your duties here. It's what is expected of you.'

'My sister and I will not follow the wishes of the King.'

'He is your father. He will not listen to his children.'

'Then he will die alone and unmourned.' Leperdandy rose to leave. 'While my sister sets off into the world beyond, I shall lock myself away with my plays and my costumes.'

'So she will run and you will hide.' She pushed aside the tapestry, suddenly tired. 'You will lose everyone you hold dear. And it will come to pass much sooner than you think.'

Dwinoline's prophecy was about to prove correct, but not in a way that any of them could ever have anticipated.

PART TWO:
Family

31

A Spy in the House

This was what he had dreamed of for so long?

Watborn no longer smelled of the dungeons' shit-water. He now smelled of rancid moat. It was a marginal improvement. He had lost his horn and arrow-pouch. Pulling strands of pond-weed from his ear, he raised his head and looked about. His heroic rescue had gone unnoticed.

He lay on flagstones behind a buttress at the edge of the moat. Watery sunshine had stiffened his reeking clothes and he was hungry, but he felt whole in body and spirit. He wondered what had happened to the lady in the lake. Would she remember him?

The drawbridge was still down, its boards smashed and its wind-lass damaged. It meant he could get inside – but then what? *Here's an idea*, he thought. *When you break into someone's home, try to have an alibi prepared, idiot birdcatcher.*

Rising, he crept along the wall to the open gateway and peered inside.

Beyond the cobbled courtyard there was no keep but a pile of buildings dumped one on top of the other, some stretched, some squat. They appeared to have been raised by a hundred different builders. He would risk exposure crossing the courtyard. *Don't stop*, he told himself, *don't think*.

Here no canticles sounded, no bells were rung. His first glimpses were mightily disappointing. A motley jumble of rain-green stones and makeshift rafters crushed together without grace or practical-ity. The higher floors were built out over the lowest so that the alleyways between them were in perpetual night. Rain gutters emp-tied into neighbours' windows and chimneys belched smoke into nurseries. Paupers clung to doorsteps, scared of being beaten. Ragged grey figures flitted past, afraid to be seen. Dogs sniffed each other warily and fought. An old woman kicked a dead rat out of a doorway. A child so ugly that at first he thought it was a tiny old man stared at him from beneath a cart. Few lights shone. There was a smell of rancid meat.

It was not the palatial vision promised in his mosaic floor. If such a gilded place existed, it had to be hidden far above or behind these hovels.

He walked purposefully towards a colonnade of arches and slipped into their shadows. He was still deciding where to head next when two men stopped almost in front of him. One was reddish and knotted and highly scrubbed, as if he had been buffed along with his weaponry that morning. The other was shorter, older, smellier and wearing so much military braid that it probably outweighed him. Watborn pushed himself back behind a pillar.

'I would feel happier if we were speaking before His Majesty,' said the scrubbed one in a secretive tone.

'I understand your loyalty, Manticore,' said the other, 'but the situation will not be contained for much longer. The Sheathwing armies are training to the south. They are not yet of sufficient strength, but they will be avenged.'

'One piddling earl.' The yeoman shook his head in disbelief. 'He should have realized he was in danger just by coming here.'

'Lord Carapace was not a leader of men, just a name on a list. We might yet try to take his land.'

'Then I must start recruiting.'

Grand-Marshal Timmorian considered the point. 'What do you need?'

'Archers, first and foremost. Our regiment is shamefully depleted and our ordnance is in poor order. One good man could teach the rest, but most of them could not hit a horse.'

Without thinking, Watborn stepped forward, surprising both men but shocking himself more. 'Sirs, I could not help overhearing. I am a fine bowman and would be happy to propose myself—'

'Who in the name of St Smaculus is this?' asked Timmorian. 'How long have you been spying on us? Who sent you? How did you get in?'

Watborn realized he had made a fatal mistake. 'I'm not spying, sir, I just overheard a phrase or two as I was passing—'

'On your way to where, exactly?'

'I – ah – over there.' He pointed vaguely to the building at their backs.

'The kennels? Are you working for Lady Phileuse?'

'I don't know who that is, sirs, I just—'

'I am the Yeoman of the Guard,' said Manticore. 'Who are you? Are you a spy?' He turned to the Commander of the Army. 'Hell's teeth, Timmorian, we have a Sheathwing in our midst.'

'Spies don't announce themselves,' the Grand-Marshal pointed out.

Watborn tried to think fast. 'I saw the Earl riding here but I did not speak to him.'

'Then explain yourself, before we have you thrown into the— Why are you all wet?'

Before Watborn could think of an answer, the yeoman grabbed at him. 'We should remove his tongue before he has a chance to use it.'

'There you are,' cried a portly fellow hung about in white aprons like a ship in full sail, sweeping down the colonnade. 'I have been looking for you everywhere! This stout fellow is mine, gentlemen, the new pastryman and very overdue for work. Thank you for detaining him.' He turned to Watborn with a scowl. 'One minute later and you would have been out of a job. Come with me at once.'

The yeoman and the commander watched in astonishment as Watborn, who had remained silent throughout this exchange, was led off at great speed by a man smelling of baked bread.

'Do you want to get yourself killed?' the cook hissed as he hurried the birdcatcher away through the arches. 'Do you know who they are? The commander of the army and his right-hand man. Why, they would put a man's eyes out for a side-glance. Turn here.' He swept them into a steam-filled alleyway. He was so fat that he could not walk with his legs together, but was surprisingly fleet of foot.

'I amn't your pastryman,' said Watborn, hurrying to keep up.

'Of course you are not.'

'Then why are you doing this?'

'How could I leave you like that? I saw what you did, diving into the moat. I don't suppose anyone else did, for I was opening a window in the scullery and happened to glance down. Although I cannot be sure, I think you saved the life of the King's daughter. If you really seek to be an archer, you have a dangerous way of petitioning for the post.' He held out his hand without slowing. 'I am Goldhawk, the head cook. Who am I addressing?'

'I am called Watborn, sir.'

'A Marshland name. What are you doing here?'

'My village was lost to me and so I came here.'

'Well! That is quite a turn-up. Most people try to get out of this place, not in.'

'I was raised within sight of it, Mr Goldhawk. It has always been before me.'

'And so you decided to see for yourself what was inside. To what end?'

'Sir?'

'There is only ever one question here, my fellow. Are you friend or foe?'

'Friend,' Watborn replied, though it was clear that those who lived within these walls cruelly used those without and deserved to suffer for it.

Goldhawk kept up the pace, turning into corridor after corridor. 'You will need a profession. What can you do?'

'I'm a fine birdcatcher.'

'There's not much call for that up here. Only the useful are allowed to stay, unless of course they are royals, most of whom serve no purpose except to excite the people with pageantry. You look like a blacksmith. Do you think you could pass for a pastryman if it will save your neck?'

'I don't know. Could I?'

'You could pound some dough with those fists.'

And so it was decided. Watborn would be taken to the kitchens and set at a long table where cooks slammed bread like pugilists. His course was taking an unexpected direction, but for now it would at least keep him alive.

32

The Foot on the Throne

Giniva sat in her window in a dressing robe, looking down at the bitten drawbridge. Her arms bore the bruises of her imprisonment in the calculating engine. If that was what stepping into the free world meant, perhaps she was safer up here for the time being.

She thought of the swimmer dipping gracefully down towards her and breathing air into her shocked mouth. Why had he helped her, where had he gone?

Plum and Split, her fat little wardrobe valets, were fussing with the sartorial plan for the day: an outfit to please the King, jewels to please her mother and Aunt Asphyxia, a pre-luncheon outfit for her riding lesson, simple luncheonwear, a practical afternoon lounging smock for her homework (singing and needlepoint), an elegant formal dinner robe looped and laced with gold chains (unusual for midweek, more commonly used for sitting portraits, but the Great Wound had acted quickly and was bringing another potential suitor to the table), followed by her retiring lace, virgin-white samite. This was her world, now and for ever.

She looked to the painting on her wall.

Biblius had taught her its meaning. It showed King Athelbrynn VI, the last of his line before Scarabold, crowned and seated upon his throne, on a raised dais beset with a thousand blood rubies.

It was said that Athelbrynn had had four hundred wives and 649 children, and owned a third of the known world. Beside him, seated at a more lowly height (for everyone in the kingdom was required to keep a lower profile than the absolute ruler) was Rudolpho Oldenberg, a representative of the Marshlands who had come to present trading terms to the King. Unbeknown to Athelbrynn, Oldenberg had raised his right boot and placed it on the pedestal of the King's dais.

The symbolism of the discreet gesture did not pass unnoticed; it was understood by all who saw the painting, and news spread fast. By displaying his relaxed familiarity, it showed that Oldenberg had the King's ear. It said he was a confidant. It said he had the right to trade.

He had no such thing.

The painting took a year to finish, but long before its unveiling the artist showed his sketches to Oldenberg, and the trader sent despatches to his homelands, so that when King Athelbrynn finally spotted the foot on the throne and was incensed, calling him a disrespectful usurper, it was too late to take revenge. Oldenberg's position had become unassailable and he was awarded a fortune in contracts.

Athelbrynn watched as the foreign trader's power grew and kept his counsel, biding his time. His spies listened day and night at the windows of Oldenberg's palace apartment until they heard him boast to an ambassador that the King could do nothing without him, for all had seen his foot touch the throne. Then they reported back.

Athelbrynn inflicted a special punishment for such words of treason. He had Oldenberg placed naked and spreadeagled inside a canoe, together with a canister of water that he could reach with his mouth. He cut off his feet and hands and tarred them, then spread sticky spices on his torso.

Athelbrynn's men emptied six wasps' nests into the boat by beating each one with a stick. The wasps became very angered. The boat was pushed out into the old lake and abandoned. It was said that the trader's cries continued for nine days and nights, but the story had been embellished over time.

Thus Athelbrynn reasserted his power and the wrong was righted. After that, all those who suffered from the affliction of a burning ambition thought twice about getting too close to those in power.

To Giniva, the painting was a reminder of her heritage, and a warning. To touch the Crown was to bring it down from heaven to earth. Doing so brought great rewards and the bitterest of deaths.

33

The Pleading Ape

Leperdandy's eyes were small and his night vision was poor. He was forced to grope his way along the stairwell leading to the dungeon. His elegant grey suede boots had become coated in guano. When he raised his eyes to the ceiling he saw that it was entirely covered with pendant bats, hanging like ham-hocks.

Once he would have fled for the safety of his rooms, but he was spurred on by the thought of discovering something that could help Giniva escape. He could not bear to think of life without her, but could not deny her the chance to be free.

Ahead he saw the flickering glow of the dungeon's wall-lanthorns. Carapace must have approached from this direction. What, he wondered, could he have discovered?

The dripping corridor opened out into a long rectangular room with a low stone ceiling and rusted cages along one side. The cobbles beneath his feet were slippery with emptied slops and outcrops of moss. Gulleys of rushing water ran across the floor. The delicate membranes of his nostrils were assailed by the scent of unwashed bodies, and beneath it an animal stench. Withdrawing his handkerchief, he pinned it over his nose. He could not help noticing that his hands were shaking.

Fumblegut's office was at the end of the hall and had no door. A bare table and a single wooden chair stood in the room, lit by one mean candle, marked down its side into hours. Even through the lavender linen, Leperdandy could sniff the aroma of wood alcohol. There was a drink the labourers made from fermented garlic leaves that blotted out all other odours. He turned and looked beyond the room.

On one side was an unmarked door with a mean little window. Opening it, he found himself in what was clearly a torture chamber, with a large oaken X-frame mounted against the far wall. A cabinet contained worn leather harnesses and straps, hammers, pliers, clamps, nails and lengths of wire. The floor was dimpled towards its centre so that blood could run down to a grating. Wooden sluicing buckets stood to one side.

Leaving the ghastly room in the greatest haste, he hurried on and peered into each of the prisoners' cages in turn.

It was hard to see within them. The floors were covered in straw-stippled ordure. Immobile figures were secreted into corners like spiders' nests. There were no nameplates, but a blackboard hung in the hall:

WARNING! CELL 15 HAS INFLATION OF THE TRIPES.

CELL 21 TO BE HANGED AGAIN ON THURSDAY.

He heard faint shiftings and whimperings but saw little movement. The thought crossed his mind that the commoners had a worse diet than his own. Dressed into puddings, pies, jellies and junkets, human meat bore no resemblance to the muck set before these desperate wretches.

He had reached the cage.

M'Lin was a black-haired orang-utan the size of a small man, except that his arms were of an abnormal length. He sat within, perched on a little wicker stool, his palms facing upwards in his hairy lap, elbows sticking out. He chewed at his fur, catching a flea and delicately pinning it between great white incisors. As the princeling passed, M'Lin raised his black-button eyes and rolled them in the direction of the door lock, welling with pitiful tears.

'I'm not going to let you out,' Leperdandy whispered, moving on. 'I know all about you.'

The orang-utan pouted and more tears spilled. He looked so desperate and gentle, but that was the trick of the pleading apes of Sumavera-Sum; these creatures were as malicious as they were intelligent. He pointed down at his right leg, which was manacled to the floor, and ran the back of a finger gently over the fitting in a pathetic gesture. A sudden thought occurred to Leperdandy and he returned to the cage.

'There was a man here – the Beetle Earl . . .'

Leperdandy did his best to impersonate Carapace's strange scuttling step. M'Lin studied the walk carefully and gave the appearance of understanding.

'He came to see the prisoners.' Here Leperdandy mimed looking into the cells. 'Which cell did he look into? Which cell, M'Lin?'

The orang-utan knew the answer, but pointed at the lock on the manacle with a powerful hand.

'I'll let you move about more freely if you show me.' He was aware that the offer sounded unconvincing, but he had no talent for subterfuge, and besides, he was talking to an ape.

M'Lin stabbed a finger at the chain again and rolled his eyes even more tragically.

'Only after you show me which cage. Anyway, I don't have the key.'

A flick of those small black eyes pointed to Fumblegut's office.

With a sigh Leperdandy made his way back along the cells. Without realizing it, he was already being manipulated by the primate. For although it was still pinioned to the floor with a steel chain, the door to its cell was unlocked.

34

A Man of Some Use

Watborn followed the head cook through arches dyed crimson by torches in stained-glass lanthorns. They passed through Hanging Sword Alley, past a painted wooden statue of a great bat being consumed by spiders. *No human beings belong here*, he thought. Netherworld creatures, perhaps. Finmoor's demons.

In front of them rose the great armoured suit of the first warrior-chancellor, one arm raised high with his spiked mace still gripped in a gauntlet, the other perched awkwardly on his hip.

'That fellow's mummified corpse is still inside the suit,' said Goldhawk as they passed. 'If you raise the visor, you will see that he turned himself around so that he is facing back to front – a sign of cowardice, some say.'

They hurried on. The head cook pushed at a protesting iron door and invited him inside.

Watborn found himself in a vaulted chamber with tall, deep-set windows that cast diagonal shafts of light along its length. He could smell cinnamon and cloves, pork and rosemary. The steamy air was filled with the noise of chopping, the clang of pots and pans, the boom of belching flames. Cooks ran in every direction, somehow managing to avoid each other even though their arms were filled with boiling pots and turrets of plates.

'Think you can fit in here?' asked Goldhawk. 'We're not known for fancy fare but we can pull a fine banquet out of our arses when we need to.'

'I have cooked,' said Watborn, thinking of communal meals in the village.

'Enjoy it, or no wife?' Goldhawk led him over to the stoves

without giving him time to answer. 'There's to be a feast for some visiting dignitaries. I don't suppose you can read, by any chance?'

'Yes, I taught myself.'

'By the Devil's yard, you may prove yourself more useful than half these flour-faced dripping-brains. I need someone to explain the menu to them. Have you a favourite dish of your own?'

'I can bake hedgehogs and preserve dormice.'

'We'll need something more sophisticated than that. Here, read this back. It was prepared for Carapace Sheathwing's banquet. It didn't go down well.' He tossed over a scroll of parchment.

'Rooks in vinegar'd vine leaves,' Watborn read obediently. 'Cod bladders with egg sauce, viper soup, rabbit bone-marrow in lemon cream, otter ham with bruised snails.' It all sounded quite disgusting.

'What about desserts?'

'I once made a sweet frumenty to be served with the fat of venison,' he admitted.

'Like the cobnut broth with wheat and fruits? It's one of the Princess's favourite dishes.' Goldhawk watched his face for a reaction but none came. 'There should be a centrepiece, like marzipan bacon and golden flummery. The ladies love to be surprised by exploding sparrows and ocean scenes made of roasted sugar-butter. You do know it was the Princess you saved in the moat?'

The birdcatcher blinked as if someone had blown air in his face. 'I had no idea.'

'Then why did you dive in?'

The question puzzled him. 'Surely you would not have let a young lady drown?'

'I'm afraid the moat is something of a clearing-house for those who displease the King,' said Goldhawk confidentially. 'We never know who will bob up in there next. I was going to set you to rolling out sweetmeats but help with the menu is far more valuable. Come.'

Goldhawk's kindness was all the more pronounced because of the burden he had to bear. Only a few trusted souls knew about the King's special dietary requirements. As the keeper of the royal menus, Goldhawk sought to make amends for this sin by helping as many of the kitchen staff as he could.

'You will be safe with us, Mr Watborn, whoever you are and from wherever you hail. You are a man of some use and that will keep you safe.' He sorted through a stack of staff uniforms loaded on a trestle table.

'I'm thankful for your faith in me, sir,' said Watborn, touched.

'Don't be,' laughed Goldhawk. 'There are strange times ahead, lad, and we may need all the allies we can find. There could come a time when friends are pitted against each other. Everyone here is scheming. The castle is filled with those who mean to succeed by climbing on the bodies of the dead.'

Remembering his escape from the sewer, Watborn kept his counsel and accepted the crimson uniform of the King's kitcheners.

35

A Fine Catch

It might have been a typical royal family scene of honourable husband and dutiful wife, except that their meeting was held at the great circular table in the Tournament Room and Scarabold was polishing his mace, for this was a council of war.

The Mater was all sharp angles and dark shades. The King was befurred with choleric temper. The atmosphere was acidic with rancour. The valets stayed out of smiting distance and even the spies Spackle and Peut knew better than to be caught lurking for fear of losing an earlobe.

Moribund examined her list again. 'Do we really need Phileuse Bose-Trunckly and Dr Fangle both around the same table? She is staggeringly boring and he is liable to bring up his feet.'

'It is your job to arrange the event,' said Scarabold dismissively. 'I have no interest in witless table chatter.'

Moribund sighed and pushed the table plan away. 'We cannot have a baron like Sir Archie F'Arcy attending a formal dinner without companions. He is not conversationally adroit and will sit there like a stewed pear unless someone engages him.'

'I don't know why we have to have a dinner at all,' Scarabold complained, pushing back his chair and swinging his mace experimentally.

'The F'Arcys are not like the Sheathwing. They are one of the oldest families in the land. They demand a certain degree of ceremony to accompany their arrangements.'

'Put Sir Archie somewhere beyond my range of sight. He looks like he had his chin blown off in battle.'

'And yet you consider him a worthy suitor for our daughter,' said Moribund tartly.

'It is said that his land cannot be ridden across in under seven fine horses, and thirty times our army is under his command. How many more qualifications does he need?'

Scarabold rested his case, the matter closed. Satisfied that the mace was as sharp and shiny as it could be, he set it aside. It was important that the last thing an opponent saw swinging towards him was a well-honed weapon.

Moribund arched an eyebrow. She was becoming quite theatrical with age. 'Very well, I will put him next to the Bishop of Wexerley. He won't be able to get a word in edgeways once the bishop starts on about Satan. How is F'Arcy to be presented?'

'To Giniva?' The Great Wound sucked his moustaches. 'I'll say she's available.'

'Why don't you get her to wear a sign around her neck, too? Really, you are quite impossible.' Moribund made a cryptic note against one of the names on her list, raised her quill and admired her work. 'You had better let me do the talking. Stick to things you're good at – explaining battle tactics and smacking the servants. I'll handle the rest.'

'Sir Archie is a fine catch,' Scarabold decided. 'Not conventionally attractive, perhaps, but his family is ancient, his orchards are young and his wealth is immeasurable. We should close the brothels while he's here, to keep him clean and build up his desire.'

'Will he have to come and live with us?' Moribund asked.

'I can hardly see him whisking her away and us having to explain about her, ah, dietary situation,' her husband replied. 'We could always send her with her own kitchen staff. They could prepare her meals separately. I would be happier if he remained where we could keep an eye on him.'

Moribund eyed him with suspicion. 'I don't suppose anything unpleasant could happen to him after he has discharged his duties? Once she is seeded, could there not be a slip on the North Turret staircase? The stairs are very worn. Or perhaps an unfortunate misunderstanding on the archery range?'

'I think that's rather jumping the gun, don't you?' Scarabold commented. 'He hasn't even met her yet.'

'I suppose you're right. Our intentions may appear too obvious.' Moribund snatched up her pen once more. 'I have it. We'll invite his parents. If the Duke and Duchess are here from the moment he sets eyes on her, they will know he initiated the union. So far he has seen only a cameo. And do not underestimate the fact that she out-ranks him.'

Scarabold had had enough. He wanted to get outside and smite something. 'I need an heir before the armies of the Marshlands start setting their ladders against our walls. If I fall in battle before then, the result would be catastrophic. Just get the wretched girl plump with spawn as quickly as possible.'

Enemies were gathering like crows settling on branches all around them, but so long as they remained unaware of each other's existence, Scarabold could regain control one skirmish at a time. His greatest fear was not that they would set aside their local quarrels and form an alliance against him, but that he would undermine his own position. He was a warrior, not a strategist, and inclined to act rashly without taking advice.

Scarabold needed to be saved from himself, but who could save their home?

36

The Whip and the Chain

Leperdandy returned to Fumblegut's office and looked among the dungeon-keeper's belongings. Where were the keys? And where, for that matter, was Fumblegut himself? Might there be a further jail chamber he had overlooked?

A black-feathered jerkin lay in the corner of the room. Feeling in its pockets, his fist closed over a ring of iron. Before he set off to seal his deal with M'Lin, he stepped outside and turned in the opposite direction.

The sweating cobbles led to a further row of cells darker than the first. Behind these bars the inmates were more animated, groaning and shuffling away from the doors as he passed, backing off like frightened dogs.

From one of the furthest cells a rhythmic mewling sounded. Leperdandy walked towards it. He looked and saw.

Slender feet, scarred and bloody, turned down and scraping against the floor. Heavy boots on top, pushing back and forth. A great cloth shape crushed on top of a pale naked one, shoving down into it loins-first. Tears and stifled cries of pain, filth and blood and body fluids, mixed with the stench of alcohol and something that bore no thinking about.

Horrified, Leperdandy turned away and ran back. The jailer was taking his pleasure, and such deeds were too dark to be witnessed without leaving a stain.

M'Lin was sitting with his great arms raised in L-shapes, waiting to be freed. Rattled by what he had just seen, Leperdandy removed the only key that could possibly fit the ape's manacle and threw it into the cage.

'You must lead me to the cell found by Carapace,' he instructed, but M'Lin was only intent on connecting the key to its lock. Panicked, the princeling ran back to the blackboard and tried to read Fumblegut's scrawl, knowing that it had to provide a code to the cells. One number was set apart.

The piteous figure he found lying on its straw in a foetal position was dressed more elegantly than the others. His features were not recognizable, for the prisoner wore a branks, an iron framework that fitted closely over his shaven skull like the struts of a helmet. On the front, below the nosepiece, a spiked shaft protruded into his mouth, preventing speech. A rusted lock sealed the infernal device in place.

Leperdandy sifted through the keys, looking for one small enough to fit. First it was necessary to find a way inside the cell, but that proved the easiest part, as the cell keys had cruciform bittings that protruded from their blades. Now he saw how the pairs of numbers corresponded to the keys.

He unlocked the cell door and entered. The prisoner was young and in great pain. 'I don't have the key for the branks,' Leperdandy whispered. 'These are only for the cells. What can I do?'

The inmate pointed down urgently, indicating his right boot. Leperdandy knelt and examined his ankle. The foot beneath it was of riveted metal.

A distant memory sounded like a bell in fog and died away. He knew there was something special about this prisoner. Carapace had known it too. 'We have to get you out of here,' he said. 'Can you walk?'

The young man shook his head and pointed again.

What Leperdandy had taken to be a torture device designed to spout blood when tightened by a screw was in fact the replacement for a lost foot, but its heel had been soldered to a long chain which led to an iron peg embedded in the ground. There was no lock to be opened.

'Who are you?' asked Leperdandy. The young man gestured at his foot once again. Before anything more could be discovered, they both heard a sound that caused them to freeze.

M'Lin was loose.

When he rose to full erectness, the orang-utan was immensely tall. He came towards them with his arms held high, walking with a peculiar gait that made Leperdandy think of a door being tilted from one corner of its base to another. The primate could not help but smile – that was how his face was formed – but his eyes were dead and dark. He knew that the easiest way to stop interlopers was to tear off their arms and legs.

Leperdandy possessed little traditional sense of courage. His battles were conducted in the pages of books, his victories won on the stage of make-believe. He valued the sharpness of his wit above that of his sword. Seeing the orang-utan rolling towards him, arms raised high, his instinct was to protect himself rather than the unfortunate prisoner, but he dragged the boy across the cell.

M'Lin gave an angry roar and rushed towards him. Perceiving Leperdandy's plan, the prisoner hauled himself around the ape so that the chain wrapped his leg. M'Lin was obliged to raise the links in his hands and pull them apart.

Although he was now free, the prisoner still had the scold's bridle closed tightly over his head and the bit protruding between his teeth, preventing him from speaking.

Leperdandy was trying to think of some way that he could trick the orang-utan into tearing it off without ruining the prisoner's features when the great ape swung at him. He felt the air punched from his ribcage as he was slammed against the bars of the cell.

The prisoner fell to his knees, rattling the chain at M'Lin, trying to draw his attention. The orang-utan swung around. Fumblegut appeared in the corridor, buttoning his trews and swearing to split the heavens.

Leperdandy glanced from one menace to the other, wondering which of them would get him killed. M'Lin looked back at his foam-mouthed master, then at the cowering prisoner. He did not wish to feel the bite of the jailer's chain-whip, but could not allow anyone to escape the cell.

A stand-off, then.

'What have we here?' asked Fumblegut. 'Slip your chain again, did you, you filthy brute?' He advanced on the primate.

Hidden in the shadows, the winded Leperdandy decided that his best option was to watch and wait. The jailer's attention was entirely focused on his pet. M'Lin bellowed and threw his fists high.

Fumblegut drew out his chain-whip and lashed at the ape, but the whip and the creature's chain became entangled.

M'Lin hauled his master towards him as if he weighed nothing. As Fumblegut pulled frantically at the chain, trying to unknot it,

Leperdandy stepped from the shadows. Freeing the whip, Fumblegut lashed out at the ape, scoring a bloody slice across its back. M'Lin roared in pain and dropped his arms. A moment later, Fumblegut caught the end of his chain and hauled him back to his cage.

M'Lin's furtive eyes darted hither and thither, weighing opportunities for escape until another lash from the chain-whip drove him inside and his cell door was slammed shut. The masked prisoner fell into a corner and made himself invisible.

The beast shot his jailer a look of blank hatred, but saved his cruellest glances for the princeling. He turned his great head in Leperdandy's direction and sniffed the air extravagantly, as if to say, 'I'll remember your scent.'

'Your Royal Princeling, I had no idea . . .' Fumblegut polished his voice. 'We have never had the pleasure of you in the dungeons before. We so rarely get any visitors.'

'And yet the Beetle Earl came to see you just a few days ago,' said Leperdandy, dusting himself down. 'Whom did he come to talk with?'

'Oh, no one in particular. I think he was just taking the air. He was due to marry the Princess, was he not? Forgive me, news travels slowly to these low quarters.'

'And who is the prisoner you've been keeping chained up in such a torturous device?'

Fumblegut pawed nervously at his mouth, wiping away spittle. 'Ah yes, sir, Your Royal Graciousness, a jolly good question indeed. He doesn't belong in the larder, sire. He's to be kept separate with the traitors.'

'But who is he?' Leperdandy persisted.

'I don't know.' He hastily rebuttoned his filthy doublet and wiped himself down. 'The Decrepend brought him to me three moons ago and said he would bring further instructions, but none have been forthcoming. I had to bar his mouth, for he made such a noise. I did it for his own good.' He dug out a receipt creased soft with filth and pretended to read it but the effect was spoiled; he might have been a cow staring at a signpost.

'On whose authority was the Decrepend acting?' asked the princeling. 'Where was the young man before he was brought here? Is he from the outside?'

'I cannot say, sire. I am but a poor deprived warden kept far from sunlight and company, who does what he is asked for the greater good of the fambly. I keep the stock fit and healthy until such time as the head cook needs them in the kitchens. Not that I know what he does with them there, you understand.'

'Then I would have you remove the branks from the poor wretch's head and allow him to speak for himself.' The princeling tried to sound confident, even though he knew he was counter-manding instructions left by the chancellor. He and Fumblegut looked about themselves. The broken section of chain remained on the floor of the prisoner's cage, but of him there was no sign.

Leperdandy was distraught. 'We have to find him.'

'He won't get far, sire,' Fumblegut assured him. 'With that thing in his mouth he can neither eat nor drink without my help.'

'Did you never think to ask who he might be?'

Fumblegut grew emboldened. 'Why should I? In all the years I have been here, none of you has ever asked a single question about the members of my wretched flock before.'

37

A Steady Hand

Before dawn the kitchens clanged and hissed with activity. Under cover of darkness, several half-dressed scullery maids scurried from shared blankets back to their duties. Watborn had passed a short night with the other cooks, who lived, slept and washed together in an antechamber near the stoves, where it was warmest.

'Usually we'd seethe a badger,' said Goldhawk, peering under the lid of a tureen. 'A substantial meal, but it doesn't look good on a banquet table.'

Watborn could understand why. After being set in a pie with its head sticking above the crust, the beast was left with bared yellow teeth and boiled white eyes.

'The Princess's last suitor expired at the table, so this time we'll try to dispel the memory by making the menu unmanly and fussy with lots of colour – pomegranates and cherries in the vinegar – and a few spun-sugar ships as centrepieces, to make the ladies squeal. Do you have any thoughts on that?'

Watborn looked down the table. At each point along the middle was a small clay model of a dish. Their labels read: *Swan (feathers on) – Roasted Boar on a Trencher – Pike in Ale and Figs – Burning Ginger Lozenges.*

'I can make a dainty dish of linnet birds in smoked honey,' he suggested. Watborn knew the importance of making himself useful. As a birdcatcher he had often prepared meals in the village.

'A fine idea,' Goldhawk concurred. 'It will please the ladies. Our efforts are wasted on the men, for they tear at their food without tasting it. One would think they have contests to see who can swallow everything and shit it out the fastest. This meal must be perfect. We cannot afford to have another death at the feast.'

'Does someone not wish the Princess to be betrothed?' Watborn asked, puzzled.

'It's worse than that,' Goldhawk replied. 'She is nothing more than a pretty little peg in a board, to be moved and traded between allies and enemies. She is too sweet and innocent for strategies. She has been heard begging Scarabold to release her from her obligations.'

'But she is not free to do as she pleases.'

'Less so than any of us. She must be dutiful, for it is all she was born for. It is important that the new suitor finds her alluring. In truth, she fails to see the danger she is in.'

'Who acts for her?'

'Her guard was removed for reasons I know not.' He slapped flour from his chest. 'To the task at hand. We need some special treat to catch the Princess's favour.'

'I could create her likeness in almond paste.'

Goldhawk narrowed his eyes. 'How do you know about almonds?'

'Manderfill, your under-chef, showed them to me. If you beat them with sugar and eggs, a moulding paste can be made.'

He considered the idea. 'The Princess loves seeing her portrait, for she is young and vain.'

'I am prepared to take the task.'

'Very well. I shall request a likeness from her mother and you can copy that.'

'It would be better if I sketched her features from life,' Watborn said.

'Royals and commoners never mingle. But I suppose you could ask the Decrepend. Do you have handwriting?'

'Well enough to draw the menus.'

'Good. Our last scribe lost some fingers in a fight.' Goldhawk pinched his new worker as if testing dough. 'Don't get ideas above your station. Until your summons, you're peeling turnips.'

Watborn knew that the key to his advancement was duty and excellence, and decided to practise calligraphy with a pot of pigment and a fine brush. He was sent to the chancellor's chambers to ask permission to draw the Princess.

The old man was hunched at his high desk with a white plume and a vast roll of parchment. He wore a red velvet four-cornered hat and a robe like an old curtain, and looked like a statue that was crumbling to dust. His desk had been so worked upon that its centre was worn away like a butcher's block.

'You wish an audience with the Princess Giniva,' said the Decrepend without looking up. 'Don't ask how I know. I am the record-keeper; it is my job to know everything and everyone. You are Watborn the birdcatcher, are you not?'

'I am, sir.'

'Ambitious, aren't you, never staying in one place. I suppose you'll want to become an archer with those arms. You're doing well for a commoner. They usually get big ideas and end up separated from their heads. The Princess never gets to meet them. A commoner could do some good here, and much harm.'

'I can do good, sir.'

The Decrepend peered at him as if unused to seeing anything beyond the printed page. He looked for the greedy light of ambition in the newcomer's eyes and found none. After much thought he gave the faintest nod of approval. 'You have an open face. I make no promises. I need to check you further. We've had spies in the past. They tend to come in over the drawbridge and go out through the sewer pipes.'

'Thank you, sir—' Watborn began.

The Decrepend handed him a roll of paper. 'You'll need this. And a lot more than a steady sketching hand, if you are to keep moving up.'

'What makes you think—'

The chancellor tapped the side of his bulbous nose. 'You're not the first one to come here seeking a better life. I know about you all, and what happens to you. I'll be watching.'

38

Others Will Be Blamed

'She wants to leave,' said Peticia, unfolding a coverlet of silver brocade and laying it across the end of the Princess's bed. 'That's all I know, and more than I should know.' Behind her, Plum and Split beat out the pillowcases. Nobody knew if they were male or female, but they were very efficient valets.

'But don't you wonder?' asked Cradleigh, the under-footman. 'You're her chief dresser. Surely you're privy to all her secrets.'

'The Princess does not confide in me,' Peticia sniffed. 'She told her secrets to her halfling brother and to Nurse Mentle, in whom she has confided since she was little more than a swaddled infant. Why don't you ask her?'

'The nurse is too old and frail to leave her room any more, and you know it. She drinks Forget-the-Pain and her wits are wandering. She can't receive visitors. Nobody goes near her any more—'

'If the Princess chooses to disappear, I fancy there will be no keeping her.' Peticia pushed past the under-footman and gathered up the remaining pillows for the bed, arranging them upon a sea of black silk and fretted damask. 'She is a woman now, in age and form at least, and females have little say here, royal or no.'

'The prince won't supply an heir.' Cradleigh chuckled darkly. 'I hear he can't abide the thought of pronging.'

'That is nothing to do with you nor I. Royals are different. They have better blood. It's thicker and of a different hue.' Peticia shook out the coverlet and tried to shake him out of the room along with it. She could forgive Cradleigh for being new to the royal household, but not for asking so many impertinent questions.

'So the future of the family hinges on the Princess's potency,'

Cradleigh mused, stepping out of her way. 'A new royal line must be started before his enemies realize the truth.'

'And what truth might that be?' Peticia bustled past with a warming pan.

'That until a child is born, the House has no armour,' he said. 'It is as exposed and vulnerable as any day-old fleshling. I hear tell the Sheathwing armies have been called from their outposts to meet with their king. It can only be about the loss of his son. Errors have been made; others will be blamed. There have been overtures to Scarabold but he denies all audiences. That is the way to start a war.'

'Just think, if you were not an under-footman you might command the entire army,' said Peticia innocently. 'Politics is not my world, nor yours. Getting the Princess ready to meet her suitors – corsets and cords and fine lace – now, that's something I understand. I know my place and I suggest you learn to do the same.'

'You'll understand more if you walk over to that window one fine morning and see five thousand men assembling beyond the grounds,' muttered Cradleigh. 'This has been a long time coming. Preparations are being made for an invasion, mark my words. And guess who will be the first ones thrown from the ramparts?'

But the dresser had gone to the linen room to gather pomanders and was already beyond earshot.

39

To Raise an Army

Scarabold waited for Spackle to finish lighting the pipe for him, then snatched it up. Opium helped to muzzle the pain in his lower back. He felt the blood draining from his nose and neck.

The Huntsman's Lodge was the King's domain; over two hundred wild animals had been captured in mid-snarl, their skulls removed, their flesh cleansed and wired and made to appear fiercer, then mounted on the walls of the octagonal chamber. Even the rabbits had had deer-horns pushed into their eye sockets to make them appear fierce. Their corpses had made fine pies for the family's retinue and staff.

'Bring me the map.'

Spackle wrestled the roll from its leather tube on the desk and brought it to the King. Scarabold spanned it across his knees and studied the landscape.

Beyond the lowlands rose the jade hills of Flemmstede, over one thousand acres currently known as the Infected Hills due to an outbreak of plague, and to their east in Exerley, where the air was bare and cold, lay the kingdom of the Sheathwing. In the vale below were the river towns, where les Sœurs aux Cadeaux Étranges, ruled over by Lady Lavinia Travernum, guarded their treasure. To the west lay the F'Arcy lands and the other kingdoms of the Fraternity, few of whom could be counted as allies.

'This map is preposterous,' Scarabold growled. 'It's completely out of scale and everything is in a different place, and all the names are wrong. There are no flying dragons or sea monsters, so why draw them in?'

If the Sheathwing was to raise its army against Scarabold, the

King knew he would have to rely on the Sisters to aid him. The only reason they would agree to help was because they feared the Sheath-wing's army passing through their territory.

Scarabold had no choice. A single royal male (for no others were allowed to enter the sanctuary of Cadeaux Étranges) had to be chosen for the mission at once, and the help of the Sisters elicited before war was declared.

Scarabold puffed on the pipe and sat back in his ancient leather chair. He was growing old and tired and did not wish to lead his men in battle, but what choice did he have?

He decided to call a full council of war with Grand-Marshal Timmorian. Weapons which had not been wielded in decades would have to be patched, repaired and made ready for use, ammu-nition stockpiled, provisions gathered in, conscripts press-ganged, oaths of loyalty sworn, rituals of obeisance conducted.

That would be just the start of it.

Calmora the Seer would have to be enticed into making a proc-lamation. The temple gods would require appeasement, and there were so many of them to remember. Bulls would have to be slaugh-tered, the priests would require reassurance, the staff would need to be calmed, the defences raised, supplies laid in, the field peasants paid, the barricades manned, the vestal maidens . . . what was he meant to do with them? Something about a cauldron filled with suicide-orchids left to burn for seven days and nights . . . how was he supposed to remember all this?

The Decrepend would recall the exact ritual, but where was the money to come from? Just how much did les Sœurs aux Cadeaux Étranges have in their collective purse?

There was something else that could help save them from all being slaughtered in their beds, but as the opium took its grip he could no longer remember what it was, and his ancient head was clouded with green-and-violet dreams.

40

Into the Cistern

'Is it safe to come in?'

Leperdandy called through the great oaken door of the armoury. He cautiously pushed the door open and stuck his head around it just as an arrow thudded into the lintel.

Giniva lowered her bow. 'I nearly pinned your ears back, brother. Next time, use the bell-pull before you enter.'

She wore a fine, flexible breastplate of beaten silver and chainmail leggings that afforded protection from the target-run, a thirty-yard list that extended along one side of the armoury. Setting off along it caused volleys of grapeshot, spears and spikes to be launched. One was meant to learn from the assaults and anticipate them, but the mechanics were ancient and poorly repaired. A few had been over-greased, some barely cleaned at all. As a result, it was impossible to guess where the next volley of arrows and spikes might land. Sometimes they went into the ceiling, sometimes they maimed the valets. One catapulted mace had sent an equerry out of the window.

The Princess endured her mornings of combat training, having been taught to treat them as abstract exercises, for it was unlikely such skills would be needed in her lifetime. Even if the threat of invasion was real, as a royal personage she would never be allowed contact with the enemy. 'Taking the mace', she had been taught, was what foot-soldiers were for. Better a thousand should lose their jawbones than one hair be harmed on the head of a member of the royal family.

'Where have you been, anyway?' Giniva set aside her weapon with distaste. Behind the list her courtiers stood down, removed their straw suits and left the hall, for they were not allowed to hear royal conversation, however innocuous.

'There's a prisoner in the dungeons who is kept separate from the rest,' said Leperdandy. 'Carapace discovered something just before I . . . well, you know. Fumblegut has him fitted with a branks so that he can't speak.'

'What concern is that of yours?' Giniva pulled off her helmet and shook out her flaxen hair.

'You sent him down there to release the proof of our vice,' he reminded her. 'But that is not all that he saw. I found the prisoner and tried to free him.'

'Who was he?'

Leperdandy looked sheepish. 'I don't know – and yet I feel as if I should.'

'Well, what did he look like?'

'I'm not entirely sure. He was locked tight into the iron bridle.'

'And what happened?'

'I lost him. But he means something. He is important enough to be kept separate from the other prisoners. We could talk to the Great Wound.'

'If this man is being kept in the dungeons, Scarabold will know why, for Fumblegut would never act of his own volition, and that means our father wants him to remain there. Now that he has escaped, he could be anywhere.'

'He can't long survive without our help. We must find him, but I don't know how. There are a hundred thousand places to look. If only there was some way—'

'The speaking-tubes,' said Giniva without hesitation. 'They run beside the pipes. Spackle and Peut use them all the time. They hear everything that's going on around here.'

As children they had sat beside the pipes to keep warm. Criss-crossing the castle in an iron labyrinth, they pumped hot air from the basement furnace to the eaves, but when they ran beside the speaking-tubes they conducted sounds strange and wonderful: declarations of passion and anger, snatches of song, proposals and protests, incomplete secrets and fragments of phrases.

'There is only one other safe way out of the dungeon that I know, via the under-basement staircase,' said Giniva. 'There's a water-duct connecting it to the cisterns.'

'I have a map in my rooms.' Leperdandy grabbed her hand and pulled her from the armoury.

They needed to avoid their family. It meant ducking away from the household suites, where Mater Moribund was making the final arrangements for the reception of the F'Arcys, and avoiding the War Chamber where Scarabold was meeting his councillors.

It also meant keeping an eye out for Aunt Asphyxia's spies, but nobody knew the place better than Leperdandy; he treated it with the respect accorded to a fine old theatre, darting through the back-stage area, the flies and wings, flats and scenery, the mechanics of pomp and fakery. There was still much he had yet to uncover, but the royal passages were as familiar as his own blue veins.

'Listen,' he said, pausing to press his left ear against a crusted furlong of pipework. 'I'd recognize that sound anywhere. It's the Decrepend flushing his guts. The prisoner escaped through the drains. I know the way.'

They set off up steps and over a little arched bridge filled with glowing sconces, around a spiral staircase encasing a ruined marble pulpit, past the perfumed pink corridor that led to the staff brothel, on to the hivernarium, where a great curving iron pipe rose from among the foliage. Here carrion-plants and pitcher-flowers lured mice towards their sticky stamen and dissolved their flesh while they still wriggled and thrashed.

'This is it,' said Giniva. They listened at the pipes.

A faint scratch, and another.

A clang and a muffled oath.

The sound of a man making his laborious ascent through the plumbing, hampered by the cage attached to his face.

'Look for a ventilation grille,' said Leperdandy. From somewhere far below they heard the howl of M'Lin in the dark of the dungeons. 'It's here – do you have a knife?' He showed her the bolted square set in the steel sheeting.

'No, I have an awl.' The Princess dug into her bodice and produced the lengthy spike. 'A knife is no use against enemy chainmail. This can be pushed straight into an eyeball.'

Leperdandy pulled a face. 'You had better do it. Nails.' He held up an immaculate hand.

The noise of her blow was tremendous and echoed down the length of the pipe. 'So much for keeping our operation clandestine,' he sighed. 'You might as well do it again and as quickly as possible.'

Three further blows tore the rusted bolts from their holes and dropped the panel. Giniva peered inside. 'I can't see anything, and it stinks.'

'That will be the Decrepend. He drops turds the size of turnips.'

'Pass me a lanthorn.'

Leperdandy obeyed the command and hung on to Giniva's legs as she leaned further in. 'He's there,' she called back, 'but he's stuck. The branks has caught against the side of the pipe. I'm going in.'

'What are you going to do?' hissed Leperdandy, alarmed.

'I shall land on him and see if that does the trick. I'll try not to break his neck.' And with that she let go. Leperdandy marvelled at the behaviour of a girl who usually complained if her pillow was not scented with honeysuckle. He heard a slither, a bump and a muffled cry. What, he wondered, was he supposed to do now?

Taking another lanthorn, he leaned inside the foetid pipe and held his breath, but saw nothing.

He was still trying to decide what to do when there was a terrible rumbling sound from above. Someone had opened the sluices that drained rainwater from the battlements.

He was hit hard on the back by the plunging cascade and tipped over into the pipe. The deluge slammed into all three of them (for Giniva was just as wedged as the prisoner beneath her). They were washed along the curving vent, bolts and screwheads tearing at skin and clothes, out into the great stone underground cistern beneath the court chambers.

The water was green and shockingly cold. Wave after wave hammered into them, tumbling them over one another. Leperdandy knew that the iron mask on the prisoner's head would pin him down and dove deep, grabbing his collar and hauling him to the surface.

'Leperdandy!' called the Princess, spitting out frogspawn like tapioca pudding. 'You have the makings of an adventurer after all!'

She had spoken too soon. Above them a sluice gate opened and dropped a ton of slippery brown effluvium upon their heads. Leperdandy screamed in a register so high that storks were startled off their chimneys. The blast of body-warm sewage pulled them apart, hurtling them along the canal of muck. A carpet of rats raced ahead of a flotilla of turds, dissipating itself into the nooks and crannies of the tunnels.

As soon as Leperdandy was able to right himself and open his crusted eyes, he looked for his sister. Bobbing in the cloacal molasses was a figure that might have been human. It breathed out, revealing the right end, and raised a hand in the flickering gloom.

'Where is he?' Leperdandy gasped.

Giniva's other hand held that of the prisoner. Together they dragged him to the side of the flagstone culvert and, with much slipping and slithering, up on to an iron drainage platform.

'I'll stink for weeks. I have been infected with a thousand ailments,' Leperdandy cried, before being volubly and noisily sick. He spat and spat again. 'Our captive looks done in.'

Giniva pointed out a sluice pipe of fresh rainwater cascading on to the stones. The pair of them stood beneath it with the prisoner in their support. 'Truly, I am not made for adventure,' the princeling complained, shivering. 'How is he? Can you get that thing off him?'

The prisoner's grey face and closed eyes boded ill. Folding back her sopping sleeves, Giniva dug out her awl and bashed at the branks's side-bolt. In her enthusiasm she scraped his cheek and came dangerously close to removing an eye.

The bridle was ancient and soon pummelled apart. The shaft extending on to the prisoner's tongue required more delicate extraction.

'Please,' Giniva pleaded, 'if you can hear us, open your mouth.'

The prisoner gasped and parted bloody teeth. Leperdandy slipped delicate fingers along the bit and felt for its rusted edges. At the end of the shaft was a spiked spindle that pressed into the prisoner's tongue and dug into his palate.

'I'm sorry,' he warned. 'This is going to hurt.'

The princeling wiggled the bit to dislodge it, then withdrew the scarlet steel from between the prisoner's lips, handing it to his sister. The prisoner spat blood and shreds of skin, coughing. He had no voice but a rasp.

'Here, let me.' Leperdandy massaged water from his chest and wiped his face. From beneath the bridle a young man emerged, chalk-cheeked and crimson-mouthed, half starved but, the Princess noted, undeniably handsome. They sat him up and bent him over to force more fluid from his lungs.

'We need to get him out of here,' Giniva warned as they heard the rumble of sluices opening once more above them. 'The water's contaminated and his wounds are raw.'

'There's a way through the cistern that leads past the library. Perhaps Biblius will help us.'

'No.' Giniva was firm. 'He was being kept in solitary confinement for a reason. That means somebody wants him hidden. No one can know about him.'

Leperdandy was exasperated. 'Then where on earth can we take him?'

'I don't know,' Giniva admitted. 'We have to keep him concealed until we can find out who he is.'

They lifted him to a half-standing position, but the prisoner was still bleeding from the mouth and appeared not to know where he was, or what was happening to him.

'I think I have an idea,' said Leperdandy.

41

To Keep a House Together

The doe turned a great ebony eye to Watborn and trembled. Its legs remained planted to the flagstone courtyard. It sensed danger.

'Slit its throat,' said Goldhawk, 'and we'll hang its flesh with the others in the warm air, the better to turn it.'

Watborn did not care for the task, but knew he was being tested. He gripped a blade and advanced on the creature. 'Does the Princess ever speak to you?'

'Certainly not,' replied the head chef. 'It is beneath her dignity to do so, and I would be deeply ashamed if she did. You will be advised of protocol before your meeting. Mind that you obey the rules.'

'You mean—'

'Your request to draw the Princess's likeness has been approved by the Lady Dwinoline. But you may have only the length of a sand-glass to do so. You may not speak first or approach her, nor look her directly in the eye. You must show respect and obeisance at every moment during her presence. You will be summoned tomorrow morning.'

Watborn thanked his employer and gently caressed the doe before cutting its throat. It died peacefully, so that its muscles did not clench and toughen the meat.

As he washed his hands of hot blood, he thought about the lady in the lake. If she was of royal blood, why had she been trying to escape her duty? He and she were as opposite as two people could be. He was making his way through the world she was so keen to leave, and as old in his heart as she was youthful.

Stop what you're thinking, birdcatcher, he told himself. *If you're caught staring at her, you will end up with your eyes put out.*

But the thought did not stop him from dreaming. He did not plan to spend his days as a pastryman. He acted according to his nature, operating on instinct, even though he was not sure whether his instinct would betray him. He owed no one allegiance, but kept his counsel.

While performing his new duties he watched and waited, speaking little and listening much. What he heard was mostly hearsay; stories passed up from those who dealt with the outside world.

He began to hear the same rumours repeated: that the Sheathwing army was reaching a head, that Scarabold would be taken by surprise, that only a secret signal was being waited upon before the assault could begin.

What this signal was and who might make it remained a mystery. The world beyond, which had once been all he knew, was now just a picture in a frame. He was about to be swept up in events he could not control. At such moments, split-second decisions could decide lifetimes.

Scarabold was busy kicking his valet. 'Hell's teeth, man, I'll take my own drawers off when I'm ready.'

Ratchet was quite used to being battered; under the old king he had lost his right earlobe and two toes. The missing items were medals of honour that spoke of his duty and loyalty to the family. But on some cold nights he ached fit to cry.

As Ratchet backtracked silently from the bedchamber, the Great Wound slipped beneath the embroidered coverlets and buried himself in his wife's hair. Mater Moribund was pretending to be asleep, the better to avoid the royal stabbing, a ten-minute ordeal that left her feeling soiled and revolted.

Outside, lightning splintered the night sky. Moribund's body was wintry and hard, all spiny peaks and frosty valleys. Dwinoline's was soft and rounded, like summer countryside. He needed both of them, but neither made him happy. He had not loved Dwinoline enough and had never loved the Mater at all. The marriage had been strategic, and now he was condemning his daughter to the same fate.

The war council had not gone well. Without money for men and weapons, the army would not last more than a few days against the Sheathwing. They had cannons – artillery that old never went out of date – but nothing to fire from them, and many of the muskets were lethal to the user, as the commander's third-best marksman had discovered on the firing range that morning. They still hadn't found his knees.

Scarabold feared for the future. He was ashamed that his strategy for survival depended on the selling of his daughter, but could allow no one to see the cracks in the Crown.

'We will hide the mildewed tapestries and stand armoires in front of the wettest brickwork,' said the Mater quietly. 'We'll put the valets in clean tunics, sweep out the flooded areas and unblock the latrines. Place sweet-smelling posies in all the bedchambers. We must make a good impression on the F'Arcys. The head cook was planning a menu of deer-flesh and herbs, but I told him it must be grander than that. No one from outside will know our secret, you may be assured. I wish I had never—'

'What?'

No answer came.

'I am trying to keep a House together, Moribund.'

She turned to face him. In the absence of make-up she appeared less imposing, although she still had her cheekbones. Without their kohl rims her eyes had all but disappeared, and yet there was still fire flashing in them. 'If you weighed those who wish our House to endure against those who wish us dead, what would you find?'

Scarabold stared straight ahead.

'Why must all families survive, if that is all they do? When was the last time any of us was happy, Archim?'

'It is not our duty to be happy now.'

'Then what is our duty? We need to grow strong again.'

'Perhaps in time . . .'

Moribund pulled herself up. 'In time! Do you not understand? We are out of time! A milksop son and an errant daughter – how are they to run your precious kingdom?'

Scarabold rounded on her. 'And what is the alternative? What do you do when you can only go on living? The Sheathwing will overrun the River People and force them into an alliance against us. They will invade our home and burn the lucky ones alive. Twenty-nine members of your family live here, along with forty-one of mine. Our combined retinues quadruple that sum, to which we must add the rest of the inhabitants. Would you see them all put to death because of one stupid—How did Carapace die, anyway? Did she poison him?'

Moribund looked as though the thought had never crossed her mind. 'Who?'

'Why, Giniva, of course. She is the only one who had good reason.'

'Don't be ridiculous. She's all gesture, nothing but rant and stamp and pout. She cannot do a single thing for herself. Her valets still have to wash and dress her. She is sixteen!'

'Old enough for the peasants to have spawned several times.' Scarabold plumped his pillow. 'She has never had to learn,' he muttered. 'Perhaps now she will start.'

'If she learns too much, you will lose her,' warned Moribund. 'There are fresh plots being hatched against us; I can feel it in my lights. Our own spies cannot be relied upon. You have rewarded too many and punished too few. No ruler survives without a steel glove. Loyalty is not born of love but from fear of reprisal. Are you listening?'

But if the King was still awake, he chose not to answer her.

42

Passing Spirits

Far below the royal bedchamber, the great cistern was filling with rainwater. Even the wall-sconces were in danger of being doused. Giniva and Leperdandy swam towards the library staircase with the prisoner linked between them. All were shaking violently with cold.

'It was builded so that the manuscripts in the reference section could be moved down here in the event of fire,' Leperdandy explained, out of breath. 'Magister Ambrosius brought me here when I was very small. Nobody knows about it but me.'

Much of his childhood had been passed in the Cistern Library, avoiding tourneys and Spear-the-Man challenges on the rooftop playing-fields.

'I don't know if the door will yield from this side.'

They collapsed on the steps while the princeling tried the handle of the floodgate. It gave a little. Unable to see what lay beyond it, he pushed harder and, when it opened, stepped out.

Cardinal Vespius Weem from the Overlands had made the perilous journey to Londinium with just one purpose: to examine the Tome of Saintly Harms, which had been written on human skin and was kept in the reference section of the Cistern Library.

Biblius the librarian had sealed away Orobus and unlocked the bars of the black teak bookcase. When he removed the book with long-handled callipers, he dislodged a century of dust and beetle-shells.

'It is most kind of you to afford an aged academic the opportunity of examining first-hand such a remarkable manuscript.' The

Cardinal wiped his eager hands on his cassock. 'We mere mortals are forbidden from tainting the pages with our sweat.'

'Alas, we have no call for such rarities in this godless age,' Biblius replied, setting alight a small copper pot of ambergris that would drive the leather-mites away from the volume. 'You would be amazed by the blasphemous tracts we hold here. Kingdoms were burned down because of their veneration, and burned again in the fight to preserve them. Once, entire dynasties lived and died to carry aloft their flame from one generation to the next. Now nobody gives a stuffed owl whether they survive a fire or get tossed into the moat.'

Cardinal Weem lowered his eye to the cover and examined it minutely. 'Such craftsmanship. They say it holds the spirit of a ghost which is released as the pages are turned, do they not?'

'Indeed, sire, and I fancy you will feel it pass as the cover is raised.' Donning a single calfskin glove, Biblius gingerly parted the pages.

The frontispiece depicted the Demon Vapula Licking Sins from Lepers. 'The sight of the original painting upon which this etching was based,' said Biblius, 'is said to have driven the Nuns of F'Arcy into a frenzy of self-abasement that lasted for ninety years. I don't believe the story myself, but you can see why peasants are not allowed to view it. It would only give them ideas.'

Behind their backs, Leperdandy and Giniva moved through the half-light of the library stacks on sopping tiptoes, dragging the prisoner between them. Their actions were swift and silent, burnished by years of prowling beyond their parents' sight.

The Cardinal raised himself and sniffed the air. 'Why, I believe I can sense the demon's presence!' he cried. 'An odour of gravely rot and nightmare filth corrupting the very air about us!'

Biblius sniffed the air as well. 'It smells like shit.'

They looked back and saw the puddles of muck that tracked across the herringbone brick, passing from one far wall to the other. Biblius was amazed. He had only half believed in the Spirit of Saintly Harms, but now he had evidence of its passage.

It was a pity it hadn't wiped its numerous feet.

43

Watborn's Sketch

'I know your secret,' said the head cook as Watborn was setting roasted butter on to a dish of burnt plums. 'Your fingers have bow-string scars. Were you also an archer?'

'A trapper needs a clear eye,' said Watborn, stepping back to admire his handiwork.

'And a strong arm,' said Goldhawk. 'Longbows were a bit beyond your range, I imagine. I wanted to be a bowman but I fell foul of an angry sheep.' He held up his right hand, which was missing its thumb. 'The bugger had a fair set of teeth. I cut them out of its head and turned them into dentures for the wife. Why did you leave?'

'My home burned down. I had no reason to stay.'

'But you could have gone anywhere.'

Watborn had thought about this ever since setting off. It was a good question; how best to answer it? 'The castle is the first thing I remember,' he said. 'Always in the distance, that big.' He held his fingers two inches apart.

'Then I hope you satisfy your curiosity,' said Goldhawk, admiring the dessert. 'But don't think you will advance far here. The castle is like a cake. We remain in separate layers and all the expensive ingredients are on the top. You're good at cooking but perhaps you'd make a better bowman.' He thought for a moment. 'I have an errand for you. Go and talk to the guardsmen for me. Find out if any are to be posted at the doors of the Tainted Hall. The feasting dishes will need to be carried in whole, you understand.'

'Yes, sir.' Watborn's heart lifted.

'And perhaps the commander has someone who can show you

the longbows. I suppose I could arrange for you to meet my brother, Manticore. He's the Yeoman of the Guard and a stout, fine fellow, although his tragedy is that he can never ride with his men.'

'Why not?' asked Watborn, declining to remind Goldhawk that they had met before, albeit briefly.

'He has one leg shorter than the other. It unbalances him.' Goldhawk laid a hand upon his arm. 'You must be careful, Watborn. There are some in here who would mean you harm. You cannot afford to be as trusting as you were with me.'

A breathless herald arrived at the door. 'It appears your errand is postponed,' said Goldhawk. 'The Princess is ready to grant you an audience.'

The herald turned and promptly left. 'Follow me quickly,' he instructed, snapping his fingers.

'How am I to present myself?' Watborn was barely able to keep pace with the rushing lad.

'The Princess will speak and your answers will be clear and brief. You address the Princess as "Your Highness". You will not look the Princess in the eye, nor turn your back to her. Do your duty without chatter, and speak to no one of what transpires. No more than this is expected of you. Remain in the room until after she has left. I will fetch you back then.'

The boy led him ever-upwards, along a hall and into a receiving chamber inlaid with emerald tiles. Before him was a table set with charcoal and parchment, and two chairs. The light was poor. *Just as well*, he thought. Watborn had never tried to draw. He had not expected his request to be granted.

When the Princess entered she brought light into the room. There were clematis petals in her bright curls but her clothes were simple: a white shift only, worn without jewels.

'I have not had time to dress this morning.' She raised the back of her hand to him but did not allow his lips to touch it. 'You will have to imagine my finery.'

She did not catch his eye, but placed herself in the opposite chair. 'Will it take long?'

'But a few minutes, Your Highness.' Watborn struggled to keep his eyes downcast. He took up the charcoal and made an outline, in the way he had seen an elder use such a stick in his village.

Giniva was amused. 'You may look upon me. I don't see how else you can capture my likeness.'

Watborn studied the Princess in a state of wonderment. He recognized the girl from the moat even without her black face-paint. To think that he had kissed her, if only to breathe air into her mouth! Had she seen him? Did she recall his face in the murky green depths? It was unlikely that they would ever be so close again. He would have to content himself with glimpsing her from afar.

His hand skimmed the parchment. He was not sure if he was actually drawing.

'What is your name?'

'Watborn, Your Highness.'

'That's a Marshland name, is it not?'

'It is, Your Highness.'

She pointed to his arms. 'Your skin is dark. You work in the fields.'

'I was a birdcatcher, Your Highness.'

'You may address me plainly, else you shall wear out the title from overuse. I know you. We have met before. You dove into the moat.'

Watborn remained silent and stared at his sketch.

'Answer me plainly. Are you the man who wrested the whalebone from me?'

She will have me put to death or at least thrown back into the Marshlands, he thought, his heart beating faster. 'I am, Your . . .' He cleared his thick throat. 'I am.'

'Explain yourself.'

'I brought you air, Your Highness.'

'You kissed me! You touched a royal personage. I could see you dance on the end of a hempen rope. There is hardly a greater sin.'

Watborn swallowed and concentrated hard on the charcoal in his hand.

'Look at me, Watborn.'

He raised his head.

'You brought me the breath of life.'

He gulped. His mouth was dry.

'I would be shamed if I did not acknowledge the man who saved my soul.' She held his gaze. 'You must have asked yourself what I was doing in such a situation.'

'It is not my place—'

'Nor mine to explain, yet I find myself desiring to do so. I was trying to get away from here. Does that shock you?'

It was best to say nothing.

'Where you see a princess, I see a prisoner.'

He prayed she would say no more. He could not be privy to her secrets without risking his neck.

'I have no allies save for my brother. I find myself quite unprotected. Perhaps next time I will find someone to help me. Someone I can trust. Can I trust you?'

He held his breath but kept his eyes on hers. 'You can, my— You can.'

A full minute passed between them.

'I'm afraid your time is up.'

As she rose to leave, the door of the receiving room swung open. The herald had been discreetly watching her, at the ready.

'I wonder if we'll see each other again,' she said softly. 'I shall remember your face.' With that, she slipped away.

If the Princess had got herself into difficulties by trying to leave, she was liable to place herself at risk again, he thought. He resolved to act as her guardian whenever he could, even though he had no authority to do so. She was in a position to reward him mightily, but could also take everything from him.

He looked down at the page through scrunched eyes and was amazed to find that he had drawn a reasonable likeness of her. At least the eyes were right. She held the sky in her gaze.

He knew it was the wrong thing to do. As soon as he was released from the receiving room he set off after her. She was wearing plain pattens that sounded against the floors, providing a beat of wood on stone.

The corridors were treacherous. Some parted only to rejoin, others tailed off into brick ginnels and vanished altogether. The Princess moved with the speed of habit, finally stopping in the archway leading to a windswept bailey surrounded by dead trees.

An angular young man stepped out to greet her. Watborn ducked back behind the arch support and listened.

Someone else surveyed the scene. Ormond the Steady of the Devil's Tongue was still pressed against the stones in his coney coat, his twin-crossbow in his arms, waiting for an opportunity to strike at the Princess. Now he had found her meeting her brother on the staircase directly before him, and prepared a second arrow.

44

The Museum of the Dead

Giniva was too preoccupied to realize she was being followed. She found herself thinking about the birdcatcher-turned-cook. Why had he risked his life for a stranger? He could not possibly have known who she was, and had therefore not been seeking a reward. It was a conundrum. The lower orders were not known for their loyalty, although there was a cabal of creeping royalists among them for whom the monarchs could do no wrong.

'I tied our prisoner inside a rug and had two of the under-servants remove it.' Leperdandy took the Princess's hand in his. 'They carried it to the Museum of the Dead. The place hasn't been used since the old king sailed to the sky. The staircases aren't safe. One fell down and flattened some visiting novices, but I know how to cross them. I paid our new friend a visit.'

'Was he awake?' Giniva asked.

'Not entirely. I tried to feed him some soup but it was too hot and his mouth was too sore. Come, I'll show you.'

As they moved off, Ormond stepped out, raised his twin-crossbow and loaded both shafts. The Scarabold children had a notable family feature: their necks, which were long, white and vulnerable. As he locked the arrows in place, he anticipated the couple's forward motion and took careful aim. He could bring them down together.

Watborn saw the scene unfolding before him. He needed to fell the assassin in such a way that the Princess would notice nothing untoward. A sharp kick to the back of Ormond's left knee did the trick. The limb folded instantly, spinning him about and loosing the arrows up into the rafters, where their sound was lost in the clatter of pigeon wings.

Watborn's right hand seized a startled face and held it close. He shook his head in warning, making sure he was fully understood, then released Ormond, sending him down the stairs. The assassin tumbled over himself a few times, emitted a feeble groan and lay still. He bore an insignia on his sleeve, a horned crimson face with a forked tongue. Watborn made a mental note to sketch it and discover who had sent this man to harm the Princess. The attack would not go unavenged.

For his part, Ormond lay still and waited for the footsteps near him to retreat, thankful that he had not been attacked by one of the Kingsmen, as they would surely have run him through.

Watborn would come to regret his natural aversion to killing; the assassin was unrepentant.

'Father will be angry that we did not appear at table,' warned the oblivious Giniva. 'He'll try to find out where we are.'

Leperdandy lit a fresh lanthorn and led her to the shattered stairs beyond the Cistern Library.

'He'll never think of looking in the museum. He has no interest in the past. He only cares about ballooning you with child as soon as possible. We'll say we were at weapons practice; that will shut him up.'

They halted in a corridor that fell away on one side. In places the stone passage narrowed to a handful of crumbled bricks as soft as icing sugar. It was best not to think about the drop into darkness.

The princeling went ahead and returned with a partially unravelled coil of rope, which he tied around his sister's waist. Inching across the broken steps in single file, they reached the museum door and unbolted it.

Watborn had managed to catch them up, but could only go so far without revealing himself. What was the posturing brother hiding in there? The door had clicked shut behind them.

He could learn nothing by waiting outside. It was not right to betray the trust of his employer. He turned and loped back in the direction of the kitchens, hoping he could find his way.

Giniva looked about herself. The Museum of the Dead ran in a broad passageway across the north side. It was clear that no one had visited this spot in an age. Spiders the size of little girls' hands dropped from their webs and scuttled off into corners as the light invaded.

Here, the Devil's Tongue Cup and the Great Pot of Stern stood on pedestals amid avalanches of armour and antique weaponry. Along one wall were mounted the heads of horses that had died in the War of Seven Thousand Cuts. Only the black lacquered poison cabinet of Fatima of the Lash stood open and appeared to have been recently touched. Leperdandy was careful to avoid looking at it as he passed.

'I wrapped him in some sacred linens from the royal bedchambers,' the princeling explained. 'And I found some binding oil for his wounds.'

A rainwater pipe spiralled into a large stone font at the back of the museum. Giniva filled an earthenware bowl and brought it to the prisoner, who lay against a wall, his face as grey as the brickwork. He drank greedily, allowing the icy water to calm his inflamed lips. The Princess took some sprigs of mint and lavender from her bodice and moulded them together into a poultice, fitting it inside the prisoner's mouth.

'This will help to calm your wounds,' she said gently, placing a bolster behind his head. 'What are we to call you?'

The prisoner turned his cloud-coloured eyes towards her. 'All my life I have been known as Tinfoot,' he croaked, glancing down at his right leg, which ended at the ankle. 'But that is not my real name.'

'Then who are you?'

'Once I was called Brasslight, and I was of this kingdom. But I never reached my naming ceremony.'

'I know of only one Brasslight and he was a very old fellow with no ears who worked in the herb-gardens,' recalled Giniva. 'Couldn't keep a hat on to save his life. You are a relation?'

'No.' The young man gingerly touched the sides of his swollen mouth. 'I was born right here. Nobody now remembers my story. It was recorded by the doctor, Emeric Fangle, and the nurse, Minerva Mentle.'

'They are still here,' Giniva cried, 'although Nurse Mentle is now touched and confined to her bedchamber, and Dr Fangle has not been sober in years.'

'But they are my only hope.'

'What happened to you?' she asked, settling herself cross-legged beside him. 'Why were you taken to the dungeons?'

'It was the night of the blood-moon,' Tinfoot began.

45

The Prisoner's Tale

The birthing spire was octagonal and as slender as a minaret. It appeared to have been carved from a single piece of ivory, so smooth and pale was it, but there was no animal on earth large enough to have provided a tusk.

The beaten-gold sun and moon on its roof represented male and female forms. Beneath this spindle stood an arched vault with a honeycombed squinch, and beneath that an octagonal bed. There was no canopy to the bed; the four posts ended at a height of two and a half feet. It had wooden grips for hands at one end and for the soles of the feet at the other. Here a woman could push and be pushed until her child made its bloody entry into the world.

The young woman at its centre arched her back and buried her skull down into the pillows so that her golden curls covered her sweating face. She groaned and cried as the pain became unbearable, but still the baby would not come. Overhead a storm raged, flashing bolts of fire from one angry cloud to another. The noise of rain almost drowned out her urgent cries.

Dr Emeric Fangle did not know what else he could do to alleviate her suffering. He had already fed her enough tincture of bitter-root to loosen a horse. Peering between her legs, he saw the child's bloodied crown, but it simply would not appear in full.

'What's wrong?' asked Nurse Mentle. 'Can you not unbung her?'

Fangle removed his pince-nez. 'My dear lady, it is not simply a matter of "unbunging" the Lady Castilia. Her Venus opening is too small. You can't push a dog through a keyhole.'

'Then she must be cut across the belly,' said the nurse firmly. 'And quickly.'

'Very well, I'll get my—'

The nurse rose. 'Not by you. How much have you had to drink this night? I'll do it. I have performed the operation many times. We should never have allowed a man in this chamber. I said it would lead to trouble. There were only ever sisters in attendance. It worked perfectly well for three hundred years.'

'The sisters are gone to orders of silence now,' said Fangle, stung. 'It is better to have an anatomist present, someone who places his trust in science instead of all these herbs and dollies.' He swept the arrangement of straw figurines from the end of the bed and pushed down on the young mother's stomach, making her scream.

'You can't squeeze it out!' cried the nurse, searching through the doctor's linen roll of instruments and selecting the sharpest knife. Scrunching her eyes, she examined the blade. 'This is covered in rust – no, not rust, dried blood. Did no one ever tell you to wash your instruments in boiled water?'

'A little dirt is good for the mother,' said Fangle. 'It helps to build strength against the body's humours and make the child strong.'

'But not when she's in this weakened state. Fourteen hours of labour is more than any woman can stand. Give me your flask.'

Fangle looked shocked. 'No, madam, this is medicinal and allows me to maintain my high level of concentration.'

The woman on the bed released another howl of pain.

'Give it to me!' The nurse reached behind Fangle's back and snatched his silver flask, deftly opening it and tipping its contents over the blade of the knife, which she then cleaned on her apron. Grabbing a wooden candlestick from the floor, she flicked away the candle and placed the holder in the girl's mouth.

'Bite hard and place your thoughts elsewhere, my lady, for this will be your greatest pain.' She waved Fangle back. 'Stand over there and thread up some needles, if you can see clearly enough to do it. Make sure they are clean. We must end this poor girl's agony.'

And so saying, she lowered the blade and began to slice open the girl's white belly.

The procedure was conducted by the light of eight faltering candles in brass sconces, but the child was delivered. Nurse Mentle was shaking as she hacked through its cord. She had not been expecting to perform the delivery herself, and was out of practice. Raising the bloody child by its ankles, she gave it a hearty smack on the arse to clear its lungs. 'A boy,' she said. 'A fine and healthy specimen, for the most part.'

'What do you mean?' asked the doctor, coming closer to examine the infant. The mother had seen her child and fallen back into exhausted silence.

Nurse Mentle stitched her up as fast as she could, but too much blood had been lost. 'We need a strong solution of minerals, or we will lose her.'

'I have some in my bag,' the doctor remembered, as much as he could remember anything. 'I'll get it.'

'No, I'll go. There's nothing more to do. Sit here with the child and hold the mother's hand.'

The nurse ran as she had never run before, but there was no doctor's case at the bottom of the spire's staircase. 'Boy!' she called Fangle's valet. 'Where is his bag?'

The valet stopped examining whatever it was he had just pulled out of his nose. 'Whose bag, miss?'

'The doctor's, you little slug.'

'He's got it with him, miss. I saw him take it up myself.'

Nurse Mentle knew she should never have trusted Fangle. To have been saddled with a drunken physician on a night such as this! She hurtled back up the spiral staircase and arrived at the chamber door with a pain in her side.

The doctor looked at her with shame and sorrow in his eyes. 'She has gone,' he said quietly, as if not to disturb her passing spirit. 'She has boarded her ship to the skies.'

'Get out of my way, you bloody old sot!' Shoving him aside and nearly causing him to drop the baby, she hammered at the mother's chest, trying to create a rhythm that would start her heart anew, but it was not to be. The girl had already lost her life-colour. Nurse Mentle checked for the beating of blood but all was still, all breath had fled.

They sat beside her, nurse and doctor, as the baby wriggled in its slime, oblivious to the life it had replaced.

Fangle settled the mother and covered her face. Nurse Mentle washed the infant clean in the font, then swaddled it in fine white muslin and wrapped it in fur.

'He should be called Brasslight,' said Dr Fangle. 'That would have been his name.'

'What do you mean?' asked the nurse. 'If that is his name, it will be pronounced at the ceremony—'

'There will be no ceremony. Did you seek to hide this from me?'

The doctor unwrapped the muslin and showed her the stump where the boy's right foot should have been.

'The law of primogeniture ensures that the first-born boy must come to the throne, but this child cannot. For there is another law – the Law of Damage. It is one of the Three Exceptions on the family tree. The child must be born entirely sound of mind and body. He can never take his place as head of state.'

'So what is to become of him?' asked Nurse Mentle, looking into the infant's wide blue eyes as if trying to read his mother's dreams.

'The King will have to seek another for his heir,' said Fangle sadly.

'But what is to happen to the boy?'

'He must be drowned in the moat.'

The doctor busied himself with his instruments. Having not been entirely sober for a number of years, he was not sure there was still a law decreeing that the absence of a foot would end the line, but it suited his purpose to say so. There were none within who did not operate without some private purpose of their own.

'Then I will take the little thing and dispose of it,' said the nurse in haste, pulling the furry bundle away from Fangle. 'I'll smother the little squallery and weight him down for the attention of the moat pike. This is no job for a drunken old man.'

Before the rum-fuddled doctor could raise an objection, she picked up her skirts, hoisted the boy and scurried from the chamber, taking the staircase as fast as she dared. The mother had already been lost. She would not allow the child to be put to death.

Under the cover of the rampant storm, she boarded a cart with her precious cargo bundled in her lap.

Back in the birthing spire, Dr Fangle sank against the wall with tears rolling down his unshaven cheeks.

46

Hiding the Foot

Tinfoot looked from one sibling to the other. 'I was taken to les Sœurs aux Cadeaux Étranges, many furlongs from here, and raised among them in secret until they judged it was time for my return.'

'But why now?' Leperdandy asked. 'How did you end up in Fumblegut's dungeon?'

'After the arrival of my Manhood Day, I decided to try to return, but it took many moons before I could make good my escape.'

'The Sisters would not let you leave?' asked Giniva.

'They were only worried for my well-being. There were terrible stories whispered about this place. They said that once a fine civilization had existed here, builded by others on democratic principles and with all the latest appurtenances, but that Scarabold had allowed it to crumble to dust. What remained was like a pustule, where everything fair had rotted to poison.'

The Princess nodded wearily. It seemed that everyone had something bad to say about them. 'Then why did you wish to come back?'

'Why is anyone drawn home?' asked Brasslight. 'I thought I would be accepted and restored, but before I could speak to the King, Fumblegut's guards dragged me off to the dungeon, and there I have remained. At the next full moon I will reach my eighteenth birthday and be eligible to adopt my rightful place in the family. Except . . .' He pointed to the ragged stump where his right foot should have been.

'I don't understand,' said Leperdandy. 'I've never heard of your mother – Castilia, did you say? And who, pray tell, was your father?'

'You do not know our history?' asked Tinfoot, puzzled.

'Only what we see on the escutcheon and in the painting of the royal family tree,' said Giniva. 'The heredity books are locked up in the library until we come of age.'

'How old are you?'

'I am now sixteen but ineligible for the throne by dint of my sex. Only upon marriage may I adopt my duties as Queen. If I birth a male, he will become the new king at the age of seven.'

'And you?' asked Tinfoot, facing Leperdandy.

'I am also of age, but a little older than my sister.'

'And therefore due to inherit the throne?'

'No,' said the princeling, suddenly downcast. 'I am a weakling. I failed the Rite of Manhood in my thirteenth year and was removed from the royal line because of my hereditary enfeeblement.'

'Can the King do that?' Tinfoot was amazed.

'He can do whatever he likes,' replied Leperdandy.

'My brother refused to take up our father's scimitar and smite the neck of his opponent,' said Giniva. 'He was meant to spatter the walls with gore, but the thought of it made him sick. For this he paid the penalty of forfeit.'

'Enough.' Leperdandy clapped his hands together. He had no desire to relive the most humiliating moment of his young life. 'You have not fully answered our questions. Who was your father?'

'I am Tinfoot, born as Brasslight, son of Lady Castilia and Lord Perseo.'

'No.' Leperdandy shook his head. 'Doesn't ring a bell.'

'My father was Scarabold's brother,' said Tinfoot quietly. 'He died after seeding my mother and she died giving me life.'

'Wait, I know about this!' Giniva raised her hand as if attending tutorage. 'Uncle Todge! We never knew him by any other name. He fell into a ravine during a fog.'

'So some say. Others tell a different story,' said Tinfoot darkly. 'We share the same royal lineage, the three of us.'

'But as you stand the eldest,' Giniva said, 'you're in line for the throne.'

'You are forgetting my deformity,' Tinfoot replied. 'I am just as cast out as you.'

'Cruel fate,' said the princeling. 'Each banned, for each of the Three Royal Exceptions. Enfeeblement, deformity and gender.'

'Leperdandy, you do realize what this means?' cried Giniva. 'Our Uncle Perseo died without further issue and you were disbarred from inheritance, leaving my future husband in line for the throne unless we can find a way for Tinfoot to take the crown. If you adopt your rightful position, Tinfoot, I can avoid being parcelled off to the highest bidder. You were the intended future king.'

'Wait,' said Leperdandy. 'How do we know we can trust you?'

'I was thrown in jail for attempting to see your father. I was not raised in your ways, but in the loving sanctuary of the Sisters. You could speak to them.'

'Sadly not possible at the moment,' said Leperdandy.

'I can get you an audience with the King on one condition,' Giniva decided. 'That you help me to escape from here.'

'But Tinfoot is ineligible by way of the deformity exception,' Leperdandy reminded his sister. 'The statute calls for "two feet to be squarely placed beneath the throne".'

'Who needs to know?' replied Giniva. 'Only Dr Fangle and the nurse were there in the birthing spire. Poor old Mentle has lost her wits and Fangle lives inside his rum-bottle. We can take care of them. And you, my dear Leperdandy – you may be wasted on the tourney court, but when it comes to the theatrical there is no finer practitioner in the kingdom.'

'What does that mean?' asked Tinfoot.

Leperdandy grinned. 'It means I can fashion you an appendage made of jointed steel covered in the skin of a newborn calf, with toenails of mother-of-pearl, and stitch the join to your skin with animal leather, and make it so perfect that no one will ever know you were born without it.'

'Vitrolio the armourer will help you,' Giniva said. 'He owes us many favours. We hid his infidelities from his wife and lied for him from the time we were seven. But you must never use the name Tinfoot again. Your name is Brasslight because of the candle fittings in the birthing tower, yes?'

'I had to be named upon my whole appearance into the world,' said the boy. 'From then I knew little but the sound of the jade fountains, the hymnal of harp-sonnets Lady Lavinia played on her gadulka and the skittering of cat-claws on the convent flagstones. The Sisters live very purely. They don't even play football.'

'Then you are to Brasslight restored, by order of the Princess. Rest here.' Giniva's hand stayed upon his arm. 'You must let your wounds heal and recover your strength. We will bring you food and medicines. There is a jakes in the corner, and blankets. Stay out of sight until all is ready. When the time is right we will summon you to the court of the Great Wound.'

'Time is not something we have on our side,' her brother reminded her. 'Our petition must be irrefutable. Your next suitor is even now heading towards us.'

'Then there is someone I have to see,' said Giniva.

47

Two Worlds

The Sepulchre of the Oracle was hung with diaphanous veils: pink for the past, yellow for the present, blue for the future. Calmora the Seer sat within swirls of vermilion silk at its centre, like a fairy-child born inside a rose.

The problem was finding her. She was so mystical that she was virtually invisible.

'I sense a presence,' cried a mellifluous voice. 'A member of the royal family. Please, come and be seated. Not over there, that chair's still a bit damp.'

Giniva hunted through the wafting silks and found Calmora seated upon her ankles on a sunset-hued divan of Moorish damask. One of its legs was missing. The air was noxious with burning herbs.

'Calmora, it is—'

'I know who you are and why you have come back,' the seer interrupted. 'You seek my advice about the succession to the throne.'

It wasn't exactly why she had come, but she supposed it was close enough. 'There is a claimant. I want to know if his cause is a worthy one.'

'I don't predict. I can only tell you what is in my eyes.'

'And what do you see?'

Calmora sank back into the cushions, which were so soft that she almost disappeared. Giniva took a sip of blackberry tea while she waited. For a minute she thought the seer had gone to sleep.

'Calmora?'

'I'm communing with the spirits of earth and air.'

'What are they telling you?'

She opened one eye. 'That someone of the royal blood has a question about a claimant.'

'I already told you that.'

'Is he a legitimate heir? He is . . . unusual.' She peeked at Giniva. 'Not . . . normal.'

'Yes, he is . . . not his entire self.' She stopped herself from saying more.

'I see a great crown,' Calmora announced suddenly. 'An enormous golden diadem. It floats above us on the head of a lion, the ruler of us all.'

'A painting?'

'How would I know?' she snapped. 'Wait, now I see a limb – a foot, but shiny somehow. How it gleams and catches the light! The lion frowns down. He is carved from a single great rock. It is here that your destiny will be decided. But only if two worlds are joined as one.'

She sat up, shook her head hard and took a drink of tea. 'There. Was that any help?'

'Two worlds joined as one,' Giniva repeated. 'What else do you see?'

'Not a lot, frankly.'

'I'm not sure it makes much sense. But I thank you.'

'Glad I could help,' said Calmora, vaguely amazed. 'Please remember that predictions are the responsibility of the interpreter and do not necessarily reflect the views of the House.'

'I also wish you to tell me—'

'One prediction is enough, I think.'

'I am the daughter of your King.'

'Ask away.'

'I want to know what will happen to us.'

'Well, obviously I can't tell you that.'

'Think of it as part of my earlier question. Just tell me if you see anything else. Anything.'

'Very well.'

Calmora sank back and closed her eyes. 'Nothing very cheerful, I'm afraid. I see fire and bloodshed, betrayal and destruction. I see your family before me, one blinded, one slaughtered, one ruined, one betrayed.'

Giniva's eyes widened. 'Is there nothing I can do?'

'There is a man who will aid you – not from this place and not of royal blood. An archer, I think. At least, he's got pointed sticks with him. Low-born, most likely. He doesn't look very clean.'

'Who is he?'

'No idea. He doesn't know that he has a place in history. He won't have a clue, right up until the end. And even then he won't fully understand.'

Giniva was confused. Perhaps the seer was drunk.

Calmora fluttered her hand. 'Now you must go. Divining visions is exhausting work and your oracle needs to see the backs of her eyelids for a while. Preferably without any hellfire visions caused by your family.'

'Have a care, Calmora,' she warned. 'You are still our subject.'

'Only in your world,' the seer replied. 'In mine you are all subject to a far more powerful force.'

What a strange woman, thought the Princess as she left coins in a strategically positioned offering-tray – but oh, her first words had been so wise, so appropriate! It was a shame that she had spoiled the effect with the rest of it. Yes, she decided she could safely ignore the last part of the prediction. Next time she'd use one of the other seers.

She had always had a knack for dismissing unpleasant thoughts.

48

Dust to Dust

There was nothing worse than being in a counting chamber with nothing to count. The grand manager flicked through the mouldering balance books and released a sigh like the last breath escaping from a corpse.

'It would be much easier to run the kingdom's finances if the Great Wound didn't have everyone who disagreed with him split from crown to arse,' Thredneedle complained to his chief accountant. 'Remember the broker Scarabold had thrown in the moat? We only found his teeth.'

Canterby's men had spent the best part of a day attempting to scrape Auditor Silvercannon from the inside of the vault until Thredneedle had thrown in the towel and ordered it to be sealed for ever. It had taken all this time for the room to cool down. There was nothing to be saved; all the bills had burned and there had been no gold for years.

'What are we to do?' the chief accountant asked. 'Our home must be defended. Our soldiers are only staying at their posts because Grand-Marshal Timmorian has threatened to cut their ears off if they leave. They are dressed in little more than rags. Some are armed with sticks instead of muskets.'

'Increase their deferred wages,' said Thredneedle. 'They might as well earn a larger percentage of nothing for their troubles. The King himself is going to Cadeaux Étranges. When he returns he will hopefully be carrying gold as a down payment for protecting the Sisters.'

'That's nice, isn't it? Blackmailing nuns.' Canterby tutted. 'With the King gone for days, it will be harder to persuade the men to remain at their posts. What about the women?'

Thredneedle looked confused. 'What about the women?'

'They are paid nothing at all but virtually run the place. In this kingdom it has always been about the women. Could we not place them on the battlements?'

'I think that idea's a bit ahead of its time for us,' warned Thredneedle. 'We like our men at the cannons and our women at the stoves.'

'Then we have nothing more with which to bargain,' Canterby sighed. 'Other kingdoms are forging ahead. It is said that the Sheathwing have machines of wood and rope that can walk over the heads of men, and in the land to the north where the men dress as women, they can restore the dead to living usefulness. We remain stuck in the past because of . . .' He mouthed the three-syllable name because one never knew where Spackle and Peut were installed. 'It's this place – it's like being trapped in a mausoleum.'

Thredneedle was only half listening. His mind was running on different tracks, but now they converged. 'Mausoleum. Morgue. Museum. Is the Great Pot of Stern still in the museum?'

'Yes, of course,' said Canterby. 'But it cannot be touched. It is sacred. You couldn't possibly mean—'

'I wasn't thinking of selling it, just raising capital on it. We'd get it back when the King brings money.'

'But it's a holy relic.'

'Holy is just another word for valuable.'

'The ashes of the Scarabolds were mixed with the spirits of our ancestors. Whoever removes them—'

'Oh, rules, rules.' Thredneedle looked sceptical. 'The good thing about ashes is that you cannot tell one pile from the next. Why, I could top it up from the grate over there and you would not be able to pick out a monarch. I'll find a money-lender who'd like to avoid a dip in the moat. Is Peter Maggot still lurking around the embankment looking for deals?'

'I believe he has managed to stay out of jail, sir.'

'Perfect. You go up to the museum and make sure the pot is still there. When you find it, think of a way to bring it to me, but tell no one of our plan.'

'But if I am discovered . . .'

Thredneedle flapped the thought away. 'Stop being ridiculous. Who could discover you? Museums are not for visiting, they're for putting stolen things in and forgetting about.'

Armed with a map of his route, Canterby headed off into the ill-lit corridors. He could not help feeling that he was about to commit an act of treason. As he walked, a trifle unsteadily, he passed a stout fellow carrying a great stone basin filled with almonds.

'May I?' he asked, dropping a few into his fist. 'Are you making frumenty?'

'That I am, sir,' said Watborn, trying to identify his companion. This weedy fellow had been standing on the drawbridge when the calculating engine fell through it.

'It always takes me back to my childhood,' said Canterby. 'Could you bring some up to the Counting Chamber?'

'I'll have to ask Mr Goldhawk, but I'm sure I can arrange it.'

'Most kind. Your name?'

'Watborn, sir.'

Canterby scurried off into a side-passage. The alcoves were missing several statues which had been removed on the grounds of vulgarity, for they depicted nuns collecting tree-penises in fruit baskets. In two of the empty niches sat Spackle and Peut, watching the exchange take place below.

'Who's he?' asked Spackle. 'We've not seen him before.'

'A pastryman,' said Peut. 'It's on his apron insignia.'

'That's no pastryman. They're always fat.' Spackle watched as Watborn turned back towards the kitchens. 'He looks too strong. He was watching like a hawk. Mark his name well. He's one to keep an eye on.'

Canterby stood before the Great Pot of Stern and realized that he was faced with a more serious problem than the morality of hawking ancestral ashes to arm soldiers. The thing was on a tall dais and stood four feet high, and would require at least two strong men to lift it. Carved from stone and riveted with pewter bands, it defeated the chief accountant's efforts to shift it even a quarter-inch.

He found a box and climbed up. Standing on the tips of his pattens, he removed the filigree lid and peered inside. The entire line was reduced to a soft grey corporeal mulch. Were they as weighty in death as they had been in life?

He gave the rim of the pot an experimental nudge to see if he might tip it on its side, empty it, then refill the thing after he had rolled it back to Thredneedle. In truth, the base was far narrower than the neck. If he could shove it over on its dais and spoon out the monarchs into a heap on the floor, he might just be able to lower the pot, remove it and return with a sack for the kings and queens.

I will surely go to hell for this, he thought. *If only I could explain to the gods that I am acting for the greater good.*

He started pushing, which set the pot gently rocking, for its base was not entirely flat, and only stopped when he heard the ring of metal on stone.

Clambering back down, venturing across the museum floor and peering around the corner, who did he see but—

'Tinfoot?'

For there was no mistaking the identity of the golden young man lying asleep in the corner, his metal heel clinking against the flag-stones as he slept.

Canterby had long heard stories about the malformed prince who had vanished from the birthing tower. There was a melancholy painting in the counting hall of this very boy aged eighteen, or rather how he would have looked if he had survived. It had been painted by Lady Dwinoline, who was fond of preserving and ame-liorating lost parts of history in the form of paintings and tapestries, and scattering them through the castle like autopsied dreams.

Why, the boy was lying in that very position, a reverie come true, and with the same metal appendage shown in the oils! How was it possible, and why was he here? Why had his presence been kept a secret?

Canterby realized he was probably the only person who might ever have noticed the resemblance. What an extraordinary thing!

It became a matter of the greatest urgency to convey his discov-ery to Thredneedle. The grand manager would know how best to make capital from the information. He would return to the bank with all possible despatch, and later bring back a couple of stout fellows to carry out the pot.

A dream of glory flooded Canterby's senses. He would be feted as the finder of the true king. A simple change in the law would allow the five-toed lad to rule. What rewards could he not ask for as the saviour of Londinium's finances? There was money to be made here. Nothing would ever be denied him again.

But while the chief accountant stood beneath it dreaming, the Great Pot of Stern had been set to rocking, its contents shifting as if all the kings and queens were pushing at it. Slowly and silently it rolled about its base as the plastered support beneath it was whittled away by the weight. When it reached its tipping point, it froze for a moment before continuing over the side of the dais, dropping its open neck neatly over Canterby's own to form a perfect seal.

The shocked chief accountant was suddenly enclosed on all sides. Under the weight of the pot's contents, he dropped to his knees with a crack, suffocating in the dust of generations. The remains of royal personages swirled about his head, filling his mouth and ears and eyes, silently choking off dissent as they had so often done in the past, when they had interfered in the lives of commoners. Canterby's body fell forward and the stone pot rolled, twisting him over and over.

The kings proved as lethal in death as they had been in life. Now only the chief accountant's dusty thighs protruded from the pot. He gave one final kick and fell still, his spirit departing to join the monarchs who would have shunned him in life.

49

Orobus of the Rotunda

'What can I supply you with?' asked Mater Moribund. 'It is a two-day ride, and then only if the weather is with you.'

'My riders can only be beaten by white eagles, and we haven't seen one of those in years,' said Scarabold, raising his arms while Ratchet strapped him into his leathers. 'I'll tell the men that we plan to cross the high valley of the Rushing River before first light tomorrow.'

'What if you encounter the Sheathwing?' Moribund rose from her bed and went to the window.

'It's unlikely they could act so quickly. The Beetle Earl's family would have to hold a council before undertaking an action with such serious consequences.' He swatted Ratchet away.

'But they may need no allies. There are more of them, as many as the insects in the soil from which they take their name—'

'Why do you worry so?' Scarabold joined her, taking her pale face in his rough hands. 'While we still slumber, on the far side of the world it is already light. The future has happened before we awake, and another day has already begun, so our fate has been decided. We can only perform what the gods wish.'

'Don't start that again.' Moribund's features never lost their resistance. 'We have no more gods. We are reviled, so let us be reviled and rule all. It is in our own hands. We must take what we can and crush all who oppose us.'

'I don't understand what makes you so determined,' said Scarabold. 'Do you not have everything you want? Are you not well cared for here?'

'That is hardly the point. You ask what I want? I want them all to know that we have not been made weak by our habits but stronger, that we are not outcasts but survivors, and that this is the right thing to do, and woe betide any who fail to follow our way. I want them to know that in a thousand years our family will still rule over them.'

Scarabold studied the scars that crosshatched the backs of his hands. 'An absolute conviction of what is right is what eventually makes every man wrong. Each kingdom wishes to subjugate its enemies. That is the way of the world. But you want more than that.'

'Yes, I wish to look into their eyes and feel their fear. A woman has the power to make this happen more easily than a man, if she chooses to exercise it.' Moribund's dark eyes grew distant. 'If we do nothing, we will be besieged on all sides. I will keep us strong, Archim. The only way to stay on top is to keep climbing. Go to les Sœurs aux Cadeaux Étranges and raise your army. Bring us the gold we need to win a war. And try to stay away from harlots.'

She laced him into his cape and pressed her cold lips against his ruddy cheek, and sent him from the bedchamber, bolting the door behind him. *Of course I have the will to survive*, she thought. *After all, what else is left for us now?*

After the adventures of the past week, Leperdandy was not so easily affrighted as he had been of yore. Knowing that Biblius the Librarian would not allow him the keys to the Rotunda Library, he resolved to find another way in. Unless he had proof of lineage, Scarabold would dismiss Brasslight's claim.

A moisture-panel had been set in the wall of the rotunda to prevent the volumes inside from drying out, and a small wooden ladder balanced on some map books got him up to it. As he folded it back and wriggled through, he heard a bone button tear loose from his quilted brocade waistcoat and bounce upon the floor. Once, this would have been enough to spiral him into a state of sartorial panic. Now he merely shrugged and kept going.

The chamber within was perfectly circular, with tall curved bookcases set at intervals around the room. Cut into the edges of the cases were iron steps held aloft by scaled snakes finished in jade enamel. There were no markings on any of the shelves. Leperdandy looked back at the main door and wondered if Biblius sat studying on the other side.

He checked the books at the lowest level, but these were the least interesting or useful, being unreliable, unpronounceable and inde-cipherable histories of forgotten royals who had once ruled beyond the river towns.

The books became rarer and more disturbing the higher he rose. As he climbed, the snakes disappeared with a click and the steps retracted behind him, leaving him stranded. He discovered that each level housed a false wooden book which, when correctly manipulated, returned the steps to their positions. A smattering of sand on the floor suggested that the system worked by shifting weights.

At the top of one stack he found *The Auto-Culinaire: A History of Eating Humans* and *Power of the Flesh: Being a Historie of the Cannibal Tribe of the Rushing River Tamesis*. But the volume he needed most was to be found in the uppermost corner of the high-est stack: *A True Accounte of the Scarabold Familie Lineage* was written in quill and violet ink. The last of its pages were yet to be filled in.

He recognized the Squeam's handwriting as soon as he studied it. The tome began with a family tree similar to the one in the Tainted Hall, complicated by the profusion of issue that arose from each spouse having two partners.

He found the section he was looking for. Under a painting of a severe-looking woman was written:

> *Lady Castilia Urethnia,*
> *Betrothed to Perseo Lionhead Adolfus,*
> *Elder brother of Archim Scarabold III,*
> *Adolfus being deceased owing to a fall from his mount,*
> *Which had been affrighted by a bear in the fogge.*

So the King's brother died while his wife was fat with child, Lep-erdandy thought. The conclusion was clear. Any son of Perseo's was directly in line to the throne.

He read on.

'The line is contingent upon the health and wholesomeness of the incumbent. Two feet must rest beneath the throne, two limbs must lie along its arms, two eyes must gaze upon the multitude with fairness, and under the crown must fit a head of knowledge, wisdom and forbearance.'

Leperdandy closed the book. *Two feet*, he thought. *It doesn't say that they must be made of flesh and bone. We must find a way to restore Brasslight before the moon starts to wax.*

Another thought struck him with such force that he very nearly lost his footing. *Brasslight is the true heir presumptive but is not directly related to Giniva. He is at most a half-cousin, and even full cousins may marry. He is of roughly the same age, which means that they could be legally betrothed and restore the dynasty.*

He tried to imagine his sister as a marriageable commodity but failed. Lately she had become too independent of thought. Surely Brasslight could be tricked into loving her before he discovered her vexing demeanour?

Against this thought emerged a green-eyed notion. Namely: *The upstart will take her from me.* Of course, he wanted what was best for her, but not at the expense of his own happiness.

He was about to put the book back when he noticed a single loose sheet of vellum wedged within it. A handwritten codicil had been added to the last full page.

As he tried to hold the book with one hand, hanging on to the shelf with the other, the codicil slipped loose and fluttered past his knees.

He watched the sheet spiral past the remaining steps, and searched out the volume that would put the first step back in place, that he might descend. The page settled face down on the parquet floor beneath him.

As it did so, something slithered across the wooden blocks.

Perhaps one of the library radiators had a crack in it, for his ears picked up a distant sound like steam escaping, soft and sinuous.

Leperdandy negotiated his way down the hidden library staircase step by step, and stopped again to listen.

The sound of scales scraping wood was growing louder.

50

Preparations for the Feast

The final arrangements were in place. Dwinoline had plumped for lemon brocade but Spattersley was dickering with fuchsia silk. The over-butler had a way with colours but lemon seemed less depressing. 'A birthday banquet should reflect a year of happiness,' Dwinoline told him. 'Fuchsia is too ripe somehow. We don't want to give the wrong impression. There's something of the bawd about that shade.'

Spattersley had never visited a bawd in his life, and was mystified by the idea. 'I'm attaching the table ribbons to clove-covered pome-granates,' he said, without explaining that his reason for doing so was to reduce the meaty odour of the King. He might have been one of the few to notice the odd aroma that pervaded the castle. While the other guests at royal occasions were always served roasted hogs or sheep, the family's meals arrived in separate salvers from Goldhawk and smelled unwholesome to his delicate nostrils.

'I thought we could offer our guests fainting duck,' said Dwino-line. Spattersley was squeamish, and this was not his favourite dish to watch being prepared. On each table a large duck, plucked while still alive, was nailed by its left foot to a circular board, and hot coals banked around it so that the protesting fowl turned its least-singed side to the heat at all times. When it finally collapsed it was thus perfectly roasted, and was carved and served at once, its heart still beating.

'Perhaps some strawberry ice to follow,' he suggested.

There were so few cheerful events to cater for these days that the Princess's feast had quite put a spring in his step. Like most of the staff, he so rarely saw anyone from beyond the immediate field of his duties that visitors were a novelty. Their arrival processions were like visiting carnivals. 'I thought we would seat the Decrepend and Father Sesquinatius together at the far end,' he said tentatively.

'Good idea,' Dwinoline agreed. 'Better to keep them downwind of the F'Arcys. I'm not sure how many Sir Archie is bringing or what he may surprise us with, but after the Beetle Earl it is better to assume the worst.'

'Lord Carapace chose not to pursue his ambitions for the Princess, I understand?' probed Spattersley.

'No, he ate something that disagreed with him.' It made a change; too often around here people ate someone who disagreed with them. Dwinoline anxiously sought to change the subject. She clapped her hands. 'Now,' she said cheerfully, 'curtains.'

'I was thinking of green silk on the balustrades in the Hall of Arrows,' said Mater Moribund as Putney the butler poured fern tea into her cup. 'To go with your eyes.'

'My eyes are opal,' Giniva pointed out, waving Putney away. 'When will Father be back?'

'As soon as he has reached an amicable agreement with the good Sisters,' said Moribund. 'Try not to think about affairs of state. They will only give you crow's feet.'

They were seated inside the crystal solarium, which was used for needlework and reading because of its fresh evening light. Below them a suppurating fog hung like snot in the crenellations of the keep and the gnarled dead oaks that lined the upper parade grounds.

'I was more concerned with the contrast,' said the Mater, raising her sample book of fabrics once more. 'And yellow velvet banners embroidered with the escutcheon. They'll flutter prettily in the breeze and can be swagged around the table tureens.'

'Moths!' shrieked Aunt Asphyxia, who was fitfully dozing in a nearby armchair.

'So my royal birthday dinner is a state function,' Giniva complained.

'An opportunity to show your prowess in deportment and . . . cheerful conversation,' the Mater finished unconvincingly.

'And to whom shall I show off these debutante skills? The courtiers? A deputation of farmers? Some frightened servants? What is the point if you only invite guests who are strategically useful to you and Father? I have no friends of my own.'

'Selfish!' squawked Asphyxia. 'Make the foolish girl understand. It is to parade her virgin parts before possible suitors, for with each passing day her womb dries a little more and another alliance is lost.'

'We have matters of security to think of,' said the Mater, pulling free a sliver of material and holding it up to the autumn light. 'White broderie, I think. Suppose someone were to infiltrate the receiving line? Why would I risk my beloved daughter in her happiest hour?'

'It won't be my happiest hour,' Giniva muttered, refusing an offer of mustard biscuits. 'What is the use of dressing the courtiers one sees every day in silly hats and jerkins, and watching them caper about to lutes, pretending all is well?'

'All will be well when your father returns.' Mater Moribund gave a little nod, folded her hands and pressed her lips together tightly.

'So he will take money from a holy order to finance the blowing off of men's heads.'

'Why do you give her voice, Moribund?' yelped Asphyxia. 'Women have no opinions worth listening to. Nobody listens to me.'

Giniva stamped her slipper and rose. 'I warned you, I will not be sold off so that my father can gain a few battalions.' She longed to spit out Brasslight's name but knew that the time was not yet right.

Moribund shot her a look so venomous that it might have nailed her mouth shut. 'Your new suitor will be seated at the head table, where I can keep an eye on him, and the deal will be sealed over dinner,' she said. Discussion of the matter was over. 'Now be silent all while I choose the table materials.'

She pulled open her book of patterns. 'There's alpaca, astrakhan, batiste and brocade. Calico, cambric, cheviot and chenille . . .'

'Your hand moves like a bird in flight.' Goldhawk held up Watborn's finished menu. 'The penmanship is exquisitely illegible. You have interpreted my requirements to the letter.'

'There are spelling mistakes,' said Watborn.

'Nobody cares. Written words have not yet been finalized. I'll find out how many copies you need to make. The women don't get menus, of course.'

'They say the Princess will be wed before the dessert arrives,' Watborn ventured.

'Sir Archie F'Arcy is so high-born that nobody can understand a word he says,' Goldhawk confided. 'Our vintner once supplied his cellars, and told me that his lordship has so little experience of the real world that he fainted when a bottle was dropped. It seems a shame that the Princess must become his wife, but there it is. Royals never marry for love.'

Watborn had not realized there was so much to discover. He wondered how many other assassins and hidden enemies there were hiding in these walls. He had become adept at picking up passing conversations, overhearing arguments, witnessing friendships and fall-outs. His fellow cooks in the kitchen dormitory talked in their sleep. Everybody had an opinion.

One of the cooks had cropped Watborn's hair and shaved his beard short. Several of the female cooks took a renewed interest in him. For some reason that he could not fathom, he was popular.

He tried to repay Goldhawk's kindness by working hard and finding ways to improve the hygiene in the kitchen, for in truth it was not a clean place. He laid rat traps and encouraged the maids to clear their serving tables of insects and mouse droppings. The children who scrubbed the pots and pans needed to be taken better care of; he built them bunks and taught them to share instead of fight. He ran errands around the floors, but failed to catch any further glimpses of the Princess.

One section of the kitchens was closed to him: the private chamber where the royal family's food was prepared. Goldhawk had suggested it was not wise to know what went on there, and Watborn knew better than to risk his position by disobeying.

'. . . for you to be there,' said Goldhawk, finishing some conversation he had missed.

'I'm sorry, sir?'

'Pay attention, man. The dinner for Sir Archie. I have to be down here timing the staff. We need someone presentable to attend to the tables. The servants are only good for protocol and cutlery. A cook must be present to answer questions. You have clean fingernails. Do you think you're up to it?'

'I am happy to serve,' said Watborn.

51

The Confrontation in the Library

Leperdandy was still trapped in the library. He tentatively lowered a leg again.

The bookcase ladder appeared to have a mind of its own, and kept retracting its steps. He was still ten feet above the floor when he heard the sound of steam escaping once more, and knew that Orobus had circled around to guard the rotunda.

The diamond head of the great reticulated snake, a form of adder that had become all but extinct owing to its ungainly size, slithered into view.

Its black tongue flickered, tasting the air. When it scented lavender it opened its jaws in anticipation of a meal. It had four rows of backward-curving teeth and appeared to be smiling. It was in the last generation of the great serpents, and its body was wracked with the pain of age. It was almost fifteen feet long and covered in shreds of moulting skin. In centuries to come it would shrink to a mere three feet.

'Nice snake, good snake,' soothed Leperdandy, trying not to tremble. He wasn't sure how much longer he could hold on to the shelves, and the step beneath his right foot was sliding back into place.

The serpent's body grew as it continued to appear from between the stacks. The coils that started forming at one end rose and repeated until they lay over the codicil in concentric loops. It seemed to him that Orobus would never allow a document to leave the library.

Another bookcase step began its silent retraction. Did adders eat their prey or merely bite them to death? If he could find the strength to hang here from the wooden shelves a while longer, perhaps the creature would grow bored and sleepy, and slide away to the warmth of the stone boilers.

Orobus's body had stopped moving. Its mouth was slowly opening beneath him, ready to receive a dropped treat like a ripened apricot falling from a tree. Its eyes never moved from him. It seemed especially attracted to his bony bare ankles.

Just as Leperdandy had convinced himself that he could continue to dangle from the bookcase by his toes and the tips of his fingers, something brown and tiny ran along the shelf above him and hopped beneath his left cuff. He knew he should never have worn trumpet sleeves. Their fashion was long past.

The mouse wriggled deeper, tickling with tiny claws. He began to sweat. He had always been ticklish. As the sensation became excruciating, he was forced to cast his left arm out and shake it violently, swinging by his right hand as both feet slipped from the vanishing steps.

The mouse shot out of his sleeve and executed a graceful somersault, straight into Orobus's gaping mouth. Its jaws snapped shut like the slamming of a Bible.

Leperdandy dropped into the coils and grabbed the codicil just as the serpent's body began to constrict. Clambering over it, he ran for the library door. The diamond head whipped around and fixed him with one golden eye.

Unnerved, he stumbled to his knees. The snake's tail lashed about. The princeling tipped over, tumbling across the parquet. His head singing, he balled the codicil into his jerkin and clambered upright. But as he tried to move away, the adder slithered towards him, smoothly raising its head.

Leperdandy wondered if he should feint left and dart right, but doubted he had the guile even to fool a snake. When he attempted to vault a case of choirbooks in a single smooth leap, he missed, taking most of the books with him and landing painfully on his bony knees.

Smoothing back his hair, he stuck up his head. Orobus was still watching him, its head and eyes quite motionless, its body seething.

They stayed like that for what felt like an hour.

With his legs cramping, Leperdandy rose to his feet and turned slowly towards the door, ready to run, but his way was barred by the serpent's diamond head, which had somehow moved without moving. The golden discs observed him dispassionately. The mouth opened a crack and the forked tongue flickered out to taste him.

One of us has to act, he thought. *What is this, a staring contest?*

Using the freestanding bookcases as stepping stones, he tried to rise above the serpent, but the head continued to follow him like a shadow. He was about to jump to the next shelf when he realized that the gap was too wide.

One foot betrayed his command, moving ahead and planting itself on the top of a shelf before he could stop it so that now he was straddled, wobbling, between two unstable bookcases.

'You wouldn't want to eat me, Orobus. I am an acquired taste,' he blustered as the pink maw opened slowly, wider and wider, revealing internal fleshy layers of gynaecological complexity as it manoeuvred itself beneath Leperdandy's legs. And there it remained, motionless beneath him, patiently awaiting the drop of its prey.

Orobus was in no hurry. Its muscles were tightly locked in position. It could stay like this for weeks. It was growing sluggish and lazy, factors that would eventually lead to its becoming extinct.

Without thinking, Leperdandy picked up the nearest book he could reach and dropped it into the creature's mouth. Orobus released a mighty hiss of rushing air, but seemed unconcerned about ridding itself of the hymnal.

He searched around for more, his terrified eyes alighting on a mammoth Bible beside his right foot. He had once seen it used by the visiting Priests of Hibernia in their reversion service at the chapel. It had taken forty years for all the chapels to be deconsecrated, and theirs had been the last. The clergymen had left behind the leather-clad tome as a parting gift for Scarabold, hoping that he would one day give up his ways and return to the fold. The thing weighed as much as a child thanks to its extra unauthorized testaments, but fear gave Leperdandy strength as he reached down (feeling his gracilis muscles sear in the process) and pulled it over the serpent's mouth.

Then he let it go.

Seven thousand illuminated onion-skin pages of religious instruction dropped down into its open throat, blocking its air passage. The jaw clamped shut with a bang.

As Leperdandy ran for the rotunda doors, the serpent contracted its muscles and coughed. It was an eerily human sound.

Orobus had once eaten an entire donkey without gagging, even though it had taken it a day to get it fully into its mouth and it should probably have started at the other end, but the Bible was dust-dry and dense and could not be consumed like moist meat. As it snorted and choked, a few shredded pieces of Old Testament blew from the sides of its jaws.

Orobus sneezed violently. Several saints were blasted from its nostrils. The great golden eyes began to water. It spat miracles and portents. It dry-hawked plagues, parables and prophecies. Pages of psalms approving the abuse of women and the dashing of infants against rocks stuck themselves over its tongue.

The Holy Scripture proved quite impossible to digest. To their acolytes, the integrity of such sacred texts was indisputable, but even non-believers could see that they had the power to choke a snake.

Leperdandy closed the door behind him and fled.

52

The Decision of the Sisters

King Scarabold was not used to being kept waiting.

The black-robed Sisters of Cadeaux Étranges were considering his request. They had ensconced themselves in one of the prayer-chambers to try to reach a decision about the war loan. They moved about the chamber like birds in flight, their white headdresses resembling the wings of albatrosses, bobbing up and down as they scurried past.

The Sisters were in turmoil. As a peaceful order, it was against their principles to comply with the King's demands, but they could not risk being stormed by the army of the Marshlands. They needed to maintain their neutrality, just as they needed to protect the sacred Vessel of All Counted Sorrows, and the thought of being overrun by the Beetle Earl's vengeful family filled them with terror.

Lady Lavinia Travernum acted as their representative. She had been granted the honorary title of Reverend Mother, so that although she wore the surplice and wimple of the order, she stood apart from it. This allowed her to bring a certain amount of business acumen to the convent, whose residents were not known for their ability to follow logical lines of reasoning, although they were adept at baking exceptionally dry biscuits.

She sat before the disgruntled King with her hands folded in the lap of her gown of midnight-blue dimity. 'It is beyond my own power to grant your request. I merely act as a go-between, for you must know that the Sisters have taken a vow of silence, and have no dealings with outsiders. We have no affinity with the Sheath-wing, but to foment a war sits uneasily with us.'

'My visit here is not with the intention of initiating war, Lady

Lavinia,' Scarabold assured her. 'I wish only to defend and hold what belongs to our kingdom.'

'Be that as it may, all seven members of our senior council need to reach unanimous agreement.'

'I also wish to safekeep the Sisters from harm,' Scarabold added. 'I know how important are your mystic rituals, and I offer you protection. Should the Beetle Earl's troops rise up from the Marshlands, there could be terrible consequences for your young virgins.'

'Quite,' said Lady Lavinia, who did not feel the need for their plight to be spelled out. The Great Wound's bluntness was legendary, but he was drawn from different stock. The warrior-kings came from a realm toned in more violent hues.

The pair were still sitting beside each other as the sun began to set behind the great stained-glass windows depicting the hideous martyrdom of St Gregorious, who had suffered an insertion of serpents for impiousness.

The prayer-chamber was bathed in deepening ruby light. Scarabold was starving and bored, and had a flat arse. The chamber reeked of rancid tallow and ambergris incense. In seven hours he had been offered a handful of dry, sour biscuits and a lukewarm carafe of elderflower tea. Anyone else would have felt the rough side of his tongue by now, but he was powerless. Without consent, he could not return with the means to fund his forces.

Finally the doors to the chamber opened and the seven sisters tripped in, standing in a line before him. They ranged in age from twenty to ninety, each representing a division of the sisterhood under their care.

Lady Lavinia rose and stood before them. 'Sisters of Cadeaux Étranges, have you reached a decision?'

An almost imperceptible nod trembled along the line. Scarabold was thankful that this part of the decision-making process seemed to be free of lengthy rituals. He craned forward in anticipation of the verdict.

'Then please will you inform our esteemed King of your opinion.'

One by one, the sisters each withdrew a small wooden paddle, one side of which was painted black, the other white, and raised it. Few things in this world unnerved him, so perhaps the wait had made him uncomfortable. He was, after all, a man of action. Subtlety confused him.

One by one, the sisters turned over their paddles. White, white, white, white, white, white . . .

Of course, he should have known that they would never vote in favour of killing an enemy, even if it meant consigning members of their own order to a fate worse than death.

The final sister, the youngest, turned over her paddle.

Black.

'Thank you, sisters. Your decision has been heeded.' Lady Lavinia turned to address the Great Wound. 'The vote was close, Your Highness. Six approvals—'

'I thought black was an approval,' said the King, shocked.

'Black is the colour of darkness and denial. White has the purity of accord. As you can see, only Sister Vitalia voted against you and the vote must be unanimous. I am sorry, but there is nothing more I can do. Although she is the youngest member of the senior council, Sister Vitalia is in many ways the most considerate and kindly of our order, and we must abide by her decision.'

'Wait,' said the King, rising stiffly. 'Could I at least have a word with the sister in private?'

'I'm afraid that is not possible,' said their representative. 'The sisters have discussed your proposal and have arrived at their conclusions.'

'But if I could just speak to the sister alone for a few moments, I feel sure I could explain the situation more clearly.'

'I'm afraid it would be impracticable to allow any members of the sisterhood to be left with an outsider, even Your Majesty,' Lady Lavinia replied. 'If only there was some other way that we could help. Perhaps some more elderflower tea and biscuits before you go—'

'So be it.' Scarabold slapped his hands on his thighs, punching life back into them. Leaving empty-handed would doom him to insurrection and defeat. A thought occurred to him.

'Perhaps at least the good sister would consent to showing me the Vessel of All Counted Sorrows? It would be a shame if after my visit I had not seen its glory for myself.'

Behind her, Sister Vitalia smiled and raised her paddle high in an indication of granted permission. To have royal interest shown in the relic was a powerful sign of approval, and most beneficial. Lady Lavinia went to her side and some kind of communication passed between them, although Scarabold could not see how such a thing was possible when the Sisters were mute.

Lady Lavinia returned. 'I would think myself remiss if you were denied the opportunity of seeing our greatest and most sacred treasure. After all, it was in your possession once, although that was many years ago. Sister Vitalia will escort you and remind you of its importance, for she is particularly well versed in the art of mime.'

The Great Wound followed the little sister from the chamber and down through a low tunnel that opened into a granite colonnade. Sister Vitalia beckoned him on, for although she was small of bone she took many tiny mincing steps and kept moving ahead of him, her white bonnet flapping.

As they walked, Scarabold attempted conversation. 'You know, the future safety of our kingdom may be at stake,' he said. 'Thousands may die. I suppose there is no way of making you change your mind?

The sister looked back and humbly shook her head before continuing onwards. Finally, after the opening of many oaken doors, they reached a five-sided stone altar that could have passed for a baptismal font. It was set beside the green lily-covered waters of the Lake of Contemplation.

At the centre of the altar, in a shaft of dappled light refracted from the lake, sat a small, plain, stemmed bowl of ochre-coloured metal.

'Is that it?' said Scarabold, shocked. 'It would fit into a teacup!'

Sister Vitalia held out her hands to make the shape of the vessel, then stretched them wide to encompass the world.

'You mean this small object has great influence because of what it represents,' he said.

The sister smiled benignly and nodded, pleased that he had understood.

'In that case . . .' Scarabold reached forward and grasped it in his meaty fist. The sister's hands flew to her mouth but no sound came out. 'I'm sorry,' he said, 'but one vote against me cannot be allowed to stand. This is for the greater good.'

He tucked the vessel inside his leather jerkin and reached out for Sister Vitalia's slender neck, snapping it as easily as one would a wheat straw. Then he picked her up and tossed her into the Lake of Contemplation.

She barely made a splash. He waited until the ripples had vanished and nothing could be seen of the sister, then returned to the prayer-chamber.

'Thank you for seeing me, Lady Lavinia,' he said to the surprised go-between. 'Sister Vitalia was most instructive and helped me to understand much about your order. Indeed, she may even have saved the day.'

'Well, I'm glad we could be of—' Lady Lavinia began, but Scarabold was off out through the convent doors and looking for his horse before she could finish returning the compliment.

The King meant what he had said. Sister Vitalia had taught him that a single obstruction could not be allowed to stand in the way of a far more urgent need.

With the Vessel of All Counted Sorrows in his possession, he now had an asset that would allow the Royal Counting Chamber to print all the money it needed to finance his defences. With the coffers full again he would even offer to return the relic, and perhaps throw in a few of St Arbuthnot's sacred fingers. The Bishop of Wexerley was bound to remember what they had done with them.

53

The Proof of Birthright

'How was your quest, my lord?' asked Grand-Marshal Timmorian, the head of the army, when the Great Wound returned. Timmorian noted that his mount was steaming and the King himself was covered in mud, as if he had been riding hard without a stop.

'A job well done,' Scarabold replied. 'There had better be some scoff about; I'm bloody starving. Here – a gift from the nuns. Eat 'em with a glass of water handy.'

He handed Timmorian a bag of convent biscuits, patted his jerkin and headed off to see Thredneedle with the good news.

Leperdandy skidded to a halt in the corridor.

Ahead were Spackle and Peut, walking side by side. They stopped to check each other's hair for lice, then continued. As they talked they examined everything around them, as if recording notes for their mother.

The princeling forced himself to stroll casually past them and even attempted to whistle a nonchalant tune before hurtling once more towards Giniva's dream-suite.

'Gin, I think I have something that will help us to restore Brasslight to his rightful place,' he began.

The bedchamber was empty. He pulled the codicil from his pocket and tried to decipher it, but the page consisted of brightly coloured pictograms that made no sense to him. The Princess would know what to do. Her knowledge of languages, codes and hiero-glyphs was unsurpassed.

But where was she?

*

Vitrolio was the head of the armoury. Glistening and furnace-burnished, as high as he was broad, his arms as thick and sinewy as tree roots, he could heat and forge any steel into a breastplate or broadsword.

He had long been an ally of the Princess. He had hoped that one day she would prove to be the only girl at court who could wield a weapon with the dexterity of a knight, while all the other ladies occupied themselves with gossip and synchronized embroidery. Unfortunately, Giniva had no accuracy in her swing and had nearly taken off the top of his head like a boiled egg, but she made up for much with a natural cunning. He felt sure she had a warrior heart even if she did not quite know it. Although, of course, she might just have been attracted to the outfits.

In the casting vault, the ringing of mallets on metal hurt the ears. White iron poured from the cauldrons into stone channels that crossed the floor, rapidly cooling to crimson and orange, and down to crusted grey. There was a cuprous tang in the air that curdled spit in the mouth.

Vitrolio had worked all night under the instruction of his Princess, and had taken pleasure in doing so. He unwrapped the chamois package with unusual delicacy. 'I made this myself under your brother's express instructions, my lady, for it is better that no one else knows of your discovery.'

Inside the soft cloth was a silver-coloured right foot with jointed toes and a delicate arched heel. 'It is made of tin, lined inside with buckskin and adjusted with these buckles,' he explained. 'Once you have ensured that it fits without chafing, please bring it back and I will cover the metal with a fine alabaster calf-leather. Then we sew it into place.'

'Do you think it can be made real enough to pass a test?'

'I pride myself on reproducing nature exactly. My wife is preparing oyster shells to make the toenails from slivers of mother-of-pearl. When do you require it to be finished?'

'By the day after tomorrow,' said Giniva. 'I have no time to return before then. I must endure my grand banquet, and an encounter with another unsuitable suitor.'

'Your mother's doing, I imagine,' said Vitrolio. He had fallen foul of the Mater Moribund in days long past and still bore the whip-mark across his back.

'She would have me marry a syphilitic centenarian if he could still provide a weakling heir with half a brain and at least one of his eyes facing the right way.'

'I am sorry for your pain, my Princess,' he said, lowering his voice, 'but perhaps the owner of this slipper may provide a prince to save the kingdom.'

Giniva returned to the Museum of the Dead and unbolted the door leading to the storage quarters.

Brasslight was recovering on the bed of furs she had made for him. He was lying beneath the latticed window, breathing lightly. In the faint glow of watery autumn sunlight, his freshly washed hair shone and his eyelids appeared to be dusted with gold.

She set down his meal-basket and woke him gently. He looked about himself for a moment, then remembered.

He raised himself on one elbow. 'Why is it not possible to see the Marshlands from here?'

'The mists from the swamp are born aloft by gas and heat,' said Giniva. 'Magister Ambrosius explained it to me. He taught us everything we know. We can never see further than a few furlongs. The poorest live to the east, where the foul odours are strong-est. How I long for clear warm skies! I have a surprise for you. Put out your leg.'

Taking the foot from her pocket, she unwrapped it and knelt before him, tenderly cleansing his scarred stump. 'With this you will be able to pass for perfect. The finishing touches will be added after your final fitting.'

Brasslight pulled the straps tight and twisted the metal foot this way and that, his eyes filling with tears. 'It is a flawless fit. To think that you would risk so much—'

She stopped his gratitude. 'Please, do not speak of what we may do for you, but of what you may do for us. Now, how do you regard yourself?'

Brasslight thought for a moment. 'I think I am a fair and honest fellow,' he replied. 'I was raised in kindness and only known as Tinfoot so that none would know my true identity.'

'That could be a problem,' Giniva said. 'If you are not recog-nized, you could be denied your birthright by plotters who seek to keep the reins of power tight.'

A cloud crossed Brasslight's gilded brow. 'Are you sure my claim cannot be proved by Dr Fangle and Nurse Mentle?'

'They cannot help us now.'

'There must be some other way. I was told that during my mother's term she was examined by birthing wives.'

Giniva adjusted the foot's straps. 'If they speak of their charges, they have their tongues removed. Too many infants are born out of wedlock to our high ladies. Vows of secrecy must be maintained.'

'I still have the name the Sisters stitched for me.' Brasslight raised the embroidered bracelet attached to his left wrist. 'Is this not proof enough? Perhaps if I go back and speak to them—'

'Anyone can stitch a bracelet, and they will not lose their positions over you no matter how much they care for you,' Giniva warned. 'We need the testament of someone whose opinion will bear weight with my father.' She worried a nail between perfect teeth. 'Sadly, I am no diplomat. If there is an argument with the Great Wound, I'm sure to lose my temper and say something dreadful. It would be the end of our scheme.'

'But you have a secret weapon.' Brasslight brushed her bare arm with the back of his hand. 'Your brother is stronger than he thinks. Perhaps he can come up with a way to unpick this knot.'

'We don't have much time,' Giniva warned. 'I am to be formally introduced to Sir Archie at my banquet tomorrow night, and if he consents to be my spouse, we will have no time to put you on the throne. Scarabold must fully support your claim.' Reaching down, she unbuckled his foot and placed it in her bag once more. 'Your right foot will soon appear as smooth as your left and none will discover the truth before you are placed where you belong.'

'It is a deception.'

'An expedience.' Giniva was firmly set upon the point. 'If our subterfuge comes to light, we'll find a way to have the archaic law overturned.'

'Only if I can find a way of validating my birthright,' said Brasslight disconsolately. 'Without the proof to convince your father, there can be no coronation.'

When she watched him deftly moving on a single foot, she felt something shift in her breast. The heart was where all feeling resided; it was pear-shaped and hot and had eyes with which to see the future.

And it was trying to tell her something about Brasslight.

*

In the Convent of Cadeaux Étranges, a slender white nose broke the surface of the water in the Lake of Contemplation, and an iridescent green dragonfly alighted upon it. Lady Lavinia Travernum watched the insect meditatively, then screamed as she realized what it was sitting upon.

The dragonfly failed to notice the pale broken body in the green water, and flexed its sparkling emerald wings towards the sunlight.

PART THREE:
War

54

Treasonous Acts

Lady Lavinia Travernum paced about the vestibule, passing and repassing the bare pedestal where the Vessel of All Counted Sorrows had sat untouched for centuries.

'To think that this should happen in such a holy place,' she said again. 'Poor Sister Vitalia, hurled into the duckweed – and for what?'

'To stay within the letter of the law,' said Thorax Sheathwing, the younger, more deathly brother of the Beetle Earl.

Like his sibling, he was clad in an exoskeleton of black leather that accentuated his similarity to an insect, clicking and tapping as he walked back and forth. 'Six votes were cast in favour of the King and one against, and now the vote is unanimous and legally in his favour.'

'How can we control a kingdom when we cannot even keep our House together?' Lady Lavinia demanded. 'Scarabold broke the neck of a holy sister and stole the treasure our order had sworn to guard.'

'Well, you didn't do a very good job of it, did you?' Thorax replied.

Lady Lavinia glared at him. 'He is the King. We didn't think we'd need added security.'

'Then I take it I have your permission to go forward with my plan?' asked Thorax.

'I cannot condone the use of violence.' Lady Lavinia firmly flattened her hand in the air before him. 'But if in the course of this coming battle you happen to mislay Scarabold's head, I'm sure the Sisters will support you. I'll instruct the seven – or rather, the six – to open their coffers to you. And if, after you have disjointed the

Great Wound, you could return the Vessel of All Counted Sorrows, we will be most anxious to show our appreciation.'

'Then we have a deal,' said Thorax, clicking his heels together. 'There will be others joining us in this covenant. The time has come to rid the land of its tyrant.'

Yeoman Manticore might have been his brother's twin, except that in place of a white apron he wore a doublet of pigeon-grey leather and had the look of a man who had been gritting his teeth for most of his life.

'How does the old bastard fare?' he asked. 'I hope you don't presume upon his good nature. Goldhawk is too easily taken advantage of. We are military men up here, and far less forgiving. He says you have a good bow arm, but he is a chef, not a soldier. Show me.'

They were standing in a long brick hall lined with archery equipment, but much of it was old and broken. Manticore limped over to a rack of immense bows and took one down. 'Have you ever seen one of these before?'

'No, sir,' said Watborn.

'The longbow must be of sufficient length to draw the string to the face or body, hence the length of the bow varies with the user. It must be made from the yew tree and is usually six feet high. It will draw a weight of one hundred pounds. You'll do no harm with this one.' He handed over the longbow, which was far past its best days.

Watborn positioned himself behind the bow and awaited instruction.

'You do not draw the string with the strength of your arms, but by laying your body into the bow. By which I mean you do not keep your left hand still and draw with the right, but keep your right at rest upon the nerve, pressing the whole weight of your body into the horns of the bow.'

Watborn followed his instruction and was surprised to find that the string could be pulled back to the tip of his nose.

'Well, well,' muttered Manticore. 'I have not seen that since . . .' He let the sentence trail off. Watborn released the arrowless string and stood down. 'And you have not had previous instruction?'

'No, sir.'

'Let's try it loaded and see what your aim is like.'

The arrow shaft was longer than any he had released before, but its weight and length felt proportionate to the bowstring, and it found its mark in a distant straw-horse.

Manticore studied the target and sucked his teeth. 'I think we have use for you. Now the nearer mark.' He indicated a bull's eye and handed Watborn a short bow. 'Don't over-power it or you will lose accuracy.'

Watborn followed Manticore's instruction and reduced his pull. Even so, the arrow carried too much charge and buried itself deep in the centre of the target.

'And you're self-taught?'

He nodded.

'Hm. You don't say much, do you?'

Watborn waited patiently.

'No man shoots well unless he is brought up to it. A fellow with your reach and strength is a rare thing. My men lack practical experience, but I must make the best of it. We do not have time to choose our champions.' He scratched at his cheek, thinking. 'Could you get the others to do this?'

'I can show them how to use their arms and their heads.'

'Why would they need to use their heads?'

'Target practice is not hunting. They must think quickly but calmly.'

'I doubt you can teach them that. Tell me, would my brother be vexed if I removed you from his command in the kitchens?'

'It was his intention in sending me here.'

'So you could start at once?'

'I have one obligation: to serve at the banquet tomorrow night.' Since the assassin's attack, Watborn thought of himself less as a waiter, more as a guard to the Princess.

'Very well,' said Manticore. 'Vitrolio, the head of the armoury, will accept my recommendation. You should begin training as soon as possible, for a battle is coming that may see the end of us all.'

'Gin, I know you have to be refurbished, but this is terribly important,' said Leperdandy, prancing back and forth as Plum and Split sewed the Princess into her yellow brocade rehearsal dress.

'Oh, do try to keep still,' said Giniva, 'you're making me giddy. Why on earth do women wear these things so tight?'

'A smallness of the waist is desirable in courtship, my lady,' Plum said through a mouthful of pins.

'I would have thought a display of broad hips would be more important as proof of birthing capabilities.' She waved the dressers away. 'Plum, Split, leave us be for a minute. Dando, whatever is the matter with you?'

'I need you to decipher something,' he explained, pulling the page from his doublet. 'I had to fight Orobus to get it, so it's important.'

'I don't know what you're talking about. Show me.' Giniva laid the sheet on her vanity stand and pressed it flat. 'This is in the Old Language.'

'Can you decipher it?'

'I have some understanding. After that, the characters are just mirrorgrams – it's not terribly hard,' she said. 'Pass me that hand glass.'

She tipped the oval surface against the letters and read it back, blanching. 'A codicil.'

'So I believe.'

'It is an instruction upon the King's death.'

'Read it aloud.'

'"In the event of there being no living male heir, the throne may default to the most recent living Queen."' She thought for a moment. 'Do you know what you've found? This is the Fourth Exception.'

'But what it suggests has never happened.'

'That doesn't mean it can't.'

'If Mater Moribund stands to take the throne, then surely it's in her interest to ensure—'

'—that a male heir cannot place the crown upon his head.' Giniva completed the thought.

Leperdandy worried at a cuticle. 'What did Brasslight say about his incarceration?'

'He says he left the Sisters even though they warned him not to go. That when he arrived here and tried to petition the King, he was promptly thrown in jail.'

'It was rather naive of him.'

'He was presumably versed in strategy, having been raised by nuns.'

'Then we must find out upon whose orders Fumblegut acted. I can't imagine he had the brains to do it himself. It must have been the King. Who else knew him as Tinfoot? Wasn't it the last thing Carapace uttered before he exploded?'

'There is so much we cannot know,' said Giniva vaguely, pulling a loose thread at her bust and then wishing she hadn't. 'I doubt our father was even aware of his sister-in-law's child. He relies on the women to tell him these things.' A terrible thought struck her. 'Suppose Moribund knows about the codicil? As the Queen-in-Waiting, only the King still stands in her way.'

Leperdandy's horrified eyebrows rose even higher than where they usually stood. 'You can't mean she intends to kill our father?'

Giniva pulled at her neckline impatiently. 'Even she could not do that. There are too many eyes upon her. But something strange is in the wind. We shall have to be very careful. We need a spy of our own. You and I can't be everywhere. Who could we recruit?'

'What about Ratchet?' Leperdandy suggested.

'The Great Wound's valet? He'd never help us. Even though he is treated like a dog, it is all too clear where his loyalties lie. What about Trotter? I know he's only a knocker-wiper but he hears everything that's going on, and he's a little in love with me.'

Leperdandy clapped. 'That's a brilliant idea.'

'Trotter will be our eyes and ears. I'll put him to work at once.'

To the horror of Plum and Split, Giniva tore apart the stitches of her dress and stepped from it. 'Boils and buboes! Will someone get me out of this ribboned corset and find me some plain hose?'

Leperdandy stared at his sister and began to wonder whether she had been replaced by a changeling. 'I have never seen you like this before.'

She touched his chin tenderly. 'It has been a season of revelations, and I suspect they've only just begun.'

'But we are burrowing from within,' Leperdandy cautioned. 'Our actions could bring charges of treason down upon us both.'

'This nation was builded upon treasonous acts,' she answered. 'Soon its people may decide more than its kings.'

55

Priceless

The Great Wound removed his glass eye, breathed on it and scuffed it on his sleeve. The puckered crimson cavity it left behind was disconcerting. 'Come on, then, what's it worth?' he demanded to know.

Craftsley Thredneedle looked over at the usurer. Peter Maggot was hard-set and narrow, with a mouth like the end of a whistle. He was a necessary evil in a kingdom that was regularly required to fence its treasures in order to raise money for arms. The Tainted Hall had already been stripped of its most valuable statues and paintings, leaving behind only the disreputable daubs, like *Hag-Witch Pissing Away a Plague of Rats*, which no one wanted upon their wall.

Maggot examined the little ochre cup and picked at a sealed panel on its stem. He was only just prevented from opening it.

'It represents the Spirit of the Archangel,' Scarabold warned. 'The Religiouses had another name for it; I forget what. We have a relic from the Archangel's body knocking about in one of the chapels.'

'Which part?' asked Maggot.

'A bit of his stomach lining, I think.' He licked his eye and reinserted it. 'The Vessel is far more sacred. There are legends builded around it. For example, it's said to contain the Papyrus of the End of Days.'

'It must be a very small document.'

Scarabold waved the thought away. 'It's purely symbolic. The compartment must never be opened.'

'How am I to assess its worth if I cannot examine its contents?' Maggot pleaded. 'The container itself is of no intrinsic value, therefore I must see what is inside.'

'The papyrus is untranslatable and the spirit is invisible to mortals, you baboon-faced extortionist,' he snapped, rolling his eye so that the pupil faced forward. 'You have to take these things on faith. One doesn't judge a painting by the cost of the pigments, or a piece of music by how many notes it has. The Vessel is a symbol of great power.'

'But the contents are not quantifiable in monetary terms,' Maggot countered.

'By the hell-hound of Gash, if you don't place an enormous value on this relic in the next five minutes, I'll charge you with obstructing the King and have you thrown into the Well of Walled-Up Children.'

Maggot's mullet-grey face was sheened in sweat. He needed to find a privy in order to inject his usual solution of poppy-oil mixed with fluids drained from otter spleen; it was all that kept him from collapsing. 'I shall need provenance on the, er, spirit-pot, in order to prove that it was obtained through legal means.'

'Of course it wasn't, you drug-addled tossbag. It was taken by force. Where do you think the spoils of war usually come from? The man's an imbecile, Thredneedle – do we really have to go through with this charade?'

'I think what Master Maggot is trying to say,' said Thredneedle, hoping to pour oil on troubled waters, 'is that although the Vessel of All Counted Sorrows is priceless, it is also valueless. If a price cannot be fixed, it is of no worth to anyone except those who value its intrinsic nature.'

Scarabold rolled his good eye. 'I can't just give it back now, seeing as the person I took it from is dead, can I?'

'I cannot hear this,' Thredneedle warned, covering his ears.

'Hell's teeth, if you won't give me money I'll have to kill someone else,' said the Great Wound. 'Maggot, have you got anything valuable?'

'No, Your Supremity,' gasped the usurer.

'Oh, get out of my sight, the pair of you.' Scarabold scornfully waved them away. *Our fate now hangs entirely on Sir Archie F'Arcy agreeing to marry my daughter,* he thought, *and then we can get a little peace and quiet around here, which the ladies always like.*

From somewhere in the darkened corridors came a terrified scream. The bear on the roof had finally broken free of its tether and had eaten the first person to come within its range.

56

Thrust

Trotter the knocker-wiper balanced on the footstool, which in turn stood on three stacks of books and an upturned vinegar jug.

He had never been entrusted with a secret mission before, and was extremely nervous. Ensconced inside a herb cupboard, peeping through a gap in the curtainage, he watched as Mater Moribund swept about the cobwebbed dispensary. He wondered if he should take notes, or whether he could remember everything accurately enough for the Princess.

'You were charged with taking care of the Lady Castilia,' Moribund cried. 'You had enough adder juice in your bag to wipe out every cow in the land. You were meant to pour boiling lead in her ear when you had finished, to hide the stain and seal it.'

'I did not have time, my lady.'

'Give me that.' She snapped the leather rum-bottle from Dr Fangle's lips and threw it across the room.

'But it had the desired effect,' slurred Fangle, staring sadly after his literally dashed spirits. 'Her death in the birthing tower was not without pain. Mercifully, her features were already contorted from the effort of expelling the cripple.'

'Nobody saw her face, you old fool. I should never have entrusted the work to a dingle-wiping drunk.'

'She was bundled away by skivvies and fed to the moat pike that same night,' Dr Fangle reminded her. 'The lads charged with this task naturally followed her into the water.'

'There was no chance of them getting out?'

'Not with rocks tied around their ankles, ma'am.'

'Then why am I hearing from the half-wit Fumblegut that a man called Tinfoot lives and, more than that, has escaped from his dungeon?' When she drew herself up, trembling with threat, her eyes reddened and her long teeth bared, she caused scrotums to tighten and crows to fall from the skies.

'The infant was not placed in my care,' pleaded Fangle, almost in tears. 'Minerva Mentle took him away to be disposed of, as we agreed.'

'Well, she obviously didn't, did she? It's no use talking to her.' Mater Moribund looked around for something to break. 'One might as well attempt a conversation with a cat.'

Trotter shifted uncomfortably behind the bunches of bladderwort. This was not mere gossip but the kind of treasonous talk that could have everyone within its radius murdered. He wished that the Princess had never come to him. The stool rocked and he only just managed to right it in time, but not before its legs clonked on the floor. He issued a silent prayer.

'Of course, poor Nurse Mentle has lost her wits, so we must be gentle with her,' said Moribund, suddenly placatory. 'Yes, we must chat with her and draw out the truth. I do hope she found a way to protect the poor mite from harm.'

Dr Fangle was puzzled. The Mater was moving back one step at a time as she spoke. 'I think if we have the patience to but listen, we'll understand the thrust of her argument.'

On 'thrust', the Queen swung her arm into the curtained opening behind her. There was a crash and a yell as she snatched back the arras to reveal the fallen Trotter with a brooch pin pushed through his right cheek.

Mater Moribund reached down her long claws and pulled the bejewelled trinket free. Trotter yelled, his face gushing scarlet between his fingers. 'Amethysts are not your colour, boy,' she warned, kicking the mewling lad towards the door.

Trotter would have to be watched carefully from now on. Moribund had no doubt that her husband had asked him to spy on her. Her permanent state of uxorial indignation meant that this was the sort of assumption to which she always leaped.

In thinking she knew everything, Moribund made mistakes that were about to settle the dark wings of death across the land. There are none so blind as those who lead.

57

The Suitor's Banquet

Watborn's tunic itched. He tried to slide a finger under its harshly starched neck, but popped a button off. It skittered across the tiled floor, beyond reach.

He snapped back to attention beside the opened doors. Goldhawk had been rather vague about his duties. With no instruction forthcoming, he positioned himself within reach of the Princess, the better to protect her.

The Tainted Hall gleamed and shone and sparkled. There were no pigs indoors, no jakes in the corners. There were goblets made of thick green glass, and cutlery enough to start a war over. At first glance it was laid out in fine array. On closer examination, however, peculiarities were revealed.

Every other painting was missing, represented only by dust-free space. On the table, the croquembouche of glazed figs was revealed to be a mountain of glazed frogs, for Goldhawk had misunderstood his instructions. Dwinoline wondered what this boded for the semolina.

Priding himself on thriftiness, Goldhawk had also dyed a chestnut pudding with cochineal made from the crushed remains of Carapace's beetles, not thinking for a moment that they might be poisonous.

The band wasn't just out of tune. It was playing two distinctly separate pieces of entrance music. One side performed Stanislav's 'Wedding Dirge' on tambour, psaltery, flageolet, sackbut and flugelhorn, and the other side played the Sunandanese 'Funeral Of A Warrior' on lyre, glockenspiel, bladder-pipe and mouth organ, with the occasional thump on a gong.

'Tell them to play a gavotte or something before I go up there and beat them to death,' Scarabold instructed the Squeam, pointing to the minstrels' gallery.

The chimney in the vast fireplace that dominated one end of the hall had needed cleaning for the last seventeen years, ever since a pair of young sweeps had vanished into the flue never to return, and emitted downfalls of soot that periodically clouded the room. A servant attacked it with a poker and a tiny shoe dropped into the grate.

Extra guests meant extra tables, so the over-butler's wife had brought trestles in from a barn and covered them, not realizing they were filled with bore weevils, which tended to vanish inside the guests' clothes as the room warmed up.

A handful of carefully chosen commoners had been coerced into attendance, although it had been a challenge locating presentable ones with the full complement of limbs and nothing actively contagious. Those who passed the test and could be trusted not to start fighting each other for ale during the speeches were scrubbed, scented and forced into clean clothes.

Unfortunately it was not always possible to understand them or even determine their sex, so a milkmaid had ended up in a doublet and a blacksmith in a blouse. They sat uncomfortably throughout the proceedings like hostages required to recant their sins in public, and applauded long after the correct moment had passed. Even the lowest peasants had been carefully rehearsed in the etiquette of dining, but no one had realized they would try to piss under the tables between courses.

The Baron had arrived with a retinue of sixteen, including his aged parents, superannuated grandparents and primordial great-grandparents. Sir Archie had a bad cold, and when presented to the Princess creaked down on to one knee, a pose which he was required to hold for some fifteen minutes without wiping his nose, so that when he was finally helped up he sneezed violently, spraying the gathering with dew.

It was said that he had the features of a fine mansion, which meant he had the complexion of old bricks, being pockmarked and partially eaten away. His yellowed moustaches looked as if they had been used to clean something inaccessible. His eyes were bad oysters. His breath could take down a buck from nine yards, or at least make it very ill. His years were impossible to measure, but it was safe to assume that he had passed the age when a man could rely on his knees.

His wealth, however, was vast and indisputable. And there was a glimmer of hope for the Princess: given the number of steep stairs up to the Chapel of Betrothment, there was a strong chance that Sir Archie would not make it to the ceremony.

Behind, below and between the formalities, the dancing of sarabands and galliards, the serving of forcemeats and mortrews, Watborn could see that anxious negotiations were taking place.

It was obvious to him that the family needed money but had nothing with which to bargain, save for a few strange old relics that meant little to those from outside. Apparently, the priests had made off with most of the chapel treasures upon their expulsion, the remaining relics were worthless bits of bone and wood, and the bank had auctioned everything else. Scarabold was therefore reduced to selling off members of the family.

Giniva sat back in her chair and surveyed the hall. When she was a little girl Londinium had been famous for the opulence of its ceremonies; the glint of steel against chased gold, the sharp stepping of the guards, the ornate formality of court rituals. Now the ragged receiving line, the ill-concealed disdain of the guests, the tattered drabness of the court colours, the unseemly fighting for slices of carved peccary and the drunken snatching at wine flasks made her long for the gilded innocence of childhood.

To be the bartered bride at the centre of this farrago was undignified and mortifying. She was not by nature romantic – heaven knows, the Mater had disabused her of any pastel notions – but there had to be a place in the world where minds and spirits could be aligned in grace, or at least where people ate with their mouths closed.

Watborn kept a careful eye on the room.

Dinner was not well received.

The F'Arcy family was descended from old money, mostly seized in questionable battles along with land and property, but its bloodlines were weak. Too much inbreeding had produced a chain of sickly, short-lived children who generally went mad and were locked away. As a consequence, Sir Archie's relatives had agreed to allow intermarriage. They were under no illusions about their new alliance, and were determined to keep Scarabold at arm's length. Sir Archie would produce an heir and his bride would be despatched soon after, the F'Arcys being rather good with rare poisons and wildly off-target arrows.

Each family studied its counterparts with ill-disguised distaste, like courtesans viewing the night's final customers. The F'Arcys saw a sour-faced matriarch and her fidgeting warrior-husband, strange lumpen courtiers in ill-fitting outfits and a princess who looked as if she was trying to work out which of them had trodden in something. Sir Archie's grandmother found a mouse in her décolletage. Everyone stared into their food with suspicion.

Dressed in spidery black bombazine, Madame Arachnia F'Arcy, Sir Archie's mother, examined her sirloin as if questioning its pedigree. To her left, the drugged Peter Maggot suddenly rose, failed to reach the vomitorium in time and threw up volubly in a corner. The King broke wind more discreetly than usual but drew attention by fanning the tablecloth. Mercifully, he had not had his padded chair replaced with a seat of easement; he planned to keep the meal as short as possible before heading off for a good clear-out. The state of the royal bowels had determined many a commoner's fate.

On the squires' table, Spackle and Peut were firing Brussels sprouts into duchesses' wigs. The painted harridans of the high court sniped among themselves, oblivious of their surroundings and barely cognizant of the event's purpose. What had once been spectacular was now mere spectacle.

At least dessert was a success. Everyone commented on the delightful likeness of the Princess on the almond cake, although the effect was spoiled when a knife descended upon her head. As Watborn directed the arrival of the remaining sweetmeats, he studied the families on either side.

The royal escutcheon, a vivid shade of pink, was displayed on the wall above King Scarabold's head, and marked out the land still under his ownership. Sir Archie's grandfather loudly announced that they possessed an exaggerated idea of their importance in the world. What was now left beyond poor old Londinium, the old man disrespectfully asked – a handful of swamps, a marsh or two?

Sir Archie F'Arcy was well aware that he was the best they could hope for, and despite his age and unprepossessing appearance all the bargaining power was on his side. As a consequence, Giniva had been seated next to him. When he openly picked what was left of his teeth with a chicken bone, she pretended not to notice. When he told a pointless story very slowly and blasted her with his rancorous exhalations, she smiled with her lips tightly shut. When he placed a corpse-hand on her thigh and gave it a squeeze while leaning forward to look down her dress, she was forced to drop a carving fork on to his bony ankle.

'Can't I sweeten his breath with one of those?' she asked Dwino-line, pointing to a salver of lurid, bulbous fruits. 'What are they?'

'They are carved from wax,' said the Second Wife. 'The orchard-women would not sell fresh produce to us. There's a green lemon.'

The Quaff rose and tinged his knife against the side of his glass, putting a crack in it. 'Your Royal Highnesses, Lord and Ladies, Knights of the Realm, peasants, et cetera, please charge your glasses and be upstanding for the loyal toast.'

He turned to face Giniva, but wasn't wearing his eye-pieces and instead addressed the Mistress of Hounds, who was letting her dog pluck sweetmeats from her mouth. 'To the radiant Princess Giniva, on the occasion of her sixteenth birthday, which has already passed, but better late than never.'

There followed much scraping of chairs and mumbling of the awkward toast, 'Better late than never.' Giniva might have been moved to speak if everyone had not sat down before she could rise.

The evening ground on. Watborn's back ached from maintaining his rigid stance. Being so large, he knew he would be noticed if he moved. He could not stand down until the last of the F'Arcys had left the hall. Instead, he observed and listened. The heat of the dishes, the chatter of the families, the suspicious glances and insincere smiles; he missed nothing.

Scarabold's obvious attempts at diplomacy were met with indifference. His awkwardly raised topics concerning political alliances and property rights fell on literally deaf ears. It was clear that Sir Archie was only interested in the physical aspect of his nuptials. He rarely stopped wetting his lips.

'So, are we all agreed?' asked Moribund as the band came to a cadence of discordant halts in a Ladies' Excuse-Me. 'Sir Archie will have the hand of my beautiful daughter in marriage—'

Giniva raised a finger. 'Mother, I—'

'And the Baron's property holdings beyond the Marshlands, his land, cavalry, farms, crops and mills to be divided as agreed.'

'Luscious,' said Sir Archie, reaching out a hand to Giniva's belly.

'No touching yet!' shrieked Asphyxia as the Princess shrank beneath her suitor's leaky stare.

'When do I get to ride her?' asked the Baron.

'Old man stinks,' squawked Asphyxia, nothing if not succinct.

'The necessary documentation has been drawn up,' the Squeam pointed out after draining his glass. 'If you would care to counter-sign the court rolls, we can arrange for the ceremony to take place in a matter of days.'

Lessons had been learned from the court's disastrous encounter with the Beetle Earl. Moribund had decided that the introduction ceremony was too risky to stage a second time. Sir Archie was not to be allowed a taste of his reward before legal ratification. The problem was that nobody had told him earlier.

'Days?' he cried. 'I can't wait that long! I've already taken certain herbal precautions to ensure that my connubial agility will last the entire night.' He pointed at what appeared to be a stick in his gusset.

'Perhaps a stroll to the pergola with the Princess,' Scarabold suggested, 'if the rain has eased.'

Sir Archie considered the idea. 'I don't know. Is it secluded?'

'Very.'

Without another word, the Baron rose sharply, seized Giniva by the hand and dragged her away from the table, scattering bowls and goblets. 'Come with me,' he instructed, 'and prepare to be boarded.'

'Why did you do that?' Moribund hissed at her husband, knowing the answer full well.

Leperdandy was about to go after them when Scarabold grabbed the flesh of his arm. 'Leave them alone,' he warned. 'We need this to happen. It's no time for your machinations. What on earth is that in your hair?'

The boy touched his curls in mock bewilderment. He had scraped gold leaf from the feet of a statue depicting the Madonna of the Rats in the chapel and ground it into his pomade. 'I wanted to look nice for Giniva – is that so wrong? You can't just leave her in the hands of that rancid old codfish!'

'That rancid old codfish is going to restore our fortunes, don't you understand? Of course not, you're the weakling child – how could you?' He cast a baleful glance at Dwinoline.

Watborn watched and listened. The Princess's brother was trapped in the coils of the family. He would never be able to slip away. He needed a distraction.

Their affairs are not yours, Watborn reminded himself. *You think you are as good as them because you taught yourself to read and*

write, but you're a mongrel and they have pure blood. If you inter-
fere, you will be blamed. You are inside their walls now. If you
watch your step, you will be protected in here and you can keep
moving upwards. Whatever its drawbacks, isn't life better? The
food is hot, the beds are clean, the work is easy. You cannot go
back.

And then there is her.

'I'm still in line to the throne,' the princeling was indignantly telling Scarabold.

'Only if Giniva is without issue,' he replied. 'And she should be
as fertile as a marsh.'

'She is your daughter.'

'Yes, and for the first sixteen years of her life she has been ornamental. Now she will finally prove herself useful.'

Watborn had been watching and listening in silence since he had
arrived. He came from a simple world where intrigue and subterfuge were unknown. *Do something to protect her*, a voice inside
him whispered. *Do something.*

Behind them, the butler Putney was tottering beneath the weight
of a stack of serving bowls. Watborn only had to thrust out his foot
for a second as he passed. He grabbed the old man before he hit the
floor and set him upright, but the chaos of cracking crockery
stopped everyone in their tracks.

It was long enough to allow Leperdandy to slip from the hall.
The boy took his cue with perfect timing.

And so, without thinking or planning or even being conscious of
the fact, Watborn, a commoner bred from the primeval roots of the
kingdom, interfered in the affairs of high state for the third time.

It was not to be the last.

58

By the Pool of Lost Virgins

Leperdandy knew his sister was headstrong and prone to take unnecessary risks. The only way she would allow herself to be dragged to the pergola was if she could see a way of escaping her suitor.

The walkway to the trysting spot ran through a rockery garden of vines, creepers and fly-crusted carnivorous plants that Magister Ambrosius employed in his experiments. Beyond it was the Pool of Lost Virgins, a place of contemplation frequented by Lady Dolorio and her Repenters, another wayward sect whom the castle had taken under its wing during the last famine.

The place was never warm, but in winter, when the rising damp met the sinking mildew, it was even more miserable, so the ladies retired to their pool to luxuriate and titivate. It was not a natural spring but a royal folly – the waterfall and lagoon were heated by an ingenious system of metal pans laid across hot coals, and most of the shrubbery surrounding the pool was made of green satin – but it was a secluded female oasis.

The Baron had arrived at the gates in a cart-and-four with arm-chairs roped on to it, and the stables were just behind the pool – the smell was a constant source of complaint for Dolorio and her repenting ladies as they bathed. The pergola was shielded from prying eyes by a wall of tough, tall reeds. Giniva eyed the exits, trying to decide upon a flight strategy.

'Tell me, my dear,' said Sir Archie, taking her reluctant hand and stroking it, 'what do you know of the ways of love? There is much that I could teach you. Are you familiar with the thirty-seven positions of aroused frenzy?'

'Please excuse me while I avail myself of the ablution room,' said

Giniva demurely, wriggling her hand free from Sir Archie's sweaty grip.

'You needn't wash for me,' leered the Baron, plucking at the ends of his yellowed moustaches in frenzied carphology.

'Perhaps not, but I need a piss.'

'You, boy.' F'Arcy pointed blearily at Leperdandy's pomaded head, which had protruded too far through an arrangement of artificial lilies. 'Go with her and make sure she comes straight back here.'

Not needing to be asked twice, Leperdandy hopped after his sister and cornered her by a bloodstone garderobe.

'You're not supposed to be in here; it belongs to the Lost Virgins,' Giniva warned, looking about. 'You're not lost.'

'Sir Archie sent me. He doesn't trust you.'

'Maybe he's not so stupid after all.' She peeped beneath the lilies. 'I have to get out of here, Dando. I may never get another chance. Will you help me?'

He threw his arms about helplessly. 'I don't see what I can do.'

'He's old, he can't be that strong, but I'd rather not end up straddle-punching him while he yells for his guards and you look on with your hands at your mouth.'

'I say, that's unfair.'

'I'm sorry, you're right. You've been uncommonly brave of late.'

'Then what are you going to do?'

'I don't know.' She sighed exhaustedly. 'Perhaps I should just go through with the marriage. It's what everybody wants. I could make my escape after he's been emptied. Men are supposed to lose their ability to concentrate in the minutes that follow.'

'That's not what you want.'

'I could think of nothing more repellent. Wait, I have an idea.' In Giniva's head a plan began to form. 'Can you get to his carriage? He probably has a pair of footmen on it but we outrank them. Send them off for a glass of malmsey with my permission. No, they're footmen – make it flagons of ale.' She bent down and twisted an iron key set in the ground.

'But how will I know that you're safe?'

'You'll be able to keep watch – the stable is just behind that clump of nasturtiums. When you see me wave a handkerchief – my crimson damask – be ready with the carriage.'

Leperdandy raised a slender digit questioningly. 'What do you mean exactly, be ready?'

59

Into the Maze

Centuries of confiscation conducted on an epic scale had turned the F'Arcys' servants into kleptomaniacs, so while the aged son was negotiating his betrothment terms in the Tainted Hall, they obtained a map from Cradleigh the under-butler, who served as a spy to anyone who would pay him enough. Then they positioned the Baron's carriage directly beneath one of the treasure rooms. Finding no treasures, they seized anything that was heavy, shiny or carved.

When Leperdandy burst through the reed-screen and came to a halt before them, half a dozen footmen, the coach driver and the postilion froze in mid-haul. They could not have looked more guilty. Two of them were balanced halfway through a window with an immense wardrobe on their shoulders, while a third struggled with an inferior statue.

For a few moments nobody moved. Then, realizing that they were facing a lone, lanky fop dressed in blue-and-silver leggings with glitter in his high-curled hair, they closed in on him, no longer magpies but wolverines.

Sir Archie had waited long enough.

What on earth was the girl doing in there? What did females get up to in their powdering places? Behind him the waterfall piddled feebly and the pool gave an intestinal gurgle. The effects of the horned goat weed he had consumed prior to the meal were supposed to last for six hours, but he could already feel his hose starting to deflate.

Giniva's appearance, lit by torches against the sparkling shower of the waterfall, restored his vitality. 'My little daffodil.' He sneezed and licked his moustaches.

'I feel wonderfully refreshed,' she said. 'Perhaps you should bathe before we discuss our forthcoming nuptials—'

'Oh, no need for that.' Sir Archie began tearing at his stained doublet.

'Bathe,' Giniva instructed, loosening her waist-chain. The Baron did not need to be asked twice, although he did have trouble standing on one leg to remove his anklets. After some struggles with buttons, clasps and knots, he balanced before her in his undervest and codpiece.

She stepped closer, teasing a forefinger between her breasts. 'Everything.'

The removal of the codpiece made a sound like a poultice coming off. Sir Archie stood before her naked, looking like the last plucked chicken at a provincial banquet. Giniva could barely bring herself to look. There were things on his legs that should not have been there. Surely his veins were meant to be on the inside?

He outstretched his scrawny arms, white and bristling with sparse black hairs, like a boiled crab. 'Come to me, my cooing doveling.'

She pushed him into the pool.

As the waterfall increased from a trickle to a torrent, his yell turned into a scream. Giniva quickly reached out a foot and placed it on his head. She had stoked the coals beneath the water-plates. The waters were already hot enough to boil a potato. Sir Archie's flesh blushed, then bubbled. A frantic hand rose above the seething cauldron. Soon it would begin to peel itself into component parts.

Giniva tore her eyes away and closed her nostrils to the stench of her stewing suitor. Grabbing his piled clothing, she searched for her brother.

She flapped her handkerchief furiously, but there was no sign of Leperdandy anywhere.

In the Tainted Hall, the discordant music had tumbled to another halt and Scarabold could be heard shouting indistinctly. It seemed highly likely that he had grown suspicious of Sir Archie's extended absence and was demanding a search party.

She heard a horse whinny and something that sounded like a wardrobe falling from a considerable height. She looked about frantically. Behind her, the boiled Baron squeaked and farted. Another cacophonous crash followed.

Come on, Dando, she prayed. *I asked you to do one little thing for me. This is no time for your silly games now!*

Beyond the walkway, the doors to the Tainted Hall burst apart with a dull boom as the Kingsmen came pouring out.

The carriage had been stuffed full of looted furniture. Its crew had the look of angry men caught doing something wrong. They tried hard to produce a simple spontaneous explanation as to why they were carrying dining chairs on their backs, but failed.

Leperdandy knew he would always be a peacock, but in the last few days another creature had started to show through. Instead of quailing before these thieving rooks, he took careful stock of the situation, noting that although they were of feral disposition, they were all small and weakly formed. True, there were six of them, but he was armed. His sword-stick was a weapon that required his exact delicacy of touch. Tonight it formed part of his dress uniform, but it was not purely ceremonial; it contained a blade that could whittle a dragonfly into a fritillary.

Even so, the sword's flexibility took him by surprise, and before he had come to terms with its speed of response, he had damaged several of the rogues, severing a thigh tendon, splitting a forearm and lopping off an earlobe.

Attacking the footmen who were balancing the wardrobe on the window-edge above them proved to be a good idea, as they fell on the pair below and all four vanished beneath their prize. This just left the two coachmen, one of whom scrambled over the side of the carriage, landing in the mud where Leperdandy was able to skewer a buttock.

The carriage driver was older, wider and of finer mettle. Producing a weapon that resembled a cutlass and setting it across his heavy chest, he stood his ground, daring the princeling to approach.

He was still deciding what to do when a blade of light cast itself across the carriage. Watborn had opened the doors to the Tainted Hall. The coachman looked back at his men, with only their boots protruding from under their haul, and knew that he was moments from exposure. If he was caught taking a slice out of a member of the royal family, he doubted his head would remain in the neighbourhood of his shoulders for long, so, without removing his eyes from his opponent, he clambered down and backed away.

Leperdandy advanced, whipping his sword back and forth. *For Giniva*, he told himself, *I am a prince and the warrior-blood of centuries flows through my veins, even though my knees are knocking.*

From this point on, there can be no going back. It is as if there is a divine light that guides us.

The coach driver had disappeared but his scimitar had not. It shot through the air and pinned Leperdandy to the coach door by a puffed sleeve. Then the startled horses took off.

The princeling had no empathy with stallions. Hanging by his shirt from the coach door as they took fright and charged away, he covered his eyes and screamed. The carriage smashed through the reed-wall in the direction of the Pool of Lost Virgins.

He swung helplessly as his sleeve shredded, but at least the motion allowed him to grab the carriage frame just as the rest of his shirt was torn away.

He attempted to control the reins of the team. The perfect carriage horse, he had been told, was a steady, gentle old beast that was hard to surprise when being steered by someone sitting twenty feet from its mouth. These were young, frisky and extremely tense. They bridled, stamped, snorted, whinnied and reared up, rolling their great brown eyes back in their heads. With Leperdandy holding on for dear life, they leaped over the boiling stream and took the coach with them, which started throwing off its looted treasures.

As the carriage-and-four showed no sign of slowing before it reached her, Giniva climbed the rockery and took a blind leap. She landed on a set of satin bolsters, half a wardrobe and a bloody, one-eared footman.

'Gin, help me – I can't control them!' As the horses careened, Leperdandy was flung from side to side. Only the leather straps that he had wrapped around his wrists prevented him from being hurled into the trees.

'They won't bolt from the road,' Giniva shouted back. 'Give them their head.'

'I couldn't hold them back if I tried!'

The carriage hurtled on, leaping and smashing about on the causeway, firing stones and spraying chunks of shattered furniture. A marble bust of Mater Moribund bounced out of the carriage and shattered. A china peacock flew into a hundred iridescent shards when it hit a fig tree.

The forecourt gates stood open while staff moved the banquet's produce in and out. Servants and villagers scattered as the coach shot out into the curving green corridor beyond. The cypresses were gold-tipped pfitzers, a type of tree more commonly planted in cemeteries. They were packed as tightly as fence-staves, so there was nothing else the horses could do but follow their line.

Giniva tried to raise herself up but the rocking carriage kept knocking her back. Behind her, a footman clambered from the wreckage of the wardrobe and threw himself at her, his hands locking tightly around her pale throat.

When one wheel of the coach side-swiped a cypress trunk, Leperdandy was thrown up in the air and landed hard on his chest, cracking a rib. Still he would not release the reins. Seeing the Princess belayed by the Baron's man, he tried to throw her his sword-stick, but found it impossible to reach.

The spittle-flecked horses followed the tree-edge as Giniva fought off her attacker. Bringing her knee up, she flattened his codpiece and tipped him off the carriage.

'It's no use,' Leperdandy cried, the reins searing his wrists. 'We'll never be able to slow them.'

'Then we can only hang on and wait until they are winded. Dando, you are trapped with me.'

She and Leperdandy clung to each other as the wall of trees rushed past. *Now we shall be truly alone,* she thought. *What are we leaving behind? Did they think I would stay for love or duty?* But the main question lodged in her mind: *How will we survive?* For this there was no answer.

The tall green corridor curved in a great arc. It should then have turned left, away toward the marshes. Something was wrong. Giniva looked up. Above she could see the great yellow moon flashing through the tops of the branches.

'Dando, why haven't we come out into the open fields towards the Stew-Fens?'

'We're in the Pfitzer Maze,' he yelled. 'I've seen drawings of it in the map room.'

'How do we escape?'

Leperdandy pulled at the reins. The horses had started to tire and were slowing down. 'Do you see any turn-offs? I don't.'

'Perhaps the other paths have become overgrown.'

'It was designed by the First Lord to keep out invaders.'

'And to keep us in,' she cried, pointing ahead.

Before them reared the great black walls once more.

The carriage thundered towards the main gate as they were brought back home.

From the doors to the Tainted Hall, Watborn watched them return with a sinking heart. *We are all trapped here*, he thought. *Men usually go to war. Now the war has come to us.*

60

To Leave or Stay

'Are you saying my son has been . . . boiled?' Madame Arachnia F'Arcy leaned over the bubbling water of the Pool of Lost Virgins and sniffed the Baron's soupy aroma. 'Are you sure that's him? It smells like potatoes.'

'He appears to have fallen in,' said the Decrepend unnecessarily. The sight reminded him of an anatomical illustration he had seen. The Baron had drifted apart and now appeared before the horrified group serially, his blanched remains bobbing to the surface in sections: first an arm, then a foot, then something flaccid with grey hairs attached. Each part was discreetly fished out by one of the gardeners and dropped into a sack.

'Where is your daughter?' Arachnia demanded. 'If she had anything to do with this . . .'

Scarabold was immune to threats. Word had already reached him that Thorax Sheathwing, the younger brother of the Beetle Earl, was vowing revenge with the backing of les Sœurs aux Cadeaux Étranges, and now the F'Arcys had good reason to join them. Once again, it seemed that his errant daughter was to blame.

'Rest assured, my lady,' said the King. 'If I discover that the Princess had anything to do with this, she will be severely disciplined.'

'Disciplined?' shrieked the Baron's mother. 'Discipline is something you do to a child who has broken a plate, not one who has stewed a man's flesh from his skull. She has turned my first-born to a broth!'

She rounded on the King with venom in her heart. 'I should have known this would happen. To think I ever imagined that our venerable dynasty should be coupled with such a disreputable tribe of low-born brigands—'

'I take exception to *low-born*, my lady.'

'And all because you occupy a strategic position on the Rushing River.'

'Is that what this was about?' Scarabold asked, genuinely amazed. 'Geography?'

'What else would it be for? We own land to the east and west. We can't get around you! You are nothing more to us than a blockage. You will pay for this day, and your daughter – if yours she is – will die a thousand times over. You will suffer for the outrage until the end of your life!'

Turning away, she instructed her father to gather the clan. The family drew itself together like a herd of threatened animals.

Behind them, the minstrel band struck up a merry, discordant mazurka.

'We have to hide,' Leperdandy warned, pushing his sister into the steam-filled alleyway that ran between the kitchens. 'Scarabold's anger will reach down and tear us out of any safe cranny.'

Thunder roared and the sky whitened as a storm collapsed over them.

'I will not be shut away, Dando.' The Princess ran ahead of him in her bloodied, tattered dress. 'He will never seal me in that room again.'

'You can't afford to have any more suitors. You're down to your last one. They have made murderers of us. But we still have Brasslight. It's time to play our hand.' Leperdandy slowed to a walk, clutching his ribs. 'I can get you to the Museum of the Dead from here.'

The Princess took a torch from one of the alley's embrasures and held it aloft. Its wind-flickered light made the steps dance treacherously.

'You wonder how I know so much,' said her brother. 'When you were young and still being dandled on our father's thigh, I was studying the history books with Ambrosius. Most were censored, of course, but they proved instructive. I was never invited out with you. The Great Wound gave up on me at a very early age.'

Giniva softened. 'I'm sorry, Dando. I've put you through so much and you've asked for so little in return. I will find a way out, and you must come too. You do see that now? There is nothing for you here.'

'We can't both go,' said Leperdandy sadly. 'I have to think of Lady Dwinoline. Our stepmother has been good to us. She sacrificed everything – her name, her status, her power – and she accepted her humiliating position as Second Wife to ensure that we would remain safe. I at least owe her my loyalty. You are the strong one, not I.'

Giniva reached out in the light from the guttering flame and touched his face tenderly. 'You are all the kindness I have known. We shouldn't be parted, but my mind is fully made up. War is at our doorstep and the fight for what remains will be terrifying to behold.'

'Suppose there was a way?' He searched her eyes. 'Suppose I told you there could be an end to all this?'

'But how?'

'We must talk to the only people who can tell us the truth. Dr Fangle was already drunk when he arrived at the banquet. He'll be under the table by now, and the Great Wound will be looking for you. But we still have the nurse. Minerva Mentle was there the night Brasslight was born.'

Leperdandy pushed open the door to the museum and bade her enter.

In the torchlight Giniva could make out the sleeping body of the boy-prince, wrapped in the damask cloak she had found for him.

Leperdandy saw him too and felt an increasingly familiar twinge of jealousy. 'Stay here tonight,' he instructed. 'I'll let you have the key but you must promise not to leave. There's no point in both of us taking the risk. Open the door to no one but me. I'll use our special knock. And if I don't appear, do not worry. Let us meet first thing tomorrow at the Bellcharter Chantry.'

'Dando,' she whispered, 'Father had no right to call you a fop. You are a hero.'

'I take my inspiration from you,' said her brother. 'Guard Brasslight with your life. I'll be back as fast as I can.'

Closing the door quietly, he waited until he heard the key turn in the lock before running back down the circular staircase.

61

Blood of My Blood

He found the Tainted Hall in uproar.

The F'Arcys had been rounded up by the King's Guard and were being held inside the immense fireplace that dominated one end of the hall.

Threats, counter-threats, entreaties and oaths flew back and forth as Scarabold held a council of war with Manticore and Grand-Marshal Timmorian. When the Great Wound spotted his son he released a bellow that shook tallow from the candelabras.

'You! Where is your sister? Is she responsible for this?'

'I've taken her to a place of safety, Father, to protect her from harm.'

'You've taken her? Since when did you do anything more than design your own clothes? Bring her to us at once, that she may look me in the face and deny the murder of the Baron!'

Though his knees trembled, Leperdandy stood his ground. 'I can't. She knows too well where your loyalties lie.'

Scarabold prowled menacingly around his dripwit son like a half-starved tiger. Could this really be the child who was once too weak to flense an enemy with his rapier? 'Bring her to me, fopling. Neither of you fully understands what she has done this night. She has placed us all in deadly peril.'

'She can't be punished for fighting off her attacker,' the prince-ling ventured. 'She has decided she will only give the kingdom a child on her terms.'

Scarabold cupped his ear. 'Am I going mad? Am I hearing things? She has decided? Is a sixteen-year-old girl dictating her will to the King? Tell me where she is.'

Leperdandy cleared his throat and spoke out. 'I can't do that, Father.'

'I desired the smallest sacrifice for the greatest gain. She is the inkwell into which a suitor must dip his quill in order to scratch out a future for our dynasty.'

'And that future is to be written on her body? Well, she is of age now, and it is her body to do with as she sees fit.'

For a second, the princeling thought Scarabold was going to swipe at him with his great fist. Everyone else in the room was discreetly backing away, knowing that at moments like this others could be caught in the fallout.

As the King advanced he seemed to grow larger. 'You will tell me,' he warned, a thunderstorm rising within him, 'or I will find a way of getting the information from you, do you understand?'

Leperdandy understood all too well. He had seen the dungeon filled with tongueless, eyeless, toeless prisoners, poor creatures gouged and blackened by Fumblegut's torturer. 'But I am the blood of your blood—' he began.

'Then you should understand where your loyalties lie. This is your last chance to speak out without suffering the consequences of your actions.'

'I can't, my King.'

'Very well.' Scarabold cast his good eye down. 'It pains me to take this action, blood of my blood.'

All this Watborn witnessed from his station at the door.

He was constrained by his position. There was nothing he could do until he had been released from his duties by Goldhawk. It was the lot of the servants to stay silent and watch, no matter how chaotic the proceedings. He was thankful that no one had seen him create the diversion, but the time for watching was fast coming to an end.

Beyond the mullioned windows of the great Tainted Hall, lightning turned the sky to day. Three seconds later, thunder broke like boulders being run across the rooftops. He looked about helplessly. By allowing the princeling to escape and take action, he had made matters worse. *Don't meddle in matters you can't control, birdcatcher*, he told himself. *Who will help the boy now? Who will protect the Princess?*

Guards were summoned at the clap of the King's hands. Leperdandy's thin arms were seized and he was dragged out of the hall.

He cast one final glance back at the outraged F'Arcys, shrieking and smothered in wet soot, held under guard in the great fireplace. Then a black hood was placed over his head.

He would see nothing more until it was removed in Torque's keep.

62

At the Mercy of Torque

Although Migor Torque held the title of Royal Torturer, he considered himself to be an explorer of the new sciences.

He was required to create instruments that could inflict pain in such subtle shades that he had also been appointed weaponsmaster. He considered his victims in theoretical abstraction, never seeing them as children or parents, sons or daughters, and was able to sleep like a baby after a hard day's work – albeit a very drunk one.

Catching sight of himself in the keep's mottled mirrors, he admired the carefully coloured and plaited beard that touched his belt-buckle, his gold earrings, the puckered, shiny scars that crossed his features, giving him the appearance of a creature assembled rather than birthed.

Torque considered himself an artist and was proud of the fact that he had never once visited the dungeons. No blood ever spurted, no gouts of gore marked him, and to prove the point he wore a silver-threaded jerkin in a delicate sky-blue fabric. The jailer Fumblegut was little more than an animal in comparison.

When he looked at Leperdandy strapped on the great oaken X-frame in his domain, he saw not a member of the royal family but a procedural problem. The lad had arms like wet string and a neck so thin that it looked as if it might snap under the weight of a hat. There was so little spare meat on him that the torturer's most useful instrument, the Skin Shearer, which could cut rhomboidal pinches of flesh from all over a body, would prove unserviceable. How then to proceed? He might have favoured something basic like the Sprinkler, which could cascade droplets of molten lead on to an upturned face, had Scarabold not asked him to avoid leaving outward marks.

Torque looked over his rack of instruments.

The Fidget might do the trick. It consisted of a spiked steel ring that could be clipped around any part of the body so that the metal just brushed the skin. It would do no harm if the victim remained absolutely still, which nobody managed for long. Once the first cut was inflicted, the body tended to flinch and jolt, causing further mutilation; in the right hands it could be a truly fascinating method of extracting information.

But no; any instrument that left scars had to be ruled out. Besides, the boy looked as if he would crack and sing at the first available opportunity. Torque finally settled on a weapon he had not used for some years.

'Cut him down,' he instructed Spank, his over-eager helper. 'Take him to the Cake-Stand.'

Spank severed the princeling's ties and draped his limp form over his shoulder. Leperdandy had passed out after merely imagining his fate. Was it even worth the effort of torturing him?

Spank needed the boy awake and enjoyed slapping him hard around the face. Leading Leperdandy to the centre of a bare stone cell sunk into a corner of the keep, he lifted him on to a circular iron disc placed three feet from the ground, and stripped him naked. *Look at him,* Torque thought. *Without his finery he's nothing more than a collection of bleached bones.*

Leperdandy wavered and looked as if he might fall. 'I'd stay upright if I were you,' Spank warned, then closed the cell door on him so that Torque could open the valves.

Water began to well up from the floor grate. The cell quickly flooded until the tide lapped just below the edge of the cold metal disc. The room's temperature fell sharply. Leperdandy's senses came into focus. He was standing unclothed but unbound on a tiny disc in the centre of an indoor pond.

Torque's voice emerged from a speaking-tube in the ceiling. 'My lord, the King requires information about his daughter. The water below you is liquefied ice. You are required to remain on the stand. If you fall, you must immediately climb back on to the stand. If you fail to do so, you will quickly freeze to death. So, if you would kindly tell me now – where is the Princess Giniva?'

Torque considered the elegance of his device. By his reckoning, the hardiest prisoners could last up to three hours before losing their bearings and wearily slipping off.

Leperdandy fell off after two and a half minutes.

Torque and Spank peered through the porthole cut in the cellar door and watched with interest. Without making a sound, the princeling climbed back on to his perch and stood shivering on the stand once more.

'He has stamina,' said Spank.

'The obese can never clamber up,' replied Torque. 'This one weighs next to nothing.'

Leperdandy quickly fell off again, but began to gain a certain agility from his plunges and climbs. After the third fall he lasted almost half an hour before losing concentration and dropping into the icy black water. He was slower to climb out and slipped back several times, but managed it in the end. His eyes were blank, for he had placed his mind somewhere else.

Torque knew that this was not a good sign. If the princeling was not mentally strong, he might lose his wits and prove unable to answer questions.

Leperdandy looked as if a draught might unseat him, but a reed is tougher than a bough, and the next time he stayed on the Cake-Stand for one hour and forty-two minutes before dropping off. Torque was having his supper when he heard the splash, and hurried to the window of the cell.

The boy was under the water for so long that Torque feared he might drown. Then one hand appeared, and another, and up he climbed, pulling himself out inch by painful inch in total silence, unrolling to an upright position on the stand once more.

'The stripling is shivering like a moth, but unbroken,' Torque muttered, pleased that his device was bringing out the best in a subject. 'Fill the water with more ice.'

The temperature in the cell dropped further. Leperdandy began to shake uncontrollably. 'Will you tell us where the Princess is?' Spank shouted through the bars of the cell door.

Leperdandy had barely heard the question. It felt as if he was floating above himself somehow, looking down at his distant, wavering body. This time he fell without a sound and sank deep. No bubble, no ripple of movement appeared on the surface of the dark water. The torturer and his assistant watched and waited, then waited a little longer.

'Get him out,' Torque instructed. 'If he drowns, our heads will roll.' Spank hurriedly opened the water valve.

The boy was dragged from the draining water and laid on the icy floor of the keep. His skin was a delicate cornflower-blue. Water dribbled from his nose and mouth.

'For the last time, will you instruct us as to where the Princess is hiding?' Torque asked hopefully.

A water-beetle crawled from between Leperdandy's frosted white lips.

'He looks dead,' said Spank. 'Now what do we do?'

63

Phosphorescence

Brasslight reached out and touched the sleeping Princess on her neck, so long and pale that she might have been born to swans. Wrapped in a pleated cloak of midnight-blue satin trimmed with coney, Giniva was lost in the stars.

'My lady,' he said softly, 'please awaken.'

She opened her eyes and saw an anxious blue glaze above her.

'Your brother has not returned and I fear the worst. We must search for him.'

She sat up, rubbing sleep from her eyes. 'You can't leave, Brasslight – not until I've fetched your foot. You must be perfect before your presentation. If you're caught now you will be cast out, and the fight will be lost.' The armourer was still working on his new tin foot to gauge an accurate measurement for the final fitting.

'There must be something I can do for you,' said Brasslight. 'I have been nothing but a burden.'

'There's been no word at all from my brother?' She rose stiffly and stretched. 'Why has he not returned? He must have failed to locate Nurse Mentle. He could be in trouble. I have to find him.'

'But how? We have no idea where he went.' Brasslight gamely attempted to balance on one leg.

'You can't leave like that. Even with a stick you would not be able to keep up with me, and how would you manage the staircases? Stay here. I'll return shortly.'

'No, I must come,' Brasslight whispered, hopping. 'Suppose something was to happen to you?'

She held him by the shoulders. 'I have to go alone. This is my family, Brasslight. They can't hurt me any more than they already have done.' She unlocked the door and threw him the key. 'Lock it behind me and answer to no one else.'

As the Princess left and hurried off down the corridor she passed Watborn, and only realized she had done so after turning the next corner. Surely there could not be two such men? The curious merman who had freed her in the moat was also an artist and a pastry chef. What was he doing up here? Was he following her? She felt herself in the presence of a silent guardian and was oddly reassured.

When she turned to glance back, he had gone.

Watborn had been equally struck by the encounter.

After Goldhawk had failed to appear in the Tainted Hall, he had finally abandoned his post. Searching the corridors above, he had heard a door unlock and had seen the Princess leave the Museum of the Dead. He checked for signs of the strange assassin. Although there were muddy bootprints beside the door, Ormond the Steady of the Devil's Tongue was not to be seen.

It was the way she moved that struck Watborn most. The King and his Queen behaved much as he'd expected, but Giniva was different. She had an inner energy that marked her as more than mortal. She was phosphorescent with goodness, although at times she seemed to hide it well. He wondered if her tread would leave golden traces, or if her touch could heal the sick.

Then he remembered who he was. Nobody.

The Princess had passed by and he was left standing on the landing of the corner turret, looking out into the tempestuous night.

The storm was now directly overhead. The cisterns were failing to cope. Rain fell in great gouts, blinding men and horses, wiping away the view as if it were a charcoal picture. One of the laundresses had been washed straight over a battlement and was still hanging from her clothes line.

As he watched from the window, he saw a great blackness shimmering behind the distant trees. It had no shape but was moving slowly forward. How long had the army been waiting there? He saw crimson pennants rising, horses champing. Even through the rainfall he heard the war drums.

So it starts, he told himself, setting off for the armoury with renewed vigour. *Remember your purpose. You are an archer now. But more than that, you have undertaken a solemn duty. The Princess must be protected at all times.*

The idea made no sense but was bred in his bones like a superstition of the blood.

64

The Assault in the Tainted Hall

As the trees cleared to reveal the iron gates, still neglectfully left wide, Thorax Sheathwing turned to his platoon.

His ebony stallion was covered in the iridescent wings of beetles, shimmering blue and green on glossy black. Storm water cascaded over his armour like liquid mercury. Raising his visor, he studied each of the warriors in his regiment.

'On this night we bring the corrupt rule of Scarabold to the end it so richly deserves,' he cried. 'The King's reign is over. We will leave no one alive.'

As he waved his company forward, the laundress fell past him along with several pairs of drawers and landed in the only dry part of the moat with a smack.

The portcullis was up. As he rode into the courtyard, dark thoughts clouded Sheathwing's brain. Where was everyone? They must have heard the army approaching. Had they laid a trap?

Inside the Tainted Hall Scarabold was trying to control the situation, but for once even his great roar could not be heard beneath the ear-piercing shrieks of the F'Arcy matriarchs.

Rain was pounding down the chimney of the great fireplace, soaking his soot-caked captives. Some bricks fell in, bringing clouds of filth into the room and blasting black muck over everything. The blackened courtiers floundered about, looking like seagulls that had been dipped in tar.

Moribund, Dwinoline, Asphyxia and the others fled with their begrimed retinues, leaving the men to deal with the mayhem. The Squeam rolled his occluded eyes and sank beneath the banquet table, coughing out ashes. Everyone was getting to their feet and trying to wipe themselves down when Thorax Sheathwing appeared in the hall doorway with his broadsword raised.

Scarabold himself could not be harmed – he had earned that right as the crowned head – but his family was fair game. His guards fought valiantly against the Sheathwing, but they sported no battle-dress and were unprepared for the viciousness of the sudden assault.

Thorax ran through the servants as they tried to flee, without pausing to wipe his sword, then sliced a swathe through the minor guests along one side of the banquet tables until he reached the blackened mob of F'Arcys huddled together in the fireplace.

The soot-covered creatures wailed pitifully but it was impossible to identify them or to understand a single word they said. Sheath-wing and his soldiers merely saw tiaras and golden chains, so they separated their visages from their bodies as if plucking the heads from daisies. The F'Arcys dropped in a great mound of crimson and black, and the hall finally fell silent.

It was not only the F'Arcys who suffered. Dr Emeric Fangle was pinned through his guts to a carving chair and bled out on to a cream blancmange in the shape of a sleeping swan. Peter Maggot, the bank's usurer, was fitted intravenously with the fireplace poker and expired in great indignation. Cradleigh, the duplicitous under-footman, got a toasting fork for his troubles, and the Mistress of Hounds was taken to the water-garden for the pleasure of Sheath-wing's men. She fought back and survived, only to suffer a far stranger fate at a later time.

After such a vanquishment it was traditional to take tokens, the spoils of victory to be displayed upon returning home, but Thorax Sheathwing could see nothing worthy of the haul. He did not real-ize that he had interrupted a birthday banquet, and that all valuables had been removed from the temptation of light-fingered villagers. It merely seemed that they were bereft of treasures, so he called his men and they returned to their horses, leaving the Great Wound and most of his retinue alive behind arrases and under tables, having slaughtered the wrong family.

Thus were the Sheathwing briefly avenged for the loss of their son, and the F'Arcys ignominiously put to death for doing nothing more than attending a celebration dinner. Kingdoms rose and fell on such caprices, and so mere accidents of fate were written into legend. Even before the night was over, the balladeers from the minstrel gallery were working on a rhyme for 'massacre'.

One more paradox occurred that thunderstruck night.

After they left, the Sheathwing were halted by a F'Arcy platoon awaiting news of their leader, Sir Archie. They were informed, quite erroneously, that he had been brutally murdered by the Cannibal King.

The F'Arcys set off home to raise an army of their own, promising to form an immediate alliance with the Sheathwing if it would bring an end to Scarabold's reign of terror.

And so, preparations for a far greater conflict began.

65

Wheels in Motion

The corridors leading to the keep had turned into turbulent streams. Water pushed through the crevices and cracks, dissolving mortar and loosening stones. In Torque's keep, rainwater was bubbling up through the grating in the Cake-Stand cell and spraying under the door.

Torque dragged the princeling to dry stone and punched at his chest. He was determined to extract the intelligence required by his master while making sure that his informant did not expire in the process. The boy coughed up several pints of filthy water and fluttered awake.

'My lord, do you feel well enough to continue?' Torque asked, concerned.

Leperdandy nodded weakly.

'Very well – that's the spirit, eh?' He threw a sackcloth over the lad's shaking body, so white and translucent that his veins appeared like distant rivers seen through mist. 'Your father requires us to carry on until he is provided with a satisfactory answer. Spank, would you kindly fetch the Scorching Truss?'

Behind them, the wooden cell door gave way under the weight of rainwater. The deluge roared in and flooded the keep. Torque was bowled head-over-heels across the floor. Spank was thrown through the far embrasure, where his head became wedged in an arrow-slit and he was left hanging by his neck as the water receded, whereupon it snapped with a sound like wood being chopped.

Leperdandy was washed off his feet and managed to slither out of the door. He did not stop to look back but allowed himself to be carried away, bashing along the corridor and down a flight of steps that had been transformed into a series of ornamental cascades. As the water ebbed into flues and gratings, he slipped about on the wet flagstones until he could regain his bearings. His delicacy worked in his favour; light and flexible, he was like a fish or a reed, flipping this way and that under force to suit his surroundings. It would, he prayed, be the saving of him.

Leperdandy had proved his mettle. He was frozen, exhausted, aching and hungry, but for once the thought of his hereditary diet made him feel sick. Returning to his apartment, he wrapped himself in a dressing robe and collapsed into his deep and downy mattress, falling asleep in seconds. Nothing more could be done until morning light.

But the new generation, aided by an intruder from the lowlands, had set in motion wheels that would not be braked.

The banners were soon to rise on the outward walls, the cannons oiled and recalibrated. The armourers were already hammering rivets in preparation. The fire of war could not be blown out by the same weak wind that had kindled it.

Now that he had left behind the kitchens, Watborn made his way to the great armoury. There he found Manticore, Vitrolio and the others drawing up battle plans. Halberds, maces, polearms and broadswords were pinned along the walls in iron brackets, rising all the way up to the hall's ribbed roof.

'So, serving dumplings lost its appeal, did it?' asked Manticore, amused. 'You've arrived at the right time. Thorax knew he was not yet facing the real enemy. There's no pleasure to be took from killing kitchen boys. They'll be back, and we won't let our guard down next time.'

'Come,' said Vitrolio, 'show us what you can do.'

Watborn surprised himself as much as the others. After he split his first logs with a longbow in a matter of seconds, the other archers came in to watch.

'A fine longbow can be crafted from a single length of elm or yew in fifteen hours,' said Manticore. 'The heartwood – that is to say, the centre of the tree – compresses, while the sapwood, which is its outer layer, functions best in tension.'

'He doesn't need to learn the science,' said Vitrolio. 'Not with that arm.'

'Fair enough,' Manticore agreed, 'but there's no room here for heroes. We fight together as one. Your time will come, Watborn. The King does not understand what he has done and is unprepared, so we must plan for him. Are you with us?'

Watborn knew he could no longer sleep in the kitchens. His place was here. He remembered climbing a tor with his father and being told not to look back. It still seemed like good advice.

'May I stay here?' he asked.

'Vitrolio will outline your duties and show you to the archers' quarters. And much else, no doubt.' Manticore and the others laughed. Watborn had heard of the brothel set aside for the Kingsmen. It was not where his interest lay. The archers' court was within a short distance of the Princess's route to her apartment. He needed to track the assassin.

'Our hours are long,' said Vitrolio. 'When we're not training, we're on guard duty. Much of the castle is poorly secured. We must protect the royal family.'

'Does the Princess have her own guard?'

'Not any more. That is a duty none of us wishes to perform.'

'Is it dangerous?'

'It is dull. She goes nowhere and does nothing. She is decorative.'

'She is at risk.'

'And what makes a man from the Marshlands think that?'

Watborn took the sketch of Ormond the Steady from his tunic and showed them. 'He was stalking the Princess.'

'This insignia belongs to the Devil's Tongue of St Stanivar,' said Manticore. 'They are a ruthless order of fanatics. They believe their so-called saint is the one true supreme being. The King offended them some years ago and they swore to take revenge.'

'Somehow he manages to offend everyone,' said Watborn.

'But this is worrisome. To gain entrance to the grounds in his military sigil suggests they have grown bold and desperate.'

'I will take on the extra duty,' announced Watborn.

Vitrolio looked surprised. 'Very well. But remember to keep your distance and watch your own back. In an attack, the Princess will expect you to die for her. It'll be added to your regular hours here.'

The birdcatcher stayed silent.

'You'll be shown your post and given shifts, but for now I think a quenching ale is in order.' Clapping his newest recruit on the back, he led him off to the archers' favourite hostelry.

What did Watborn truly want?

In Breornsey he had seen that every little life that began in joy ended in tragedy. He had always known that Londinium, looming large above his village, would affect his life in ways he could not understand. It was a cliff that had to be climbed to the summit, so that he might afford himself a view of the world. But there was something else: a need to restore the natural balance and put things right.

Later that night, as he bedded down under the eaves and lake-flies buzzed through the rafters, he fell to wondering where this puzzling ambition had come from, and where it would take him. But before he could reach an answer, he fell into a deep, exhausted sleep.

66

The Nurse's Tale

Nurse Minerva Mentle lived in apartments reserved for those who were no longer allowed to participate in the daily affairs of the court. The wet-maid to all the royal children had served with astonishing commitment and fierce loyalty, loving her charges like a mother. As a consequence, she had been confined to her quarters, to remain there until the day she died.

For once, good fortune aided Giniva. A washerwoman with a huge goitre at her throat passed her on the stairs with a laden basket, having lost her way in the chaos of the attack. The Princess smelled camphor and burnt wax, laundry soap and peppermint, scents that took her back to days wrapped in swaddling in the nurse's care.

'Oh yes, saving Your Grace,' said the old washerwoman, curtseying awkwardly, 'she lives on in the Tower of the Forgotten.'

'I've never heard of such a place.'

'Begging your pardon, Worshipfulness, it's what we call it, but I think you know it as the Tower of the Faithful.'

'Do you have other names for all the parts of the castle?'

'I'm sure I wouldn't know, Your Majesticity.' The washerwoman was nervous, for she knew all the other names and few were flattering. 'You'll find her there. Just go to the head of this staircase, then left and left again, and left once more, for it folds in on itself like a periwinkle. And you may wish to give these to her, for they are her favourites.' She handed the Princess a small cloth bag.

'Very well,' said Giniva. 'You may go, and don't let me catch you using these stairs again.'

For the first time, as she climbed the steps leading to the tower,

Giniva wondered how many others were kept locked up and hidden from view. The paintwork on the wooden beams and stair-rails ended abruptly at the foot of the turret, a sure sign that the inhabitants had been dismissed and abandoned even by the decorators.

After following the washerwoman's instructions she found herself in a stone corridor of doors, each bearing a wooden tablet upon which was chalked a name. She discovered the nurse's quarters at the end of the turret, beyond twenty similar apartments. There was no bell or knocker, so she tried the handle and pushed.

'Who is there?' called a cracked and querulous voice from within. Giniva tried to see through the gloom.

'Wait, visitor, let me find a candle,' said the voice.

The Princess flinched, dreading what she might be forced to confront. Instead the flame revealed a cosy, patterned nest of woven purple bedspreads and indigo valances, yellow shutters and pea-green tapestries.

Nurse Mentle had shrunk considerably – she was all but lost in her immense feathered bed beneath a string of clove pomanders – but her eyes were lively with intelligence. Her hair was the colour of clouds and there were more lines on her yellowed face than there were stones on a beach, but this merely added to her character.

'Little Giniva, my precious creature! My duckling!' Throwing out her thin arms, she gave the girl a hug, tears squeezing from old eyes. Giniva felt as if she was holding a sparrow.

'They tell me nothing of court life,' the nurse whispered. 'I am not allowed communication. You must not be caught on this floor, for we may have no contact with the outside world.'

'I neither,' said Giniva sadly. 'We are as much prisoners as you, Nursie. They told us you were mad.'

Minerva's eyes acknowledged the sad truth. 'It is the easiest way to avoid visitations,' she said. 'We are none of us mad but a little touched, certainly, after being detained here for so many years. Let in some light, will you?'

Giniva opened the shutters. 'Do they treat you well? You survive?'

'Surviving is not living, my petal-dove. We are fed and watered and cultivated like plants in the nursery. That is to say, if we stretch too far towards sunlight, we are liable to be lopped back.' She dismissed the thought. 'But look at you – how fine you have grown!'

'Nursie, I need your help. My father has adopted a stratagem to save the kingdom. Only you and Dr Fangle know the truth.'

'I have not seen that dreadful old soak in years,' Minerva mused. 'Given the amount he drank, I'm surprised that anything more than his liver survives.' She looked into Giniva's opal eyes. 'This is about the Lady Castilia, wife to Perseo, mother of Brasslight, is it not?'

The Princess nodded, surprised.

'I thought as much. He would be of age now.' Minerva struggled to raise herself a little. 'No doubt you wish to know what happened. Make sure the corridor is empty. It is time you knew the truth.'

'Your laundress gave me these for you. Your favourite: sweet rosemary biscuits.' Giniva emptied the bag upon a plate and set a glass of nettle tea beside her. 'Please go on.'

'Poor Lady Dwinoline, Scarabold's first wife, was rejected by the King's brother.' Nurse Mentle's toothless mouth felt its way tentatively around the edges of a biscuit, in the manner of all old ladies, but despite her best efforts crumbs still fell everywhere.

'I did not know that,' said Giniva.

'Oh, there is much you do not know, and much that has been kept from us all. The Lady Castilia was young and untested. Her birthing canal was not wide enough to emit the infant and the doctor was in his cups, so I took charge and cut the mother's belly open. I hacked through the cord myself and sewed her shut.' She brushed crumbs from her quilt. 'When I returned with the doctor's bag I found Castilia dead. I was suspicious, of course. She had lost much blood but she should have survived. After Fangle drank from his rum-flask and fell asleep, I went through his bag and found an empty distillate of adder juice. It is a lethal poison used to put wounded soldiers down, and quite undetectable except that it leaves a greenish stain. I checked inside Castilia's mouth and found nothing, but when I looked in her ears I found that the right one was marked.'

'Her ears! But why would he kill her?' Giniva asked, taking the nurse's mummified hand.

'Fangle knew it would be better to tell the King that both mother and child had died in the birthing.'

'Are you sure of this?'

'Nobody royal ever has an accident. Kings and queens are always attended by their most trusted valets. Our kingdom has sunk into murder and deceit.'

'But Fangle could not have been working under his own recognizance,' said Giniva. 'Who instructed him to take the mother's life?'

The nurse gave a dry cough and sipped some nettle tea. 'Who else but the Mater Moribund? The boy was born deformed and could not reign according to the Rules of Exception. There was a speaking-tube in the birthing spire. Dr Fangle told me the baby had to be killed, that Moribund had given him clear instructions. Brasslight and his mother could not be allowed to live. He said the King knew nothing of the matter.'

'Do they know you stole the child away?'

'It was a terrible storm-swept night. To my knowledge, no one followed me.' Minerva lifted herself so that her pillows could be arranged. 'I couldn't let the poor mite die just because he was lame. My first thought was to take him to the sanitarium where the sick servants are nursed. Then I decided it would be safer to place him with les Sœurs aux Cadeaux Étranges, to be raised by Lady Lavinia until he came of age. Soon after, I was moved up here with the other inconvenient members of the household. I never discovered what became of him, save that the Sisters had fashioned him an append-age and named him after it.'

'What if I were to tell you that we have the boy they called Tin-foot,' said Giniva, 'and that we intend to put him on the throne?'

Minerva waved the thought aside. 'It is not possible, my dear. You know the law.'

'Only a handful of people know that he was born incomplete. Nobody else ever has to learn the truth.'

'Mater Moribund knows. Dr Fangle told her that the boy was deformed and had to be smothered. If he turns up now, the first thing she will do is check his foot.'

'We will fashion a foot and teach him to walk with such perfec-tion that she will never suspect a thing.'

'Then you would base the royal line on another lie. And you would go against your own father, who is at heart a good man, no matter how he seems.' Even though she was a prisoner in her apart-ment, Nurse Mentle still staunchly supported the King.

Giniva was confounded. 'You agree with me that our kingdom has rotted into corruption, yet you would do nothing to save it from itself.'

'I am a nurse, my lady, nothing more,' said Minerva. 'These are matters for those with purer blood and sharper minds than mine.'

'And I am the heir-princess,' Giniva replied. 'I have seen in these past few days horrors that would shame the world.'

Nurse Mentle's head fell back upon her pillow. She looked old and frail. 'I brought each of you into this life, hoping you would do great things. I am just the deliverer. Everything else is up to you. Perhaps you will see a way.'

After she had finished speaking she closed her eyes and sank into the bolster, so that her head was lost from view. Giniva tiptoed from the cloying room and closed the door quietly behind her.

Minerva Mentle turned her head to the view from her window. The clouds had lifted and blue starlight filled the room.

'I had expected . . .' she murmured to herself, catching sight of the sweet rosemary biscuits on the plate, of which she had taken but a single bite.

The nurse's eyes were drifting in mist. 'I had expected . . . a better end to my life than this.'

As she sank, her hand caught the plate of biscuits that had been glazed with a greenish distillate and sent it to the floor.

67

Wayward Creatures

As arranged, Giniva and Leperdandy met at dawn in the Bellcharter Chantry, a chapel dominated by a rose-window that depicted dancing martyrs with spikes through their tongues. It was one of the quietest and safest places they knew. Only the former clergy came here to commiserate over their lost faiths and the fact that they were trapped in their denominations like peacocks in cages. Even Spackle and Peut had no access here.

'We can't just turn up with Brasslight and demand that he takes his place on the throne,' said Giniva. 'The nurse's words gave me pause. Moribund demanded his death. No matter how well we disguise it, she will discover the truth. She controls our father, but she has a weakness.'

'Tell me,' the princeling demanded, his vigour restored after his freezing ordeal. 'I will fight so long as I can wield my sword-stick. It's terribly good, you know. It takes ears off.'

The Princess grabbed his lapel and drew him to her, the better to hold his attention. 'We must use diplomacy. If we fail to go through the proper channels, our petition will not be honoured.' She glanced at the rose-window, seeing how the light had moved. 'Magister Ambrosius will know what to do. But first we must appear as dutiful children before the family.'

Breakfast was awkward.

When Giniva and Leperdandy appeared on the steps and made their way to their usual places around the dining table, a deathly hush settled over the hall.

Everyone was there, and all eyes turned to watch them. Scarabold scowled so hard that his good eye almost sprang out, but was hampered from speaking by the shame of having ordered his own son's torture. Mater Moribund looked as if there was a thunderstorm taking place inside her hair.

Leperdandy unfolded his napkin and glanced about for coddled eggs.

Giniva poured peach tea.

Everyone else stared.

Something was obviously very wrong. The walls, tapestries and windows were blackened with explosions of soot. Several suits of armour had vanished and the axes over the fireplace were now mere silhouettes. The fireplace was filled with a great heap of charred rags and sticks, and the reek of burnt flesh hung in the air. The flagstones were still bloodstained. What had happened here?

To ask directly about the party would have been foolhardy. Giniva resolved to broach the subject in a roundabout way. 'I hope our guests enjoyed the banquet,' she said airily. 'Where is Dr Fangle this morning?'

'You're sitting on him,' said Mater Moribund.

The Squeam spat his nutmeg juice across the table. Aunt Asphyxia turned even paler than usual. Scarabold growled.

'Putney sponged the last of him out of your cushion an hour ago. Your escapade cost us twenty-three lives, including the most senior members of Sir Archie's family. I don't know if you had a chance to meet them, but you may make the acquaintance of his mother by stoking the fire – her wig is over there in the coal scuttle. We had to burn as much of the evidence as we could. Madame Arachnia kept the room warm all night.'

'What happened?' asked Leperdandy, unable to contain himself.

'I'm glad you asked.' Moribund peered into a pot of marmalade and was disgusted to find a beetle squirming within it. 'It appears Thorax Sheathwing was not best pleased about his brother being turned inside out at our dinner table, and decided to stage a surprise attack. He did not realize that another suitor for my daughter's hand was being stewed alive while we dined. He mistook the F'Arcys for us and slaughtered them all.'

'I'm sorry I missed all the excitement,' said Leperdandy.

Scarabold could contain himself no longer. 'Two suitors dead, a house wiped out, and what was the other thing? Oh yes, a declaration of war. If either of you had the guts, I would think you'd planned it. What happened when you went to the pergola?'

'We decided to bathe,' said Giniva. 'I went to change and when I returned Sir Archie had gone. I was so disappointed that I stayed with Leperdandy.'

'Lascivious liar!' screamed Asphyxia. 'My nephews saw you leaving in the Baron's carriage!'

Giniva affected mock puzzlement. 'And yet I am here, Auntie, so how could that be?'

'And you.' The Great Wound rounded on Leperdandy. 'You were left in the hands of Torque.'

'Did you not expect me to fight back?' the prince cried hotly.

'Frankly, no.' Scarabold shrugged. 'What has the world come to, when the two weakest members of my dynasty despatch my most dangerous foes?'

'They always rebel,' said Moribund sadly. 'Troublesome, wayward youth.' Dwinoline looked down into her plate and kept her counsel. The Princess hid some toast in her gown for Brasslight.

'Now history must be unpicked and rewritten. You have damned us all, the pair of you!' Scarabold slammed his fist on the table, spattering marmalade everywhere. From the hearth, part of a F'Arcy servant peered sightlessly at the scene, passing silent comment. 'You were nourished on the souls of your enemies, fattened and given strength by the weak. Perhaps the meats proved too rich for you.'

'We shall have to think of an appropriate chastisement,' said Mater Moribund, her dark eyes crinkling at the thought.

'Oh no,' cried Dwinoline. 'Is that really necessary?'

'A real mother does not think of her children in terms of punishment,' said Leperdandy, wrapping several slices of roasted bacon in a napkin. 'For us there will be no more eating of flesh. We are not barbarians. Giniva, let us leave the family to consider the ghastly error of their ways.'

He held out his slender hand and the Princess joined him, tripping from the hall.

'Betrayers. Wayward creatures,' muttered Asphyxia, but this morning her usual epithets lacked force.

'You have to admit they have some spine,' said Scarabold, looking after his children in some wonder and a little admiration.

68

Shapeshifter

Magister Ambrosius peered between his unguent pots at the newcomer.

In one of Dwinoline's tapestries he appeared to be wearing a black frock coat and a tall stovepipe hat, but obviously this was incorrect. Sometimes his hat was pointed and his coat was ermine, depending on whether he was teaching that the world was round or whether he was in his laboratorium.

Ambrosius knew that the former priests and the King himself disapproved of modern scientific thinking, but his discoveries were far ahead of their time. His meticulously copied papers would soon be lost to the world, wiped away by war, famine and fire.

'By the blessed virgins,' he said delightedly, 'it's rare that I receive a visit from my best pupil these days. To what do I owe the pleasure?'

Leperdandy walked around the equipment, pausing before a shaved cat with a glass tube protruding from its fat little stomach. 'What is this?' he asked.

'I'm decanting his blood,' said Ambrosius. 'There is much to be learned from feline humours. Cats have a limited genealogy that can be traced by the colour of their eyes, their bile, their phlegm and the markings on their fur. It's a pity the King ordered all the gingers to be burned.' He grabbed a white kitten and opened its eyes. 'Look – one blue eye, the other amber.'

'Why would you want to do that?'

'It provides us with clues about who we are. Royal families are no more complex, because they marry within themselves. I'm recreating your complete family tree. You have very unusual blood, you know.'

'I can imagine,' said Leperdandy. 'Are you sure it's a good idea to be poking about in our family history? People who do that have a habit of turning up in the sewer.'

'It's a scientific exercise, nothing more,' said the magister, un-alarmed. 'I'm hoping that my findings will one day prove helpful to your father.' He absently set the cat down in a bowl of apples. 'But I'm sure you didn't come here to discuss your abnormalities.'

'I wondered if you could help us . . . me.' He picked up a silver tube and looked along its length.

'I'll certainly try, my lord.'

'The Very Reverend Trebuthnot Skank-Damply.'

The magister thought for a minute but nothing came. 'I am not familiar.'

'He married my parents. Elderly, lives in the West Quadrant.'

'Boil on the forehead, trembling hands, hairy ears? Got into trouble for selling choirboys?'

'That's the one. I need you to speak to him.'

'Why me?'

'Because I cannot.'

Ambrosius was puzzled. 'But my lord, surely you may talk to whomever you please.'

'Not in this case. There is a scroll of betrothment. I need to know where it is. My position is delicate.' He tapped the side of his long nose.

The magister swallowed. 'May I ask if this is something that would incur the wrath of your father if he knew?'

'Yes, I imagine it would.'

Ambrosius feared his position would be much more delicate if he was caught countermanding the King's wishes. But he had fond memories of bouncing the boy on his knee when he was young, of showing him how birds fly, why flames scorch, how water turns solid. Watching his curiosity grow, his eyes widen with delight, his hands reaching out to touch a leaf and ask why it recoiled.

'Very well, my lord,' he said finally. 'I will do whatever I can to help you.'

Watborn was waiting in the shadows. When Giniva checked to make sure she was not being followed before returning to the Museum of the Dead the following morning, she failed to spot him. For a large man, he was good at being quiet, and was so motionless that he became almost invisible. However, tracking birds was easier than following a princess. The girl had a habit of stopping, turning about suddenly and going back, questioning herself all the way. He felt for her; there was no one she could trust or turn to except her brother, and for all his brave words Leperdandy seemed ill equipped to wage a war.

But war it would have to be. He had seen the dark crowds amassing beyond the treeline. He had also looked inside the kitchen pots and seen the reason. The stories that had been whispered in the village for so many years were true. Not that he was especially shocked; the result of power was unending appetite.

When Giniva turned on her heel again he was forced to drop back behind a statue of a horned demon embracing a goat. She paused for a moment, then took a step towards him. Watborn was aware that he had not washed. He remained motionless, holding his breath until she moved on.

He tracked her up staircases and across courtyards to the museum. At one point he was so close that he could almost reach out and touch her.

Instead, she suddenly faced him. 'You are not very discreet, are you? Why are you still following me?'

'It's best not to travel alone, Your Highness,' said Watborn. 'Your retinue—'

'—are silly ladies who would flee if a mouse ran across their path. You need a bath. Who are you now? You seem to have many identities. Come out where I can see you.'

He stepped from the shadows.

'You're wearing the insignia of the Imperial Archery and the ribbon of the King's Guard. You have shapeshifted again. Does this mean you have been set to guard me?'

'I go where I am needed,' said Watborn.

'And I need to be watched.'

'Not watched. Aided.'

'If I fight my father, whose side will you be on?'

'I will protect you.'

'You make it sound so simple. My father is taking us into a war he cannot win.'

'And yet I hope he will not,' Watborn ventured, 'because I can help you in your cause.'

'What cause is this?'

Watborn remembered to cast his eyes down. 'I speak out of turn.'

Her hands went to her hips. 'No, continue. I'm interested. Pray give me the benefit of your wisdom.'

'If you stay, you will be sold to the highest bidder. If you leave, the monarchy will fall.'

'And you have observed this, have you? Four hundred years of rule is about to end because you have decided to take an interest.'

'I meant no disrespect.'

Her voice was full of quiet fury. 'Why should we survive? We are reviled. We rule nothing. We have no lands, no assets, no reason to exist. So what would you have me do, commoner?'

Watborn was chastened. He had thought she would be pleased to find an ally. He saw that there could be only two positions within the court – master or servant – and was happy to be the latter. But even that role was not easily granted.

'It's true I know nothing of courtly politics,' he said, lowering his eyes. 'But I know when someone is at risk from enemies.'

Giniva was outraged. 'Do I look as if I need you to follow me about like a stray dog? You know nothing of our lives because we choose not to let you know. Now go about your business and stay away, shapeshifter, or we shall both have to pay the price.'

As she turned aside he glimpsed a flicker of fear in her eyes. He had been told to expect her protestations. He would bide his time and wait for an opportunity to prove himself.

But for now he had to stand by helplessly as she closed the door on him.

69

The Unchained Heart

She found Brasslight by the window, anxiously looking down into the grey mist. 'You must come with me now, while the coast is clear,' she said, taking his hand and leading him out into the corridor. 'Lean on me.'

'Where are we going?' Brasslight asked.

'To my suite. I have taken back my dressers' keys so no one else can gain access. I have a surprise for you.'

Brasslight was more agile than she had expected. He had bound his ankle in soft cloth and was able to walk upon it for a few paces at a time, even climbing the circular staircase to Giniva's apartment.

She unlocked the door and guided him inside the scented emporium.

'I have it,' she said excitedly, unwrapping the oilskin and removing the calf-covered foot. 'Vitrolio kept the tin one and will destroy it, so your secret is safe. Sit here by the grate and let me put it on for you.'

She placed Brasslight on a low stool by the fireplace and stooped to one knee in the cinders, tenderly unwinding the cloth from his stump. Then she slipped the foot beneath his ruined ankle.

'It's a perfect fit,' she said, pleased, doing up the straps. 'You must warn me if I bind you too tightly.'

'No,' said Brasslight, 'it feels as soft as a newborn lamb.'

'You'll have to stay here a while longer while you learn how to walk upon it. No one must suspect for a moment that your real foot is absent. The final stage will be to sew it to the flesh of your leg and make it part of you.'

Brasslight leaned on the Princess's arm and rose, finding his balance. 'I will repay your kindness a thousandfold.' He wavered, then lowered his right foot to the ground, slowly increasing his weight on it. The straps held fast. He took a step forward and lurched. 'The top one, just a little tighter.'

Giniva dropped and adjusted the buckle. 'Try again.'

Brasslight stepped forward once more. This time the movement was smoother, more natural. The joints had been oiled to copy the pulsation of the muscles.

'Better, but your right shoulder dipped. You must keep your carriage upright. Don't try to compensate with your other leg. Start by squaring your shoulders.' She rose and placed her hands either side of his collarbone. 'Now walk with me.' She stepped back, allowing him to move forward.

He found it difficult to stay in a straight line. 'I don't think my right ankle is strong enough.'

'You should see how I am shod by my mother for dances.' For the first time he smiled. She lightened her grip. 'Keep going.'

Leaning on her, he wavered forward. His posture straightened. His step quickened.

'Now we add soft leather shoes,' she said. 'Can't have you going around barefoot.' The learning process began again. With her hands on his shoulders she walked backwards, gently quickening the pace. 'I think you have the hang of it. Can you turn?'

It seemed he could not. He fell to the floor and looked up at her sheepishly. 'It's no good – I'll never walk like a normal person. No one will ever believe me.'

Giniva helped him up. 'You have to keep trying. You cannot give up now. See this?' She raised the chained golden heart at her neck. 'You know why it is criss-crossed with chains? It shows I am a captive. It was made for a martyred abbess, St Osyth. She was beheaded, and where she fell a spring issued forth from the ground. She picked up her head and walked to the door of her nunnery, and knocked three times on the door before collapsing. On her dying instructions, the heart was made and attached to her. But see here, on the reverse.'

She turned the heart over between two fingers and pressed the centre. The silver chains dropped away.

'It shows that the heart may be unbound. It is why you must never abandon hope.'

He examined the trinket, watching in fascination as she relocked it in place.

'Then I will not be bound either.'

His grave demeanour amused her. 'Wait,' she said, 'I have an idea. Something Ambrosius invented. He calls himself a teacher but we think of him as a magician.' Taking an ivory box from the shelf, she wound it and they began again. 'It is a system of cogs that strike different lengths of metal. There is no other in the land.'

A lilting tune allowed him to find his footing and keep time. 'And one, two, three – and one, two, three,' she said softly. 'Turn and reverse with me. Follow the rhythm.'

Soon they found themselves matching each other in perfect synchronization. She rewound the box and they continued around the room in a smooth circuit, then in a figure of eight.

'Watch my steps,' said Giniva. Brasslight lifted his right foot in time with the music. As the spring unwound and the song began to slow, she slowed with him. He slipped slightly, and she caught him under the arm, gently righting him. His armpit was warm and safe, like a sparrow's nest.

The music had come to a stop. Giniva's heart was beating hard in her breast. She raised her face and looked into his eyes. His hands moved from her waist to her shoulders.

'They speak of having me seeded, as if it were a matter of animal husbandry, without a kind eye or a warm touch. I have heard that when you look upon the one you love, your eyes soften and you see the world as a better place, that the very air changes its composition.'

'I believe that to be true,' Brasslight replied.

'Then why should I not be allowed that happiness?'

'Perhaps you will be, Giniva.'

She glanced towards the run-down music box. 'It has ended.'

'No.' He leaned forward and kissed her. The movement was as natural to him as breathing.

She opened her eyes and studied his, exhaling. There was a sharp flitter of lightning outside. As the storm rolled around them, her heartbeat joined his.

The way ahead is dangerous, she thought, breaking away in confusion. *Vigilance must be my watchword.*

She wondered if Watborn was still close by.

Her eye fell upon the coverlet of variegated silver damask,

beneath the clock of Fascinus. An odd fear settled over her, that their flirtation could turn to courtship and an impulsive consummation that would be the ruination of them all.

'You can't stay,' she warned.

'I have dreamed of such a moment as this,' said Brasslight happily, not hearing her.

70

The Outsider

'How soon can we get him up to the terraces?' asked Manticore, studying Watborn's form from the courtyard arch.

Vitrolio replaced a mace in the armoury rack. From without came the sound of soldiers in training. 'Why are you so convinced about this man?'

'He has a way of looking,' Manticore replied. 'There's much going on inside him. But he has no experience of combat. I'll not have him felled by the first green foot-soldier who approaches. He is unproven in battle.'

'If you place too much trust in him too quickly, the men will resent you.'

'I care not what they think. Their hearts are blind. They grew up under the King's protection and care only for their own comfort. Watborn is a different breed. The eyes of his heart have begun to see. He has a watchful spirit, although I doubt he knows where it is leading him.'

'Then let's test him,' Vitrolio replied, calling the birdcatcher over. Watborn had been at practice all morning but showed no sign of fatigue.

'Do you scare easily, lad, or can you keep your wits about you? The next thing you split will not be a log but another man's head.'

Watborn did not reply.

'There is to be a council of war with Grand-Marshal Timmorian tonight,' said Manticore. 'Better late than never, I suppose. We can take the Sheathwing if they come alone, but if they persuade others to their cause, we will be besieged by an endless wave of fighters.'

'Who else will join them?'

'The F'Arcys, certainly, and now les Sœurs aux Cadeaux Étranges, who already have an alliance with the Fraternity of the Green Corpse. The assassins of the Devil's Tongue have a history of working alone but could be persuaded to fight for spoils. The Martyrs of the Apocalypse live in the hills far above us but hate Scarabold for taking their slaves. The Army of Redeemers are fanatical Religiouses who seek new acolytes. All can be turned to attack the King.'

'So many tribes.' Watborn was awed.

'That's just the start of it. You should try travelling further north. They're all mad up there.'

'Does the King know about them?'

'He will not notice them until they pass a flaming spear beneath his whiskers.'

Manticore looked behind the birdcatcher. His opponents were watching him. He led the young man to one side.

'We have not been called upon to withstand a siege in centuries. I fear we are about to be sorely tested. There have been signs and portents. Comets have been seen, and it is said a maid gave birth to a three-headed dog.' He thought for a moment. 'Tell me, what do you think of those fine fellows you train with?'

Watborn knew when to hold his tongue. 'I was not raised within these walls, sir. We are as different as milk and mead.'

'You need to speak freely here.'

Watborn's tone was low and measured. 'I have not broken sweat.'

'Is it because they are weak?'

'They lack neither strength nor discipline, sir.' Watborn glanced back uneasily. 'They don't observe. I always see what they are about to do next. If they watch me, they will know where to strike and how hard.'

'Is it not something you can teach them?' asked Vitrolio. 'What if you instructed me and I passed on the advice as my own?'

Watborn gave an almost imperceptible nod.

'Then, as you have no lost breath to get back, we should start at once.' He sent the birdcatcher to his fellow archers.

'Speak to your brother,' Vitrolio now urged Manticore. 'He will know how much the pantries can provide if there is a blockade. Our preparations must be stepped up. The King's foolishness will be the undoing of us all.' He did not mention the part he had played in these political machinations.

'I hope they have a plan for us,' said Manticore. 'Later, Watborn can come with me to the munitions keep. We have no quartermaster and must make an inventory.'

Watborn remembered his times in the village hall when he had pressed upon his elders the importance of stockpiling supplies for the hard winter months. They had ignored him until he proved them right, then fell silent and resentful, their misguided beliefs unchanged.

When practice ended he followed Manticore to the keep.

A spiral staircase took them down six floors to a square chamber of grey granite. As they pushed back the doors, Watborn saw that no one had been inside for years. Cordite, gunpowder, dust and rot – their odours were knitted into the stale air.

Manticore limped over to the inner keep, an iron cage with a great lock, and searched among his keys. 'Here we keep the ammunition supplies. It's ruinous for an armoury to undergo an extended period of peace.'

'Let me try,' Watborn offered. The key would not fit because the ancient lock had rusted. Gripping it in his fists, he was able to smash it apart against the bars. He dropped the pieces with an air of apology. Mice scattered in every direction.

Inside, one end of the sloping floor was filled with stagnant water. They uncovered the corroded, soaked remains of shells and bombs, brown and black and green, once volatile, now as dead as the rodents surrounding them. Less than a quarter of the supply was salvageable, and most of that would be too dangerous to use.

'Is there time to cast new ammunition?' Watborn asked.

'We can start.' Manticore brushed back his moustaches as he considered the problem. 'The furnaces are lit and Malleus the blacksmith will be able to muster men with enough skill to help him, but we have no idea when the enemy will strike, or how numerous they will be. They wait on the ridges in silence, but as soon as their plans are formulated they will start to move. I fear our rulers will act rashly and tell us nothing until it is too late.'

'Why can't they keep us all informed?'

'That is not the way we do things here,' said Manticore with a helpless shrug. 'The rulers keep their subjects in ignorance. It makes life easier. As for our men, each has but a single task to perform and knows no other. They have had too much time on their hands. They have grown soft.'

'It is not my place—' Watborn began.

'It is not, yet you may pass on your observations. As an outsider, you are well situated to do so.'

Manticore brought his company of archers down to the keep to help with the moving of the munitions. He watched as Watborn shifted a cradle of explosives that three men would have had trouble lifting. Eager and tireless, he performed each task with quiet determination, switching to help the others whenever they struggled. The birdcatcher's attitude was so different that they decided he must have been raised outside. If that was the case, they had broken the law in taking him on – what if he was a spy? Manticore had noted three neat gashes on Watborn's right forearm, long healed.

'How did you get those scars?'

'It was my own fault,' Watborn replied. 'It will not happen again.'

'You are not from here.'

'I am of this land, and have seen this place every day of my life.'

'But from a great distance.' Manticore took his silence to be an affirmation. 'So why come here now?'

'My village is gone.'

'And you would lay down your life for the King?'

'I know I am rough-mannered, for I was not raised in your ways, but I will fight with my fellow countrymen against strange invaders. I am no mercenary.'

'Well put, lad. Our fighting force is mostly made up of men who can brawl and do little else. You will be valuable to us in the dark days ahead.'

Watborn was humbled. 'You and your brother have been kind to me.'

'Not kind, I think,' said Manticore. 'You are useful. We understand what will happen if we fall. Londinium is the heart of the land, and while it endures, our position will be maintained.'

'So we are to be tested.' Watborn unsealed an oilskin that covered dozens of small bombs in perfect condition.

Manticore helped him open the dry stock. 'The commander and his general carry out the instruction of the King, but all will be for naught if the King's judgement is clouded. You must look for infiltrators and assassins.' He tapped the iron disc on Watborn's jerkin. 'As a King's militiaman, that gets you entry to any part of the castle.

Tell me what you see. Then we will decide whether to await orders or act alone.'

'Am I to spy?'

'No,' said Manticore emphatically, 'you are to provide us with the sight we do not have. Report back to me before practice tomorrow. We may yet be able to save the King from himself.'

71

Holy Orders

'You realize this goes against everything we stand for,' said Sister Devotia, hurrying to keep up with the Reverend Mother.

Lady Lavinia Travernum ducked beneath the low arch to avoid snagging her bonnet. 'Our Lord and Saviour was not a man of peace, sister,' she said as they rushed along the corridor. 'He was a warrior who believed that only by vanquishing our enemies could we spread the one true religion. Surely I don't have to tell you that?'

'But we are an order of penance and reflective calm, of unity and respect, utterly opposed to conflict and factionalism.'

'Don't use long words with me,' the Reverend Mother warned. 'Religion provides no refuge for the intellect. Our acolytes follow us because they lack the ability to make sense of the world. It is easier to become devotional than to think for yourself.'

'That is heresy, my lady.' Sister Devotia dropped low to avoid being hit in the head with a latticework thurible.

'Nonsense, it is pragmatic. Through their dedication we find enlightenment. What, did you think faith was classless? The ones who suffer most are at the bottom because they expect to be. We will unite the kingdom and prepare it for Paradise, you can be quite sure of that, but they will suffer heavy casualties. This is a holy war, sister, and it is no time to shrink from the more unpleasant aspects of our duty.'

It might also have been considered heresy to tell the King that they were a silent order, thought Sister Devotia. They were quite happy to speak aloud to one another when circumstances required it. These were, she reflected, hypocritical times.

They had arrived at the chancery, a plain chamber of inlaid

wooden benches and candelabras where les Sœurs aux Cadeaux Étranges settled legal matters pertaining to their order. Sister Devotia took her place beside the other members of the senior council as Lady Lavinia rose to address them.

'Sisters, you know of the outrages visited upon us by King Scarabold. Now word reaches me of further crimes against our covenant. The Great Wound has defied our demand to return the treasure he stole from us, and through his wayward actions has united the armies of Sheathwing, F'Arcy and St Stanivar against him. Now we too have a just cause. The Vessel of All Counted Sorrows was left in our sacred trust and for the sake of our land must remain with us in perpetuity. For the faithful it represents tangible evidence of their belief.'

'And for us too, Reverend Mother,' piped up Sister Minimus.

'Quite so,' said Lady Lavinia, moving swiftly on. Her own belief was rooted in pragmatism. 'Our mission is therefore a holy one: to return the vessel to its rightful place here at Cadeaux Étranges, and to end once and for all the tyranny of the royal family.'

Sister Minimus raised a timid hand. 'We are a peaceful order, Reverend Mother. How can we achieve this aim without breaking our vows?'

'Quite obviously, we cannot,' said Lady Lavinia impatiently, 'but there are others who can act for us. I have spoken with several of our greatest allies, including the Fraternity of the Green Corpse. We have reached an agreement to send our oldest friend, Sir Roger de la Zleuze, to see the King at once and demand the return of the vessel.'

'There can be no further bloodshed,' warned Sister Devotia.

'Rest assured that Sir Roger has been specifically instructed to do no more than is required to defend himself and his warriors.'

'Why should any man help us?' asked Sister Thrushgrave, who could display remarkable cynicism for a woman under holy orders.

'You forget that his mother served Cadeaux Étranges loyally for many years before succumbing to putrefaction. Sir Roger is a man of peace but he assures me he will cut off his enemy's danglements if he has to. We will regain what is rightfully ours, usurping Scarabold in the process. If we fail, our allies will join with all those who seek vengeance against him.'

She studied each of them in turn, the better to impress upon them her point. 'One way or the other, the House will be returned to the watchful hearts of the gods.'

285

72

A Foolproof System

Magister Ambrosius tended to hurtle. His legs were as thin as stalks. His long chin was thrust purposefully forward, and his robe flew out behind him. He moved like a heron striding across mud-flats as he approached the door of the basilica.

The Very Reverend Trebuthnot Skank-Damply appeared as worn down as the stones that surrounded him. He was sponging soup from his soutane in the vestibule of the chapel dining hall when Ambrosius arrived, and was flustered by the unannounced visit.

'You must excuse me,' he apologized. 'I've been serving the midday meal. You never know what you'll get down your cassock around choirboys. We had a chef and a waiter once, but Mr Thredneedle said it was unprofitable to retain them. Won't you walk with me? I must attend to my ecclesiastical duties.' Not that he had any.

He led the way through a hall so dark that it had to be torch-lit at the height of summer. In the nave of his basilica the crystal sanctuary-lamps burned sweat-grass incense, casting a blood-red glow across the walls.

The castle-city held within itself the remains of an old church constructed over a temple. There were chapels of every shape and size, but none of them was legally sanctioned for prayer. It made being a man of the cloth terribly trying. Worship would return, he felt sure, but only after the faithless had been obliterated.

Skank-Damply pushed open the chapel door and led the way to an altar so covered in ancient candle-wax that it looked like a range of mountains.

'I hope Father Sesquinatius and the Bishop are fully recovered after the Princess's banquet,' said Ambrosius, doffing his hat.

'What a misfortune,' opined the reverend. 'So many dead, and at a birthday celebration, too. Poor Cardinal Weem was invited at the last minute and got a bannister through his head. What can I do for you?'

'Reverend Damp-Skankly—'

'Skank-Damply.'

'Yes, I understand that you officiated at the wedding service of King Scarabold and Mater Moribund.'

'Indeed, and a memorable day that was. Not a happy one, but certainly memorable. I often wonder how Lady Dwinoline felt, watching her replacement taking vows with the husband to whom she was still married.'

'It's interesting to note that polygyny is generally associated with two states: heathenism and devout religion,' commented the magister.

'Of course, the female is of naturally inferior status, but one sometimes can't help wonder what they feel.' The reverend stopped before the altar and buffed his ciborium with a freshly starched purificator.

'Reverend Dank-Scamply—'

'Skank-Damply.'

'The royal couple were not just bound by spoken ritual. There was a scroll of betrothment, was there not?'

'Indeed.' He steepled his branch-like fingers. 'Although they are the reigning monarchs they are not absolved from the laws of the land, and must sign affidavits that signify there are no impediments to the union and so on.'

Ambrosius felt the need to tread lightly. The reverend was known to have the ear of several lords, and information was freely reported back to them. 'So it was all straightforward. There were no ... anomalies ... in the written process.'

'Why are you asking?'

'Reverend Scamp-Dankly—'

'Skank-Damply.'

'—I have been asked to create a new family tree.' This was not an untruthful statement, although his own researches mainly involved bloodlines and their mutations. 'To complete this process I need to examine all documentation pertaining to the marriage.'

The reverend cast a critical eye over the altar and straightened his monstrance, which had developed a distinct lean. 'Ah yes, you mentioned the scroll of betrothment. I'm afraid I am unable to let you have access to that.'

'It is placed under lock and key, I take it?'

The vicar laughed. 'Heavens, no – there is no need. As tradition dictates, after it was signed it was placed upon the tabernacle in the Haven of the Afterlife.'

'I've never heard of such a place,' said Ambrosius. 'Is it new?'

'My dear fellow, it was probably there in the time before the First Occupation. It was builded in the bowels of the earth, accessible only via the Tunnel of the Damned – not as formidable as it sounds, but it keeps out the riff-raff – and it is guarded day and night.'

'Oh?' Ambrosius was intrigued. 'Guarded by whom?'

'Not by whom, sir – by what. It is protected at all times by Black Shag, the Hell-Hound of Gash. A most unlikely name, I know, but it serves as a warning. The vicious beast has been taught to love the taste of human flesh.'

'It must be very old,' said Ambrosius dubiously.

Skank-Damply laughed. 'No, no, it has a normal lifespan, I assure you. I've never seen it, but I believe the current hell-hound is the forty-third in its line. Heaven knows what was there before him – some sort of prehistoric creature, probably.'

Ambrosius had the distinct impression that his leg was being pulled.

'The Haven of the Afterlife houses the private correspondence that exists between Church and State, although its protection lies with us, which is why you have probably never heard of it.'

'Why would it need to be guarded so fiercely?'

The vicar gave a little squeak of laughter. 'Why, it is the very bedrock upon which the monarchy is founded. Nothing and no one may be allowed in or out of the central chamber.'

Possessing a scientifically rational turn of mind, the magister was not quite ready to be put off. 'But presumably you had to place the scroll inside it – why did the creature not attack you?'

'It most assuredly would have done, but there is a system. If you'll indulge me for a moment?'

He took a torch from the sconce and led the way behind the chancel screen to a moth-eaten tapestry. Lifting one corner of the cloth, he pointed at a peculiarly shaped stone protrusion in the floor. The magister crouched down beside him.

'This is the delivery-tube,' he explained, pointing to a two-foot-wide hole in the top. 'The documents are tied and sealed, and dropped in here. Then a system of channels sends each one into the correct receptacle.'

'This is most interesting, and useful for my research,' said Ambrosius. 'But surely someone still has to take care of the creature that stands guard?'

'Of course, and that is Fumblegut's job. It used to be the responsibility of Manticore, the Yeoman of the Guard, but since the cutbacks that task has fallen to our jailer.'

'Forgive me.' Ambrosius wondered how much more information he could extract without arousing suspicion. 'Is Fumblegut the most trustworthy subject for such an onerous task?'

'I take your point,' said the man of the cloth, resealing the arras, 'but there is a method for dealing with Black Shag.'

'And what is that?' he asked as casually as he could.

'I suppose there's no harm in telling you, magister. A silver whistle, made by the forefathers of Malleus the blacksmith. The hound is trained to be put to sleep by its sound, rather as a bell may be rung to bring the creature to its supper.'

'A most ingenious idea!' Ambrosius clapped his hands. 'Is the resourcefulness of the human mind not a wonderful thing to behold? Even so, such a clever device is only as good as its user, and I fear that in the case of Fumblegut—'

'Oh, it's not in Fumblegut's hands,' the vicar assured him. 'That's the most ingenious part of the system. It is inside the cage of his malicious orang-utan, M'Lin, attached to the chain around his foul neck.' He smiled. 'So you see, its security is quite foolproof.'

73

Heir to the Throne

Giniva ran a peacock feather across her pale ribcage and hummed a summer air. Sunlight fell from the mullioned window, spackling its shaft with golden motes of dust. She fancied the room smelled of sea and fresh-cut grass.

Her onyx jewel-casket lay open on the bed. She raised a necklace of peridots, fire opals and carnelians, watching the colours refract across the counterpane. Brasslight was by the window, walking back and forth on his new foot.

I deserve happiness, she thought. *Even if it does not last, I shall have this moment. I have been kissed, and my embrace returned.* It was impossible to know what her father would do when he discovered there was a claimant to the throne backed by his own daughter.

'It's so quiet,' she murmured. 'I can hear swallows diving past the window.'

'My foot needs oiling,' said Brasslight, tipping forward on to his toes. 'It creaks.'

'Swallows soaring high into the blue, blue sky.'

'They're not flying for joy, Giniva, they're catching insects, otherwise they would starve. Everything is fighting to survive.' Brasslight threw himself on to her eiderdown and stared into her eyes.

She tossed her hair. 'The birds can't see how beautiful I am.'

'They should be able to; they have very good eyesight. Don't you see, though? Together we could be invincible. Two acting as one. We could rule the world. Don't you feel it? You and I – we can bring an end to all of this.'

'It may not be as easy as you think,' the Princess warned, sitting up a little. 'You were raised by the Sisters in contemplative iso-lation. You know little of the true world.'

'You mean this place.'

'Indeed, for it is my world. A place of blood and shadows where treachery and deceit lie in wait for the innocent.'

'Fortune favours the brave.' He jumped up and began walking about once more.

'We must tread warily.' As she watched him teeter back and forth on the false foot, her words took on an alarming new meaning. One misstep could destroy them both. 'Scarabold has a way of effortlessly vanquishing his enemies. Look how he got rid of F'Arcy and the Sheathwing.'

'He didn't get rid of them, Giniva. You and your brother did. You two are your father's saviours. The old man must know now that he is a spent force.'

'You have no idea what my father is like,' she said.

'You are the blood of his blood. Surely he would allow no harm to come to you.'

'He had my brother tortured.'

'Leperdandy was branded a weakling at birth; look at the name he was given, that came to define him! It suited your family to remove him from favour. You are your father's love-apple.'

'And where does that leave you, Brasslight?' she asked. 'He has no reason to hold you dear. There was no love lost between the Great Wound and his brother.'

'Perhaps, but he must honour the line of the Crown, and *I*' – here Brasslight thumped his chest – 'I am the natural heir. There is no proof that I was born without a foot.'

'Dr Fangle knew. No one listened to him, or indeed could under-stand him, and now he is gone.'

'If we can convince Scarabold that the doctor lied, we have a case.'

'Why not tell the truth and say that Minerva stole you away to be raised by the Sisters?' Giniva suggested. 'He would not have to be informed of your missing appendage.'

'Then why would she have stolen me away?' He lowered himself to one knee and listened for the creak.

'We could say she is secretly a Religious. But no, he would have her burned alive.'

'Your father will listen to you, whatever you say. And with you at my side, your belly ripe with an heir to the throne, he will find it hard to refuse our entitlement.'

She touched her bare stomach. For a moment, a chill breeze stippled her flesh. What if she had exchanged one trap for another, albeit one that was lined with silk?

Brasslight warmed to his subject. 'I mean, you wouldn't even need to have children at once, don't you see? It will take time to get everything working properly again. These things can't happen overnight without a revolution, and this place has seen enough bloodshed. Imagine, Giniva, a new order rising with your children in line to make sure that it survives for a thousand years!'

She watched the boy earnestly pressing heel to toe, heel to toe, trying to move with natural grace, and suddenly began to fear for them both.

74

The Inconsequence of Sir Roger

The head cook, Goldhawk, gave Watborn a map, although parts of it were scorched, stained or simply missing. The main buildings were marked but as for who lived where, it was impossible to know.

Luckily the kitchen staff possessed a second map showing the passageways, tunnels and backstairs routes they used to avoid running into those whom they served. Many of these cut-throughs had gaps in their brickwork or statues that could be moved to reveal peepholes into private chambers.

'Don't hide and sneak like Asphyxia's twins,' Manticore told him. 'Your best defence is your honesty. As a King's militiaman you are allowed everywhere. You are here to protect us all.'

Watborn was despatched to the upper reaches to learn what he could. He marked down the inhabitants of every floor, and although he quickly discovered that the castle was a hotbed of amorous activity, he paid no heed to gossip or hearsay. There was something about his sturdy appearance and open looks that made others want to befriend him, so he listened while they talked.

The next morning, before he headed off to make his first report to Manticore, he stood on the chill battlements and watched as Sir Roger de la Zleuze reached the drawbridge.

Watborn had never seen the like. The knight was clad in spectacular dress-armour of finely beaten copper that gleamed even in the autumnal half-light. He was immaculate but for his scruffy grey beard, which he kept as an indication of his affinity with peasants. Like all politicians, he liked to pretend that he had the common touch.

However, the arrival of Sir Roger from the Fraternity of the

Green Corpse should not occupy us for long; he turns out to be a sidebar, a dangling participle, an appendix, nothing more.

The birdcatcher looked down from the battlements and saw all, and what happened was this:

Dismounting outside one of the gates, Sir Roger raised his visor and looked up at the great stone lion that bestrode the peak of Londinium. It seemed designed to strike fear into the hearts of all who saw it. Undeterred, he demanded entry.

Unfortunately he spoke so quietly and inconspicuously that nobody heard him. Half a dozen guards stood leaning on the crenellations, buffing their bayonets and honking out the contents of their noses, watching his arrival with disinterest.

Setting aside his standard, Sir Roger waved his cavalry back. The standard featured a red spear piercing the chest of a green man on a white background. The man's liver was on the end of the spear.

'You can let me deal with these upstarts alone,' he called to his men in a voice no louder than that of a mouse in a drainpipe.

'You can't come in,' shouted one of the guards, nodding to his mate. 'They can't come in, can they?'

'I am here to hold parley with your crown sovereign,' called Sir Roger.

The guard raised a leg and broke wind. 'I'm afraid you just missed him. He's gone out.'

'What do you mean, he's gone out? Kings don't go out.'

'He went for a walk.'

Sir Roger looked around, something he had trouble doing, for his helmet was fitted too low and partially obscured his vision. 'Without his retinue?'

'He's the King. It's not our business to ask why.'

'Well, do you know when he's likely to be back?'

'What time do the shops shut?' the guard asked his mate. Manticore the yeoman appeared beside them and joined in the laughter.

Sir Roger was not so easily mollified. 'Sir, I am of the royal family of Zleuze of the Fraternity of the Green Corpse, founder of the Grand Order of the Holy Star, and I demand entry. If the King is absent, I will speak with his minister of war.'

'I'm sorry, he went out as well,' said Manticore. 'We could get you someone in the judicial department.'

Sir Roger looked back at his troops. 'What do you think?' he asked. But they did not like having their opinions canvassed. They were waiting for him to take the lead. Watborn peered over the parapet, watching in fascination.

'Look here, who is your most senior official?'

'That would be Grand Judge Pandergreen,' said Manticore.

'Well, can you get him?'

'I don't know. We'll see what we can do. Who did you say was calling again?'

'Sir Roger de la Zleuze.'

One of the guards spat his chewing root, spattering it beside Sir Roger's foot. 'He's probably at stool around this time, but we'll try him for you.'

'Then kindly do so.' Sir Roger waved them away impatiently.

'You'll have to give us a few minutes,' said Manticore. 'The judge is old and moves slowly. We'll fetch him up.' Two heads disappeared. The remaining guards continued to look down over the wall, studying Sir Roger's finely attired cavalry soldiers as if planning to barter for their pennants.

Sir Roger had only brought six of his own men, for in truth he had somewhat exaggerated his resources to les Sœurs aux Cadeaux Étranges in the hope that they would reward him upon his return with the vessel. He had many more troops in Green Corpse, but they were not presently motivated for a fight as they had not been paid in over a year.

The knight was not concerned by the peculiar confidence of the guards, for it did not cross his mind that there might be subterfuge. He assumed that they were merely in awe of him.

Sir Roger waited patiently with his troops. A wind began to rise in the cypress avenue behind them. The golden pennants lifted and fluttered magnificently. *Tap, tap, tap.* A curious squeaking sound emanated from behind the crenellations of the battlements.

Eventually the two missing guards reappeared. 'They've brought the judge,' said Manticore. 'He's only got one leg and can't manage the stairs. He can talk to you through the wall. Stand over here.' He pointed to a bare spot close to one of the shut gates.

Sir Roger reluctantly did as he was told and took two long strides forward.

'A bit to the left.'

He moved slightly, feeling himself losing the respect of his men.

'A bit more.'

The squeaking from above stopped and a new grinding noise replaced it. The knight looked up in time to see the machicolation, the gap between the wall's corbels, filling with turbulent vermilion liquid.

A thick rope of boiling lead fell perfectly downwards, into the upturned helmet of Sir Roger, searing away his visor, skin, meat, guts and sundry organs right through the copper suit until it settled into the tips of his gauntlets and the toes of his boots, at which point it rapidly cooled and hardened, leaving him a statue of his former self.

After a few minutes one of the guards opened a side gate, wandered out and raised his boot high, kicking the suit over so that it fell into the outer moat with a bang and a sizzle. Then he went back inside and slammed the gate shut.

The cavalry soldiers looked at one another, wondering what to do. Along the battlements there were now twenty archers with drawn bows. There was no point in fighting back, as it seemed certain that they would be slaughtered before they could reach the avenue of cypresses.

'We like your pennants,' said Manticore. 'We'll let you go if you give them to us. How about that?'

75

To Halt the Reckoning

Lady Dwinoline was attempting to fold a length of cretonne embroidery, but her kitten insisted on trying to pull threads. 'I don't see what you expect me to do,' she told Mater Moribund, who had glided in just as the sun was starting to sink. 'Light the candelabra, will you?'

'You have people to do that sort of thing for you, Dwinoline – did you never learn in all these years?' The Mater plucked up a taper and struck it alight with distaste.

'It's a small job and hardly worth disturbing the staff,' she said. 'I never had long enough to adjust to servants. I was Queen for such a short time before you came along.' If it sounded like a rebuke, Moribund failed to notice, as she was busy touching each of the tallows in turn.

'You have seen the moon. You do understand what will happen tomorrow night if Giniva continues to behave in this flagrant fashion,' the Mater warned. 'But of course, you don't. She is my daughter, not yours, so how could you be expected to understand? Whatever else you may think of me, I am a caring mother.' She kicked the kitten aside and seated herself in a whisper of black chenille.

Dwinoline knotted the last thread and bit it off between her teeth. 'I agree that Giniva's ways have been errant of late, but I'm sure she can be encouraged to show remorse.'

'How?' asked Moribund. 'She has run out of time.'

'She is allowed three suitors, and the Reckoning has yet to be scheduled. The ceremony has not been performed in my lifetime. Perhaps it is little more than a phantasm created to frighten the young into proper behaviour.'

Moribund leaned forward in a conspiratorial manner. 'It strikes me that we could do something.'

'What can we do?' asked Dwinoline hopelessly. 'We are but women.'

'We have power, even you,' she said grudgingly. 'We could force Scarabold to stop the ritual.'

'How would we do that?'

'Not everything is achievable by force alone.' Moribund settled back in her high chair. For once she had no easy answer for the situation, because no situation like this had ever arisen before. Silence filled the room. A candle popped and guttered.

'We must halt the Reckoning before it becomes a legal necessity.' Dwinoline examined her hands, knotted from years of holding her tapestry needle. 'What exactly is it?'

Moribund gave a shrug. 'It has no standard form. If the Princess is unwilling to take an appointed suitor, the Reckoning will punish her for making her own decisions. I believe it is a ritual intended to teach the meaning of control. We could insist that it passes through the due process of the law. Then it would have to be given the seal of approval by Grand Judge Arnelthus Pandergreen himself, not one of his lawyers.'

'So we should ask for clemency?'

'Good Lord, no, but I may be able to blackmail him.' Moribund stroked her chin, thinking. 'Leave this to me.'

76

Strength and Compassion

At the setting of the sun, the conspirators met in the chantry. Ambrosius, the most reluctant of the rebels, took his place between the Princess, her brother and the young claimant to the crown.

'This is dangerous knowledge,' the magister warned, setting aside the white clay pipe that was always to be found clenched between his teeth when he needed to think. 'The bats are gathering around us.' It was an expression the older generation usually used to describe the approach of death, and felt far from encouraging. 'Apart from the personal risk to yourselves, you will be jeopardizing the realm. You must temper your ambition with caution.'

Giniva sought to reassure him. 'We are a family. Behind the titles we are still mothers, father, daughter, sons. What we are embarking upon is a mission to save the family, not destroy it.'

'The Great Wound may not see it that way. If you countermand his desires and act against the accordance of his wishes, he will be forced to decide between the survival of the line and the behaviour of his children.'

Giniva made fists of frustration. 'Why do the old never understand the views of the young?'

'You think we have not travelled the same roads, reached the same junctions in our lives?' The magister's eyes held the wisdom of his years. 'The old know all the secrets of the young. Kingdoms do not hang upon our decisions, but what we choose alters how we are seen by those we love – in that respect we are all cut from the same cloth. The heart unites monarchs and farmers.'

'There is a difference,' said Leperdandy. 'The King must place duty above all or his subjects will think him weak. We have to show something more. Strength first, compassion after.'

'Strength and compassion,' repeated Brasslight, holding out his arm and making a fist.

'Strength and compassion.' Giniva placed her hand tightly over his.

'Strength and compassion.' Leperdandy made the union triumvirate.

Ambrosius rose. 'Very well. If you three are to act, it must be before moonrise tomorrow, for the lunar cycle is at its close and your destiny must be fulfilled by then. If not . . .'

'What?' asked Giniva.

'Why, I thought you knew,' said the mage, shifting uncomfortably. 'If there is no marriage agreement by the time of the new moon, the Reckoning will take place.'

'I don't understand.' Giniva looked to the others in puzzlement. 'What is this Reckoning?'

'A test,' said Ambrosius. His hands fluttered evasively.

'We don't do tests,' said Leperdandy. 'We're high-borns.'

'This is a special test, my lord. It has mystical origins. No one knows what it is or how it works. It simply happens when the time is most propitious. The Crown has failed to, ah, ensure the Princess's fertility, as it were, and so she must be tested.'

Giniva stared at him in disbelief for a few seconds, then laughed bitterly. 'What, I am to be punished for avoiding rapine?'

'I am only the keeper of records, not the archives – that is the province of the Decrepend. I am required to ratify the scientific.'

'Could this test harm my sister?' Leperdandy demanded.

'Heavenfall, no, not physically.' The magister looked mortified. He turned to Giniva, anxious to reassure her. 'The Reckoning is a dark prophecy. It has not taken place in my long lifetime but it exists in different forms throughout our history, since the time of the ghosts who existed here, and it is not arranged by kings but by Fate itself. Your refusal to provide an heir from the available choices means that you must be brought to a reconciliation.'

'Doctor, you're talking in riddles. This ritual is sanctioned by my parents?'

'It merely exists. Only the seers know all of it. You comprehend that for every action there is a consequence, yes? And that some of these consequences can last for generations?'

'Of course,' said Giniva. 'You taught us this as children.'

'Then you know what the Reckoning is for. It is a cancelling out. It draws power through your choices and closes them off so that all can move on.' He cast his gaze to the floor. 'Two suitors of the King's choosing are dead, two chances gone, and no further choice left in sight ere moonrise. I'm afraid it does not bode well for you.'

'I still don't understand what you're saying,' said Giniva softly. 'If you are loyal to me still, you must reveal my fate.'

In the gathering darkness Ambrosius could barely be seen beneath the brim of his hat. 'The Reckoning is different for everyone who undergoes it. Calmora the Seer says that for you the event is already foretold. You will meet Pok-Pok, the One Who Moves in the Shadows.'

'Where? When?'

'The time and place cannot be known.'

'I have never heard of such a being.'

'No, I don't think anyone has. Perhaps he does not exist.'

'Oh, this is nonsense,' Leperdandy cried impatiently.

'Will I survive?' Giniva asked.

'You will, but you will not be . . . the same.'

A cloud passed across the dying sun, and the chantry sank into darkness. 'Talk to the seer,' said Ambrosius. 'She may be able to tell you more.'

When Giniva left the presence of the magister, Watborn moved silently in her wake.

He glimpsed her in the embrasures between aumbry and candlestick and reredos, slipping through archways and up staircases, flashing through stripes of light and shadow. He saw her step around a tortoise and dispel a cloud of blackflies. He was meant to be watching the King's council chamber but the Princess, though wayward and dismissive, had imprinted herself upon his heart.

One trusts the things one understands.

77

The Heart Has Its Reasons

Calmora the Seer had been waiting for the Princess to appear, although in truth she had been warned of her imminent arrival and had had time to arrange the Sepulchre of the Oracle to its best effect. There were very few comings and goings here that somebody somewhere did not know about.

'You again,' said Calmora, who was so white of face and hair, so soft of feature and transparent of skin that she barely seemed to exist.

'Where are you?' asked Giniva.

'Over here.'

'Ah. You are impossible to separate from your surroundings.'

In her hands Calmora held a ball of cool alabaster, which she passed from palm to palm. Giniva noticed a tall pile of ancient volumes stacked behind her.

'Do those books belong to ancient mystics?' she asked.

'No, to the library,' said Calmora. 'I must remember to take them back. I'm exhausted. Did you bring anything to eat with you?'

The Princess dug a cloth packet from her dress and handed it over. 'You have worn yourself out issuing predictions.'

'No, I drank too much last night. What is this?'

'A fennel sugar-pastry.'

Calmora peered inside the sweetmeat. 'Has it got nuts in?'

'I wish to know about the Reckoning and what may be required of me.' Giniva barely possessed the patience needed to seat herself for the interview.

'Well, it's a test,' Calmora replied with her mouth full.

'So I hear. When will it take place?'

'When you least expect it.'

'And where will this be?'

'In the place where you feel most safe.' She ran a finger around the inside of her mouth, then wiped her hands on her gown.

'It's a bit vague.'

'I'm a seer,' Calmora reminded her. 'We're always a bit vague.' She picked up the alabaster ball and rolled it from one hand to the other.

Giniva pouted. 'Why should it be me who has to pass a test?'

'Because you are destined to do so. Princess and so forth.' The ball rolled backward and forward.

This is hopeless, she thought, *the woman talks in riddles that may be interpreted in any manner.* 'I must have one clear answer to a question,' she warned.

Calmora sighed wearily and clutched her head. 'Very well. Ask it of me.'

'I wish to know if I will survive this ordeal,' Giniva said.

'Tell me what you feel.' Calmora leaned forward and placed the alabaster ball in her palms.

One side of the stone ball grew hot under her fingers. With a yelp she transferred her hands to the cool side, which grew colder. Calmora watched her for a moment, then took back the ball. Its heat did not appear to bother her.

'There. You have your answer,' she said. 'Part of you will live, and part of you will die.'

Watborn kept his eye on the King from a window above the minstrels' gallery, but it sat ill with him to do so. Spying was sly and unmanly, a coward's profession that risked betrayal. He could not hear the others but the King's words boomed so loudly through the clear air that he might have been making a speech before thousands.

Scarabold was struggling to remove the labrys from above the fireplace. The double-bitted axe was three feet long and either of its blades could shave the bristles from a badger.

'I do not give a ferryman's fart for Sir Roger of the Sluice or whatever he's called,' he bellowed. 'I would not give one of my arse-hairs to know if he was diced, minced, shredded, staked, baked, blasted or regurgitated by pigs. What I care about is that *you* gave the order to have him evaporated, and not your King.'

Manticore blanched. The Yeoman of the Guard had not intended to incur the wrath of his sovereign. He knew that his new observer was watching and feared a loss of face in every sense. 'Your Majesty, I did not imagine that you would care to deal with such a trifling problem as Sir Roger yourself.'

Scarabold hefted the shaft of the axe in his palm and gave it an exploratory swing that caused Manticore to move beyond his reach. 'If I had decided he was beneath our concern, I would have dealt with him accordingly, which would very likely not have involved filling him full of boiling lead and booting him to the bottom of the moat.'

'I know Your Majesty has a great many affairs of state to which he must attend, and sought to alleviate him – I mean, you – of his . . . ah, that is, your . . .' Manticore strangled himself with the grammatical demands of correctly addressing a monarch and decided to shut up.

'Did it ever occur to you that he might have made a decent suitor for my daughter? He could have been the third choice.' He swung the labrys and embedded its head deep in a prayer-table, sending a spray of splinters across the room. 'Time has almost run out. Do you think I want to sacrifice my daughter to some kind of red-eyed thing that reputedly wanders about the undercrypt looking for victims just because it's mentioned in the Royal Charter? What kind of monster do you think I am?' He pulled the axe free and the table fell apart.

Manticore decided not to prostrate himself so long as the labrys was in the King's hands. 'What can I do to make amends, Your Majesty?' he asked anxiously.

'Find me someone who can marry her before moonrise tomorrow and prevent our line from coming to an end.' The Great Wound dropped the axe with a clang and ran his great dry palms over his scarred face. 'I can't leave it to her. You know what the young are like, as thin-skinned as onions and full of grand ideas, but incapable of pissing out a fire in their own breeches.'

'What qualifications do you seek in this . . . person?' Manticore enquired.

Scarabold breathed out between his fingers. It was the sound of a storm-wind breaching a line of trees. 'He must be free of the pox, full-membered and fertile, and he must stay alive long enough to complete the act,' he murmured. 'He must also be from a royal bloodline without too many intermarried cousins, with full treasury coffers and plenty of land. Why is it so hard to find anyone with those qualifications?'

'Your Majesty, perhaps under the circumstances it might be best to take another approach,' Manticore suggested, 'and petition the lawyers to reinterpret the law.'

'Our laws were set by long-dead men,' said Scarabold. 'The King of all I survey and yet I would be bounded in a walnut shell. Do you have children, Manticore?'

'No, Your Majesty.' It was most unlike the King to enquire about anyone else. Was he ill?

'There is nothing you can explain about them to others that does not wither the attention. Yet they are your world and purpose. My daughter does not care about continuing the line or staying here in the bosom of her family. Perhaps she is a changeling. She renders me powerless. I would do anything to stop this Reckoning but I don't even know what it is.' The Great Wound sighed. The sound was like pebbles being dragged by lunar tides. 'Go on, get out.'

Scarabold turned away, his great gnarled head slumping between his shoulders. Manticore did not need to be told twice. He fled the room, grateful to find his own head still atop his neck, and met with Watborn on the stairs.

'You understand the problem?' he asked as they descended the slippery steps. 'A King heeds no advice. It is beyond his ability to follow the words of others.' He stopped at an embrasure and allowed the cool updraught to dry his sweat. 'If our enemies arrive at a mutual accord, they will strike as a single force. In my dreams I see a bony white creature with a scythe, ragged and flyblown, stepping towards us over the hedgerows. All we can do is be prepared.'

'The Princess is trying to escape,' said Watborn.

'Are you surprised, when the King uses her so cruelly?'

'Yet through her the kingdom can be saved.'

Manticore's brow furrowed. 'Hold your tongue, archer. Strategies are not for us.'

Watborn tempered his thoughts. He would do whatever was necessary to restore the balance of the land, even if it meant sacrificing his own life. If anyone asked him why, he would say he had his reasons and nothing more.

Watborn had a chance to prove himself later the same day, when he passed through an arched walkway filled with old gods. As he moved among them, he unthinkingly counted the crumbling statues.

There was one too many.

He halted and returned, counting back.

Ormond the Steady was as good as his name, but was given away by the fact that he was the only statue wearing a coat. Watborn reached for the assassin's bow, forcing Ormond into action. He struck out with the butt of the twin-crossbow, catching Watborn on the jaw and sending him floorwards.

The assassin had been waiting for the Princess to pass, but she appeared to have taken another route. Watborn was unarmed. Ormond had taken so many young lives in fits of screaming rage that the birdcatcher seemed beneath his attention.

'Stay away from the Princess or I will hurt you,' warned Watborn, rising.

'I am protected by the incantations of the Devil's Tongue,' Ormond warned.

'That means nothing to me.' The birdcatcher lifted a broadsword from the stone hands of St Winifred the Uncertain and swung it at the assassin, who watched with vague interest as his opponent attempted to wield it in an arc.

Ormond stepped beyond its reach with ease. 'I cannot be stopped, so it is best you keep out of my way. I have no quarrel with you.' It was obvious that Watborn had never taken such a weapon to an enemy before. The assassin could predict every move before he had even thought of it.

Watborn cast the sword aside and lunged at Ormond, tearing the crossbow from his hands and smashing it to splinters on the stones at his feet. Ormond was appalled; no one had ever done such a thing before.

He moved around the birdcatcher and slipped away into the shadows. His target was Giniva Scarabold, not this green underling. But if Watborn got in the way again, he would be made to suffer before he died.

78

The Binding of the Kingdom

Snear, Muzzle & Crouch lurked in an endless corridor of polished mahogany, cutting deals with their defendants and plaintiffs, according to who would pay what and for how long. It was an alley usually awash with misery and outrage, but tonight only Mater Moribund was here.

Grand Judge Arnelthus Pandergreen had agreed to meet her in the courtroom where he was preparing papers for his cases in the morning. He had no office or private apartment; under the law he was required to live in the courtroom itself, so that after sunset it was strung with washing lines of undergarments. The witness box was filled with pillows and eiderdowns, and the back row of the jury bench had been made up into a bed. Where the court recorder sat by day there was now a small stove with a pot of broth set upon it. The judge had just finished eating, and was still batting breadcrumbs from his robes when the Queen entered.

Pandergreen knew he was unkempt; his eyes were crusted from lack of sleep and there were patches of white bristles upon his chin, but lately work had been taking its toll. The legal battle over promissory notes between Craftsley Thredneedle and the army paymaster had grown bitter and vindictive.

He rose to attention as the Queen strode past, casting disapproving looks around the courtroom. 'Milady, this is an unexpected honour,' he said, trying to smooth himself into a state of presentability.

'So it appears. Of course, I imagine you see enough of my husband.' Moribund forced herself to be amiable.

'I'm afraid the Great Wound feels that the wheels of justice grind too slowly for him,' said Pandergreen. 'He tends to nod off.'

'Yes, I find that,' she said vaguely. 'I shan't keep you long. Without a suitor for our daughter, I believe we are now heading for the Reckoning. Do you recall this ritual?'

'Indeed I do, milady,' the judge replied, hurriedly searching his reference books, 'although it has never been invoked in my lifetime.'

'It goes without saying that the ritual runs contrary to our wishes for our only daughter. In short, I would like it to be forestalled.' She flicked aside some stockings with distaste and perched upon the witness bench.

'I understand your concern, of course,' said the judge, 'but it would go against the law of the land to tamper with an ancient ruling in any way.'

Moribund was barely listening and determined to have her way. 'None of us knows what this ritual involves, exactly—'

'I can tell you that, milady.' Pandergreen donned his pince-nez and examined the yellowing document on his supper-desk. 'The Princess is to be left in the sole company of Pok-Pok, the One Who Moves in the Shadows, until such time as the ceremony is deemed to be concluded.'

'That's not terribly specific, is it?' said Moribund menacingly. 'Where is the meeting due to take place?'

'I thought it was possibly in the undercrypt – there was a scroll somewhere.' He swept around a pyramid of paperwork with uncertainty.

'And exactly who or what is this creature of shadows?'

The judge laughed nervously. 'Ah, there you have me, milady, for it is merely a prophecy based on our peculiar circumstances. It is said that owing to some malfunction of the optical capillaries, this creature's eyes glow red in the dark – but of his intentions or purpose, I cannot tell you.'

'Why was I not made aware that such an agent of chaos was roaming about our home?' asked Moribund with no little sarcasm.

'I don't believe he "roams", milady. He is simply where he is. He is Fate.'

'But someone must have appointed him, someone must know his purpose and control his movements. This is a monarchy, not a free state. We must halt the proceedings. What we need is an heir, not another death in the family.'

'Unfortunately, the ritual is enshrined in the legal spirit of the land,' the judge reasoned. 'It might be carved into the walls of the castle itself. The few suffer for the many. The law has always been constructed this way.'

'Laws are made to be broken.'

The judge raised a digit. 'Begging to differ, my lady, they are made to be obeyed. The kingdom is bounded by them. They apply from the highest-born to the most lowly citizen.'

'Well, I'm glad you've raised that, Arnelthus.' She turned to the door. 'Come in, children.'

Spackle and Peut had been awaiting their cue and bounded into the laundry-hung courtroom. They were neatly matched in green velvet jerkins and leggings.

'Tell me, spylings, what did you see?' She never removed her eyes from the judge.

'Grand Judge Arnelthus Pandergreen, Mater,' said Spackle, sounding pleased with himself.

'What was he doing?'

Spackle looked at Peut with a secret smile. 'Making stickybellies with Lady Dolorio.'

'And what did he say to Lady Dolorio?'

'He said, "You know you want it."'

'And what did she say?'

'She said, "Ooh ooh ooh ooh."'

'And where was this?'

Peut pointed. 'On the Sentencing Star, right where you're standing, Mater.'

Moribund stepped aside with a grimace of disgust.

'And then on the witness box, and on the jury bench,' added Peut.

'All right, Peut, that will do.' Moribund turned her iron gaze back to the accused. 'Lady Dolorio is respectably married to our chief executioner, is she not? Well, Pandergreen, what do you have to say for yourself?'

The judge was outraged. 'The court has no call upon matters of the heart.'

'Come, this hardly concerns the heart but a smaller organ more lowly placed, surely?'

Spackle and Peut sniggered.

'What is it that you want?' asked the judge stiffly.

'I want this Reckoning stopped,' replied Moribund. 'If anything happens to the Princess, my husband will be most aggrieved. This could not come at a worse time.'

Pandergreen stood his ground. 'The King must also be aware that he is bound by the laws his own family created. The statute has been in the books for centuries. He had only to strike it down.'

'Then he can do that now.'

'I'm afraid it is out of the question. The abolition would require ratification before the Inner Council and would take many months. My hands are tied.'

Moribund raised a bony finger at the judge. 'You are obstructing me,' she warned.

'You are obstructing yourself, Your Majesty. From whence do you think these laws first sprang? You all add to them. You fail to consult each other. You do not share.'

'Of course we do not share. We rule.' The Queen was fairly boiling with rage. 'Wait, has somebody added to the law concerning the Reckoning?'

'I am not allowed to answer that,' said the judge.

'Someone has enforced them.'

The judge kept his counsel.

'You have to tell me, Arnelthus,' she warned, coming closer.

'I am not under oath, Your Majesty.'

'You are always under oath when you are before your Queen,' said Moribund, drawing herself up to her full imposing height.

Even now, the judge refused to be bullied. 'You may take the action you see fit, but it will not alter the fact that this edifice exists because you have builded it so. Your forebears passed decrees that allowed the, ah, consumption of prisoners of war. By acting in defiance of the very laws of nature, the King cast his ship of state adrift.'

Moribund pushed a sharp scarlet fingernail at his chest. 'Have a care, Arnelthus. Your words have the ring of treason.' She suddenly gave him a bright smile. The effect was unnerving. 'I have an idea. Lady Dolorio is so delightful, and I'm sure she has lots of interesting stories to share. Why don't I send her to visit Torque? He's very good at getting people to open up.'

Judge Pandergreen changed colour. 'If Lady Dolorio spoke about us, her husband would have me killed.'

'Then revoke the Reckoning.'

'I cannot. It is not a parliamentary act but an event of spiritual significance. To tamper with the timings is to alter Fate itself. To influence it in any way would be to change all our destinies.'

Moribund's voice took on a tone he had never heard before. 'Help me in this, Arnelthus. The girl has become more dear to me than I had ever expected.'

Shooing Aunt Asphyxia's spies ahead of her, she swept from the courtroom before Pandergreen could see her glistening eyes.

79

Stealing the Silver Whistle

Fumblegut had consumed half a dozen baked rats, two badger pies and four quarts of strong ale, and was still not asleep. He was, however, feeling extremely bilious. He turned on his foetid bunk, trying to get comfortable, but a ball of hot muck roiled in his stomach, driving off dreams. Forcibly breaking wind produced an unwelcome surprise, so he rose and waddled off to find a wash-bucket.

It was the moment they had been waiting for; Brasslight, Leperdandy and Giniva slipped past his cell, then headed toward M'Lin's cage. On their way, they passed the cells of a dozen pitiful prisoners.

'Who are they?' asked Brasslight as the princeling clutched his arm.

'Best not to look,' he replied. 'The cage we seek is just ahead.' As they left behind the reek of damaged bodies, the air became pungent with animal musk. Remembering the orang-utan's powerfully developed sense of smell, Leperdandy had scrubbed the lavender oil from his skin.

The creature was asleep in the corner with its back to them. The diagonal whip-scar across its shoulders was still sore and weeping. He would not easily forget their last encounter.

'Where is the whistle?' whispered Giniva.

'The chain must be buried under all that hair.' Leperdandy dug into his jerkin. 'I still have the key to his cell but I can't just root around looking for the thing – he'll tear my ears off.'

'Leave that to me,' said Giniva, removing the cap from the slender glass cylinder that Ambrosius had prepared for her. She checked its spike. 'Open the door.'

'Keep your wits about you, Gin. He's a trickster. He's just

waiting for you to let your guard down. If he starts to open his mouth, you must run. His incisors can bite through bone.'

Leperdandy tied a piece of fine silk over the end of the key and inserted it gently into the lock. It turned without squeaking. M'Lin emitted a deep rumbling snore.

He recalled that last time the hinges of the cage had whined. He needed to oil them. The only thing he had in his pocket was a vial of rose oil for his eyelids. It was delicately scented but he decided it would have to do. After smearing it on the hinges, he slowly opened the cage door.

M'Lin had not moved. If they could have seen the creature from the other side of the cell, they would have known that his watchful eyes were wide open.

Giniva pushed Brasslight back, fearing that he was not yet agile enough on his new appendage, and advanced into the cage. She held the bone needle ahead of her, moving towards the exposed grey sole of M'Lin's left foot. Leperdandy stepped aside and gave the signal.

She plunged the spike into the orang-utan's sole.

She had not realized how thick his skin was, and the tip snapped off before she could depress its plunger. M'Lin flipped over with astonishing speed and threw out one immense arm, grabbing Leperdandy by the throat.

Brasslight dropped on to M'Lin's legs to try to hold the ape down, but had underestimated his strength and was hurled across the bars of the cage. M'Lin remained concentrated and silent, ignoring his attackers as he pushed the air from Leperdandy's chest. The princeling gasped; his ribs were still cracked from the fall in the F'Arcy carriage.

M'Lin slowly insinuated himself from his resting place and lifted the princeling off the floor. Brasslight was lying on the stones, gathering his wits. Giniva searched for a vulnerable spot on the great ape's carcass and found none. Thick folds of grey skin were covered in a heavy layer of coarse black hair.

M'Lin studied the choking Leperdandy, the ape's ever-present grin playing on its crescent lips. Slowly he opened his mouth. His jaw appeared to hinge to an impossible degree – and opened yet further. Leperdandy coughed and gasped, trying to pull stale air into his lungs. His sight dimmed, then vanished altogether.

As M'Lin lifted the boy higher still, Giniva saw her only chance and seized it. M'Lin had exposed a vulnerable spot, for he had no hair in his armpits, where his skin was thinnest. She rammed the broken end of the spike into the cavity and emptied the whole of the tube directly into M'Lin's bloodstream.

The toxin hit the great orang-utan like an electric shock. He convulsed, his fingers springing open, and dropped Leperdandy to the floor.

'Run, Dando!' Giniva cried, dragging Brasslight with her.

M'Lin spun towards them and kept spinning, releasing a scream that shook the walls of his cell. Around he thrashed, his hands hitting the bars, fingers cracking, and still he spun, snapping and biting, poisoned grey spittle flying in every direction.

The Princess fell to her knees and crawled to Brasslight, trying to drag him beyond reach.

Leperdandy climbed to his feet. He was not prepared to abandon their goal. He watched in horror as M'Lin drew in his long arms and clawed at his face, burning from the inside out.

Thick, dark blood poured from between his teeth, spattering on to his rush-bed. His broken hands tore at his throat, trying to reach the source of the pain. As he pulled away handfuls of hair, the fine hidden chain came with them and the whistle skittered across the floor.

Leperdandy grabbed it just as the great ape fell, his skull cracking upon the flagstones. The anger was locked behind M'Lin's eyes, and he died as he had lived, in pain and captive fury.

80

The Search for the Scroll

Watborn had lost her.

He had been returned to his duties on the windswept archery court, to test a new influx of recruits. While he and Vitrolio decided who was the least worst, watching as they whiplashed their bowstrings into their faces and dropped their arrows, Watborn tried to imagine what the Princess was planning.

He had always thought himself to be a patient man, calm and methodical, hard to enrage. Now he felt only impatience and frustration. It was hard to tell whether it was she who was changing his feelings or the castle itself. *Perhaps*, he thought, *they are one and the same.*

He was convinced that the Princess's determination to bring about change for herself was pushing her in a dangerous direction. He had caught sight of the young knight in the museum when she had slipped in and out, briefly leaving the door ajar, and wondered why he had been hidden from sight. Instinct told him that this was no secret lover, but that some kind of a ploy was at work.

The birdcatcher was no strategist, but he could scent the wind and know that trouble had arrived.

Ambrosius fretfully withdrew his pocket-bell, the chimer he had constructed as an experiment based on drawings made by his grandfather during his fateful travels across the Grey Sea, and flipped open the lid.

He could only hope that his young friends had succeeded in carrying out the first part of the plan. By now they needed to be clear of the dungeons and approaching the chapel. He feared that

Scamp-Dangly would start his evening rounds at any moment and find him lurking.

The door burst open and Giniva slid to a stop in front of him, followed by her brother. She had torn away her silken gown to less than half its usual length, exposing a pair of Leperdandy's black leggings. She thumped her chest, out of breath. 'We have the whistle,' she said. 'Why would you have us meet here?'

'Because this is the fastest way in,' said the magister. 'Where is Brasslight?'

'We've sent him back to my suite. His instability is too much of a hindrance on this part of the journey.'

'Very well.' Ambrosius pointed. 'Go through to the rear of the chapel and you'll find the tapestry of the Divine Ecstasy of St Graticus – you can't miss it; he's having his eyes torn out with red-hot pincers. Behind the tapestry is the delivery-tube that should take you straight into the Haven of the Afterlife, but you won't be able to come back up that way. After you've put the hound to sleep and located the scroll, you'll have to find a way to climb back out. Use the Tunnel of the Damned. Take this.' He handed them his golden pocket-bell. 'You must head north. The whistle will work immediately but I don't know how long its effect lasts. Hurry, I hear the reverend approaching.'

The pair slipped beneath the tapestry and Giniva lowered her toes over the edge of the delivery-tube. 'Make sure you're right behind me, Dando,' she cautioned. 'You must be ready to blow that whistle.'

She pushed off from the lip of the tube.

The Very Reverend Trebuthnot Skank-Damply appeared in the chapel doorway. 'Magister Ambrosius, again! To what do I owe the pleasure this time?' There was more than a little suspicion in his voice.

'I . . . I was passing and thought you might enjoy a game of mumbly-bill over a glass of sherry,' said the mage, who was not a very proficient liar.

'Forgive me, but having only nodded to you at ceremonial dinners for the last three or four years, I am at a loss to understand why our paths should cross twice in two days.'

'Um, well, the late Dr Fangle – so unfortunate that he should have been caught in that frightful business with the F'Arcys – advised that I should take some regular exercise, and as my laboratory is near by, I find myself passing the chapel. I've brought a rather fine sixty-three Raisinvine.' He held up the amber bottle he had secreted in his jacket.

'Indeed.' The reverend strode past him and furled the tapestry, stepping inside. He looked down the delivery-tube, listened for a moment, saw nothing, then re-emerged. 'Well,' he said finally, 'perhaps one game. Let me see if I can find some glasses.'

'Not here,' said Ambrosius. 'It is a fine evening with only a light touch of drizzle. I thought we should play in the arboretum.'

'No,' said Skank-Damply slyly. 'Let us play right here.'

Giniva and Leperdandy hurtled through darkness. Rough stone walls scratched and snatched at their clothing, buffeting their bones, tumbling and tearing. They passed gravel-worms and spider-balls, and some strange eyeless birds in a creviced nest. As they fell, both had the same thought: that there would indeed be no climbing back this way.

They landed on sawdust sacks and rolled out on to the stone floor. As Ambrosius had suspected, the system could not place them by size and shape, and had deposited them into a zone where miscellaneous items fetched up.

Giniva spat wood-powder from her mouth, and rose. Leperdandy examined a bruise through his torn sleeve. They were in a low tunnel with a faint light, cold and blue. The temperature had fallen with the passing distance.

'We're in the undercrypt,' Leperdandy whispered, taking her hand. 'Look, the walls follow the shape of the corridors above us, narrower to the left and right, long this way and that.'

Giniva opened the golden pocket-bell and studied the dial. 'It's a divining compass, too,' she said. 'That's why he told us to head north.'

As they set off, they became aware of a soft padding sound following them, punctuated by a deep sniffing of air.

81

Nuns at War

At their emergency meeting, the Sisters were informed of the igno-
minious death of Sir Roger de la Zleuze. His men had reported the
offhand way in which his armour had been booted into the moat.

'This is what they think of us,' said Lady Lavinia, furiously
pacing the black-robed inner circle. 'We try to bring piety to this
godless land but our efforts are as naught. We hold a sacred trust to
protect the treasures of the knight-mages but it means nothing to
the great despot. He tramples upon our calling and our authority.'

'Then what are we to do?' asked Sister Devotia. 'Londinium follows no faith. It has no reverence for our order. And there is no use
in sending further allies to try to regain what is rightfully ours.
They will simply be slaughtered.'

'They must be taught that they cannot disrespect us,' replied
Lady Lavinia. 'They are beyond nature and beyond salvation, and
so we must use force, but of a different kind.'

Sister Minima looked around the circle. 'I'm not sure any of us
understands what you mean, Lady Lavinia.'

'It is against the natural laws for us to take up arms and fight,'
Lady Lavinia said, as if having to explain to inattentive pupils. 'If
we send champions to carry out our bidding, they will be despatched without a second thought. We have an alliance of armies,
but without their leaders they are as eels with their heads cut off.
There is only one way to deal with the King that will allow us to act
in accordance with our personal vows.'

She stopped before each and every one of them in turn. 'We will
have Londinium placed under a state of siege.'

'A siege!' repeated Sister Minima. 'We know nothing of warfare.

It is the province of men. How would we go about conducting such a manoeuvre?'

'The battalions upon whom we can call to maintain a blockade are many. The armies of F'Arcy and Sheathwing will soon be joined by the Green Corpse and many others. We will smooth the way between them to make a single mighty force. The access points to Londinium will be sealed suddenly and surely.'

'Will they not be able to hold out?' asked Sister Commotia. 'There are a great many of them and they are within mighty walls, after all.'

'They make nothing and grow nothing,' Lady Lavinia replied. 'Everything is brought to them from outside. I am told they are so used to being supplied with all their needs that they have become as soft as calves. Without grain and water, they will die within days, as all beings must. They have to surrender and return what is ours. In this way we can strike not through violence but abstinence. Cast your votes, my sisters.'

While she waited for the decision to be made, she considered their position.

The Sisters knew a thing or two about removing access; they had immured so many recalcitrant nuns in the walls of Cadeaux Étranges that the corridors once resounded with muffled wails and the weak thumping of fists.

She had in mind a broader agenda. The castle-city was a strong-hold of devilry. Its influence was felt throughout the Marshlands. If it could be undermined, the true religion would have a chance to take hold and grow.

'Sisters, please show me your verdicts,' she said, stopping at the centre of the circle. One by one the paddles were turned over.

This time there was no dissent.

'Very well,' said Lady Lavinia. 'Tonight when we meet with the commanders we will give them our full consent for a siege, to begin immediately.'

82

The Secret of the Scroll

'He's behind us,' said Leperdandy, taking a torch from a sconce and creeping forward. 'I can feel his breath on my neck.'

'Don't turn around,' Giniva warned, checking the pocket-bell. 'It can't be much further.'

As they turned the corner they sensed that the arched brick roof was rising. The stone walls wept dark tears. Before them stood reed-woven baskets filled with scrolls in red leather cases. As Giniva raised the light she saw with a sinking heart that they went on for ever.

'There are thousands of them. Every decree ever made must be here. How will we ever find what we need?'

'There must be an easy way.' Leperdandy handed her the torch. 'The reverend told Ambrosius that the system directed each scroll to its rightful place. How could it do that?'

'There's only one way it could work with guaranteed assurance.' Giniva stooped to examine the edges of the baskets, checking each one.

'Well, what?' Leperdandy was becoming panicked. He could hear the canine breath drawing closer.

'Time. The system requires measurement. It divides by centuries, decades, months, weeks, hours. Look.' She raised one scroll case and ran a finger along its edge. The dust was half an inch thick. 'We know when Scarabold married my mother, down to the exact minute. All we have to do is find the right basket.'

'That's all.' Leperdandy was starting to feel that the situation was slipping beyond their control.

They could no longer hear the scraping of paws. As they turned left and right, steadily following the compass north, the baskets of scrolls became newer. Above each stack was a delivery-pipe with a numeral stamped on it. The first baskets were so old that they fell apart when touched. The ones they passed next were woven from fresher rushes.

'They run in order,' said Giniva. 'We must be close.'

They searched for an age.

'Here,' called Leperdandy. 'Over here. The right day, even the hour of signing. Give me the light.'

Throwing himself over the side of a wicker basket, he hauled up a scroll-case bearing the royal seal. 'Wait, there are others. This may take a few minutes.' He dug deeper, vanishing inside the basket. When he rose again he was triumphant. In his left hand was the dated scroll. 'The number matches. Should we look at it now?'

'Best to wait,' said the Princess. 'Hold it tight.'

'How do we get out?'

'Not the way we entered, that's for sure.' Giniva looked around but the gloom refused to yield its secrets.

'I think there's something over here,' said Leperdandy. He began to search the walls. 'Why is it that no one has ever seen this hell-hound? It's like your mythical being who attends the Reckoning. They're just trying to frighten us. And Black Shag – what a ridiculous name. I know the Knights of Gash had a thirst for blood, but who calls their dog Black Shag? It's not the sort of name you'd give a real dog, is it?'

'Dando—'

'I mean, what's wrong with Toby or Lucky?'

'Dando—'

'It's just to keep us away, which means that they have something to hide.'

'Hold the light higher,' Giniva commanded.

The princeling did as he was instructed. He found himself looking into the face of an immense creature, standing about five feet above his own head. He saw the glint of open jaws and dripping saliva, felt the blast of chill breath. The beast roared, sounding distinctly un-houndlike. Odder still, it smelled not of dog but of damp cloth.

Leperdandy screamed. Clutching each other's hands, the pair turned and ran.

There, straight ahead of them, torch-lit, was a circular brick chamber with a wooden platform at its centre. 'The Tunnel of the Damned,' said Giniva.

With the hell-hound close on their heels, they climbed on to the platform. 'Now what?' asked the princeling.

The hound's great brown-and-grey face loomed suddenly before them, its jaw dropping.

'The whistle, Dando. Blow it now!'

Leperdandy raised the whistle and blew as hard as he could. A piercing high note stilled the hound in its tracks. It did not fall, but simply froze in place with its great head lowered. The effect was odd indeed. The beast wavered about in a most un-beastlike manner.

Giniva stopped. 'We've been tricked.'

Behind them the creature roared weakly and pawed, an immobile mass of fur and teeth and claws.

'What do you mean?'

'Its breath is cold. Black Shag is not moving at all. Look at his feet. They aren't even touching the ground.' She grabbed the princeling's arm. 'If he's such a terrifying monster, how does the reverend keep all these torches lit? He didn't have the whistle.' Taking the torch from her brother, she held it high.

The creature was nothing more than an armature of wood and iron, covered with stitched fur pelts, bolted together over struts and ribs like sails on a boat, and hung from ropes like an immense string puppet.

'The whistle just trips the operating lever – look.' She pointed to the hound's interior, at a fine strip of tin sewn atop some delicately balanced wooden pegs. It responded to the whistle's pitch by vibrating, tipping the pegs to block the forward movement of the great dog-puppet.

'There's nothing to be afraid of, Dando – they're the ones who are afraid of us, afraid of what we might find out. That's why they builded the hound there. The chamber is filled with documents they don't want anyone to see. These secrets reach back into our past.'

How many secrets could be held in such an ancient kingdom? How many lies could be inscribed on parchment and accepted as law? Giniva hauled on the ropes at the side of the platform and they slowly ascended.

Once they were safely back in Leperdandy's bedchamber, they unribboned the scroll from its cover and laid it out on the counterpane. The princeling produced a magnifying glass and they read the document together in silence.

Giniva turned to her brother. 'The contract of betrothment has no signature from Moribund. Why not?'

'Look.' He indicated the document's codicil. 'A blank space. She couldn't provide all the details of her bloodline.'

'But that would mean . . .'

'. . . she's an outsider.'

'Moribund has no power to rule herself, so she seeks to rule through another.'

'That's why she needs you married off and pregnant, to control your heir.'

'I always felt Moribund was distant towards me, but this . . . I am betrayed by my own mother?'

Giniva sank down into the mattress, horrified. The lies had risen in a tide through Londinium and had come to lap at her own door.

83

The Start of the Siege

It began seven minutes after midnight.

As the waxing moon was swallowed behind battlements of black cloud, soldiers crept on to the surrounding paths.

They blockaded the avenue of gold-tipped pfitzers with a barrier of ash trees. The stone bridges that stood at the corners were obstructed with dragged elm-trunks. The ungravelled roads that led through swamps and forests were sealed with fallen oaks and pines, their branches sharpened. Before the first blackbirds had risen, before Watborn and the other archers had tumbled from their beds, every escape route had been sealed off.

By the time dawn approached, the rivers had been dammed and the reservoir pipes blocked so that there could be no more fresh water drawn in. All that could be heard was the gurgling of tanks as they were drained.

Everything was carried out at great speed with a minimum of noise and fuss. Before the residents came to realize what was happening, the bridges had been barred, the roads dug with spikes, the gates wedged shut.

The soldiers had appeared as if from nowhere. They lined the roads, marching in columns, busily dragging and building and blocking the routes, working in silence. Later, once their intentions were known, they would blast apart the bridges and bring trees crashing down.

The military tribes of Sheathwing, F'Arcy and Green Corpse could be spotted stacking their weapons in separate piles between the misted trees. They had been joined by a group of wild-eyed zealots known as the Red Heretics. Although they were unhappy about working together, they shared a common aim.

Now a murmuration began. It was the last day of the month, when all the farmers brought their wares for the coming season, and suddenly nothing could get through.

Due to their parlous finances the merchants always allowed rations to run low just as fresh supplies arrived, so there was nothing put aside except for the ice-crusted wares in the basement cold-store.

Armed with an agreement brokered by the Sœurs, the armies now turned everyone away.

At the same time, the Red Heretics gathered rats from the cesspits and infiltrated the food cellars through wood-chutes at the rear of the kitchens. They released the half-starved creatures into the wheat bales, bran tubs, vegetable truckles and fruit baskets. With so many rodents on the loose it seemed likely that at least a few of them would be carrying a disease.

The rodents scampered into the cool-rooms where the remaining meat, fish and game was stored, tearing bites from dead flesh, spreading germs and shitting poison. This more virulent action had not been sanctioned by the Sœurs. They did not know that it was taking place. A siege, it had seemed to them, was a passive form of battle acceptable to all deities. They had not realized that it could be infinitely more protracted and much crueller.

Throughout the mild but airless day, lines of soldiers assembled along the south side, deepening by the hour. They stood motionless but remained at attention, awaiting further orders.

After depositing the rats, the Red Heretics went to join the other platoons at the barricades but were rebuffed; they were regarded as dangerous fanatics, and fanatics were not welcome in the disciplined military ranks of Sheathwing and F'Arcy, so they joined the soldiers of St Stanivar and Green Corpse.

With their mission carried out, most of them dispersed into the trees to make other plans, but not before they had fired a few infected rat corpses over the walls for good measure.

Inside, as the sun's pale beams penetrated the walls, the first meals of the morning were served to the servants and sickness began to spread.

As soon as it was realized that there was something wrong with the food, Goldhawk and Spattersley hurried to check the kitchens. They saw rat-bites in sides of beef, overturned grain buckets and rat-turds in the pastries.

They had dealt with rodents many times before – the creatures sought dry places on the lower levels during the flood season – but they had never seen such strangely infected ones. A peculiar smell quickly pervaded the floors: the odour of the sickroom, of rotten-ness, of scuttling death.

Word spread through the floors at the speed of the pot-boys' legs. The scullery maids called up the stove flues to their friends. The serving girls passed messages to their beaux in the stables and stockrooms.

The hearsay became increasingly grotesque and exaggerated.

It was suggested that the King and Queen had decided to take their own lives in their bedchamber rather than surrender to the gathering armies, and were taking their unwilling retinues with them. Some of the servants gathered in a deconsecrated chapel and rediscovered their ability to pray. A shrine had already appeared outside one of the chapels. Two washerwomen held hands and jumped from the battlements.

The swirling rumours caught up with Watborn in the armoury.

The platoon had raggedly assembled itself, still half asleep. Everyone had heard something different and no one could make sense of it. Foreign invaders had arrived at the port from the east and were murdering all who crossed their path. Tall blond devils from the Frozen Lands were taking away all the girls. Somebody saw a flock of birds flying backwards. What could be done?

Observing Scarabold's army, the birdcatcher saw at once that it had forgotten how to defend itself. There were no rules of engage-ment. Its equipment was outdated and there was no clear chain of command.

Searching through Manticore's war chest, he found defence maps from two hundred years earlier. Luckily, the layout had changed little and the plans were still valid. The bigger problem was the attitude of the men. They had grown up without any sense of comradeship or community. In Breornsey, the villagers watched each other's backs. If one went hunting, another guarded his hearth. The women had their own secret methods of protection. Nobody left the village exposed. Here, the women and children were invis-ible and the men only assembled to train together.

Vitrolio gathered his company and warned them that no more longbows could be made, as the supplies of yew wood were depleted.

'From this height it doesn't look as if we are surrounded,' Watborn told the armourer. 'There are fewer platoons at the rear and they have not yet been given a signal to move. I can lead a sortie to the woods and cut down some branches. Is there a gate?'

'The smallest is the most hidden but it has not been used in years,' warned Vitrolio.

'We must try to break through it. Can any of these men cut wood?'

'Most were trained to make their own bows. But it will take an hour or two to fit them into their chainmail.'

'Then we go as we stand,' said Watborn. Without waiting for permission, he gathered half a dozen men and led them out with machetes, saws and axes.

The rear gate was little wider than a horse. It had been covered with ivy planted by a gardener who had lived one hundred and seventy years ago, and was set within a four-foot-thick wall that proved invisible from most angles. The path to it was completely overgrown. After hacking their way to the door, they were unable to prise it open.

Watborn reached down and rubbed at the baseboard. The ivy had kept it dry. He struck his flint and lit the splintered wood. After burning the lowest planks they were able to tear open the gate. A lone curlew sat in the branches of a lime bush; no troops had reached here.

Watborn and his men crossed the moat into the dense woodland beyond.

From here he could see the incomplete ring of soldiers encircling the walls. They had no need to attend to the rear parts because trees and rocks blocked the path. Pointing out the suitable yews and elms, he set to work beside the men. He could not allow them to take the larger branches; they would make too much noise as they fell and would never fit back through the gateway.

They had been working for nearly three hours in silence when one of the woodsmen brought down his branch with a great splintering crash. Climbing on to the stump of an elm, Watborn scrambled as high as he could and looked out.

The soldiers of Green Corpse were running towards them. Over two hundred screaming men with emerald faces, most hefting a notched weapon that appeared to be a cross between a battleaxe and a spear.

'Back, now!' Watborn called to the others. 'Take nothing more. Drop whatever you are carrying and leave.'

The men obeyed and ran towards the gate. Sliding down from his perch, Watborn saw his team through the embrasure. Four men – two were missing.

The soldiers crashed through the tall green ferns at the edge of the woodland and began their battle cry as one. Watborn looked around for the last two, wondering how long he should wait before resealing the gate.

The first lad appeared, dragging a huge bough with untrimmed branches that had become entangled in the bushes. 'Let it go, Brock!' he called to the boy.

It was too late. Brock was intent upon his task. As he struggled with the bough, a spear-axe hit him in the back of the neck with such force that it partly severed his head. He remained quite still with his head on one side, then dropped forward into the ferns as more missiles rained down.

Behind him was another terrified boy even younger. He hopped across the cleared path near the gate until an arrow hit the back of his right leg, felling him.

Watborn held a saw-blade above his own vulnerable neck as he ran into the ferns and seized the lad by the arm. Hauling him back under the barrage was almost as difficult as moving the elm bough. The air was filled with the shouts of soldiers celebrating their first kill.

The other archers were waiting at the gate in fear and confusion. None of them thought to move the obstructing branch. As Watborn plunged into the leaves they reached out their arms to grab the pair. The moment all were inside, torn but whole, the gate was slammed shut and rocks were piled against it.

'We need something stronger,' said Watborn. 'They know it's here now.'

They sacrificed the grandest elm bough and wedged it in such a way that the garden gate could not be opened from outside. The Sheathwing arrows failed to penetrate the cover of trees that grew within the wall.

As they dragged back the branches, Watborn carried the dazed boy on his shoulders. Setting him down, he oiled the arrow shaft and withdrew it without leaving splinters.

'Where is your infirmary?' he asked Vitrolio.

'We don't have one,' replied the armourer, amazed by the question. 'There are wise women who take care of the wounded and the dead.'

Watborn found half a dozen matrons in brown aprons and caps waiting on the floor above. They knew what to do. After a thatch of herbs and a poultice, the boy was set to rest.

'He'll live,' said one of them, 'no thanks to men like you taking a child into war.'

'You need to be ready for many more patients,' Watborn warned her.

'We are not a hospital!' They looked at each other, affronted.

'You are now,' said Watborn.

84

The Plague

As the first purple buboes appeared on the faces of those who had eaten, it became obvious that plague had found its way in. Those with long memories knew it could cut a swathe through the populace in a single day. Urgent action had to be taken.

The castle-city's sanitation system was sophisticated; the royal suites on the top floors had private latrines with their own cesspits, but there were only shared wooden troughs below. Too many remembered how Richard the Raker had fallen through the rotten boards and drowned in filth.

Poisons were laid but the sewers ran deep beneath the kitchens, and were filled with crevices, cracks, tunnels, passages and pipes along which the rats could travel anywhere they pleased. They could flatten their bones and slip into the most tightly sealed rooms, fleeing into the servants' nursery, where they bit the babies in their cots.

King Scarabold was informed and the hiring of scavengers was sanctioned. These poor souls were the lowest of the low, and were given instructions to 'remove all noxious substances from the blocked latrines and jettison them over the walls forthwith'. They wore horsehair gloves to protect their hands but soon became sick.

In the absence of orders from above, which he knew would arrive too late, Watborn took it upon himself to issue some basic instructions. He ordered all eating surfaces to be scrubbed with hot water, then partitioned off corridors to separate the sick from the well and had sheets soaked in vinegar hung wherever children gathered. The maids strewed dried herbs around their beds. Crude wax effigies of the Blessed Virgin began to appear in doorways.

There was no other defence against the plague but flight, and as they were now in a state of siege it was impossible to escape. Manticore agreed that the next best remedy was containment.

Consequently, he and Watborn set out to trace everyone who had come into contact with the food and brought them to the kitchens, whether they had eaten or not. They were searched for signs of sickness, and if found to be ill were led into the largest vaulted store-room, which was then bricked up. The few below had to be sacrificed for the many above.

Goldhawk tried to get his staff out before the bricks went in and most of the scullery maids managed to make their escape, but the head cook remained behind with his workers, the youngest of whom was just seven. They were held at knifepoint as the wall rose before them. Goldhawk tried to calm them by giving them tasks to perform, but as the last of the light disappeared only the stoutest hearts remained unpanicked. Watborn agreed it was for the best, but the sound of crying children could not be stoppered.

Soon other chambers had to be set aside for the infected, and were quickly filled and sealed. The Bishop of Wexerley was called upon to give benediction to the wailing mortals being shut up in suffocating darkness, but suddenly proved unavailable.

'Don't worry,' the Very Reverend Trebuthnot Skank-Damply yelled through a boarded-up door, 'we shall not abandon you in this desperate time.' Then he plastered a carbolic towel beneath his nose and fled back to his chapel, where he had hoarded enough festival offerings and communion wine to see him through the crisis. Unfortunately, he failed to notice the rat-nibblings on a votive bun and later died alone in the nave, his tripes knotted with boils.

On every level, doors were nailed shut, cracks were blocked and chimneys were closed. Pipes were stuffed, sinks plugged, sewers sealed. The castle-city had always been good at making itself impregnable. Watborn cut up cloths, soaked them in vinegar and handed them out to anyone who was required to pass through the infected areas.

With the disease speedily brought under control, a new and even more alarming discovery was made.

When the taps were turned on, they gasped and squeaked and emitted a brief burst of water followed by a few brown droplets and rattles of rust. Bath-pipes clanged and rang like bells, sink taps whined and groaned but nothing came out. Bowls, basins and bogs were dry.

The farmers beyond having all been turned away, there was nothing to eat from the store-rooms above the kitchens except potted chutneys bitter with spice, heels of stale bread and tainted scraps of meat. Several plague-rats had landed in the open water-cistern, so it had to be drained and disinfected. There was nothing to drink now except ale and wine, and the dregs in vases, which could be boiled but still stank. In a cruel twist, the ever-present rain had mysteriously ceased, so that the gutters were no longer filled.

How was it possible that such a mighty edifice could be laid low so quickly by a few chopped trees and dead rats? To Watborn the answer seemed obvious. Its inhabitants existed in a fug of mental stagnation; nothing had changed for so long that the past hundred years were considered in the same breath as the present. Everyone expected things to work without considering why they should. As a result, daily life ceased with shocking suddenness.

At the gates, various divisions of the besieging armies were warily introduced to one another, and found that although they had minor differences they also had much in common. After all, they were now united by their determination to destroy the 'King-dom Against Nature', and vowed to work towards this single cause.

As the word spread, their numbers swelled, with new legions and detachments joining throughout the day. Even the men from Green Corpse began to be welcomed, for they were no longer the stran-gest warriors to arrive; that honour belonged to the Martyrs of Antioch, who threw poisoned tridents at their enemies and happily sacrificed themselves in battle, singing merrily as they died.

The logistics of engagement proved tricky, as the raised apron of hardened earth beyond the gates led only to the maze-avenue, and the sides fell away to rocky ground where it was impossible to pitch tents.

The troops formed narrow columns taking up most of the road. This had the advantage of protecting them from Grand-Marshal Timmorian's archers, not that a shot had yet been fired from the castle-city. Everyone was waiting for a sign that hostilities should lawfully commence.

Scarabold held another council of war with Timmorian. He was much happier now that war had been declared. He had a purpose, if not a plan.

'Who exactly are we dealing with?' he asked, leaning from the window. 'There are so many flags down there it looks like a bloody carnival.'

'Your Majesty, in addition to the F'Arcys and the Sheathwing, we have counted troops from the Green Corpse and Devil's Tongue, the Martyrs of Antioch, the Knights of the Awful Conception, the Faceless Ones, the Red Heretics and the Hangmen of Westmere,' said Timmorian. 'There are many other pennants, but none of us can work out who they belong to. There's an unofficial division of crossbowmen down there wearing the pelts of dead cats.'

'Basically everyone, then,' said the King. 'I'm surprised there hasn't been an uprising of the poor. They usually make themselves available for a scrap. Well, I suppose we must arrange a sortie.'

A ragtag platoon was assembled and sent to the entrance hall. It did not take long to ascertain that all access routes had been cut off. As soon as the soldiers of Cadeaux Étranges saw the royal inhabitants arrive on the battlements, they knew there was no more point in subterfuge and dynamited four of the seven stone bridges, further isolating the castle. They wanted to blow up the widest bridge across the Rushing River but too many of the latecomers were still using it.

As the numbers surrounding the walls continued to grow, more anxious faces appeared at windows above. The air was still and silent. All birdsong had ceased, as if the thrushes and wood pigeons had sensed that it was now too dangerous to fly anywhere near the accursed spot.

The fortress had become an island, alone in a treacherous sea of enemies.

Watborn was sent on a fool's errand by Grand-Marshal Timmorian, to study a hopelessly inaccurate model of their defences made with wooden blocks. From one of the arrow-slits in the archery, he watched with trepidation as, to the sound of a steady drumbeat, half a dozen soldiers from the Sheathwing army raised a battering ram and approached one of the seven gates.

Watborn could not understand it. What was everyone waiting for? A search of the enemy camp through his lens gave him a clue: the newly allied leaders were arguing among themselves.

He ran out into the archers' courtyard and loaded a shaft into his longbow. Dragging it to a crenellation, he aligned its tip and pointed it down into the gesticulating throng. If he could fire it now and kill one leader to prevent the loss of a hundred men, he knew he would do so – but which of them was in charge?

It was no use. He could not act under his own command without committing an act of treason. The great rampant lion appeared to be glaring at him from its home on the blackstone arch, daring him to defy his King.

85

So Much for Diplomacy

A tremendous roar went up and the crowd surged forward. A cannon boomed. Giniva heard the explosion from her bedchamber and ran to the window.

Looking down, she saw the stanchions of the bridge split apart in clouds of dust and tumble into the river below. The dust cleared to reveal the battering ram and its bearers.

'It has begun,' she said with finality. 'Who are they all? Have we made yet more enemies? They all look so *aggressive*. This is my mother's doing.'

'I don't think it's your mother,' said Brasslight, watching the great rush forward. 'They're wearing the purple-and-gold insignia of Cadeaux Étranges, but also their own colours. Look, black and green there – that's the Sheathwing – and the crimson and black of the F'Arcys. The armies have joined together to defeat your father.'

It would have been pleasing to imagine that war brought out the best in everyone involved. Instead, alliances appeared where there had been none before, ancient rivalries were freshly minted and friends smote each other for causes they neither understood nor cared about.

Giniva considered abandoning her ethereal chiffons and damasks. 'Brave warrior-princess,' she mused to the mirror. 'I think the look would suit me. Perhaps not just yet, though.' She turned to Brasslight. 'We need to put you before the King as soon as possible. The matter must be resolved at once. If he knows that the line will be continued, his resolve will be strengthened and he will be spurred on to defeat our enemies.'

It also meant that she would not be allowed to leave, but she had never considered such strategies and her thoughts were nothing if not contradictory. She went to the handbasin and opened the tap, but only a dribble of mud sputtered out. 'Why is there no water?'

'You must have noticed that we are under siege,' said Brasslight peevishly. 'Your father will have no time to deal with you today.'

'But we have to stop the Reckoning!'

He came to her side. 'Think, Giniva. Even if we could distract him for long enough, how am I to be presented, suddenly appearing from nowhere without cause or provenance? Who am I meant to be? We need someone who knows the law. There may be a clause that says it can be suspended in times of conflict.'

Giniva closed the shutter. 'I'll ask the Decrepend; he's bound to have an answer. Who could you be – a twin to Tinfoot born with sound limbs but mislaid as a child? I'm sure we'll think of something marvellous. We must talk to the magister. Thank goodness we have a handful of allies we can trust.'

The Leperdandy who burst in at that moment was now barely recognizable. Usually he had not a thread out of place, but in the last few days he had begun a transformation into an altogether wilder creature. In a suit of scuffed buckskin, with his hair washed but unpomaded, he could have taken his place at the battlements without too much comment. Though he was still a skinny thing in silver rings, there was now a whip-wire strength to him.

'They've poisoned the food and cut off our water,' he said. 'The whole place is in uproar. You must come to the Tainted Hall at once. General Bullmarsh has refused to hold a council with the King. Father's about to give the order for the commencement of hostilities on our side. He's bellowing and roaring so hard I think he may detonate. Mater Moribund is screaming at him and poor Dwinoline has all but retreated into one of her own tapestries.'

'Dando, what do you think we should do about Brasslight?' Giniva asked. 'Could we introduce him?'

'Really, Gin, this is the worst possible time you could pick.' In truth he was becoming more and more annoyed by the way his sister fawned over her perfect prince. Without saying or doing much at all, Brasslight was getting in the way of everything. Leperdandy had preferred it when it had just been the two of them, siblings left to their own devices. Every time she looked at Brasslight now she seemed to glow. It really was most peculiar. Had something happened that he did not know about?

335

'Let's work out how we can survive first,' he said, 'then get the Reckoning off your back, then worry about how we may save the kingdom. No, wait – other way around.'

To think that they had lived in a world of indolence only a short time ago! Their lives had passed in lake-like stillness and they were now tumbling, one disastrous event following the next like a pack of prediction cards.

Giniva realized that she had not been bored enough to pick up a lesson book for several days. What had happened to her was nightmarish, appalling and really rather wonderful. It felt as if her life had finally started. She opened the shutter and saw that the Sheathwing soldiers were scrambling to enter through one of the shattered gates.

'I'll lead the way,' she said excitedly, her blood rising, although when she opened the door of her bedchamber and ventured into the corridor she stopped in horror, for there right in front of her was a servant vomiting amid the most terrible smell of shit.

'We have a partial inventory of water vessels and foodstuffs, Your Highness,' noted the Squeam, slapping a pile of yellowed pages. He had placed them on the immense longbench of the council chamber before the King and Queen.

'What the blazes do you mean, a partial inventory?' Scarabold demanded. 'It is either an inventory or it is not.'

'It is impossible to account for our supplies,' the Squeam explained. 'There are some doors for which we have no keys. There are others which have no handles, or are stuck, or tarred and painted shut. We have larders full of clouded jars and clay pots with sealed lids, and no way of knowing what is inside without breaking them. They could contain marmalade or nails or poison. There are pickles and preserves and a few hanging sausages, although the ones that are not green have been hanging so long that they have turned to stone. The dogs have some meat put aside, of course, and there's a bear around somewhere. Many bottles in the cellar are without labels. They could be filled with vintage wines or cleaning acids. Nobody remembers what was put down there.'

'Water, Squeam, we need water!' Scarabold boomed, smashing his fists on the longbench and shivering the papers.

'There are ornamental lakes, basins and fountains,' said Mater

Moribund sensibly, 'but the water will need to be sieved for potability.'

'We have fire, have we not? Then boil it! Surely that will dissolve the insects. As for the rest, pour it into the dunnies. We cannot shit into dry pots, woman, there is already enough disease in here.'

Moribund flinched and turned her husband aside. 'Everyone we can spare is working on the problem. As for food, I assume the dungeons are still full.'

'The prisoners will not last long, and they are only for the inner royal circle,' warned Scarabold. 'The Decrepend holds a document to be followed in the event of emergency, a pecking order of willing sacrifice, as it were.'

'We have to feed everyone else,' said the Mater. 'What about the fish in the moat?'

'We have no way of reaching them,' said the Squeam. 'There are soldiers posted across the drawbridge.'

Moribund whirled about. 'What is my Grand-Marshal doing?'

'I am here, Your Ladyship,' said Timmorian, clicking his heels. His uniform had been polished and his moustaches trimmed. Unfortunately, appearances mattered more to Timmorian than decisions.

'Why aren't you confronting those men below? Has the main gate been breached?'

'A few slipped through but my men are working on resealing it.'

'How? I see nobody working there.'

'I have sent Watborn to the planning chamber to study a scale model of the castle that will test the feasibility of their schemes.'

'There are more troops arriving with every passing minute and you have sent off your best hope to play with a toy fort? How numerous are these barbarians? What are their demands?'

'We have no answers to those questions yet,' Timmorian admitted. 'They are an amalgam force.'

'An amalgam of whom?' asked Moribund.

'Of all your enemies, Your Majesty,' he replied, helpless. 'It would seem you are under attack from everyone.'

'I think you mean "we", Commander. And it can't be everyone – most are under the double-ensign of Cadeaux Étranges. It's obvious what they want.' She turned to Scarabold. 'You have to give them back the Vessel of All Counted Sorrows, Archim. It's the sacred symbol of their order and belongs to them by divine right. We cannot keep it here.'

Scarabold punched one spiked glove into the other. 'I am their sovereign. My line to the heavens is more direct than theirs.'

'I don't care about the hierarchy of the deities; I just think you should return it, for everyone's sake.'

'The Vessel once belonged to us,' he said stubbornly. 'The Heart of All Counted Sorrows was builded to house it. Do you know what will happen if I give in to them?' He made a noise like a cornered wolf.

'I know what will happen if you don't,' said Moribund reasonably. 'This will turn into a holy war, and I need hardly remind you what happened during the last one. There must be a diplomatic solution that will satisfy both sides.'

'I will have their soldiers' heads sawn off and fed to the pigs,' Scarabold muttered.

The Mater sighed. So much for diplomacy. During the last disastrous siege they had been forced to discover a taste for human flesh. She had no desire to see what might happen this time.

86

A Desperate Deal

Spackle and Peut were smoking rats.

Spackle held the tin canister close to the split in the brickwork and started pumping, then Peut trapped them in his cage as they shot out. After each cage was filled, they lowered it down the tower into the moat until all were drowned. The rats were strong and it sometimes took two or three submersions to kill them.

They had also run fishing lines down to the water. Folgate, the King's equerry, had commanded everyone to stay away from the windows, but the twins were adept in ways of hiding themselves. They had managed to draw up several fat gleaming perch before an arrow had almost clipped Peut's left ear. They stayed away from the front line now.

'There's water and food for the taking if they opened their eyes,' said Spackle. 'It'll rain again soon and there are always cockroaches to be caught. The army can keep us locked in for days, months, years – we'll get by.'

'Where's the proper food?' Peut was always hungry.

'Hidden away in the cold-store. Nobody goes there but Gold-hawk and he's all bricked up now. He keeps the keys.'

Peut's eyes, already as tiny and black as a rat's, grew even meaner. His hand rubbed the ear he had nearly lost. 'How can we get them from him?'

'By giving him something he needs,' said Spackle, beckoning. 'There's ways and ways. Come.'

Together they scurried off along the corridor that led to the sealed kitchens. The main archway had been crudely closed off with stones, wood and tar, but here and there were dark holes and cracks against which the pair pressed their ears and eyes. They heard nothing at first, but as they reached the battened side-windows they could hear a low moaning beyond the planks, like the pleading of the sick in a field hospital as the only available doctor passes. A sickly putridity emanated from within.

'Mr Goldhawk,' hissed Spackle through every crevice. 'Ergenio Goldhawk – where is he?'

A reply came back. 'Help us; it's black as night in here. The rats are attacking our sick. They come in the dark to gnaw our bones. We hear the scraping of their teeth.'

'Where is your head cook?' called Peut. 'We need to speak to him.'

They heard the cry pass through the kitchens: 'Where is Mr Goldhawk?'

'Go to the end,' a voice hissed back. 'To the far window.'

The pair found a gap between the tarred slats and rocks. 'I am Goldhawk,' came a weak voice through the dark slit. 'Who is there?'

'Are you well, Mr Goldhawk?' asked Spackle.

'I think so, yes, but many of us are dead and the rats grow bolder by the hour. Can you unseal us?'

'No,' said Spackle, truthfully. 'We are only two, but we could get food and water to sustain you. Can you make a larger hole in the wall to pass things through?'

'Perhaps. Some of the wood is rotten and was nailed in haste. But it is impossible to see.'

'You have knives there, yes? If we pass you a taper and flint, you could see to tear open a hole, just a small one, and give us the key to the cold-store.'

'No,' came the emphatic reply. 'If I give you the key, you will not return to free us.'

'You need to be fed and watered until we can release you,' said Peut. 'How many of you are sick with plague?'

'We have placed the most severely ill to one end of the kitchen,' said Goldhawk. 'I fear the rats are feasting upon them. Their cries are pitiful and we can do nothing to help them. Those who remain at this end are well.'

'Then give us the key and we will save you.'

'How can I trust you?'

'You have no choice.'

A thick silence followed. Spackle pressed his ear to the gap and listened for any sound that might hint at compliance. Goldhawk was holding a conference with his fellow chefs. Finally he returned.

'You must find a man called Watborn. He will be with the archers on the roof. I want him to be my emissary. Have him bring us poison to kill the rats, and water sealed in stoppered pouches, and then I will give you the key from around my neck.'

Peut made a face at Spackle and they both fought to stop themselves from laughing. 'Very well,' Spackle answered, adopting a serious tone. 'We will fetch your trusted friend, give him what you need and return. Allow us one hour.'

'Hurry,' cried Goldhawk, betraying his desperation.

The kitchens had always resounded to the clank of copper cauldrons and the slither of knives being sharpened. Now, in the blackness, new sounds were heard.

A wet cough. A low moan. A stomach being emptied. The sound of skittering paws and teeth gnawing against bone.

Goldhawk turned the spill and watched its fluttering light expand about him. A red-eyed rat, hunched over the opened arm of a young girl, raised its sleek head and carried on feasting, knowing that it was in no danger of being trapped. Around the great stoves lay a scree of small bodies, the kitchen boys who had tumbled down and been partially devoured as they lay dying of thirst.

What a terrible end to the mighty kitchens, thought Goldhawk, where once a commemorative cake had been baked containing a thousand plover eggs. To rot apart in darkness and disease ... unless those boys kept their whispered vow, and returned with flasks of water and a way of fighting off the rats.

After working tirelessly in the gloom to segregate the afflicted from the healthy, Goldhawk felt his own strength fading. He had placed all his faith in Watborn, and prayed that the birdcatcher would reach them in time.

Pulling himself up against a cupboard filled with pastry tongs and icing flutes, now looking like ancient artefacts, he drifted off into turbulent nightmares.

87

The Ambrosius Assassin

Magister Ambrosius had failed to notice the intrusion of war and plague. Surrounded by his dishes of mildews and bowls of blood, he trusted only the numerals and figures he scribbled out in rows. He believed nothing else, certainly not his rulers, to whom lying came as naturally as breathing.

As he stared into his magnifying lens he released a murmur of satisfaction or gave a hoot of complaint. When he reached a conclusion he would sit back and issue a grunt of comprehension.

Today, though, he was stumped. Getting the blood samples had taken for ever. At one point he had been forced to jab Dwinoline with an embroidery needle. Neatly arranged in a row along his windowsill were pots containing blood from almost every member of the dynasty. Scarabold's had been easiest to obtain because he was forever cutting himself. Now that Ambrosius had tabulated all the results, he was most alarmed by his findings.

He pulled loose a fresh sheet of fool's cap, dipped his quill and began to write down ... what, exactly? There was no point in simply repeating his research; no one would be able to understand it. He needed something simpler. Instead, he described what it proved in a single short statement. This he dusted with fine sand, folded up and pressed against his seal, leaving a blob of vermilion wax.

He needed to put the note somewhere safe. As the last scientific paper he had left in his laboratory had been eaten by mice, he decided to take it to Leperdandy's apartment. His reasoning was simple: the princeling had been his favourite pupil, able to recognize him before he was old enough to walk, and good faith had always existed between them. The boy had long considered him a magician, not realizing that he was being bamboozled by scientific experiments.

Arriving at the bedchamber, he knocked but received no answer. He was about to slip the letter under the door when he thought better of it.

The royal offspring were both away from their rooms; Leper-dandy was searching the royal larders for food to take to his servants and Giniva was sounding out the Decrepend, trying to discover a way of bringing Brasslight to the attention of the family. Ambrosius decided to leave his letter in the one spot where he could be sure it was protected: in the strange chapel once known as the Heart of All Counted Sorrows.

The Vessel had been restored to its original site. After making the sign of the cross (he was not a religious man but it was better to be on the safe side when dealing with something so venerable), he examined it. The Vessel was far too small to hide a letter. Out of curiosity, he turned it in his hand. In doing so he unwittingly broke its seal, and the lid opened.

Inside was a thimbleful of papyrus shreds mostly crumbled to a fine grey powder. He resealed the pot, not realizing that his action would be a subject of heated discussion for the next thousand years.

Off set the magister to find a new hiding place for his treatise, and so the only remaining ecclesiastical guidelines for what to do at the end of the world were lost for ever.

The secret spot he finally picked for the Ambrosius Hypothesis was cleverly thought out but mistimed, so it passed unnoticed until luck pressed it into service.

The magister returned to his laboratory and swept away all signs of the experiment, tipping his dishes and pots into a muslin bag that he smashed and burned in his fireplace along with his papers. Then he emptied out everything from the cupboard in which he kept his most useful inventions and buried them under the floor.

Afterwards, his hands still shaking, he poured himself a large pepper brandy and sank back into his chair.

Perhaps he had not been explicit enough. If Giniva and her brother read the note, would they even understand it? And if they did, what could they do to change the path of history? He had noticed there appeared to be a siege under way. Their protestations would not be heard. In times of war, leaders only listened to each other.

He was still contemplating the problem when he heard a strange new sound. Raising his head from the cushion that supported his thin neck, he was surprised to see a flash of darkness in the room and find a blade at his throat.

The crimson mouth that opened below his Adam's apple almost complemented the cushion cover, which was finished in a racy shade of heliotrope. Before the knife descended again and the mage's mouth hotly overflowed, he forced out one last exhalation of air. As he died, he tried to turn and identify his assassin.

A raw, half-starved face stared back at him.

Ormond the Steady, the assassin from the Devil's Tongue, had not eaten for days, but was determined to carry out his orders. He did not understand them and did not care to, for he existed only to serve and kill.

88

The Cruelty of Hope

From his perch on the roof beside the archers' platforms, Watborn had seen the siege escalate.

Men were surging forward in ever-greater numbers, pressing up against the walls. Soon they would be forced to climb upon each others' backs. The Martyrs of Antioch and the Red Heretics were more interested in slashing at each other than concentrating on a common enemy, but their commanders were unable to control them.

The gate directly below him needed to be sealed correctly; if tree limbs were stacked against it, the troops would soon be able to climb over. Recalling the traps he had set in the meadows at the edge of Breornsey, he showed Timmorian a simple way of interlocking branches so that they could not be broken apart.

His diligence paid off. Timmorian's men-at-arms held their enemies at bay while they slid a stronger barrier into place. With the lattice firmly set, the Sheathwing failed to break through. The new thicket flexed greatly but held. Soldiers rushed it a dozen at a time and were repulsed.

Although General Bullmarsh was now the commander of the entire allied attack force, he was no strategist. He failed to realize that there were other gates with greater flaws that could grant entry. Instead of studying his reconnaissance reports, he berated his men and gave the order to attack with airborne missiles.

A phalanx of discordant bugles sounded. A ragged cry went up through the crowds as the onslaught began afresh. A dense wave of arrows darkened the sky as it passed overhead.

Scarabold's men were meant to have three archers for every

man-at-arms, but numbers were depleted and many of their arrows proved to be warped. Timmorian gave the order to return fire.

'Make every shot count, lads,' he cried. 'We can't fetch back the wasted shafts.'

Watborn stood with the archers and repeated his fire so quickly that he required two arrow-boys to keep him supplied. He set about disrupting gatherings of officers, breaking their concentration so that they were unable to control their troops.

Few of the shafts that sailed in over the walls found their mark; they either went wide or fell short. One burst a poor lad's head open like a marrow, but most of the King's archers were able to safely return fire from leather hides mounted on the crenellations that protected them.

The constant raining-down of missiles made it dangerous to be outside on any of the exposed bridges or walkways. Watborn worked methodically, taking out the infantrymen who seemed most likely to effect a breach, and encouraged the others to follow his lead. As he fired he recalled his days in the village, catching birds and badgers first for his grandparents, then for his parents. He needed to employ the same attention to detail now.

Once he was satisfied that the other archers were copying his style, thinking about their intended targets and not merely firing indiscriminately, he headed back down into the halls below to see how everyone else was coping, first looking in on Goldhawk and checking the store-rooms.

As he marched along a gangrenous, sweating corridor that led to the kitchens, he passed Spackle and Peut, who were dancing along in the same direction.

'You – children,' called Watborn, unsure how to address the twins. 'Have you seen the head cook, Goldhawk?'

'Goldhawk?' Peut glanced at his brother and stifled a giggle. 'He's not seeing anyone today.'

'Or ever again,' Spackle could not resist adding.

'Why, has something happened to him?' Watborn asked.

'Not yet,' said Peut.

'If you see him, please tell him that Watborn is looking for him.'

Realizing that they had stumbled across the very man they had been instructed to find, they grew crafty.

'We think he went to the Chapel of the Grey Goddess,' said

Spackle. 'To pray for the victims of the plague. Straight ahead, turn left three times, keep going for ever – you can't miss it.'

Watborn gave them a curious look. He knew something was amiss, but anyone in a velvet suit was his superior, so he bowed to their knowledge. 'Thank you, sirs,' he said, turning and striding away from the bricked-up kitchens.

'He's not from around here,' said Peut with narrowed eyes. 'I don't trust outsiders. I told you we should keep an eye on him. He's going to be trouble.' They set off to the kitchens once more.

'Wait, wait,' hissed Spackle, dragging his brother back. 'Before we give Goldhawk everything, we need a plan.'

The leather water-pouches slung over Peut's shoulder gurgled as he was pulled to a halt. 'What do you mean? Don't we just hand this over?'

'We keep our promise, a-course; we don't hold anything back. We just make one small change.' Spackle began to unstop the flasks. Removing the sack from his own back, he emptied a small amount of glittering black powder into each of the flasks, wiping the tops, restopping them and giving them a good shake before handing them to his brother. 'See? No one can say we're not as good as our word. They get the rat poison and the water just as we promised, only a bit mixed up.'

'Why?' asked Peut.

'They're going to die in the kitchens, aren't they? The Great Wound will never unbrick them and they will only ask for more help. Nobody wants to be a burden. "A sacrifice; the few for the many." This way everyone will be happy.'

'Everyone will be happy,' Peut repeated, not entirely sure what was meant.

They arrived at the crack in the filled-in window and found that Goldhawk had managed to make a fist-sized hole in the tar and boards. He could enlarge it no further, though, because granite stones blocked either edge.

Hearing their return, he called to them. Behind him a chorus of pitiful voices mewed and wailed. The stench of death from within was appalling.

Spackle held his nose, lowered his face to the hole and peered through. On the other side he saw Goldhawk's bloodshot eye.

'Where is Watborn?' the cook asked plaintively.

'He could not spare his precious time to help you,' said Spackle viciously. 'He has more important matters to attend to.'

'I don't understand it – I thought he would come to our aid. Are you sure you found the right man?'

'Big fellow, answers to the name of Watborn, didn't want anything to do with you,' Spackle confirmed.

'It seems so unlike him. So unlike . . .' Goldhawk's voice grew faint.

'Wake up!' shouted Peut. 'We have brought what you asked for. Do you have what we need?'

'The rats have already taken the weakest. We cannot see them in the dark. Our only hope is to lay down poison. Please, I beg you—'

'Here,' said Spackle, passing through the bag. 'Don't get it on your hands, for it burns.' He beckoned to Peut, who unloaded the water-pouches. 'And these will see you through until your merciful release.'

Peut giggled and was slapped on the head by Spackle.

'Thank you, fair brothers, thank you from the bottom of my heart,' cried Goldhawk pitifully, his grandly commanding voice now reduced to a gravelled croak.

After passing the last of the water-pouches through the hole to Goldhawk's bloodied fingers, Spackle pressed his lips to the opening. 'We have risked life and limb to keep our end of the bargain,' he hissed. 'Give us the key, so that we may save those who are dying without.'

'You are good, kind boys,' said Goldhawk. 'I will repay this debt, I swear.' A clear crystal key threaded its way towards them on a thin leather strap.

'It's made of glass,' said Peut in dumb surprise.

'The ice-store is for my use alone,' the chef warned. 'I have the skill to use its key, so you must be very careful with it. Slide it very slowly into the lock and turn it once with great delicacy, or else it will crack and can never be used again. Once you have unlocked the store and fed those who are most in need, you must return the key to me.'

'I will do exactly as you wish, Mr Goldhawk, of that you may be sure,' said Spackle, whose promises might well have been written on dry oak leaves over an autumn bonfire. Pocketing his prize, he rose to his feet, grabbed his brother's hand and led him off down the corridor, bouncing away from the men and women who were dying in the darkness of the great kitchens.

89

The Four Foundations

Giniva and Brasslight were still barricaded in the bedchamber, high above the fighting. Most of it was taking place on the other side of the castle-city, so they heard very little from below.

The rooms had become claustrophobic, the air stale. The looping patterns of blue ceanothus and clematis were oppressive. It was time to leave.

'You have to remain out of sight,' the Princess warned, opening the door to check that the coast was clear. 'At heart my father is a fair man, but he has a temper that burns like starlight and he will not hesitate to have you killed if you impede his plans.'

'Then we must discover his intentions first,' said Brasslight, taking her hand as they headed into the passage. 'We are bonded, you and I. When you finally lose your . . .' He struggled with the word.

'You may say it. My intactitude,' Giniva offered. 'Without my maidenhead I will no longer be of value. My father will be unable to forge new alliances based on access to my body.'

'If you care for me,' said Brasslight, 'we can show the King that you and I are the last hope for the kingdom. If I can prove who I am . . .'

Giniva looked down at his foot. There was nothing that now suggested it was artificial. The edges had been sewn so that flesh and leather appeared as part of the same limb.

'The only way you can reveal your true identity is by removing your foot. That is the cruel paradox of your birthright, Brasslight. To prove yourself the rightful heir you must reveal your ineligibility. You cannot rule because of it.'

Brasslight started to look most concerned. 'We must both be

careful. Without your mark of purity, you would have no power to control your father.'

'My virtue is in my gift to give,' said Giniva. 'The time must be right. I shall await a sign.'

She held Brasslight back as a pair of archers raced across the passage, heading for the ramparts.

'For years I watched my family scrabble and claw at one another, making new enemies as they tried to preserve our way of life. But what is there left that's worth preserving? They are so eaten with ambition that they have quite forgot what they are fighting for. If the country could unite its tribes in peace as the new alliance has in war, we could regain our strength of purpose.'

They set off once more. Giniva took a torch from a sconce and led the way.

I have done what all the royal children do, she thought angrily, stalking onwards through the penumbral gloom. *I have sulked and complained from my tower in a state of perpetual powerlessness. I have achieved nothing for myself, relying on others to alter my fate. Well, no more. I watch them trot one after the other, each thinking they can get their foot on the throne, but none of them succeeds. It has to be me, the one everybody dismissed, who brings us out of darkness.*

'I won't do what they expect,' she said aloud. 'I won't be imprisoned here, oh no.'

'You would not stay even for a while?' asked Brasslight.

She shook her head violently. 'They can plot all they want to keep me here, but they will stay and I will go. I will go, Brasslight, out to the wide world with skies so blue they can make you cry, and no one will ever be able to hold me back again.'

Brasslight frowned. 'You say "I will do this" and "I will do that", but we must work together. We are as one now, you and I. You haven't told me what was written in the scroll of betrothment. You need an ally and I can help. Leperdandy is not strong enough to survive alone.'

'He has strengths no one but I can see. We talk even when we are apart.' She glanced at a ribbed speaking-tube mounted on the passageway wall.

'Then think of me, Giniva.' Brasslight suddenly pulled her close. 'Think of what we can achieve together. I have given my heart to you.'

'There is much to be done before we can be happy.' The Princess searched his sky-wide eyes. 'If you really love me, you will have to be patient.'

'Only if you tell me everything with absolute honesty.'

I can never tell him all of our secrets, she thought. *What if he discovered I am descended from eaters of their own kind, and that my family still practises its rituals?*

Now she was beset with another fear. If Mater Moribund had been prevented from signing the scroll of betrothment because she was not a trueblood, then she and Scarabold were not married and that made their daughter a bastard, and a bastard could not inherit a kingdom.

Paradox upon paradox.

Founding a new dynasty with a bastard and a cripple – had she not sensed in her bones all along that this was a plot doomed to failure? Was it not why she longed to flee and have nothing more to do with the family? How would Brasslight feel when she was publicly disinherited?

Their child, if a male child she bore, could only rule if his father was accepted into the bloodline, and that would rely upon a deception. The idea sat uneasily with her. The plan was void in its own plotting. Brasslight would be using trickery to take the crown, doubling the number of his feet to a workable pair when he had but one.

Oh, her head swam and swirled with deceptions! She and Leper-dandy, both so young and high-a-mighty, determined to grow up better than their parents, had become just like them. Transforming into a warrior-princess was not to be as easy as changing one's clothes.

Miserable, she kept her counsel.

They had by complex means arrived before the door of the Decrepend's mouldering apartment. Giniva lifted the dead-hand knocker and let it fall.

A boom echoed in the hall beyond. Eventually there was a painful creak, like the sound of an ancient knight stretching his knees, and the Chancellor's rheumy eyeball peered around the door at the height of the handle. 'My lady,' he rasped, 'your father has been asking for you.'

'I shall see him in my own time,' said the Princess, determined to be oaken-hearted. 'I need your help. You are the record-keeper, are you not?'

'You know I am, Princess. Why, when you were a tiny little girl you used to—'

'Yes, no time for that now,' said Giniva, pushing past him. 'I need information.'

'Please enter, but excuse the atmosphere,' the Decrepend apologized. 'There is no water for the jakes.'

The Princess wrinkled her nose but pushed on. 'You know about the scrolls of betrothment – don't deny it, you do; I will hear no protestations. Why did Mater Moribund fail to sign her marriage covenant?'

The Decrepend looked as if someone had asked him to pull down the moon. 'That . . . that is not a matter for me to say, Your Highness. Perhaps the King—'

'My father is dealing with the siege and cannot be interrupted. Anything you say to me will not leave these walls.'

'But Your Highness, I cannot—'

'Don't make me ask again. I command you, as the ruling Princess.'

'Very well,' said the Decrepend, shaking his head with such vehemence that dust fell out of his hair. 'The scroll of betrothment was left unsigned because Mater Moribund is not a trueborn.'

'Not a—'

'So the marriage was never ratified.'

'But what does that mean?'

'She was born elsewhere. She was – ah – imported here, so to speak. There is no shame in it. We think of ourselves as trueborns all, but in faith most of Londinium's bloodlines start somewhere else. Your father thought it would matter not, but the rules clearly state—'

'You were there when she was prevented from signing!' Giniva's hand flew to her mouth. 'Why has she let you live?'

'Because I am the keeper of all records,' said the Decrepend. 'If nobody writes it down, it did not happen. I am Londinium's memory. Without me there is no past. And we are a kingdom entirely built upon four things.'

'What are the four things?'

The Decrepend shrugged as if it was obvious. 'History. Family. War. And blood.'

90

Horrible Murder

There was a time when Leperdandy would have kept a nosegay of lavender buds close to his nostrils whenever he ventured out, but now he was determined not to shy away from painful realities. He halted before the narrow oaken door to Ambrosius's laboratory. It was ajar, and a faint breeze flickered his light. He pushed the door wide and stepped inside.

'Magister?'

A tall armchair stood before the fireplace. He could see his old tutor's boots casting shadows, but there was no movement. As he walked around the chair, he was confronted by a sight that filled him with horror.

Ambrosius had been pinned to the chair by a blade that shimmered in the firelight. A handle of polished bronze protruded from his throat. Blood had run along it, finding a conduit to the floor. The old man was drained as white as alabaster.

'No,' the princeling cried, 'not him!' But there was nothing to be done. With a grimace he pulled at the handle, catching the body as it folded forward.

He laid the mage on his rug before the flickering grate. Tearing a curtain free from its encrusted moorings, he covered the corpse and said a silent prayer for the man who had always been so kind to him.

As he left the room and ran off along the corridor, his cheeks were chilled with tears.

There was a storm coming. The corridors had grown so dark that Watborn was forced to light a lanthorn.

The birdcatcher was confused. He had discovered that the

Chapel of the Grey Goddess did not exist where the twins had said it did – that was a privy. Now he was in an elevated part of the castle that was usually closed to commoners. The few people he passed were in a rush and paid him no heed; the siege was upending the rules of privilege.

The blockade and the plague were taking a terrible toll. Ghoulish shadows followed him through the gloom as he walked. Spectral courtiers lay slumped in corners, their pale mouths cracked and dry. Some had red buboes beneath their eyes. Others were still propped against their pikes, determined to remain on duty even as their insides ruptured and shrivelled.

Watborn kept a knife at his belt and a vinegar cloth tied over his nose and mouth. He was still searching for the Chapel of the Grey Goddess, but with the allied troops temporarily stopped by their reinforced gates, it was a good time to take stock for Timmorian.

He could see how separated the upper echelons had become from those who worked to keep the castle functioning. The royals and their retinues were as remote as mountains. It was clear they were avoiding the worst ravages of disease by locking themselves in their apartments.

He caught a glimpse of a finely dressed lady peering around the next corner but she gave a little scream when she spotted him, covered her mouth and fled. It was probably the fastest she had moved in years.

Watborn decided that the strange children who had directed him must have been in error; he could see nothing around here that remotely resembled a chapel or any kind of goddess.

When he turned into the next corridor he saw a spindly young man just ahead of him and was immediately aware of being in the presence of royalty. Two things gave Leperdandy away: he was flicking aside tears with a purple lace handkerchief and was wearing shoes of yellow kid.

Watborn followed as softly as if stalking a grebe. Leperdandy's ears trembled like marsh reeds and he turned to see who was behind him. He jumped when he saw the birdcatcher.

'There has been murder afoot!' he cried. 'Horrible murder!'

'Who?' Watborn asked. 'Who has been killed?'

'Why, Magister Ambrosius – he tutored me as a child. Someone has speared his poor throat.' He took stock of the man before him. 'Who are you?'

'Someone sworn to protect your sister, sir,' said Watborn, because the family resemblance was undeniable and he had heard much talk of the fopling prince.

'The misfortune in the moat. You are the one who came to her aid. Then you are to be trusted, whoever you are.'

'I am Watborn, sir, archer under Grand-Marshal Timmorian and at your command.'

'You have your work cut out. We face a dark hour. You must forgive my ignorance. I know few men of common stock. I mean no disrespect. My sister – there are malign forces at work.'

Seeing the boy struggle, Watborn sought to reassure him. 'I will do everything in my power to protect the Princess.'

'She is precious to me. I will give you whatever you want.'

'I don't want payment. I want things to be right.' He felt foolish saying it. He had lived his life without ever expecting to have the luxury of choice. To come here and be offered it felt unnatural.

'Promise me, Watborn. Find her. Save her however you can. She is blind to the dangers she faces. You may think we don't deserve your help.'

'I hold no opinion on the matter.'

'I'm glad to hear you say so. The old order is at an end but we can't build a new one alone. What do you hear down there in . . . wherever it is you are stationed?'

'That your father must return what has been taken.'

'You're brave to say that to me.'

'We are just two people who met in a corridor.'

'His behaviour was mal-intended. I can assure you that Giniva and I are not like our parents.'

'Then you may be assured I will help you.' He clasped the boy's arm, breaking four hundred years of protocol in one gesture.

'We'll see each other again, friend.' The princeling's hand rested on Watborn's a touch too long. Then he turned and fled.

'It's here,' said Peut, stretching out his bony fingers over the icy grey rocks as smooth as shaved corpses.

His breath clouded the air. The corridor was hewn from the land itself, a dense dark mix of clay and stone. Before them stood the cold-store, its wall sparkled with ice and curved like an earthen jar.

'I can feel the cold,' said Peut. 'Lovely, refreshing cold. It comes from the river that rushes underneath. Hurry, give me the key.'

'No, you are too clumsy,' said Spackle, unlatching the crystal key from the strap around his neck. 'Let me do it.' He blew into the mortice and gently inserted the shaft.

'Are we to save them all?' asked Peut. 'We can't feed everyone, can we? This can be our secret. I like secrets.'

'We can feed the royal family because they will be grateful to us and reward us,' said Spackle, 'but nothing for people we don't like.'

'No, nothing for Meldred Moribund! Let's draw up a list of everyone who has done us wrong.' Peut made a grab for the crystal key and pulled so hard that it made an ominous cracking sound. Spackle batted his hands away.

'Leave it! We'll do an inventory, that's what we'll do, and only take out what we need. We won't tell them how we got it, and that way we can control the supply, so they'll have to come begging to us.'

Peut clapped his hands delightedly. 'They'll all come begging to us! Hurry, brother, hurry!'

Spackle carefully turned the pin in the lock. The cracked key held. He pushed at the door. It was thickly constructed but rolled smoothly inwards on wooden pegs coated in pig fat.

When he lit his watch-lanthorn and raised it, a glittering white cavern filled his vision. Dusted with frost, a banquet arose like stalagmites from the ice-braced floor. A crackling sound washed over the mountains of frosted food as warmer air rolled in from outside.

'Look,' whispered Spackle, his awe-filled voice more hushed in the cold-store than in any church, 'enough feasting meats to last us a thousand years!'

They were surrounded by geese, pullets, grouse, partridges, pheasants and plucked swans. A split bullock, several headless ewes, a staring skinned ram's head, ham-hocks hanging like the thighbones of dead soldiers, rows of gape-mouthed fish as iridescent and sumptuous as jewelled satchels serried on slabs of stone-ice, baskets of exotic sweetmeats as mysterious as foetuses in a medical drawing.

'We'll parcel it out in return for favours,' said Spackle, his face aglow, 'a little at a time, the quality depending on what we get back. But we thaw the meats first so they don't know where they're from, grind them and mix them with sawdust to make them go further.'

'And if they have no favours to trade with us?' asked Peut, his greedy little eyes narrowing to slits.

'Then we'll be fair; we'll treat everyone equally,' said his brother, setting down the lanthorn. 'We'll agree to take gold. Or fine silver. And perhaps some jewels. Let's start with the fish. Find a basket to put them in. We'll go to Craftsley Thredneedle and his accountants first – they'll strike bargains with us. Then Judge Pandergreen. Then Snear, Muzzle & Crouch, and after that the Bishop of Wexerley and Father Sesquinatius.'

Peut counted off on his fingers. 'Favours from the bank, the law, the church. Yes, that should do for a start.'

91

Moribund's Impasse

Watborn returned to the kitchens and found them gone. The elegantly carved entrance to the scullery had been replaced by a wall of rocks and rubbish, tarred into a blockade.

He moved along the barrier and listened. From somewhere within came the sound of ringing pots and pans. A filthy urchin dashed past with a stale piece of pastry in one hand. Watborn grabbed him, swinging him off the ground.

'You, boy, what happened to the kitchens?'

'Boarded up, sir,' said the child, anxious not to lose his grip on the pie crust. 'It's to protect us, for there's pestilence inside.'

'You worked at the sinks – I remember you. A lively lad. Tell me, where is Goldhawk?'

The boy pointed at the stones. 'Bricked in, sir, for his own good. No telling if he's dead or alive.'

He dropped the boy and headed back to the barrier, looking for breaks in it. 'Mr Goldhawk,' he called, 'are you in there?'

'Help us,' a papery voice croaked through a fissure, 'we have been left to die.'

'Is the head cook in there with you?'

'Yes, but he is sore ill. The humours are mal indeed. We cannot breathe without drawing in death. The boys lied to us. They said they were our friends. They brought us water but it is poisoned.'

Watborn's ears pricked up. 'Which boys?'

'I know not their names . . .'

Others knew, and called out to him.

'A pair of young lads the same age with high voices, who take turns to speak, as if they are one person?'

'That's them, Spackle and Peut. They betrayed Goldhawk. He gave them access to the cold-store.'

Watborn searched about for water and found some dregs close by in a rain-trough. He decanted it into his own pigskin bottle and found a gap to pass it through. 'Drink this,' he called. 'It is not fresh but it will not poison you. Make sure you give some to Goldhawk. Do you have flagons of vinegar within?'

'Yes, there are plentiful stores of preserves.'

'Soak the dishcloths in them and wear them around your faces. Keep a separate privy for the sick. You must make more holes in the wall to breathe fresh air.'

'Please don't leave us.'

'I must, but I'll return with help. If the boys come back, don't speak to them.'

Watborn was as good as his word. As soon as he had replenished the kitchen's prisoners, he set off again, this time to find explosives.

Mater Moribund was determined to show that the siege was not taking its toll on her. She knew how to appear fearsome, and to this end had darkened her eyes and changed into a black crystal gown of agate and onyx.

Couture was but one small weapon in her armoury. Now she awaited the rising of the portcullis to confront the battalion that stood to attention across the drawbridge, cutting off the castle from the cypress avenue beyond. Scarabold could strike fear into his enemies. He was a man; he enjoyed seeing things die. She was the cold heart of the family, and knew how to ensure its survival.

'Who is your commander?' she demanded of the first officer she saw bearing the ensign of Cadeaux Étranges.

'General Bullmarsh, Your Ladyship,' answered the astonished soldier, trying to keep his eyes set ahead. Mater Moribund was an imposing figure and towered above him.

The General was so surprised to see the Queen herself standing before him on the drawbridge that he could only cede to her desire for a meeting. He pushed aside his uneasy men, leading the way to his tented quarters at the mouth of the avenue.

Moribund seated herself across from him in a mildewed canvas chair, but her bearing still imposed. She was more than matched by the rhinoceros-like Bullmarsh, a brown, ageless cliff of a man who stood a head taller than any of his troopers, and as wide as any two. A fellow of iron principle, he believed in righteous justice and applied it rigorously in his military campaigns, without much fore-thought or skill.

'There is a new insignia on your banners,' she said. 'It appears to be a hawk in flight.'

'It is the spirit of winged vengeance, my lady,' said the General, sitting opposite. 'It represents the armies of the Alliance.'

'This siege can only harm the honour of all parties. It is undigni-fied. There is a better way for us to settle our differences.'

'My lady, we have always had differences. An unspoken state of war has existed between us almost as long as the King has been in power.'

'You have never joined forces against us before.'

'This is no mere settling of accounts. The King committed a crime, and such an act of provocation cannot be allowed to pass unpunished.'

A pot-boy brought them clean water. Moribund took a small sip even though she could have drunk the whole jug in a single draught. 'You're taking your orders from the Holy Sisters, I assume?'

'We agreed to ally ourselves with the Convent of Cadeaux Étranges,' the General replied. 'The others joined after.'

'Do the Sisters understand that a siege is not a battle but slow genocide?'

Bullmarsh spread his broad fingers widely on his thighs. 'My lady, I am glad you appreciate the situation. It is precisely because a siege is not a battle that it has been sanctioned.'

'And yet they endorse the starvation of not just the royal family but their people? General Bullmarsh, this is not justice. It will not regain the treasure that they expect to be returned to them. There is a better way to deal with the situation.'

Bullmarsh could find the wisdom in Mater Moribund's words. This was not fighting with honour but merely waiting until the other side grew too weak and malnourished to resist. It sat badly in his heart, and as a warrior stratagem it did indeed lack grace. He had approved the siege only because the Sisters were determined to prevent bloodshed. Then there was the matter of time: how long could he keep his own men fed and watered here in these narrow confines? Was he also expected to provide supplies for their allies?

'What do you suggest?' he asked.

'If I can bring you the Vessel of All Counted Sorrows, will you call off the blockade?'

Bullmarsh considered the offer. 'So the Sisters will regain what is rightfully theirs. But there are still lost lives to be avenged.'

Moribund was sanguine. 'There are lives to be avenged in every war, commander. Attrition benefits no one. The King was most wrong to have taken the Vessel as a trophy. Sometimes he acts impulsively.'

'It is the way wars are started, Your Highness,' Bullmarsh said. 'On that point we are agreed.'

'You do know that the Vessel was kept here in one of our chapels ever since the time of the invasion?'

'History does not concern me, Your Highness. History is dead. We are making a new world.'

'Well, of course, you have your orders. But I would like you to consider my offer, for which I am prepared to act as a mediator with my husband, the King.'

'Very well.' Bullmarsh rose. 'I think your offer is fair and hon-ourable, but my instructions are to return with the Vessel. Therefore I must insist that you bring it to us. You have until noon tomorrow. After that, the actions against you will be stepped up.'

'What do you mean?'

'We will summon the Diableries,' said Bullmarsh, politely hold-ing the tent open for her. 'A siege is not enough. It will be time to rain down fire upon you all.'

92

Leperdandy the Betrayer

'Pinned to his chair with a knife!' cried Leperdandy. 'A dignified old man who never hurt anyone. We have to tell someone.'

The three were together in Giniva's bedchamber once more. Brasslight had perfected his movements so that it was impossible to tell that he was wearing a false foot. He paced around them, eager to leave his brocaded prison and fight.

'No,' said Giniva flatly. 'We can't tell Father. I know he was your favourite tutor, but I doubt the Great Wound even remembers him. Right now he needs to concentrate on ending the blockade.' She knew that Scarabold was a man of sudden violent actions and would not be able to grasp the meaning of this latest news. 'If there is a viper in our midst, we must root him out ourselves. We're better suited to finding a murderer.'

'I must do something,' said Brasslight. 'I fear I have been an unnecessary distraction for you.'

'I'm sorry we imprisoned you here for so long.' Giniva took his hand. 'You exchanged one jail for another.'

'Anything is better than being kept in the dungeons, and I'm here with you. But why has Fumblegut not reported me missing?'

'The siege has stolen everyone's wits,' Leperdandy replied. 'Who can think when his throat is parched and his stomach is rumbling? I hear tell the servants are falling off the battlements in their attempts to catch sparrows. The stable-maids know that cloth masks will prevent them from breathing mal humours but refuse to do so. They believe they can be made immune by drinking water from the sewers. Ambrosius wasn't practising sedition; he was fighting ignorance, keeping his nose in his books and studying our history. There's no need to kill a man for reading.'

'Unless he discovered something that he was not supposed to know,' said Giniva.

'What, more secrets?' The princeling was exasperated. 'I made a search of his laboratory. He'd smashed everything up and burned all his papers in the fireplace.'

'Why would he do that?'

'Perhaps because what he discovered was best left unfound. Whatever he learned is lost for ever.'

'You knew him better than anyone, Dando. You must have some idea. He trusted you; he always told you his plans.'

'It's true,' Leperdandy agreed. 'When Squanderberry the postilion brought flea-worms into the castle, the magister tracked down their nests and made them sick up their own insides by feeding them special poisons, and the only person he told was me. Everyone else thought it was magick, but I knew it was science.'

'You were his favourite pupil, Dando. Perhaps he left you a message, some kind of clue as to what he'd discovered.'

The princeling shrugged helplessly. 'But where,' he asked, 'and how?'

'I won't do it!' Scarabold stalked the length of the war chamber.

The silver breastplates of long-dead kings and queens looked down upon the planning table. 'You think I will give in to this congregation of snot-faced miscreants just because they have been able to keep our merchants away from the gates? A barricade is not a war!'

Moribund had known that the Great Wound would explode when she suggested handing back the Vessel. She needed to deflect his anger into something she could use. 'Your subjects are dying, Archim. Your own family is at risk from disease and starvation. You need to concentrate on saving as many of them as you can. Of what use is the relic to you now?'

'Do I need to remind you that it is our only surety for the finances of our army?' Scarabold's empty goblet rang as it flew across the chamber.

'It has become unsaleable, Archim. We must have some forgotten treasures of our own which can be parlayed for our defence.'

'We have *nothing* left. A few rotted paintings and tapestries, some candlesticks and pewter plate. We are monarchs in name only, and that name means less and less each day. Everything we took for spoils of war was sold off years ago or promised to debtors upon our deceasement. The Vessel is priceless.'

'Then it is worthless, for it cannot be bought or sold.'

'It can be used. And it belongs here, on the site where it was forged.'

'If we fail to lift the siege, everyone will die.'

He took her shoulders in his great hands. 'I understand our predicament, Meldred. But if we give in now, our line is finished. Everything ends. Do you not see the shame in this? Not defeated on the bloody field of battle but by a bottleneck in farm supplies?'

'It amounts to the same thing,' said Moribund bitterly. 'The rotting dead will pile against the walls.'

Unable to bear the thought for a moment longer, she swept from the battle-room, determined now more than ever to end the siege behind her husband's back.

She had rarely ventured as far as her son's apartment – the smell of his perfumes and the sight of his fineries sat ill with her – but she did so now, climbing the narrow stairs to his world.

Leperdandy opened the door and ushered his mother into his bedchamber. She glanced with disapproval at the canary and crimson fripperies, the draped tableaux and silken flowers, the theatrical props and hanging costumes.

Her son stood before her in an azure harlequin suit made from some silken material that reflected the light. She had hoped the siege might have brought him to his senses, or at least made him dress more like one of the archers on the battlements. But there was something different about his bearing; he seemed more straight-spined and ready to catch her eye.

As he had never known what to call his mother, he stepped aside without greeting her.

'I want you to do something for me, boy.' She walked to the mullioned window, from where she could see Bullmarsh drilling his troops beneath the great stone lion, readying them for a renewed attack. 'You are doubtless aware that your father visited les Sœurs aux Cadeaux Étranges and took something from them.'

'The Vessel.' His gaze was steady. 'You want me to remove it from him and hand it to our enemies.'

Moribund was taken aback. Strategy had never been the boy's strongest suit. 'Do you think it is possible?'

He stood beside her at the window. 'It doesn't matter what I think. Will it end the siege?'

'Yes, although Scarabold will be maddened beyond reason.'

'I suppose we could fashion a replica and hide the original.'

'The Sisters would know the difference.'

'Then theft it must be. Why should I be entasked with this challenge?'

'Because no one can get closer to Archim except your sister.'

'Why not ask her?'

'No matter how much she protests, she is her father's child and will not act against him.'

'But I would. Leperdandy the milksop becomes Leperdandy the betrayer. Acting in revenge for being denied the throne.'

Moribund clutched at her chest. 'I don't know what has got into you, child, for I should never think—'

'Of course you would; it is what you do best. It is all you do. You strategize better than any man.' Leperdandy's jaw was set. 'To fulfil your desire I would have to snatch the Vessel.'

'If you bring it to me, I will return it.'

'And if I should fail, the sword would fall upon my neck. This you know.'

'I understand what I am asking.'

'As the Queen, you cannot afford to have any part in this.'

'Then you understand as well.'

Leperdandy sighed. 'I have nothing to win, so it stands to reason that I have nothing to lose. You have a kingdom to command.' He led her across the room.

'Then I will show you how and where—'

Leperdandy opened the door wide and all but pushed her out. 'No,' he said. 'I will discover the ways and means for myself. The less you know about what happens, the better it will go for you. And for me, probably.'

And with that, he shut the door in her startled face.

93

To Stop the Siege

The wicker basket was leaking on to the desks in the windowless office of Muzzle, Snear & Crouch. 'Three trout, no more,' said Spackle. 'And in return you will cancel the debts against me.'

'What, all of them?' asked the outraged Muzzle – or it may have been Snear, for all the lawyers looked so similar, being prim and thin and lightless.

'Every single one.' Spackle raised his basket so that they could see the glistening fish nestled within. He had sprayed their scales with precious fresh water. The trout-eyes gleamed with such clarity that they still appeared alive.

'But the paperwork alone . . .' said Snear (or it may have been Crouch) as he licked his lips and imagined a sizzling pan on an open fire.

'Three fish – one for each of you – and I'll throw in some scallops.'

'Scallops,' echoed the third lawyer. 'Six each.'

'Two each.'

'Three.'

'A deal.'

'Then perhaps we can dispense with the paperwork on this occasion.'

And so it went, as Aunt Asphyxia's twins worked their way around each floor.

In return for the cancellation of each accusation against them, the debtors received a pair of pork chops or a lamb's liver, a bottle of wine or a half-flagon of beer. A cavalry master traded his bridle medals for a pair of calves' feet. The Head of Household handed over her wedding ring for oats and potatoes. The twins swapped food for bills of promise from the clerks and furtive embraces from the frightened cleaning-girls.

Where debts were not owed they demanded brooches, necklaces, rings, bracelets, jewels and pieces of silver. Money was suddenly worthless within the walls. Nor could it be used to bribe the soldiers outside, as they were unable to leave their posts. Thus, the new order of power within Londinium began to exert itself. In desperate times, fortune favours the opportunists.

> The target is sought.
> Breath fills the chest.
> The bowstring creaks.
> The smooth wood shaft slides through calloused fingers.
> The tension stretches further, ticking.
> A moment of silence.
> A soft outward breath.
> And a rush of displaced air.
> It brings the bowstring close enough to snatch the hairs from the ear.
> The arrow arcs, its aim true.
> A figure falls in the field – or fails to fall.
> And the whole process begins again.

Watborn ran across the roof beneath a curtain of descending arrows. There was no way of avoiding them other than to move at speed and hope that the wind turned them aside. Other men ignored his instructions not to follow him across the roofs, for the slates were green with algae and they slipped over, shooting off into the sky.

Darts glanced off the gold-crowned head of the great stone lion and shot out in lethal new directions. He could not always see where his own arrows fell. There was too much madness and confusion in the crowds below. When he was able to look down to the fields beyond the moat once more, he saw that the massed armies of the Alliance had trebled in size.

Fresh troops were arriving on horseback all along the horizon. Most of the new pennants were unfamiliar. A group of female warriors was being jeered and jostled by soldiers from another county. A troop of blind guardsmen was heading towards the cesspits. Each man had his right hand on the shoulder of the one in front until, one by one, they tumbled in. Another platoon was entirely drunk, still firing missiles even though they were mostly hitting each other.

Even so, there was method in much of the madness. As the new recruits arrived they were met by General Bullmarsh's men, who assigned tasks and places in exchange for spare ammunition. Quartermasters' stores had been set up behind a stand of oaks. Ostlers were corralling injured horses into a makeshift stable.

A campaign was taking shape.

After the next wave of arrow fire had begun, the first of the siege engines trundled forward. Lumbering petraries, those great wooden stone-throwing devices, were set up beside other machines with strange names: mangonels, ballistas and trebuchets. They were all designed with a single purpose: to hurl heavy projectiles with the greatest force.

The walls were twelve feet thick in places. The gates were of wood but could not be torched because years of standing on damp ground had sodden and compressed them. Even so, Bullmarsh still had his men standing by with moat-drawn water and wet straw.

Diverted from his mission to find explosives, Watborn made his way around the ramparts, trying to spot the most vulnerable points. A few infantrymen were attempting to climb the south-east wall by throwing ropes over the sturdy stems of the buddleia that sprouted from the brickwork. He was able to take them out with three bow-draws.

A trebuchet had been set up to fire burning projectiles, but their loads fell apart when they hit the stone walls. The fortifications had been designed to prevent invaders from finding any footholds.

The archers' courtyard had not received a visit from a single member of the royal family. Vitrolio said it was because there had not yet been sufficient casualties. He expected they would turn up once the hospital was full. Watborn thought there was another reason for their absence; they were so confident about the castle-city's ability to withstand attack that they saw no point in inspecting the troops or overseeing the battle plans.

The birdcatcher had not been tested in the ways of warfare, but even he could see that the royal absence was a tactical mistake. The archers needed to be assured that they were being well led, and Timmorian did not inspire confidence. He insisted on his men presenting themselves in full regalia but was less decisive about the rules of engagement. Some of the men fired indiscriminately into the crowds while others wasted precious ammunition on targets that were unreachable.

Almost everyone was suffering from thirst. The archers were unable to concentrate. Babies had started to die. It was unlikely that anyone would survive for much longer without clean water. Watborn remembered one summer drought in the village that had turned the fields to tinder and withered the livestock. Its effects had been felt for the next three years. Some villagers had never recovered.

He noted that two more of the gates were poorly defended. The New Gate was held by a handful of skinny boys, while the Old West Gate was propped shut with a few dry-looking oak branches. He had no right to question Timmorian's tactics but he needed to do something. The frightened soldiers, many of them little more than children, were expected to hold back the hordes with only a handful of contradictory instructions. The generals were arguing among themselves.

Watborn marshalled some men and they dismantled an iron thresher, hammering its blades across the door of the New Gate to seal it tightly. When the archers shifted away from the Old West Gate they were able to climb up and attach rusted bayonets from the armoury stockpile to the top of the wall. They reinforced the wooden door with dense tangles of springy briar, and dug deep pits that quickly filled with mud.

After helping where he could, Watborn returned to the gunpowder store and poured a little of the black powder into a drawstring bag, which he tied to a flint. Then he set off for the kitchens once more.

94

To End the War

Before he went to steal back the Vessel of All Counted Sorrows, Leperdandy searched his old schoolroom, a creaky planked coffin where he and Ambrosius had passed the blowsy, overheated afternoons of late summer in verb declension and fitful dreaming.

He tried to think like the mage. If Ambrosius knew he had unravelled a secret so big that it would place his life in danger, how might he have left his favourite pupil a clue?

The princeling turned out desks and cupboards, hunted through bags and boxes but found nothing. They had shared so many scientific passions, the lonely old teacher and the isolated boy, that he hardly knew where to start. They had built a sailing boat that sank on the moat, and vanished a great many cats, and constructed a water-clock that never worked, and manufactured fireworks that detonated prematurely, burning off their hair, but nothing was now left of these endeavours except a few mummified frogs.

Recognizing that the task was hopeless, he turned to another more pressing problem. He had been outmanoeuvred by Moribund. It was time to take control of the situation.

Two hundred female carvers had created the frescoes surrounding the chapel's great golden star; it was widely acknowledged that women made the best masons for fine alabaster. They had been ritually smothered after their task was completed, with their full consent. Indeed, it had once been regarded as a great honour to serve the kingdom so. Since that time no female had set foot in the chapel. It remained unguarded. If Moribund was found inside she would have been instantly put to death, despite her royal status.

The place of the royal women in sacred sites was complex, and only partially understood by the Decrepend. Their lives were more restricted than those of the peasants who tilled the Underlands. Their subjects were forbidden to touch them, and their honour could be ruined in a hundred different ways. These constraints were meant to make them strong, but many of the women had failed to find a way through the codes of reverence that governed them. If they showed any signs of abnormal behaviour, like crying or questioning tradition, they were carted off to the madhouse.

The relic had been returned to the centre of the great star in the marble floor of the chapel, where a single shaft of light, cleverly deflected through a building where light hardly ever penetrated, spun a sparkling moon about it.

The Vessel was such an innocuous thing, and yet over this a two-hundred-year war had been fought and many thousands had died. Knowing that no one was likely to enter the chapel and stop him, the princeling lifted it and for one brief moment was tempted to remove the lid. By not doing so he showed more sense than the learned mage. Instead, he placed it gently within his jerkin and headed off to the main gate to negotiate a settlement with the enemy.

Looking out of an archers' window, he saw that the clouds were scarred with jagged black tears. Gulls were trapped in tornadoes of white and grey. The meadow grasses had flattened as if stamped upon by invisible boots.

Leperdandy was forced to dress in an iron breastplate and chain-mail gloves before he approached the main gate. He demanded that it be unlocked.

When the door swung back he saw General Bullmarsh's army standing to attention in a ragged line across the drawbridge.

Having spotted the command tent from his window, he now made his way towards it, raising the red-and-white pennant of royal ceasefire. The guards crossed their pikes, refusing him entry until they spotted the crimson insignia on his chest. Someone ran for the commander and a council was hastily convened.

'So, Scarabold sends his son to negotiate,' said Bullmarsh, entering the tent and circling him like a predator. 'Forgive me, Prince Leperdandy, but you have the reputation of a dilettante, not a warlord. Those are women's gloves, by the way.'

'I know what they are,' replied the princeling. 'I have small hands, but I can handle a mace or a broadsword if I have to.' He couldn't, of course, but it didn't hurt to say he could.

Bullmarsh smiled. 'Perhaps I have underestimated you.'

'It is always better to be underestimated, my lord,' said Leperdandy. 'Those who watch and listen can learn more than those who speak.'

Bullmarsh was surprised. 'Well, I cannot disagree with you there. How fares your House?'

'I will not lie to you. We are suffering near unto death. The people start at shadows and believe every false rumour they hear. Many have already lost their lives and many more will do so. Our troops have held back their full strength until now in the hopes of a concord. My father, King Scarabold, knows nothing of my visit.'

'Are you saying you came under your own recognizance?'

'That does not mean he would not approve, should my purpose prove successful,' he said truthfully.

'And what is your purpose?'

'To settle the matter between us in civilized circumstances.'

Bullmarsh stalked about behind him, blocking the last of the light. 'Your mother was keen to suggest that all debts could be levelled. Perhaps no one has told you of the great wrong that has been committed against les Sœurs aux Cadeaux Étranges.'

'I am all too aware of it,' said Leperdandy. 'But I must respectfully remind you that the Vessel was housed here since our time began, in the chapel that was builded for it.'

'And it was negotiated away to end a war,' Bullmarsh reminded him. 'Now its theft has started another one. The treasure has no meaning to any of you. It is just another prize. After your family abandoned the gods, they did nothing but take from the people. The predators know the old lion has reached his final days. That's why they're circling around him, not because of sacred relics or slights to their families, not even to avenge their murdered sons.'

'Then why?'

'They see a dynasty that will soon be without a head. They are licking their lips in anticipation.'

'Then they are mere pirates, ready for plunder, just as my own father once was.'

Two guardsmen appeared at the flap of the tent. It would soon be too dark to see. Leperdandy knew his time with Bullmarsh was coming to an end, and spoke carefully.

'Commander, the King refuses to heed advice. He is determined to fight to the death and is happy to take us all with him. There must be another way to negotiate a fair resolution.'

'There is only one way a conciliation can begin,' said Bullmarsh, pacing. 'That is with the treasure placed on the table between us.'

'So be it.' Leperdandy opened his jerkin and removed the ochre-hued pot, gently setting it between the two of them.

This time Bullmarsh found it impossible to conceal his amazement. 'Is that it?'

'Wars have been fought over less.'

'Not much less, I imagine.' He reached out to pick it up but stopped himself, fearful of what might happen.

'I wouldn't if I were you. Spirit of the Archangel, divine retribution and all that.'

Bullmarsh quickly withdrew his hand.

'How do I know that you'll return the Vessel and not take it for yourself?'

'I am not Scarabold,' said the commander of the Alliance. He examined the pot a little more closely and saw that the seal had been torn apart, the edges inexpertly pushed back together.

'Guards,' he called. 'Kill the boy.'

95

To Save the Line

Giniva was riven with frustration.

Nothing, it seemed, was achievable. As she unthinkingly stepped over the dehydrated corpse of the peasant woman who usually delivered sweet basil for the breakfast table, she tried to understand how this disastrous state of affairs had come to pass. Worse, she feared that the fault was hers. If she had not proved so determined to avoid delivering an heir to the throne, they would not now be at war with all their former allies.

'What can I do, Brasslight?' she asked. 'I must put right what I made so wrong.'

She studied him by the light of the torch in the hallway, keen for his approval. The heir-prince walked beside her with natural ease. His height and bearing gave him high-born grace. The crimson leather doublet he had borrowed from Leperdandy lent him grandeur even though it was too small.

'No one would think to look at your foot now,' she said.

'Mater Moribund was informed that I was born lame and put down,' Brasslight reminded her. 'She'll insist on an examination.'

'And you will pass it. Perhaps not in bright light, but if we confront everyone tonight they will see that the calfskin matches your ankle perfectly. You're walking as if two feet were second nature to you. But we need another ally. Minerva Mentle is locked away and nothing she says will be credited.'

She had no idea that the poor old nurse had been poisoned. Upon the discovery of her body the room had been barred. The House dealt with inconvenient problems by hiding them away.

'What about the doctor?'

'Dr Fangle is gone. Moribund granted the warrant for your death. It's my father we have to convince.'

'How will he accept me?' asked Brasslight doubtfully. 'I have no proof of who I am.'

'That has long bothered me,' Giniva admitted. 'How did Nurse Mentle get you from here to the Sisters' convent on such a wild night? The roads are all but impassable during storms.'

'Perhaps she had help from someone inside.'

'But who?'

He took her slender hands in his. 'Giniva, it doesn't matter. Scarabold will believe because he wants to believe, and Moribund will be forced to keep her mouth closed. If she admits the truth, she'll be owning up to an act of treason. Tampering with the royal line is punishable by death, is it not?'

'Yes, especially when the act has been committed by someone in direct line to the throne.'

'Then she can say nothing. When Scarabold sees that you and I are in love and can produce an heir, his biggest fear will be dissolved.'

'No.' Giniva tugged at his sleeve. 'There is one problem with the plan. Your poor mother, the Lady Castilia.'

Brasslight looked puzzled. 'What do you mean?'

'The green ear. Nurse Mentle told me the truth. Dr Fangle poured adder juice into Castilia's right ear and stained it green. Her coffin will be opened—'

'What kind of people would—'

'Trust me, they will open her coffin and find proof of her murder.'

'But now is not the time,' said Brasslight. 'Not when a war is being waged.'

'You are the key to ending the war, but if my father and Moribund doubt you in any way, they will happily accuse you of being an enemy of the court and have you put to death. If the Great Wound hears that Lady Castilia was murdered, he will never believe that you, a naked babe, could have escaped alive.'

'Then what are we to do?' asked Brasslight.

'We must get rid of the evidence,' said Giniva with renewed resolve. 'We must cut off your mother's ear and destroy it. It's the final barrier we must pass to ensure your safety.'

'How are we to do that?' Brasslight asked.

The Princess patted his hand reassuringly. 'We must go to the Cemetery of Rhubamon the Great. I know where the keys are kept.'

'You want us to break in.' Nothing surprised Brasslight any more.

'The old cemetery was builded in the centre of the castle-city as a mark of importance. Its vaults lie beneath a tangle of stones and roots. It existed when the earliest inhabitants were still living in caves. It is a terrible haunted place where the spirits of the unquiet dead still roam.'

'Ghosts can't hurt us.'

'It's surrounded by high railings of black iron, topped with acanthus leaves that end in razor-points. Rhubamon the Great was supposed to be a vicious warlord who could fill a cemetery in a day, but it turned out he didn't exist. All the royals are buried there.'

'Perhaps we should wait until daylight.'

'It may be our last chance to get there, Brasslight. We must act now.'

'If the allies mount another attack, all this will become pointless.'

He might as well have argued against the incoming tide. Giniva's mind was set.

'Very well,' he said. 'Lead on.'

Beyond the walls, the thunder of distant cannons moved closer.

96

Earth and Fire

As if taps had been opened in the heavens, it began to rain. A great violence of water fell, flooding the gutters, filling the cisterns and turning slopes into mudslides. Rainwater bubbled and gushed into saucepans and vases, into pots and upturned helmets, pelting over windowsills and dripping through ceilings so that the castle-city was awash once more.

The parched populace ran to place mugs and bowls under any fresh stream of rainwater, and were soon able to drink their fill. Chamberpots could be emptied and floors cleaned.

The problem was, water was not enough to fill a stomach. Only those with something to barter had been able to obtain any food. Fights quickly broke out whenever edible scraps were spotted in someone's possession, so now all eating was fast and furtive, in dark corners and behind barred doors.

A black market had sprung up among the hoarders and buyers. Sexual favours were offered for crusts of pie. Food passed through hands less as nourishment than currency. People who had once helped each other now turned on their friends.

While it was wrong to suggest that Londinium had been a friendly place, a new level of suspicion and selfishness now infested it. As trust died, factions appeared. The scullery boys had always hated the chefs. The chapel custodians detested the Counting Chamber staff. The ladies-in-waiting loathed the maids, and everyone spat behind the backs of the lords. Just when a thousand petty territorial grievances should have been set aside so that all could work towards a common purpose, Londinium was fractured into a thousand different self-interested wards, each with its own demands and disputes. Lies became the new currency.

While its leaders floundered on, the castle-city moved towards a state of ungovernability. Perhaps it had always been so, and only invaders had ever managed to impose a semblance of order. It was fundamentally disreputable and troublesome, but while it kept to itself, nobody minded much.

On his way to the kitchens Watborn traversed the parapet walks searching for the Princess, but found no sign of royal occupation anywhere. From an embrasure he watched soldiers crawling in single file through a gap in the stone curtain-wall, wrapped in ropes.

The first grappling-hook hit the wall below him but failed to find purchase. The next one caught in the mortar.

Watborn took out his knife and cut off a length of branch, trimming its leaves while he waited for the climber to reach him, then pushed him away from the wall. He sought to be humane but when another moustachioed marauder scampered towards him like a monkey, swinging his sword blade, Watborn cut his rope and let him tumble back to earth. After that, anyone else landing on the parapets was despatched with a disabling arrow in the thigh.

He searched about. Where were Timmorian's archers? Why weren't they keeping up a defence barrage to protect the residents?

As he ran between the windows looking down into the grounds, the answer became clear. The men were milling around not knowing what to do. They still had no leadership. The villagers back in Breornsey had been better organized at harvest time.

The upstart birdcatcher was in a position to see what was happening from every angle, but what could he achieve alone? *Keep to your intent and head for the kitchens*, he reminded himself, setting off at a run.

The cemetery was set in a narrow stone courtyard surrounded by high walls, a place of perpetual shadow. After Giniva had unsuccessfully tried the key in its crusted lock, Brasslight kicked at the gate and burst it wide.

'How do we find her?' Brasslight asked, peering through the rain-mist.

'There is a system. The females in the line are separate. It was thought they were impure.'

Giniva led the way. Tombstones leaned upon each other in

upheavals of soil and weeds, their plots sunk in neglect. The upthrust tubers of ancient trees wove over, under and in some cases through the serried coffins.

Black furry creatures wriggled out of the mud and fled. 'Corpse-moles,' said Giniva, kicking at them.

Brasslight looked around at the disarrayed graves. 'After so long in the earth there won't be much left of my mother.'

'She would have been sealed in a lead coffin; they are reserved for members of the royal family. And certainly not outside. One of the vaults will hold her remains.'

Giniva led the way, slipping and sliding, across the humps of mud, between ivy-gripped slabs of marble, until she reached a crypt that was veined with the tendrils of parasitic plants. The lintel was inset with small square carvings.

'These are royal emblems. The Castilia sigil is a butterfly. Your mother is here.' She pushed against the counterweighted door. As they descended the worn steps, Brasslight lifted a dry flambeau from its link and lit it with his flint.

The flame revealed a series of stone tombs, each with a title-plaque carved at its head. Corpse air crept icy fingers over their necks. The breath of the dead filled their lungs.

Brasslight removed an iron stave from a catafalque, checking its strength as a crowbar. 'I'm afraid there is no other way to do this.'

'All these women interred here.' Giniva pointed to the caskets garlanded in crumbling stone flowers. 'Mothers, wives, queens and princesses. I was meant to join them one day.'

'Over here,' Brasslight called.

Together they lifted off a lid of woven rushes to reveal a black-ened lead coffin. Brasslight located an elegant clasp riveted over the lid and inserted the end of the stave.

'The vanity of kings,' said Giniva. No one imagined that a crypt would be so disrespectfully broken open.

It took both of them to swing back the cover, and when Giniva caught sight of the contorted remains within she nearly dropped her side. The effect of the toxin on Lady Castilia was all too obvi-ous; her body, clothed in a gown of rotted red velour, was convulsed in pain, her hands raised in twisted claws, the nails all but torn off.

'My poor lady,' said Brasslight. 'The poison had not finished its work. She revived and found herself entombed.'

'She feels nothing now,' said the Princess. 'Do you have the knife?'

Leaning over the edge of the casket, she moved the flambeau nearer the corpse's right ear. Despite the ravages of the passing years, the inner canal remained a bright emerald green.

'Don't do it,' said Brasslight. 'Severing her ear will not take away all evidence of the venom. One look at her poor body would tell anyone what happened here.'

'Then what do you suggest?'

'We must obliterate her completely.'

Searching the wall cavities, Brasslight uncovered a stack of grey cotton shrouds and unravelled them, throwing them into the casket. Before Giniva could stop him, he touched his flambeau to them. They were exceedingly dry and caught fire at once, burning with a sharp blue flame, like a spirit leaving a body.

'We have to go,' she warned. 'The mal humours will be released in the smoke.' Grabbing his hand, she pulled him towards the steps.

When they reached the top they found that the door had dropped shut behind them. The flames were now spreading through the shrouds that lay all around the vault, sparks hopping from one cloth to the next. Why did it have to be the only dry place in the whole of Londinium?

The venomous smoke stung their eyes and obscured their vision. The fire crackled and spat, then began to roar. A solid scalding wall of heat pushed at them. Above the inferno could be heard the squealing of corpse-moles in panic. The roof was black with fleeing spiders.

Covering their mouths, Giniva and Brasslight clung to one another as the crypt glowed bright with blue and crimson fire. They hammered on the rapidly heating door of the vault, but it would not budge an inch.

97

Stand the Men Down

'Wait.'

Thorax Sheathwing stepped into the Alliance command tent and found one of General Bullmarsh's men about to push a tempered skewer into the princeling's white throat.

'When they ask you why you killed the King's son, what will you say? Let me deal with this.'

Leperdandy had been fixed to an upright chair with leather straps, his hands tied behind his back. Before him, the Vessel still sat on the plan-table, mocking him. As Sheathwing strode past he pushed the underling away and hit the princeling across the face, unable to contain his fury.

'You have the effrontery to bring this to us? Did you even bother to look at it? The seal is broken open. It has been defiled. For all these centuries it has remained unviolated and now you dare—'

'Not I,' said Leperdandy, spitting blood upon the soil floor. 'Someone, I know not who. The Vessel has no magical properties. We live in a time of reason, not superstition. All that matters is what it represents.'

'And therein lies its true value, heathen. It can start a holy war.'

Sheathwing called in his guards from outside the tent. 'Carry him to the wagon,' he instructed, 'and keep him securely bound.'

'Where am I to be taken?'

Thorax turned to him as he was lifted and removed. 'You are our surety, boy. It is for the Sisters to decide what to do. You thought you could reprieve yourselves by bringing us this sullied relic? What about the deaths of our lords and earls, and the sacrilegious slaughtering of an inner-council sister? You will pay for the sins of your family, stripling, that I promise you.'

He stormed out, leaving Bullmarsh to oversee Leperdandy's removal.

'Well, you have achieved what you set out to do, lad,' said Bullmarsh wearily. 'The siege will neither be continued nor ended for now. I will tell our troops to hold off from attack until a decision has been reached, but the blockade will remain in place. My men will be pleased to abandon this godforsaken swamp-hole and take their leave in the pleasanter breezes on the other side of the Tamesis, if only for a short time.'

He called to his marshal. 'Drumband, keep your men at attention. The borders must be kept sealed. Issue instructions to hold fire until we are sure that the Sisters are satisfied with the return of their pot.'

'The enemy has not ceased to fire upon us,' Marshal Drumband complained.

'They will if I send them a signal,' said the princeling. 'If they see you abduct me, they will step up their operations.'

'I doubt that.' Bullmarsh eyed him with suspicion.

'You have no one closer to your enemy than I.'

The commander spat into the earth. 'Tell the King's troops to hold off until your return.' He thrust his slab-grey face before the princeling. 'Think yourself lucky that Thorax arrived to prevent us from killing you. You're getting out before the annihilation of this mouldering, monstrous keep. Who knows, the Sisters may even elect to keep you alive.'

Leperdandy tried to assess the situation. Nobody wanted to be here. The lashing rain, something to which all who lived here were immune, was clearly affecting the waiting soldiers. The climate was so inclement that moss could grow overnight on their epaulettes. Helmets rusted, powder soaked, weapons became waterlogged and useless. One of the Sheathwing sergeants already had a duck nesting between his spare boots.

Leperdandy gave the signal to the watching men at the gate, and after a short discussion the bowmen stood down.

On one of the terraces leading to the kitchens, Watborn looked up at the bleak tumultuous skies and saw a strange black cloud in the trees. At first he thought that a convocation of eagles was clawing its way through their topmost branches.

Twisting his head, Leperdandy also watched the dark cloud nearing as his chair was manhandled on to the back of a cart. His view was replaced by the serried wall of dark-green cypresses as Drumband's driver carried him away.

'Tell the men to redouble their assault,' Bullmarsh instructed.

98

The Attack of the Diableries

Watborn had no time to think about what he had seen.

He had reached the dammed wall of the kitchens. Now he carefully decanted a large measure of gunpowder into a twist of cloth. He added a little more for luck and wedged it into a crack between the stones.

'Get as far back as you can,' he called to those inside. 'Cover your ears.'

His experience with gunpowder was limited to the rockets he had constructed for the funeral of Finmoor's father. The resulting blast had taken off his left eyebrow and turned him deaf for two days.

He lit the fuse he had made by soaking a length of string in a solution of gunpowder and oil. Darting behind a stone column, he pressed his palms over his ears.

The bang reverberated around the walls and echoed off the great stone lion. In the Tainted Hall, the Squeam was knocked off his walking stick and Aunt Asphyxia was blown to the ground in a cacophony of crockery. In her embroidery salon, a shocked Dwinoline stabbed herself with a tapestry hook. In the Magister Chamber, Mater Moribund was almost tipped out of her chair. In the royal privy, Scarabold was dislodged from his ablutions.

In the sealed kitchens, a sizeable hole had been blown in the outer wall, releasing those who remained alive within.

Watborn shook the dust from his locks, tied a vinegar-cloth across the lower half of his face and climbed inside. The sight that greeted him by the flickering red light of the stove embers was one of terrible suffering.

The plague had burned itself out by killing too quickly. Mounds of bodies had been shovelled to one end of the great scullery. The infected rats had been beaten to death with oven shovels. At the opposite end of the kitchens, a pathetic group of survivors huddled together.

'Mr Goldhawk,' said Watborn, gently helping the head cook to his feet. 'I am pleased to find you alive.'

'I knew you would come back.' Goldhawk wiped his soot-smeared cheek and hugged the birdcatcher. His left leg was bleeding from a rip but he paid it no mind. 'We were cruelly tricked. The twins lied to us and poisoned our water. They have the key that opens the door to the cold-store. May the gods blind me, I will take revenge on Spackle and Peut.'

Something bright roared past the embrasure in the wall. A ball of flaming tar and wood bounced along the corridor and exploded against a tapestry, igniting it. Watborn tore the cloth down and beat it out.

Goldhawk helped the others claw their way from the culinary tomb. The head cook cared not that fire was raining down upon him. His only thought was to track down the tricksters who had tried to murder them.

'I will find them for you,' Watborn assured him, lifting a pastry-maid to her feet. 'I will make them pay for what they did.'

'How does the war outside go?' asked a spindly boy with a bloody bald patch on his head. 'I want to fight with the archers.'

Watborn looked out. Some platoons appeared to be retreating. Others remained near the gates doing nothing. The dark cloud was moving down from the trees. He raised a finger and pointed. 'What are they?'

'Diableries,' said Goldhawk. 'Falcons of death. I have seen pictures of them but never thought they were real.'

The Diableries were one of history's less commemorated fighting machines.

As they descended, swooping closer, Watborn saw that they were simple contraptions made of wooden stilts, roughly jointed and constructed, moving with a jerky gait. Their wicker-armoured pilots hung in baskets, working in pairs to lift and move each leg in turn.

The machines were hard to keep upright and were easily tipped over, but had advantages. Although they were easy targets for archers placed on battlements, the pilots could slingshot clay bomb-balls from above before they fell.

The Diableries were operated by a platoon of small, light-limbed women from the North Hills who had heard about the fight and had come to show off their fighting skills. They were not the only people who had joined the war for the pleasure of it. Their baskets also contained spears, animals and sacred relics that they would set alight and rain down on enemies for no particular reason other than to see the world burn. Thus the plans of stiff-necked military men were cast aside by the forces of maniacal chaos.

The first of the walking machines arced close to the gates and its pilot released her load. The detonation hurled wood and stones through pillars of cascading dirt and left behind a widening column of flame.

With each descent of a Diablerie, another explosion sounded above them.

Scarabold's archers were quick to react. They were easily able to pierce the rope baskets slung between the birds of prey, although it took over a dozen shots to down one contraption, for its pilots were determined to continue onwards, though bristling with arrows. The archers hit upon the idea of dousing their own arrowheads with burning lamp-oil, which proved much more effective.

However, this was just the first wave. Behind them came half a dozen more, sweeping nearer and swinging down with increased confidence to drop their bombs within the battlements.

Scarabold, now with his girdle refastened and stockings raised, watched from the nearest window in amazement. Through the haze of whirling machines, he saw a Sheathwing carriage leaving the drawbridge and setting off into the cypress avenue. For a moment he fancied his son was aboard it, strapped to a chair.

The armies appeared to have called a halt – what was going on? Surely the archers had not run out of arrows already?

He realized that Grand-Marshal Timmorian should have invested more in the King's army, but of course the bankers had refused to release further funds. Now Scarabold saw with his own eye that the rumours were true; the monarchy had rested so long on its laurels that its financial rulers had been able to take over governance. All his bluster and thunder had only increased the general view that they were arrogant and out of touch.

Well, no more, he thought, ducking as one contraption stepped directly past a tower window. *If we get through this alive, I will personally lead the charge by sending the bankers out to battle for me. And I will take back control, even if it means that half of us have to die in the process.*

The next bomb blew out part of the central portcullis and sent debris cascading into the royal hammam. In the North-East Quadrant, four ladies-in-waiting were hiding under the stairs, trembling in fear as each cricket-legged monstrosity clanked overhead. So many bricks rained down upon them that they were entirely entombed. For the first time ever, their sworn enemies, the chambermaids, united to dig them out.

The serving staff's children were taken to the vomitorium for safekeeping. Someone tried to conduct a headcount, but nobody knew how many there were supposed to be.

A pair of curious governesses climbed aloft to watch the incredible walking machines pass by. No one ever found enough of them to bury. Three archers were caught by a bomb-ball and blown in the direction of the river. Lady Phileuse Bose-Trunckly, Mistress of Hounds, was flattened by a burning goat that dropped out of the sky and landed squarely on top of her. Many years later the act would be commemorated in a stained-glass window.

Bullmarsh's older troops were appalled by what they saw. The rules of engagement had been cast aside by these fabled wild women, and although it placed the odds in the Alliance's favour, it could not be condoned. After the princeling failed to bring peace and the fires were put out, after the castle was stormed and its remaining rulers taken captive, there would be repercussions.

But for now the interminable barrage seemed to herald the destruction of the world.

99

The Current of History

Some of the bombs landed on the parade ground, turning it into a rockery. They could not reach the royal quarters, which remained sealed as tightly as a cake-tin. The buildings surrounding the cemetery kept it protected from attack, but down below the conflagration raged.

Burning corpse-moles scurried around Giniva and Brasslight, shrieking in pain and fear. The poisoned air was compounded by the stink of scorching flesh and bubbling wood-varnish.

'I've failed you,' cried Brasslight, barely able to catch his breath. 'It was never meant to go like this.'

'Wait, I have an idea.' The Princess dropped low beneath the fumes and searched for more shrouds, which she threw into the fire.

'What are you doing?' cried Brasslight. 'You will only make it worse for us!'

The rising heat drove them back as the flames leaped higher and faster. 'We must hold our nerve and wait,' she instructed, taking his hand.

The first detonation caught them both by surprise. The stench was appalling. The newer corpses were bloating like diseased bladders and exploding in the conflagration. Innards flew everywhere.

The next gaseous body blew off its coffin lid and sent it soaring so close to their heads that they were nearly decapitated. Giniva pressed her hands over her ears and eyes. When several corpses ignited at once, the resulting eruptions put a crack in the vault's door through which light could be seen. Brasslight was able to kick out one triangle of stone, then another.

Giniva felt a rush of cold air as the door fell away. With her ears singing and her hand locked tightly in Brasslight's, she stepped out and collapsed in the mud.

They were covered in burnt crimson entrails and surrounded by fragments of smouldering cadavers. They looked like penitents in a grotesque allegorical painting designed to frighten agnostics.

But they were alive.

Leperdandy looked up at the vaulted ceiling. A long-legged orange lizard was watching him from behind a plaster acanthus leaf. He was sitting before les Sœurs aux Cadeaux Étranges in their chapel, waiting for a verdict.

His wrists and ankles were no longer tied, but the straps had bloodied his delicate skin on their journey through the Marshlands. Gingerly, he felt the pebble-lump on his forehead. He had been knocked unconscious in Bullmarsh's wagon and had awoken just as they arrived.

The Sisters were whispering and passing the Vessel between them, angrily noting its broken seal. Lady Lavinia Travernum listened to each of them in turn and finally faced the princeling, severity etched on her features.

'Leperdandy, son of King Scarabold, you have returned to us the holy treasure which is the rightful property of les Sœurs aux Cadeaux Étranges,' she said, 'for which we commend you. But it should never have been taken, and our poor sister so brutally murdered. Now we find that the Vessel's seal has been ruptured, and the papyrus foretelling the End of Days has been destroyed. What has been done can never be undone. You must tell us in truth. Who committed this terrible sacrilege?'

Leperdandy rubbed at his wrists. 'I can't tell you because I don't know. I very much doubt it was my father, for, as you know, we are no longer a religious family. We place no spiritual value on such relics. I suspect that a man of science, now tragically murdered, had been seeking to understand why the relic was venerated and opened it unthinkingly, for which he paid the price.'

'You were all devout believers once,' said Lady Lavinia sadly. 'What terrible thing happened that could lead you so far from the path of righteousness?'

'The need to survive,' said Leperdandy, staring at the ground.

'But the providence of celestial grace bestows all bounties upon those in need.'

'We were dying of starvation and the gods did not provide. They turned their backs on us, so our forefathers took another path to ensure that their children would have a future.'

'You chose the path of evil.'

Leperdandy felt his face flush hotly. 'No, my lady, we chose expedience. We became the defilers of the dead. Had we not done so, we would have ceased to exist generations ago. And now we must live with the shame until the last of us has entered the earth. We are already dead. In our family, only my sister is free of sin. She must lead the next generation.'

'You see with clear eyes, my boy,' said Lady Lavinia. 'But seeing alone cannot suffice.'

He felt a hot tear fall from his chin. He had never seen himself from outside. Now he began to form a picture of how he was perceived by others.

'Do what you must with me,' he said. 'I can't judge you. But I beg you, when all other paths have been cruelly closed to him, remember what a man must do to stay alive and find compassion in your heart.'

Leperdandy's words touched a nerve, for the Sisters well recalled how they had turned their backs and falsely declared themselves an order of silence when others had come to them in dire need. They had stood at the windows and watched as those who claimed sanctuary were put to death.

But it was not enough to turn them from their path.

'We have decided,' said Lady Lavinia, after another conference with the Sisters. 'Your rule must come to an end. Your House is mired so deeply in corruption of the soul that it cannot survive. Either Scarabold capitulates or we leave the allies to finish their work.'

'And so you would sanction the deaths of innocent peasants, women, children, maids, tradesmen, servants – for what?' said Leperdandy angrily. 'A meaningless token.'

'Meaningless to heathens, I agree,' said Lady Lavinia. 'But to the many thousands in this land who still have faith, it is everything, and belief must be counted even by those who are not in accordance. Right must prevail.'

Leperdandy burned with anger. 'You speak of *right*, but where is there happiness, where beauty, where love? There is no point in me giving him your message. Scarabold will never consider your terms.

He knowingly committed an act of war, and to him Sister Vitalia was but a faceless casualty.'

Lady Lavinia rose to signify that the meeting was at an end. 'Then heed this, Leperdandy. Now that the Vessel has been returned to its rightful place, your family's reign is at a close. Your dynasty has arrived at its own end of days. The attack will continue until all of you are destroyed.'

'But you cannot sanction violence,' he told her retreating back.

She turned to him for the last time. Silhouetted in the archway of the chapel, there was a radiance around her that was almost enough to make him believe that she possessed some kind of divinity. She was a strange mixture, ageless and wise, as sanguine and determined as Mater Moribund. He had never thought that the key to ending wars might lie with the women.

Lady Lavinia sensed that she was addressing one of the few members of the family who would heed her words. 'The Alliance ranged against you is composed of the many enemies you have made across the years, the decades, the centuries. I understand that almost everyone you have wronged is represented therein. Londinium can no longer be the property of one privileged tribe.'

'But if they understand how we are trying to change—'

'You, perhaps, but your parents are unrepentant, and they still rule. There can be no negotiation between you and your adversaries; the time for talk has passed. The tribes are arriving from the very furthest shores of the land. They are impossible to defeat, for they have no single head and will continue to arrive, wave after wave after wave, until your evil is obliterated from the very soil itself.'

'This is not making peace. You're behaving like soldiers.'

Lady Lavinia took a couple of steps towards him and folded her hands into her sleeves. 'You must always have known it would one day come to this. Your blood is not ours. You are a race apart. You are the old blood, the first blood from the land before gods, tainted and impure.'

'But I want us to change,' Leperdandy cried. 'I know about the sins we've committed, the harm we've caused. It divorced us from the people and left us isolated in a stone citadel that no one could enter or leave without risking their life.'

She placed a consoling arm around his shoulders. 'Poor princeling, you and your sister have awakened something that cannot be stopped, and now you are swept up in the current of history. But you have finally come here, to the convent that once you sought to destroy. We alone can end your shame and suffering.'

Leperdandy had never intended to cry, for it was unmanly, but the sobs came unbidden and he could not stem them. He cried not for himself but for his beloved Giniva, who deserved life and would be denied it. He cried because he would never be able to hold and comfort her again. He saw in a final flash of clarity that the only pure joy in life was caring for another.

Reaching down to his wet cheek, Lady Lavinia stroked it gently, then slashed open his pretty face, allowing his hot blood to gush over her hands in a cleansing torrent. Her fine silver blade dropped silently to the floor.

'And so the debt is paid, Leperdandy, bravest of them all,' she whispered as he dropped silently at her feet. The princeling twitched violently. The diagonal cut had split his right eye and left nostril, his mouth and his throat so broadly that blood poured down in a crimson curtain.

'Now are the repentant children forgiven and their souls set free. The old order will be overthrown and a new path to righteousness will be created.'

She looked down at her stained hands and made no attempt to clean them. Instead she pressed each palm in turn upon the pure white plaster at her back, leaving the scarlet mark of her deed for the ages.

The Sisters solemnly escorted the princeling's body to the ossuary, singing as they went. It was the sound of angels. They threw him from the ossuary window into the blade-sharp blackthorn bushes far below, to be eaten by the wolves that roamed the perimeter of the covent.

Now the war could be taken to its inevitable conclusion.

100

All Is Lost

Goldhawk's right leg was still bleeding from the blast that had opened the kitchen wall, but he paid no attention to the wound, grimacing with impatience as Watborn bound his calf. One thought filled his brain and turned his eyes scarlet: revenge.

As he hung on his apprentice's arm and picked his way across a courtyard, sections of which were burning too fiercely to look at, he was appalled by the loss of life that surrounded him. Those who had not died of thirst or plague had been scorched to death, pierced by arrows or crushed by falling brickwork. From every corner came the sound of crying children. Before the war, they had been neither seen nor heard.

As Watborn led the way he realized that most of the injured civilians were servants. The aristocracy had survived behind bolted doors, safely locked away. The old order held; selfishness ensured survival. The senior members of the court had all been raised to look after themselves. So secure were the gentry, so careful to douse fires near their living quarters and shore up their own walls, so determined to feed and water and clothe themselves at the expense of others, that Watborn could find no ingress to this private world.

He, too, was seized with a desire to avenge the deaths in the kitchens. The thought of Spackle and Peut feeding their favourites at the expense of everyone else sickened him. He was sure that the Princess would be horrified if she knew. He wondered where she was and how he could reach her.

By now the birdcatcher had grown tired and thirsty. After a

while each new corridor looked the same as the last. He saw no one else in the halls or chambers. Every door he passed was locked. Goldhawk was limping and falling behind.

Just when he was starting to despair of finding a staircase or archway leading above, Watborn smelled it: roasting bacon. An under-butler rushed past him with something sizzling under a salver, arriving at a door marked 'Royal Counting Chamber'.

'Wait, friend, where did you get that?'

The under-butler gave him a look of disdain. 'Whose master sent you?'

Watborn beckoned Goldhawk forward. As the head cook, he was known to all. Though he might not have been looking his best, his kitchen-smock torn and caked with mud and blood, he could still strike terror into any butler.

'I did,' said Goldhawk. 'Who summoned you?'

'I'm serving Craftsley Thredneedle, sir.'

'Who gave you instruction to do so?'

'Members of the royal family. Spackle and Peut told us they were acting on your express will. They have opened up the cold-store.' The under-butler was shocked to see the head cook in such a dreadful state. 'Are you all right, sir?'

Watborn seized the under-butler by the lapels. 'Where are those little lizards now?'

'I saw them just a few minutes ago. They're charging us fortunes for fresh meat,' he croaked. 'They only take gold and jewellery from the bankers. I've heard they demand favours from others in return for fine wines. It's a salmon to a gudgeon they've gone back to the cold-store to find some juicy rump-steaks for the usurers.'

Goldhawk nearly fell down the stairs in his rush to get there. 'Don't use up all your strength,' Watborn begged. 'We will find them. Tell me the way.'

They reached the bottom of the Pecheham Tower, hopping awkwardly over the narrow streams that rushed under the cold-store, providing it with the ability to make ice.

The door to the storage vault stood ajar. Spackle was inside, chipping legs of lamb free with an ice pick. Peut was waiting at the threshold and spotted Goldhawk first. He tapped his brother on the arm. They both laughed. Goldhawk alone was in no condition for a fight.

But Goldhawk was not alone. Watborn stepped into the store beside him. He was nearly twice the height of the twins.

The laughter dried in their mouths. Watborn picked up Peut as if he were a kitten and threw him so that he landed on top of his brother in an avalanche of frozen chops and ribs.

'So you'll feed the King and return the key at once, will you?' he said with menacing calm.

'It gladdens our hearts to see Mr Goldhawk so well.' Spackle struggled to his feet and dusted frost-ferns from his chest. He recalled being wary of this burly giant. It was clear that Goldhawk had found himself a champion.

'We tried to return to him but we're under bombardment, as you can hear.' Peut pointed to the ceiling and cocked an ear. 'Now that you are here, Mr Whoever-You-May-Be, we can help you distribute food to all the poor starving mothers and children.'

Goldhawk's rage started to heat the cold-store. 'First you may trouble yourselves to give me the gold and jewels you took in exchange for the items you stole from the King's larder. Then you might care to start pissing yourself with fright while my friend here decides upon your fate.'

'But Mr Goldhawk, sir, you know we have only ever had your best interests at heart,' said Spackle coolly. 'Although, of course, there's the cost of our labour and hard work in the service of the needy. We don't know this other fellow and cannot be expected to deal with him. He's not one of us.'

Before he could continue, Watborn picked them both up by their collars and spun them around, hurling them at the larder shelves, where they vanished in a cascade of ice-covered codfish, oysters and pork loins.

'Watborn, leave them for me,' Goldhawk commanded, raising his meaty fists. 'I will tear them apart with my own hands and serve their guts to the King in a stew-dumpling.'

While he was distracted, thinking about the different ways in which the boys could be served, fricasseed, baked, roasted, steamed, stewed or prepared in a pie with shallots, Spackle sprang back to his feet and snatched Peut out by the collar of his shirt.

Everything happened so quickly that Watborn had no time to react. Moments later they had swung the cold-store door shut, slamming it so hard that the crystal key shattered in the lock. The booming of the door had the cold air of finality.

Without the intact key, the lock could not be opened. The chef and the birdcatcher searched about for sticks and twigs to push into the keyhole but it was blocked with fragments of crystal.

It was the second time that Goldhawk had been condemned to death, but the first time for Watborn.

'At least there is no way for those little thieves to access the food stores any more,' said Goldhawk.

Watborn tried to see into the gloom. The cold was enough to freeze eyeballs in their sockets. 'Is there any other way out of here?'

'No, we are deep within the walls.'

'We can survive for a while.' Watborn had a mind to wrap himself and Goldhawk in the skins of sheep. He had once lasted three nights on a moor in the heart of winter, knotted inside a lamb's wool.

From somewhere behind them came moans of suffering.

'There is no escape from this cave of ice and stone.' Goldhawk watched as the only candle guttered, its thin flame flickering in the blank brown eyes of some severed cow heads. 'Watborn, we shall die in here,' he said, 'and so will everyone else. All is lost.'

The moon had risen, and the latest Diablerie raid came to an end as its crescent crept behind clouds, for the pilots could no longer see clearly enough to continue bombing the walls. An eerie hush fell across the battlements, broken only by the feasting of crows and the enfeebled cries of those trapped beneath bricks.

Although the blockade was still officially in place, various secret missions had attempted to get the farmers and fishermen to deliver their wares, but so far they had all failed. No one from the Underlands was prepared to approach with death dropping from every direction, and so the starvation continued. At least now the wells could be safely unstoppered without fear of being poisoned.

'In the morning we will assemble all for the great assault,' announced General Bullmarsh when Leperdandy did not reappear. He was from the south and hated this marsh-grey land where the sun barely existed and the people were so arrogant. 'We will lay waste to the castle and slaughter all those within, and good riddance to them. I have long been waiting for this moment and plan to enjoy it.'

Watborn sat wrapped in a bull. Its cold wet skin was stuck to the back of his neck. Its intestines had at least been arranged in a tidy pink pile. Goldhawk was covered in a sheep.

The cold-store was silent. Their hands and feet were numb. Their teeth shook. There was no telling day from night.

'I suppose you regret coming here now,' said the cook. 'Why did you come anyway?'

Watborn pulled the bull-skin closer about him. 'I had a purpose.'

'And what was that?'

'It's better not to speak of it.' He unfurled himself and reached out for the wall. 'There must be a loose brick somewhere.'

Goldhawk persisted. 'Talk to me, Watborn. So closed up, never speaking of yourself. You made the journey from your village and found a way in here, something very few ever do. You took a great risk. We will die in here side by side. Now is a good time to tell me why you did it.'

'The cow.' Watborn blew on his hands and thought for a moment. 'The Kingsmen killed our cow.'

Goldhawk was amazed. 'According to the Decrepend, we have lost half our population, and most of those who've survived have surrendered their limbs and their wits. And you are here about a cow?'

'It wasn't even a very healthy one,' he admitted, 'but it was our livelihood. It was all we owned. Without her, my father knew that we would starve. Children are only cared for in our village if they become orphans. When there was no more food left, my mother and father had no choice but to allow themselves to die.'

'That is a terrible fate to consider.'

'That is how it is in the villages. My sickly brother, Wen, and I were left at the mercy of the elders. Wen was worked to death and fast expired. I was stronger and survived. Scarabold's men killed the cow not because they needed her for food, but because a seer had issued a prophecy and they obeyed her.'

'And you came here to demand justice.'

'I knew there would be no justice,' said Watborn.

Goldhawk waited but the sentence was not resolved. 'So you came to Londinium . . .' he prompted.

'. . . to kill the King,' said Watborn.

PART FOUR:
Blood

101

A Family Reunion

Far above the armies, the royal family regrouped in the smoky grey remains of the Tainted Hall, exhausted by the continual bombardment.

'Something must be done!' shrieked Aunt Asphyxia repeatedly, to less and less effect.

'Dwinoline, if she cannot stop making that appalling noise, take her to one of the ladies' withdrawing rooms and have her neck snapped,' Scarabold instructed.

The former First Wife remained on her chair with her needlepoint. Mater Moribund paced from window to window, wondering what had happened to her son. There had been no word from him and his bed had not been slept in. Although they had never been close, she found herself worrying. What if she had inadvertently sent him to his death?

'Gods' bollocks, Moribund, can you stop marching about?' Scarabold boomed. 'I need to think. The enemy has regrouped at a distance far away enough for us to send out food-gathering parties. You never know, a few might come back alive with something edible. Where are my errant children? They should be here with us. Are they hiding? Are they safe? Where is my virgin daughter? And where are the servants, the valets, the under-footmen?'

'They're not two-a-penny these days, like they once were,' said Dwinoline distractedly. 'Some are in hiding or have fled. Many have faded to nothing. Grandfather Blackshingle had his face kicked in by someone who got in through the roof.'

'Is he dead?'

'It's hard to tell.' She bit through a silver thread.

'Archim, you must take control of this before we lose the few who remain,' warned Moribund.

The King's thoughts were following different lines. 'Meldred, I need you to locate my children. They remain our last hope for the future of this family.'

'The family, the family!' cried the Queen. 'We are being starved, blasted and crushed to death and all you can think of is the continuation of the bloodline.'

'There is nothing else left. We have lost everything we once held dear. I've a good mind to fetch that damned Vessel and hurl it from the battlements. Let's see how the Spirit of the Archangel can aid our enemies in their righteous cause.'

Moribund quailed at the thought of the Great Wound discovering the Vessel's disappearance. She was about to divert his attention elsewhere when she heard the door to the hall creak open, and looked up.

Standing on the threshold of the Tainted Hall were Giniva and a handsome young man she had never seen before.

'Father, Mother, everyone,' announced Giniva, as if she had not a care in the world, 'this is Brasslight. He is the true son of the King's brother, Perseo, and the Lady Castilia.'

She pushed the heir-prince forward, noting with pride how naturally he now moved. Brasslight had the courtly bearing of a prince. He had washed his face and brushed his blond hair, and bowed deferentially but only fractionally before the monarchs, as instructed.

Everyone in the hall stopped and stared. The Decrepend looked as if his eyes were about to fall out.

Scarabold broke the stunned silence. 'I don't know where the bloody hell you've been, but it's one o'clock in the morning. And I have absolutely no idea who this is. I've never seen him before in my life. Is Folgate missing a stable-boy?'

'It is true, Your Majesty,' said Brasslight. 'My father was your brother, Perseo Lionhead Adolfus, suivant to yourself, Archim Scarabold the Third, and my mother was Lady Castilia Urethnia Carmine.'

Moribund turned to the window, the better to hide any sign of comprehension. This was the child she had ordered to die? It was simply impossible, of course, because Dr Fangle had informed her that the boy had been born deformed and was put down.

Turning back, she studied him more closely. This wondrous angel was seemingly perfect in every feature. His eyes, his skin, his royal bearing – all perfect. She was immediately suspicious.

'My father was killed in a riding accident and my mother died in childbirth,' said Brasslight. 'I am the sole surviving heir.'

'Then where have you been all this time, child?' Dwinoline set aside her tapestry, leaving it within easy reach.

'Suspecting a plot, Brasslight's deliverers conspired to take him away under cover of darkness,' said Giniva.

'Where did you go, boy?' Scarabold demanded. 'What happened?'

'As a newborn, I was hardly in a position to remember the circumstances,' said Brasslight. 'I'm told I was delivered to les Sœurs aux Cadeaux Étranges, who raised me as a foundling.'

'Oh, this is some kind of ploy.' Moribund was no longer able to contain her anger. 'We are at war with an army raised in part by the Sisters, and now you come in here telling us this fish-and-bait tale of snatched infants and secret fosterhood? You, sir, are not who you say you are. The child was born deformed.'

'Forgive me, Your Ladyship, but how do you know this to be true?' asked Brasslight.

'Why, Dr Fangle and Nurse Mentle both swore—' The sentence curdled in her mouth as she realized how ridiculous it sounded for a reigning monarch to rely on the word of an incompetent alcoholic and a befuddled old midwife.

Brasslight pushed his advantage, knowing that he had to tread carefully. 'Your servants acted in good faith upon the instructions of an enemy. Knowing nothing but the cloisters, I was released upon my eighteenth birthday to return to a home I did not remember.'

Mater Moribund thought fast. What had Dr Fangle said about the boy's disfigurement? 'Strip,' she instructed. 'Take off your clothes. Prove yourself to us.'

Brasslight remained motionless for a moment, then removed his doublet and shirt, his boots and hose, standing before them as naked as an infant. In the candlelight his right foot blended so seamlessly with his ankle that it was impossible to tell that he was missing it. For added effect he gracefully turned each hand and foot.

'A fine performance, lad,' Scarabold exclaimed as he allowed Brasslight to dress, 'but it does not hold. If you are not deformed, then why were you not presented as the heir apparent?'

'Because, Your Majesty, you were deceived by a traitor who wished you to believe that both mother and son were dead. This traitor is doubtless the same person who staged my father's accident.'

The implication was clear to Scarabold. The finger of guilt pointed in one direction only, to Mater Moribund. Anyone could see how easily the fire of vengeance might ignite within her dark eyes.

Suddenly Moribund found herself accused of arranging the assassinations of an entire family, the revenge of a cheated woman.

Scarabold did not care about intrigues; he was a warrior, not a politician. Let the women plot while the men fought. The Great Wound spread his seed as he spread his marmalade: thickly and on many different surfaces. Some sprouted, some did not. All he needed now was one sturdy, healthy boy to carry the weight of history on his shoulders. This one looked well enough, so the circumstances of his survival hardly mattered, even if it made his own wife a murderess.

Brasslight took advantage of this impasse to cover his foot with care. Giniva tried to consider the choices open to Moribund. As Queen, she could not be executed for treason.

But she was not, technically, the Queen.

Only she and Scarabold, and possibly the Bishop, knew that the scroll of betrothment had remained unsigned. One other person knew why: the magister who had tested her blood.

'You killed Ambrosius as well, didn't you?' said Giniva. 'He was found murdered in his laboratory.'

Moribund's eyes widened in outrage. 'You dare to accuse me? I know nothing of how this came about.'

'But you ordered it.'

'You think with everything that is happening to us right now I am concerned with such intrigues?'

'But they are both connected in some way.' It was a weak gambit, and in making it Giniva revealed her hand to be empty. She flinched, sensing that the tide was turning against them.

'Leperdandy has returned the Vessel to the Sisters as you wished,' she told Moribund. 'He was seen leaving Londinium.'

The Great Wound was rendered speechless. His face was as red as a salamander. His mouth opened and shut but no sound emerged.

'The blockade is only the start. The bombardment will continue until we are overrun and defeated.'

'Are we expected to surrender?' asked Moribund in amazement.

'No, Mother. We are expected to die.'

'You.' Scarabold raised his great majestic head and pointed at the heir-prince. 'You hold no allegiance to this family. Why are you here?'

'I am in love with your daughter,' Brasslight said, taking her hand.

'In a time of war you think only of love?'

'No, Your Majesty, I think of unity.'

'Explain yourself, stripling.'

'We should be married at once and set about providing you with an heir,' Brasslight replied. 'The only way to salvation is by bringing about the birth of a new generation.'

'That is not going to solve our immediate problem,' said Scarabold. 'We'll all be dead long before then. I hope my son's peace offering is not accepted by the Sisters, for they and their pernicious religion deserve to be ground into bone-dust.'

'First things first,' said Giniva. 'We must open the cold-store and feed the troops. They need to have their humours restored. They cannot fight without food.'

'And what else would you have me do, pray tell?' asked Scarabold, in a honey-coated tone of threat.

'Since the attack is being led by an ever-expanding coalition, it is unclear which factions are now involved. All we know is that the F'Arcys and the Sheathwing are still leading the Alliance.'

'This is most fascinating,' said Scarabold, stroking his beard. 'To find that my daughter has forsaken her interest in lace and transformed overnight into a military strategist.'

The Princess knew that a storm would burst forth from these gathering clouds. Sure enough, Scarabold made a grab at the air itself.

'Do it, then, do everything you wish. Organize a damned wedding, make sure you are seeded and then get back to your boudoir. I will deal with these flittering gnats' – he indicated the patch of night sky beyond the windows where the pilots had delivered bombs from their stilts – 'and once they are crushed I will lay waste to their kingdoms. I will despoil their lands, slaughter their families and eat their children. I will wrap myself in their entrails and smash their skulls to make our bread. I will make the skies rain with blood. Do you understand?'

Giniva was now so close to the King that she found herself

checking his teeth for shreds of crimson meat. 'How?' she dared to ask. 'There are no coffers for weapons or ammunition, no food-stuffs to keep your troops alive, no potions to keep them well, no wages to keep them loyal. They are the aggressors but we are the wrongdoers. We are godless, and they have the gods on their side. We don't believe in them but they do, and so have the advantage of faith.'

Scarabold had never before struck his children, and the action surprised both of them. Giniva was sent sprawling across the room and arose with blood smeared across her lips. His ring had cut her cheek.

'You are banished, raw girl.' Scarabold growled like a dying bear. 'You will leave the royal sightline for ever. From this day forward I have no daughter.'

'No, Archim,' warned Moribund, placing a staying hand on his arm. 'Think of the child. Get the girl wed.' She knew that the people could be persuaded to accept a baby prince, and that he would be controlled by those who still wielded power. 'It's the one thing that will show them we have changed. Let the joyful day take place, and as soon as possible.'

102

A *Wedding Under Bombardment*

The morning's bombings had commenced afresh. A distant boom sounded, dropping stalactites on them.

Watborn paid no mind. He saw it now, the shadowy thing he had not been able to admit to himself. From the moment he had seen what the Kingsmen had wrought in Breornsey, some dark part of his mind had begun to think of revenge.

The cook thought the matter over. 'You are as green as a meadow, lad. A king has a thousand enemies. You think you ever had a chance? Don't you know that those who come to Londinium always fall in with it?'

'I know that vengeance is not an honourable act. He took my family. I can't go unavenged.' He dragged the bull-pelt a little more tightly around himself. It squelched and leaked. 'The King's days are numbered, anyway. It's obvious to all but him. Something new must rise.'

'I wish I had your optimism,' said Goldhawk. 'I'd settle for getting out of here with my fingers and toes intact. If we make it out of here, what are you going to do?'

'I shall confront Scarabold and ask him why I should spare his life.'

'You do understand your position, I take it? To him you are' – he held his frozen fingers a hair's breadth apart – 'less than this.'

'Everyone keeps telling me he is a great man. This means nothing. Until I got here I never knew we even had a king. I want proof of what makes him great.'

'So you plan to talk to him man to man. You will not be allowed to enter the same room as him. Your path will be blocked by guards.'

'We shall see about that,' Watborn replied with a grim set to his lips.

Many floors above, plaster fell from the arris of the chapel ceiling. It pattered over the yellow roses arranged in sprays along the altar by an enterprising warden, who had risked his life to clip them from the rose-garden. He had carried out his mission in exchange for a hunk of mildewed bread.

It was the fastest wedding ever assembled.

The entire arrangement took less than an hour. In other circumstances the bride might have looked radiant, the groom resplendent, but her periwinkle gown was in tatters and his jacket was split at the seams. They both still reeked of corpse-smoke.

The organist tackled a toccata but brick-dust had entered a number of pipes, causing filth to be blasted over the assembly when he ventured into major chords. As the couple entered he settled for 'The Bridal Penance' (anon., traditional). It was a dirge-like piece designed to last for the exact length of the crossing of the nave, but as he couldn't play all the notes, it ended too early, and as part of the nave was missing, the bride had to clamber over rubble to reach the altar.

Most painful of all to Giniva was the absence of her wayward brother. She had not heard a word from him. It was impossible to imagine that he might have fled the kingdom. He had been taken somewhere. Where was he?

The pews in the Chapel of St Bartholomew held just a handful of survivors, the more expendable members of the family being required to hold the ramparts, although for the most part they fled to their apartments and hid.

From the groom's side there was no one at all. Father Sesquinatius presided over the ceremony, as the Bishop of Wexerley had been rendered *hors de combat* by an airborne saint. In a typical paradox, the clergy were only allowed to preach sermons with all religious references removed. For the sake of expedience, hymns and readings were omitted from the nuptials so that the service preserved only the vaguest bones of the liturgy.

'As a man and woman grow together in love and fear, they shall be united in heart, body and mind until death renders them to the damp and stinking earth,' said Sesquinatius, moving through the service at a gallop. 'Companionship, maturity and so on, community and society – not applicable in this case, I think – comfort, honour, obey, protect, et cetera, for the whole of their earthly life. If anyone should know of any just impediment—'

Sesquinatius barely paused for breath here. Giniva looked around, wondering if her brother had arrived yet. From far above them came a fall of bricks. Somebody screamed.

'Let's skip that bit, too. Do you, Princess Giniva Belladonna Moribund, take Prince Brasslight Perseo the Third – I hope I've got that right – as your lawfully wedded husband?'

'I certainly do,' said Brasslight, moving to kiss the bride.

'Not yet,' said Father Sesquinatius.

'Oh, for Squeam's sake, get on with it,' rumbled Scarabold. 'They're married, yes? Have you got the scroll, Sesquinatius?'

'No, Your Majesty, it isn't ready,' said the priest. 'I think that under the circumstances we can postpone the ratification of the scroll of betrothment until a more auspicious date, when a scribe can be found.'

One of the illuminated windows in the vestry blew in, scattering iridescent fragments of coloured glass everywhere. The effect was of an exploded rainbow. Coming as it did just after the groom's affirmation, it felt like a disapproval from higher powers. The Grandmater shook a shattered martyr out of her hair and continued reading her hymnal.

'There will be no banquet,' the Squeam announced, 'unless we can open the cold-store.'

After a visit from Asphyxia's twins he had ventured down there and attempted to remove the broken crystal key from the lock, but had failed to do so. Spackle and Peut had kept up a steady barrage of conversation, diverting him so that he failed to hear Watborn striking the inner walls with a frozen leg of mutton.

Vitrolio and Manticore had both asked where he was, and sent out archers to search for him. If he was dead, they needed to raise another to his position.

The Decrepend had found a case of wine that had miraculously survived a fall of rubble in the transept but there was no one to bring up goblets, so the family drank a toast from some empty jampots that one of the wardens had left in the vestry.

Everyone was on edge with the exception of the Grandmater and

Dwinoline, who were both enjoying the occasion. Scarabold was itching to get away and tried to hurry Sesquinatius out, but he seemed intent on talking to everyone.

'So,' said the Great Wound, slapping his huge hands together, 'when can we expect a child?'

'Scarabold, I'm sure that the young couple will take care of that at the earliest opportunity,' said the Grandmater. 'Let them get out of the chapel first.'

'There's no reason why they couldn't make a start now. She could be seeded before I reach the roof. We're trying a new kind of missile.'

Giniva caught up with her father before he could leave. 'Please, Father, take back your harsh words. I beg you for this on my wedding day,' she pleaded. 'I swear I only wanted what was best for the kingdom.'

Scarabold could never resist his daughter for long. 'Leperdandy's inexperience has made him a danger to all of us, and you still have much to learn. We each have our role to play in this conflict. Mine is to ensure our victory. Yours is to provide a bratling. Now I have to go and shoot something.'

'Why must there forever be conflict?' Giniva asked. 'Is there no way we can learn to live together?'

The Great Wound shook his shaggy head with vigour. 'We were cast out too long ago. Our differences are buried deep in differences of the blood. Take your new prince to bed and return with a son. I will raise an army without allies and will destroy all those who wish to take what is not theirs. With a child at our head we will grow strong once more. Our survival is all that matters.'

As Giniva departed with her new husband, she cast a backward glance at her father. His great red head was bowed, his hands at his sides. The bone-rattling drone of the bombardment circled around them as if determined to bring his sins to life.

She began to doubt that even Scarabold believed his own misguided words. The King had blinded himself to any other course of action. There could be no reconciliation now, only a headlong rush to the end of things.

103

The Crystal Key

A team of brutal-looking labourers worked in the dark, swinging pickaxes in a steady rhythm, striking metal against the petrified ice of the cold-store, barely scratching its surface. Every few minutes they stopped, exhausted, only to restart their efforts once more.

They were not attempting a rescue; they needed food.

A face as wrinkled as an aged knee moved out of the shadows. The Squeam slipped from the alcove where he had been watching the labourers' progress. As the family retainer, he never liked to interfere, but today he felt he should say something. Having identified the foreman, he tapped him on the shoulder. The great sweating brute swung around. For a moment the Squeam thought he was about to be pinioned.

'You are Flossgrey, are you not?' he asked.

'And who are you?' The foreman had a face like a trodden-upon crab. Angry eyes stared out beneath an overhang of broken brow.

'I know this cold-store,' said the retainer. 'It is opened with a crystal key, but there are shards in the lock.'

'Why do you know this?' Flossgrey growled.

'I am from the court far above you,' said the Squeam. 'We built the store this way for security. Instruct your men to strike their picks at a spot precisely two barleycorns above the lock, but not too hard. Set up a steady rhythm like this: *tap-beat-tap-beat-tap*, and so on. It is essential to maintain this rhythm for at least a quarter-hour. If the key has broken, it is the only way to shake out the pieces.'

'And what good would that do, Mr Fancy-Clothes?' Flossgrey asked, looking him up and down.

'You will then be able to insert this.' The Squeam placed a hand inside his tunic and produced a crystal key identical to the one broken by Spackle and Peut. 'We keep a copy of everything upstairs.'

From overhead came the loudest, most devastating explosion yet. It sounded as if the tops of the buildings were being destroyed.

'Hurry, man,' the Squeam told Flossgrey, holding out the glass duplicate as stone-dust showered down upon them. 'And by the fingernails of the gods, be careful with it, on the loss of your head, for there is no other.'

'You heard the fine gentleman,' bellowed Flossgrey. 'Get ready with your picks, lads.' He looked around, but the retainer had gone.

Another deafening blast resounded across the ceiling and several chunks of granite tumbled down, narrowly missing the labourers.

Flossgrey looked down at his bloody palm. 'Hell's plagues,' he exclaimed.

He had snapped the key in two.

104

Take the Day

Manticore, the Yeoman of the Guard, delivered a status report to Grand-Marshal Timmorian in the depleted armoury, and the figures did not make for comfortable reading.

'However many archers and foot-soldiers we take out,' he explained, 'fresh ones arrive minutes later. I thought there was supposed to be a ceasefire.'

'There was, but either General Bullmarsh did not keep his word or he cannot control his allies,' said Timmorian, pushing back from his planning table. 'They are close enough to scent blood.'

Manticore examined the rusted blade of an axe that looked as if it had not been sharpened for fifty years.

'How long can we just keep firing away at them?' asked Timmorian.

'We have plenty of cannon. What we lack is ammunition. The lead shot was boiled down for use in the vats we tipped over the battlements, and that proved to be a waste of time. We have been pouring hot tar around the gates, but the enemy has learned to fill it with branches, the better to climb upon. I could set the work corps to digging oil trenches.'

'We need to attack, not defend,' said Timmorian, jutting his jaw. His table was a chaotic jumble of half-prepared strategies and unworkable plans.

'We have nothing else to launch at them, sir.'

'Use your imagination, man! Raid the dining halls and take every piece of cutlery you can lay your hands on. Don't melt them down, bundle them with wire and fire them as they are. As long as it's made of metal and can fit into a cannon mouth, use it. Stair-rods, curtain rails, catchment-hooks – distribute them among the cannon-masters. We'll shoot anything we have at them.'

'Sir, we haven't made the smallest dent in their numbers since the battle began,' Manticore pointed out. 'So many barbarians have arrived that there is no room for them to stand beyond the moat. They will overrun us.'

'Perhaps they will start to kill each other before they do that,' said Timmorian with an air of desperation. 'Furniture. We have a trebuchet, don't we? Send a few wardrobes and dining tables over.'

They went to the largest window and looked down at their own soldiers. Some were in full military attire. Others were serving boys armed with pitchforks and pikes. No two platoons wore the same colours. Word had spread that the dynasty was falling to its knees, and every jackal from here to the river was prowling around in the hopes of a bite.

Manticore leaned out. Beyond the outstretched claws of the great stone lion he saw men raising timbers and setting them against the walls, although what they intended to do with them was unclear. 'They haven't been able to breach the fortifications, even though part of the portcullis has fallen down.'

'Look, when one division tries to send up a grappling iron, another gets in the way,' said Timmorian. 'They need to thin out their troops. The moat is too wide and deep for them to cross, and the battlements are placed at such odd angles that they will not support a single ladder. How, then, can they enter?'

'You might ask how we may leave,' said the yeoman.

'We never leave,' replied Timmorian. 'This is our kingdom.' He watched the chaotic scene below, thinking. 'We must breach our own walls, here and over there.'

Manticore looked at him as if he had gone mad. 'Why would we do that?'

'It is an old trick I have seen work before. Pull the stones inwards when they fire, so that they think they have done it themselves. Arm our men with anything you can find and station them behind the walls. The enemy will funnel through the hole and keep coming even though we slaughter them. When corpses make the breaches impassable, pour tar over the whole lot and seal it shut again. We shall use their own army against them.'

'That is . . . devious,' the yeoman admitted.

'They have no head, Manticore. They lack instruction. We were unprepared, but without a common leader they are nothing. We can still take the day.'

105

The Least Expected

They circumnavigated the cold-store looking for survivors, but only found a handful, and those frozen almost to death.

'There must be a way out,' muttered Goldhawk, trying to prevent his few remaining teeth from chattering. 'We are going to die here.'

The labourers outside had gone. Without the crystal key there was no way for them to gain entry.

'We're on our own now.' Watborn cut open another sheep carcass with one of the hooked rip-knives that hung on the wall and wrapped it around a sink-boy who did not look as if he had long to live. 'You know the cold-store better than anyone.' He tried to lick his lips but his mouth was too dry. 'Our biggest problem is the lack of water.'

'There are no drainpipes in here because the ice never melts.' The head cook accepted the bloody fleece Watborn handed him and draped it around a young girl's shaking shoulders.

'The ice never melts,' Watborn repeated, thinking. He had managed to light a lanthorn and took it over to the door. He could see the pieces of the key still wedged inside the lock. Snapping off an icicle of blood, he threaded it into the keyhole and gently pushed. One small piece of the key fell out of the other end with a tinkle, but the icicle had to be withdrawn before it snapped.

'Why are you bothering to get the key out?' Goldhawk asked. 'It was specially made for me. The Squeam had the only copy. We will not find anything else that can fit.'

Watborn did not reply, but worked silently on. After an hour he had managed to push out all the pieces of the slender crystal rod, but they had fallen on the other side of the door.

'I have an idea.' He snapped off a fresh stalactite and placed it in a tray that had been used to present lamb hearts. Setting the lanthorn under the tray, he melted the icicle. 'The lock tumblers must be very delicate if they turn on glass.'

'Oh, they are,' Goldhawk assured him. 'The slightest brush is enough to open them. They are impervious to the ice for they're carved from oak-wood, but they must be touched in the right order.'

Watborn took a length of wire from a bale of straw and set it in the tray of water. He repeatedly removed the wire and replaced it until a coating of ice began to form. The next part was the hardest. Tilting the wire into the keyhole, he dripped water along it. The droplets fell where the tumblers touched the wire. He held the wire steady while ice grew, but the process was agonizingly slow, especially as continuing attacks made the walls shake.

Goldhawk went grey with cold, and his eyes became dull. Watborn tried to work faster but could no longer feel his fingers. Gradually he built up the shape of the ice spear to fit the lock, hoping it would stick to the tumblers. Once there was enough to hold the wire in place, he took the lanthorn and heated the lockplate just enough to free the ice-key.

The first time he turned the key its tines snapped off. Now he had to melt them and begin again.

The second time he waited longer and made them thicker, but they broke once more.

The third time the ice-key formed in the wrong shape.

Watborn knew that escape was a matter of trial and error, but above all, patience. He had sat in hides for days at a time and waited for partridges to pass his way. He felt sure he would eventually get the door open, if only he could stay alive for long enough.

His nerve-dead fingers threaded the wire into the keyhole for the sixth time.

'I'll make you a promise, Mr Goldhawk,' he said, determined to keep the old man awake and alive. 'If we manage to get out of here, I will confront the pair who did this to us, and it will not end happily for them.'

'You will have to avenge me,' said Goldhawk faintly, 'for I fear I am no longer in my own mind.'

Watborn worked on in silence, only to hear the ice splinter again.

*

Giniva stood by the window, being unhooked and unbuttoned by Lady Vermilia. The moment felt oddly normal, even though her dressmaker had one arm in a sling, having been affrighted on the staircase by some kind of hurled meteorite. Why was there still no word from her brother? Either he had deserted them in a state of witlessness, or he had been taken prisoner.

Brasslight was perched on the corner of the bed, divesting himself of his borrowed finery seemingly without a care.

'I keep thinking about Nurse Mentle,' she said, waving Lady Vermilia from the room. 'How did she get you to the Sisters on that terrible night? How far is it from Cadeaux Étranges to here?'

'I have no idea.'

'But you made the journey yourself only recently.'

He placed his pale arms around her shoulders. 'You're overtired, my loveling. You shouldn't fill your head with such worrying notions. Why not try to get some rest?'

Giniva stared straight ahead. The late-afternoon sky was layered in lemon and purple, and clear of fighters for once. The dying sun threw out one final streak of fire before sinking into a bank of blue cloud.

'Brasslight, you said it was never meant to go like this. When you said you'd failed me. What did you mean? Never meant to go like what?'

'When did I say that?'

'In the Cemetery of Rhubamon the Great. Where we nearly died.'

'Really? I honestly don't remember.' He eased himself away from her and bent down to rub his right foot, which was chafing his ankle. 'I have to take off the shoe for a while. It makes the foot heavier and harder to control. Did you enjoy the wedding service?'

'No,' she said absently. 'A girl might dream of such a moment all her life, only to find it does not live up to her expectations. This most certainly did not.'

'We had no choice. You don't have any regrets about marrying me, do you?'

'It was just the way it had to happen,' she said forlornly. 'Leperdandy should have been there. I miss my brother. He is wiser than anyone realizes. If only he were here with us now—'

'I'm sure he's not very far away,' said Brasslight. 'You know he would never leave you, not entirely.'

'I can't believe he volunteered for such a dangerous mission himself. Father cannot see how brave his son has become.'

'Perhaps we should have a drink to celebrate.' Brasslight pulled off his black leather boot and wriggled the calfskin foot about in relief. 'I hid a bottle of flamed plumvine so that we could celebrate our union alone.'

'At least I don't have to suffer the ordeal of the Reckoning now that I am lawfully married,' she said, unlacing her bodice. 'Although we're not, are we?'

Brasslight removed the cork with a pop. 'Not what, my loveling?'

'Lawfully married. The scroll of betrothment could not yet be signed.'

'It's just a formality, nothing more.'

'Like Mater Moribund's . . .' she murmured.

He filled a pair of ceremonial goblets. 'The important part is that we are now spiritually bound together. I give you a toast: to us, whatever may befall.'

He raised his goblet to hers. She drank but did not answer him. The room had darkened, and no candles had yet been lit. She could only see the outline of his fine head, his strong square shoulders. She came up to the middle of his chest. She needed to see his eyes, to be reassured that they had done the right thing.

'Could you brighten the room a little?' she asked. 'There are tallows and tapers in the anteroom.'

Her feeling of unease was blossoming like some poisonous flower. The air in the room felt thick and hard to breathe. Brasslight found his way in the dark and located the candles at once. He seemed at ease in the shadows.

'Brasslight, we will be happy, won't we?' she asked. 'We will be different? Kinder and fairer and free from enemies, so that we may walk in the light of the great world beyond?'

'In the light, of course,' came his reply, almost dismissive. 'After you have birthed our heir. We must protect your unborn son. That is the most important thing now. There is much at stake.'

'It may not be a boy,' she said.

'It will be, of that there is no question. There are certain herbs you can take to ensure you give birth to the right sex.'

She frowned. 'You seem to have thought this through very carefully.'

'I have had a lot of time to think.'

'Perhaps there's no need to rush.' She pressed against her stomach in the gloom. 'A child will come when the time is right. After all, we're together now, and life should take its natural course.'

'The spirit of a boy-child is already within you, Giniva.' He smiled reassuringly. 'The process has begun.'

'What do you mean?' She tried to read his face but his features remained indistinct.

'The potion is doing its work. Can't you feel it?'

'No . . .' Her fingers pressed deeper into her belly, searching. 'I thought you said—'

'It's already growing.'

She pushed until it hurt.

'But that is not possible. I haven't – *we* haven't—'

'There are other ways. The potion ensures that a healthy baby boy will grow to term in just one month.'

'But that is sorcery.'

'Can you not sense the creature feeding in your belly?' He stared at her and smiled and smiled.

She glanced down, aghast. 'What have you done?'

As he walked back towards her she heard his shoeless steel foot on the flagstone floor between the rugs. The sound was like the ticking of the ancient clock above her bed.

> *Pok . . .*
>
> > *Pok . . .*
>
> > > *Pok . . .*

Her heart skipped a beat. She remembered the advice she had been so eager to dismiss. Calmora had said it would take place when she least expected it, in the place where she felt the most safe.

Brasslight walked towards her with a burning candle in each hand. In the last strands of twilight his eyes appeared to glow red.

Pok-Pok, she thought. *The One Who Moves in the Shadows.*

106

Escape

Watborn was only a little superstitious, but the number seven had always proved auspicious for him. Now, as he prepared to turn the seventh key, he could not help but ready himself for the sound of fracturing ice.

On the last try he had pressed his ear so hard to the wall that it had stuck there. He strained to hear the tumblers clicking into place one by one. His frozen fingers turned so incrementally that they might have been petrified.

Behind him an avalanche of stone-hard swan carcasses caused him to still his fingers. Goldhawk did not respond. He had turned blue. His eyes were open but had been frozen in place.

Watborn needed to keep turning the key to stop the wet ice from refreezing and sticking. The last quarter-turn would end either in a click or a crack. He slowly turned it and squeezed his eyes shut.

Click.

Seconds after the last tumbler dropped, the door swung open as lightly and easily as a barn-gate, as if to suggest that it had only needed a loving touch.

He propped it open with a swan, then dragged Goldhawk out into the warmer hallway. The chef's clothes were as stiff as boards. Taking down the wall-torches, he pushed the hot metal cylinders beneath the sheep's skin so that it was soon hard to tell who was roasting most, Goldhawk or the sheep.

The chef's mouth hung open. His tongue was hard and dry. Watborn dripped melted ice on to it.

'Goldhawk, come back. You'll be warm now.'

There was no answer. His eyes were like grey marbles.

Watborn lowered the old man's dry eyelids. After dignifying his body by placing his hands across his breastbone, he took the sheepskin and donned it, leaving the bloody entrails to hang over his chest.

I failed you, Goldhawk, he thought. *You who accepted a stranger without questions or demands. Before I die, I swear I will avenge your death.*

He was still considering how to do so when Goldhawk spat over him, stuttering back to life. 'I smell like a bloody farmyard,' said the chef, coughing. 'I need more water.' He loosened his tongue. 'Give me a hand up.'

Overjoyed, Watborn helped him to his feet. 'You're back.'

The chef stamped life back into his feet. 'It was too damned cold to stay where I was.'

'Tell me where to go, Goldhawk.'

'You? I'll be fine now. You should return to Timmorian's archers and fight beside them.'

'Up there I will be one of a hundred. Where can I make the most difference?'

'Only the family can make decisions that change wars. You will never get close to them.'

'There must be some way . . .'

Watborn rubbed warmth back into his tingling arms. He wished to see the Princess. After making sure that the cook was well enough to find his way to safety, he doggedly set off in the direction of the royal apartments.

107

The Secrets in the Thread

Giniva turned to run but Brasslight was upon her.

He brought her down hard upon the floor. The candles spattered tiny meteors of wax and fire. He placed a hand across her mouth. She tried to gnaw his thumb.

'Be still, my love, be quiet as a mouse, for we must attract no attention and you know how much you and my little heir mean to me.'

Her wide opal eyes stared above his fingers. 'If I have a child within me, it is witchcraft.'

'You are so very clever,' he said, 'yet so innocent. If I remove my hand, you must promise not to scream. The Lady Vermilia is without and I don't want her to interfere in our affairs. Your well-being is of paramount concern to me. You are quite safe, I promise you. I have our future to think of.'

He watched her eyes, then slowly withdrew his hand.

'I have used a spell that let me feel the piercing of your egg. You are carrying the future heir within you.'

She bit his wrist to the bone.

As he rolled back she scrabbled for the door handle and slammed it open. Lady Vermilia had been listening at the keyhole and was knocked across the anteroom.

He moves in the shadows, she thought. *He will always defeat me in darkness. I must aim for lighted areas.*

She had visited every inch of the royal quarters; every chamber, gallery, oratory and bailey was known to her. Yet much of the building still remained a mystery. She knew the routes along which torches were lit at night, but only those. She ran among them now, fearing that at any second he would appear behind her. She could hear his foot steadily tapping in the hallway at her back.

The bombardments had ceased for the night. With their usual daily chores disrupted, the hungry, sickened inhabitants were trying to sleep. The only sounds as she ran onwards were her own hard breathing and the steady ticking of Brasslight's foot.

Although he had become proficient in managing the appendage, he could not move as quickly. If she stayed near the outer walls until she reached the Tainted Hall, she would keep herself safe. The Squeam slept so lightly there that he could be roused in a moment. He was old and weak but could raise the alarm.

He has not seeded me, she thought wildly, *for I would feel the thing growing. We do not believe in such things as witchcraft and demonry. We are a hard-headed and practical people.*

Perhaps the steady, unstoppable approach of her new husband clouded her mind for a moment. She had turned inwards to the royal apartments, and now found herself outside the Tapestry Room. It was the one safe haven she could truly be sure of.

Lady Dwinoline was seated alone in her usual tall-back armchair with needlework on her lap as ever, surrounded by lanthorns. She smelled of amber and oranges. An octagonal side-table held her pot of tapestry hooks. The scene was so familiar and homely that the Princess fell back against the door with a sigh of relief, locking it behind her, and fought to regain her breath.

'Giniva, my dearest duckling, how thoughtful of you to visit, but should you not be in your marital bed?' Dwinoline tilted her forehead upwards to be kissed.

'My new husband is not . . .' she began, but knew not how to express herself.

'Not what, my little cygnet? Not what you expected?'

'He is not true. He is my Reckoning.'

Dwinoline appeared not to have heard. 'Come, little dove, look at my tapestry. It is nearly completed.'

'He says I am with child. I am bewitched.'

'Over here, child. I have just the last panel to finish.' She held her needle, threaded with coppery gold, to one side.

Giniva paced nervously. 'There has been no word from my brother.'

'No. I understand he was last seen in the company of Bullmarsh.'

'Are you not afraid for him?'

'Your brother is stronger than anyone realizes. I have always known it. But it has taken this war to draw him out. Sit beside me, doveling, let me take your mind from your troubles for just a few minutes. See what I have wrought.' She patted a cushion.

Unsettled and confused, Giniva joined her stepmother. Dwinoline unravelled the tapestry – there seemed to be many yards of it – and pointed to the panels.

'The story goes back centuries, of course, before tales of sorcerers fighting dragons, all of them completely untrue. Those events are lost in the fog of the past, but for you perhaps the story starts here – now, let me see . . .' She ran a nail over the stitches. 'Ah yes, with Scarabold's older brother, Perseo, and his much younger, much more vulgar wife, Castilia. Here they are at their betrothment, see? See how badly dressed she is. And look, a child. Sadly the wrong sex. She had so wanted a boy. What use is a female to a dynasty?'

She held up a section of the intricately threaded gold-and-green tapestry in the lamplight. The stitching was so fine that it looked like brushstrokes.

'And here is Perseo falling into a ravine in the fog. Affrighted by a bear, so we're told, but there was never any proof of that so I left the bear out. I've heard there's a bear wandering around these corridors. Can that be right?' She tapped the tapestry. 'Anyway, there is your father riding with his brother. How dashing he looks. And there is Perseo, landing on his pate. How could this have happened? Kings ride before they can walk. The pair were less than half a league away. A highly unlikely tragedy, then. Perhaps we'll never know. This panel need not concern you.'

She moved the stitchwork on. 'And see here, this is Lady Castilia in the birthing tower as Dr Fangle and Nurse Mentle deliver a boy born without a foot. For this part I used scarlet and white thread. Here is the poisoning of Castilia, quite acceptable under the circumstances. A lovely emerald for the adder juice. As Perseo was dead by then, she could not bear him another child, so she had to go.'

Giniva studied the tapestry by the flickering candle flames, appalled. Dwinoline lovingly ran the gleaming material through her fingers.

'Here you see Nurse Mentle bearing the child away in the storm, and the Sisters accepting the poor deformed infant – not just missing a foot, according to poor old Minerva, but mentally deficient. Ambrosius had warned us that there was a history of derangement in Castilia's family.'

She moved the tapestry on. 'In this panel you can see les Sœurs aux Cadeaux Étranges drowning the little child in the baptismal font, for it had indeed been born a cretin, a thing without a brain at all, and the Sisters were not equipped to care for such a poor creature. There is a streak of practicality running through the convent that many would call callousness. But what is this?'

She moved the tapestry on to a newer section, displaying it to the Princess. 'More wedding days. My marriage to Scarabold when he was fine and fit and had both his eyes, a legendary warrior. So brave and handsome, I thought then. There are no threads to stitch for disappointment. And another wedding, look – Scarabold's betrothment to Moribund, with me much smaller in the background between them, do you see? I was the First Wife. Then I became the Second, always behind, always ignored. Dwinoline who is barren and therefore incomplete. Dwinoline who hears and sees nothing, but hears and sees all, and records it in the tapestry.'

She unfurled the next fold of cloth. 'I'm particularly proud of this panel – you and Leperdandy growing up, playing happily beside the great oak in the arboretum. You were lovely children – not mine, of course, but Moribund showed so little interest in motherhood that she barely noticed when I stepped in. The greens of those plants were so difficult to get right. But here now, see, I have woven vines around you – through the whole tapestry, in fact – representing your lineage. The question is not about your ancestry but your future. Leperdandy – always a sickly child, thin and weak, confined to his apartment, dismissed by the Great Wound for being too girlish and unfit to continue the line – and you, a female, unable to rule and possessing but one purpose.'

The Princess looked fearfully towards the door. There was no tapping of Brasslight's foot. She could not understand what had happened.

Dwinoline was still unfolding the tapestry. 'But here's a surprise. Look, darling, here you are at five years. The perfect little Princess who was meant to obey her parents suddenly rebels. See how she throws a tantrum! Look at the way she rants and storms about! Such a sense of privilege! So much entitlement! I knew then that you would be difficult to marry off. Alas, women get the poorer deal in courtly life. Three chances only, have they not always told you that? By law, apparently, obscure and ancient, but still a law. The Beetle Earl murdered, F'Arcy drowned, Brasslight your last chance. You see the trouble you caused? How close we came to collapse?'

Behind them, the door to the apartment opened. Brasslight stepped into the room, closed the door quietly and stood to one side. He listened respectfully with his hands folded behind his back.

'Thank goodness, then, for this handsome young man,' said Dwinoline, tapping the section of the tapestry that heralded his arrival. 'Dashing and charming, healthy and whole. But of course, that was the problem. I found him in the stables, a perfect candidate, but to pass him off as your suitor he needed a creditable lineage. There was only one possible contender in the dynasty, a malformed baby boy prevented from ascending by the Law of Damage.'

'You cut off his foot,' said Giniva, horrified.

'Oh, he agreed, didn't you, Connor Brasslight of the Groomery?'

'A small price to pay for the honour of becoming your husband,' said Brasslight, with a slight inclination of his noble brow. 'Some numbing herbs, a quick rip with a woodsaw, some stitches from my lady's fine needle, a few hours of pain, nothing more.'

Dwinoline nodded approvingly. 'A paradox – in order to prove one's eligibility, one must become ineligible. But knowing you as I do, I had faith.'

'What do you mean?' she asked.

'I told him he would have to work hard to win your heart. But he needed to succeed. How else could the Law of Damage be rescinded, unless the King's favourite herself demanded it? Perhaps it will not need to be repealed now, after all your fine efforts with the new foot. And I understand you are with child.' Dwinoline smoothed out the tapestry lovingly. 'Oh, I know there has been no official examination yet, but Brasslight assures me he was successful in your impregnation.'

'If he was, he used supernatural means,' Giniva said. 'So you will control the heir to the throne. Unless it's a girl.'

'In which case it will be drowned and you will try again.'

'And once the boy has been delivered I will die just like Castilia, so that you can control the imposter.'

Dwinoline smiled happily. 'You have undergone the Reckoning, Giniva, although you may not have realized it. The price of failing the King.'

'The One Who Walks in the Shadows . . .' she murmured.

'A silly story.' Dwinoline set aside her tapestry hook and moved the great tableau from her knees. 'The servants heard him walking about on his tin foot. You know how they love to create their own ghosts and demons. None of them knew what the Reckoning really was.'

'And what was it?' she asked dully.

'Why, what all reckonings are, my little Belladonna: a fall from innocence, of course. After the child is safely delivered, there will be a drop in the black river that rushes beneath us, unseen and unheard. Perhaps now you understand the nature of sacrifice.'

Giniva felt the bitterness of betrayal, but most of all shame – that all of her privileged, selfish life should amount to this. She had so long relied upon others that she had stopped thinking for herself. Even her refusal of the Sheathwing had simply been her revulsion at his touch. For the first time she saw her world with unclouded eyes.

'You will find me a proud and worthy father to your son, Giniva,' said Brasslight. 'I am strong and unafraid, and I can be trusted to obey the family. Did I not take care of the meddling Ambrosius?'

'A harmless old man who had never hurt anyone,' said Giniva. 'Why did you have him killed?'

'He sought to undermine the kingdom with his traitorous science. Best you stay at home and rest, my love, and leave the politics to men.'

'I have not marked out the final panels of the tapestry yet,' said Dwinoline. 'It depends upon what I decide. If you die in childbirth, Brasslight can marry again. I think it best that you should die. After the future boy-king is delivered, there are other dams better suited to breeding.'

'What about Father and Mother?'

'Scarabold's time is at an end; you must know that. And Moribund has no more cards to play. As always, the future rests upon the children and whoever controls them. I see everything so clearly.'

'You see nothing.' Giniva swept up the bundle of tapestry hooks in both fists and thrust them into Dwinoline's eyes.

Dwinoline had no time to cry out. Her tapestry slipped to the floor beside her, unspooling crimson silk across the flagstones.

Brasslight ran towards her but Giniva raised the heavy tapestry table and slammed it down upon his calfskin foot, denting it and tearing stitches. Dwinoline whimpered as she tried to remove the hooks from her ruined eyes.

Brasslight had not relocked the door. Giniva was out into the corridor before he had a chance to gather his wits and follow her.

Wiping blood from her hands to leave a shocking smear along the whitewashed wall, she fled into the darkened corridors, quickly losing herself, neither knowing nor caring where she was going. Where was there to go? Everything always led back to Londinium. Nobody ever escaped and remained alive.

She had bought herself some time. Brasslight could not easily catch up with her now. As she dashed deeper into the warren of high brick walls, without a plan, without a future, she cried out for the only one she could trust, and had ever been able to trust: Leperdandy.

108

Bombardment from Above

The corridors of wet green stone remained unresponsive and silent.

Watborn listened to a sudden cascade of masonry. He was on the lookout for armour. It had become too dangerous to venture on to the battlements without a wicker tunic. He could see Scarabold far below at the main gate, arguing with his men while Timmorian marshalled their defences, but from the look of it nothing they did made any difference at all.

He ran on through the maze of passages, hoping that he was heading in the direction of the royal apartments. Just as he recognized where he was, a shadowed figure stepped before him and raised his crossbow.

Ormond the Steady, the assassin from the Devil's Tongue, had suffered a number of excruciating misadventures since last encountering Watborn. He looked as if he had visited Hades, yet here he was, still standing and ready to complete his mission. He had finally managed to lay his hands on a new crossbow of quality after pitchforking an archer from Green Corpse into a bearpit.

Watborn was unprepared for the encounter. His arrow sheath was on his back, and on either side of him were only the corridor walls. There was nowhere to go, no way to fight back.

He did not see Ormond move but heard the air part. The first arrow punched into the meat of his shoulder. The second went wide, but only because the birdcatcher had recoiled in shock. He fell to the ground, rolling on to his undamaged side as Ormond reloaded.

I could not save her, he thought. *I cannot even save myself. I have been entrusted with a job I cannot perform.* He fought to stem the flow of blood from his shoulder.

Ormond was methodical and relentless. He enjoyed his work.

Watborn crushed his eyes shut and waited, but nothing happened. When he opened them again Ormond had been joined by another figure in even worse shape. It seemed barely able to stand upright and there was something horrifically wrong with its eyes. It was raising something in its right fist.

Ormond stood between the pair of them with his legs planted firmly on the stones, ready to strike again.

There was a sound like a snapped wire whipping through the air. The assassin's head turned around a little. One startled eye rolled up into his skull. A fine seam of crimson appeared at his throat and opened along its length like a cushion being slit. His hands tried to close the wound; too deep, too late. He dropped to the flagstones like a dumped sack of grain. Blood filled the mortar between the stones as if his body was writing a secret message.

'I believe you're looking for my sister,' said Leperdandy, returning his fine sword to its scabbard.

The breaking dawn saw the arrival of deadly new bombardiers.

The companies of archers and cannon-masters braced themselves. They had been awaiting the return of the Diableries, and now larger walking machines supported by an extra stabilizing leg were dipping rhythmically towards them, heading for the main gate once more. Although, two of them still fell over long before they reached it.

'If you can get a decent volley out there and drive them down,' said Crawthorn, a young lieutenant in charge of the roof's largest cannon, 'I'll be able to hit her square on. This thing only tips back so far.'

The cannons were immense and capable of sending a heavy stone ball nearly half a league, but they required a trajectory of no more than forty degrees. The higher the walking machines went, the more impossible it was to hit them, and the greater the chance of dropping balls on their own men. The lead had all been used up and the stonemasons were not producing granite balls fast enough, so the cannon-masters were making do with bundles of swords, knives and soup ladles.

One of the stilted falcons was toppled with a volley of toasting forks. Pinned within her own cockpit, the pilot spiralled down into the moat. Another crashed into the north-east turret in a cloud of splinters, landing with its explosive load intact. When this happened, the cadets rushed forward and seized the clay gunpowder balls, passing them to men who decanted the spheres into paper sticks, tying them to arrows which the archers tapered and lit and fired back.

But the bombardment was not much more than a game, for it made little difference to the odds. However many walking machines the battalion took down, the same number appeared beyond them. They were easy to construct and served as a distraction from the real work being carried out below.

Emerging from the mouth of the cypresses, batteries of foot-soldiers tried to reach the gates, but their numbers were limited by the width of the avenue. The moment they emerged on to clear ground, every imaginable kind of missile rained down on them, including cobblestones, railings and cats.

This was where the rank-and-file proved useful. Everything that could be lifted as high as the battlement was set on fire and tipped over. The men below were crushed beneath burning ottomans, oaken tables and cabinets. A massive three-hundred-year-old mosaic dresser still filled with iron crockery landed flat on its back, taking out half a dozen foot-soldiers. As fast as walls were turned into rubble by the Diableries, they became ammunition to be dropped on the enemy. All this falling weight had the benefit of building a barricade that proved impossible to circumvent.

'I don't know how long we can keep this up,' Crawthorn told Ramdogan, his loader. 'We're creating an engine of perpetual motion.'

'What do you mean?' asked Ramdogan, wiping his sooty face on his sleeve, for a misty rain had swept in, obscuring their view.

'They fire missiles at us, we reuse them and when everything ends up down there, they haul it all back and fire it at us again. If the troops keep coming without either side capitulating, it could go on for ever.'

He waited for Ramdogan to light his fuse again and they stood well back, holding their hands over their ears. The blast peppered a stilt-legged enemy with decorative chimney-breast spears.

'Timmorian and Bullmarsh can't conduct negotiations because King Scarabold refuses to parley with anyone. The heads of the families won't come to the front line.'

'It'll have to stop sooner or later,' said Ramdogan. 'I'm hungry, wet and knackered.'

'The last conflict lasted nearly two hundred years,' said Craw-thorn wearily. 'There was hardly anyone left standing when it ended. A war of thousands reduced down to two men, a stick and a stone. Attrition, they call it.'

Ramdogan scrunched up his face. 'What's that, then?'

'The process of diminishing an army's strength through sustained attack until there's no bastard left,' said Crawthorn.

As they watched, something great and dark slowly emerged from the clouds. It looked like the skeleton of an iron fish, with gleaming grey balloons where its guts should have been, as iridescent as mackerel-skins.

The sacks were filled with rising air from lethal-looking bonfires in baskets, the whole contraption being turned by four wide paddles. The great craft was the size and shape of an ancient underwater mammal, blind, slow and cumbersome to manoeuvre. Only the rising air appeared to be keeping it aloft. It slowly drifted past as arrows and curtain-rods bounced off its scaled under-surface.

It reminded Ramdogan of the Sheathwing shield. 'I've seen this bugger before,' he said. 'You watch, it'll only manage to stay in the sky for about a minute before it catches fire and collapses. Anything that flies through the air is propelled by demons, and that's a scientific fact.'

When the bombardier reached a point directly above the parade ground, a trapdoor was cranked open and a bomb as large as a percheron unclipped itself. It rolled over and over as it began its leisurely descent.

Crawthorn swore in a way that would have made a brothel-keeper faint.

He and Ramdogan threw themselves to the ground and covered their heads.

109

Follow the Line

The blast reverberated throughout the entire edifice, killing many soldiers and most conversation. Everyone stopped and looked heavenwards. There was an odd pattering sound; pieces of bodies were raining upon the roof above them.

The arrow seared in the meat of Watborn's shoulder. He and Leperdandy had reached the floor that belonged exclusively to the royal siblings. The pair collapsed on the floor of the princeling's apartment and caught their breath.

'The shaft has gone deep.' The boy rolled himself over and dragged a pair of crimson-painted iron pincers from under his couch. 'A prop from my stage production of *The Divine Ecstasy of St Graticus*,' he explained. 'I stole them from Malleum's foundry. They'll do the job. Hold still.' He passed Watborn his leather glove. 'This will hurt.'

Watborn bit down hard. Trying not to yell out, he concentrated on watching Leperdandy as he worked; the princeling's face was a breath-stopping ruin, slashed in half upon the diagonal, his left eye burst and scabbed, the right corner of his mouth dropped and exposed to the torn and toothless gum. A dozen smaller cuts covered his face and neck, unhealed rips made by the blackthorn bushes into which he had been thrown.

'Don't look at me unless you wish to make yourself sick,' said the princeling. 'There is no cure for vanity like it. The nuns threw me into a bush of spikes, but some pierced my throat and held the flesh together. A haywain found me. His sewing was practical but not pretty. His cart brought me back to Londinium. I felt every jolt in the track. Even that didn't hurt as much as when his child saw me and screamed.'

434

After the arrow shaft had been cleanly removed, he pushed a plug of honey-soaked cotton into the wound, causing Watborn to cry out again.

'I wasn't looking for you, by the way. But I remember you. You're quite hard to forget.' The princeling sat back on his heels and looked at his handiwork. 'That should do it, but you'll need to go carefully.'

'And what about you? Can anything be done?'

'If we get out of this alive, I shall make a fine wax mask for my face. Several, in fact, to suit my every mood.'

'The Princess must be worried about you.'

'I shall go to her.'

'No one knows where she is.'

Leperdandy rose and reached down his hand. 'Then we shall look for her together. First, we need to wash. My wounds must be cleansed and you smell like a cow's guts.'

Watborn realized he was still covered in the animal's intestinal secretions. Unsticking the stinking bull-pelt from his back and throwing it aside, he stripped and washed in a bucket of rainwater. Leperdandy gingerly bathed his bloody face. He made no fuss and did not cry out, or feel sorry for himself.

Watborn took over, carefully removing crusts of pus and blood from beneath the princeling's ruined eye. Curiously, the wound on his face matched his father's. 'It will take time to heal,' he warned. 'Maggots will keep it clean. Wait, I think there are some on the bull-skin.'

'Later, perhaps.' Leperdandy searched for his tournament uniform, the closest he had to military-wear. Watborn looked in amazement at the racks of outfits. The princeling had shed them as a lizard sheds its skin, the fretted velvet suits and robes, costumes of indolence and boredom entirely lacking purpose other than to look delicately appealing in a prone position. Now they had no worth.

Leperdandy read his mind. 'And here is the greatest offender.' He held up a pea-green gilt-threaded ceremonial tailcoat with a sapphire-studded marabou collar and prismatic fish-scale buttons edged with dragonfly wings.

Watborn knew that birds with the brightest plumage attracted the healthiest mates. As he touched it in wonder, something fell out of a pocket.

Leperdandy picked up a vellum fold marked with a red seal. 'From Magister Ambrosius.'

He opened it.

WE ARE ALL ONE

'What does it mean?'

'"We Are All One." It's written in the manner of a scientific formula.' He turned it over. On the back of the sheet was the family tree, like the one on the wall of the Tainted Hall. But this one had many more branches spreading out to over a hundred more names, all connected by a thin blood-red line of ink. 'It's not much. Do you have any idea?'

'I am just a commoner,' Watborn said. How could he be expected to know what such things meant? He had no right to look and not enough education to understand. But he had seen the red line before somewhere.

'I think I can show you where this is.'

Leperdandy looked amused. 'Very well. You are in your stockinged feet.'

In the first courtyard they reached, they found a cavalryman lying folded over a washing-trough. He had on good leather boots. The birdcatcher unlaced them and stamped them on to his feet. As he knotted them in place, he pointed up to the crimson line.

'We have to follow that.'

It ran between the stones of the floor, up the wall and over the ceiling. Watborn tried to see where it went but the shadows were too dark. 'I've seen it in other places, when I served dinner to your family.'

He had seen it made from different materials, too: glimmering bloodstones, tiles, paint, cochineal, blood. Sometimes it disappeared under a layer of paint or a wooden crossbeam, only to reappear a few feet further on.

Through corridors, across floors, around pillars, behind tapestries, it led them upwards into the castle, at one point passing into an open courtyard where half a dozen men were brawling, bloodying each others' faces with ribbed metal gloves. They were ignored as the pair cut between them.

After the courtyard came a passageway wide enough for a horse and carriage to pass along. It took the pair nearly half an hour to track the line all the way to the Tainted Hall, where it led to the original drawing of the family tree.

It did not end there, but continued outside to the Heart of All Counted Sorrows. Beneath a rotunda of elaborate crimson tiles, they followed it to the bare stone font, upon which should have stood the sacred Vessel. Here the line was no longer painted but consisted of a cord dipped in red wax. Digging it out with the tip of his knife, Watborn gave a sharp pull. It unravelled as though it had been waiting for centuries for someone to attend to it.

The waxen thread burned his fingers and reddened the palms of his hands. After crossing the wall and the domed ceiling it reached a great iron spike at the centre and stopped. Leperdandy gave him a curious look, although in truth he could not do otherwise.

Watborn looked up in puzzlement and wrapped the cord around his hand. The princeling nodded his consent. He pulled as hard as he could.

There was an explosion of dust and sand. For a moment nothing happened. Then the spike lazily divorced itself from its mounting and dropped. Still attached to the crimson cord, it swung down in an arc and embedded itself in the stained-glass window opposite. The iridescent panels fell out on to the tiles, clattering about them.

Behind the window was a brick cavity with something withered and human inside. A body, held upright in rusted iron rings.

Commoner and prince stood together. 'There's no time to understand. We need to find my sister,' said Leperdandy. 'If she is in trouble, I know where she will go. You will have to guide me. Londinium has become treacherous and I cannot see well.'

110

The Snake in the Rose

The latticed Chancel of Penwit, a slender oratory dedicated to those slain in a battle long forgotten, was her sanctuary.

Giniva ran towards it until she could run no more, the chained golden heart bouncing at her clavicle. She found herself at the spiral staircase to the North-East Quadrant, her feet scored by the spiteful brass scorpions that lined the steps. The castle-city always contrived to hold her in place. Even here, five floors down from the roof, unfamiliar shafts of light had appeared through the ceilings and walls, the fire of heaven smiting the stronghold of heathens.

Piles of stone had cracked the floors with enormous force. In one hall, a courtier's legs protruded beneath one, and when she tried to remove the rubble she found they were no longer attached to a torso. Many of the outer rooms had been entirely destroyed. Lower floors could be discerned by peering through the cracks in floors.

She could not avoid the stench of the foetid green moat. Parts of the castle had always exuded a cruel beauty but now the smell of blood, smoke, shit and scorched stone was everywhere.

Penwit was illuminated by a single immense guttering candle that could never be extinguished. It was a spidery place one rushed past on the way to somewhere else. The royal children had been threatened with banishment to its cobwebbed corners, and had dared each other to dash through it.

Giniva no longer found it disturbing. There were, she knew, more terrible things to fear. The chancel's lack of sound and sunlight made it a still, timeless place. No one would be able to find her here.

Above her, a sparrow hung upside down in a gossamer web, the spider scurrying around it, spinning it into a silvery cocoon. All that could be heard was the faint ticking of death-watch beetles as they ate their way through the wooden floor beams. The rotted boards had always been lethal for the unwary to cross.

Dust drifted down as softly as snow. Her shoes left patterns on the creaking floor. She found a pew, wiped dirt from it and sat, catching her breath, one bloodied white knuckle at her teeth. She tried to think clearly but emotions crowded in.

Londinium was her world. As permanent as the sky and stars, its halls were her streets, its columns her trees. She realized now how close to death it had been for decades, and to see parts of it smashed open tore at her heart. Even without its hands, the great lunar clock of Fascinus had controlled her life. Everything had had an hour and a place. Routine, order, discipline, tradition. Now she had no idea if the dial still stood upon its wall or if it lay shattered upon the flagstones, its governance at an end.

Everything she had been taught to believe in was false; parents were disloyal, men were liars, women were poisonous, secret motives were assigned to all. History itself was a lie.

She felt as if she had awoken from a lifelong daydream to see the world as it truly was: a place of mud, blood and terror where living was just an attempt to survive for one more day. She was finally free but it was too late to put anything right. Her tears put penny-sized patches in the dust.

'My lady.'

She raised her face and found Leperdandy standing before her. At least, he bore her brother's shape, but his ruined face and wracked body belonged to a stranger.

She fell into his arms and refused to let him go.

'Ow.' Leperdandy winced as he extricated himself.

'What happened?'

'The war.' He turned away from her.

'My poor love. You look like Father now. The wound is deep to your skull but it will heal. I'll look after you, Dando. You know how Archim got his scar? I was just a baby. He was protecting me.'

'Just as I tried to protect you.'

'And you succeeded. I have committed a dreadful crime. I have killed our stepmother.'

She tried to explain what had happened in the Tapestry Room, but none of it sounded right. It did not matter. They had been re-united, and that was everything.

The princeling pulled Watborn forward. 'I believe you know my friend.'

Her eyes widened. 'Oh. You are still alive, then.'

'So are you, my lady.'

She thought of him swimming towards her through the green murk, the silver bubbles filling her mouth as he pressed his lips over hers.

'Gin, we have something you must see. Perhaps you can make more of it than we can.' Leperdandy led his sister over to a single shaft of sparkling light. Pulling the Ambrosius Hypothesis from his pocket, he held the vellum before her eyes. A red line. A tree. Four short words in the old tutor's handwriting.

'What does it mean?'

'The bloodline. We'll show you.' Holding out his hand, he led her back to the domed chamber of crimson tiles, with Watborn following.

'This is also called the Chamber of Kinship,' said Giniva, stepping over the pieces of stained glass. 'Kinship is blood.'

'Sorry I broke the window,' said Watborn.

'It depicted the First Lord, King Something of Olbion.' She peered into the hole behind the glass. 'Oh.'

Watborn followed her eye into the dark. The monarch's cadaver was inside, fixed in its iron brace. He was nothing more than a papery husk clad in grey rags. Giniva leaned in. His heart had been cut out and replaced with a crystal facsimile. As she removed it, she saw that it contained a vial of blood that moved when tipped.

'It's been sealed inside for three and a half centuries. There's something written around the edge.'

'The blood of us all,' said Leperdandy. 'If we compare this with the magister's samples and they're the same, we'll prove the point. We are all one. Blood doesn't lie. There's no difference between royals and commoners. There's no difference between anyone.'

'We can't prove anything,' said Giniva. 'The magister is gone and no one else has the knowledge.'

Watborn looked at the message. 'You don't need to prove it.'

'What do you mean?'

He shrugged. 'You just need to believe it is true.'

The thought came as a revelation. Giniva's family history re-ordered itself, like a run of cards slotting into place. Perseo murdered, Castilia poisoned, the child taken. But Castilia had already given birth the year before – to a girl.

'And look, a child,' Dwinoline had told her. 'Sadly the wrong sex.'

'I am the first-born,' she said, stupefied. 'I am not sixteen. *I am the eldest.*'

Her head began to swim. Somewhere far above there was another fall of brick and a scream.

The eldest daughter of the eldest son.

The King had selected his first wife for maternity, his second for strength and strategy, but Dwinoline had proved barren and Moribund's son was branded sickly, aesthetic, interested only in books and finery.

The Great Wound said he did not trust Leperdandy to get through breakfast unaided, let alone command an army, and he was kept that way. Female heirs used to be drowned or locked up. Giniva had been raised to ensure that she would never become a threat. They both had.

'What am I to do? Moribund is not my mother. Everything we were told, everything we believed – all of it is wrong. Not just in blood,' she added bitterly. 'In the stitches, in the stories, in the paint, in the stones – everywhere – all false.'

She turned and suddenly shoved him in the chest. 'Your name is Watborn. Of that you can be sure. But who am I? I am not the daughter of Moribund and Scarabold.'

'I don't understand.'

'As the daughter of his older brother, I am next in line to the crown. I am the subject of the First Exception.'

She took his arm and sat him on a pew. 'I must find Scarabold. There is much to set right.'

Watborn struggled to comprehend what had occurred. It felt as if the mysterious message had broken open a door and let in daylight.

'So this is the place where you feel safest,' said a voice from the shadows. 'It doesn't look very safe to me.'

Brasslight stepped into the pale glow of a candle.

111

The Worm in the Bud

Giniva refolded the vellum note and slipped it into her doublet. She cast a final glance at Watborn before Brasslight took his place between them. Watborn had glimpsed the intruder before. It was clear now that he meant to harm the Princess. He must have made his apprehension obvious, for the intruder suddenly lashed out, sending him over a pew. Leperdandy hobbled forward but was in no condition to take up the challenge.

The birdcatcher was back on his feet in a moment. 'You must leave,' he called to Giniva, standing between them.

'Where shall I go?'

'Somewhere I can find you.'

She turned and ran.

Brasslight picked up a bejewelled monstrance and hurled it in his direction. It shattered beside him in a shower of opaline shards. Watborn noted that it gave the Princess time to vanish into the corridors.

He stepped back into the shadows as Brasslight snatched up a heavy iron thurible and swung it at him, advancing. 'So, what are you to her? Protector, commoner? You look like a farmboy to me. Oh, there's a smell of hay about you. If you have her ear, you can tell her for me. She will prove to be like her mother, too delicate for childbirth. But a healthy son will survive. The Great Wound only cares about continuance.'

Watborn kept himself out of reach while the bogus prince ranted.

'You hear that sound outside? That is war. Shout your peasant plans from the rooftops. None of them matter now.' Brasslight's eyes shone with the angry light of ambition. 'I see you born with naught, raised in the fields with burrs in your hair and the stink of shit on your hands. There are a thousand farmboys like you, ostlers and fowlers and pedlars all looking up at the towers in the distance, full of fine words when you're in the ale. Given a chance, you're just like the rest of them. You see a silken hem and can't wait to drop to your knees in obeisance. But the second the high-borns start to fall, you climb on their backs to try to take their place.'

There was no denying that Watborn had been seduced by this new world, but his deepest conviction still held: that he had been drawn here by a higher power to end a great harm.

'We might have begun in the same place, you and I, but I'm moving from the stable to the throne. I'm bringing a new bloodline into the ailing kingdom. To maintain its strength, every tribe has to kill its weak. It's the most humane thing to do, to remove the strain of impurity.'

'You talk too much for a king,' said Watborn.

Brasslight smiled and opened his arms. 'Lead me to her, farmboy. In return I won't remove your guts.'

He swung the thurible. In trying to avoid it Watborn fell on to his back.

Brasslight stepped over the upturned pews and grabbed him by the ankle, dragging him forward. He began to twist at the joint. 'I lost a foot. This is what it feels like to be without a limb.'

Watborn cried out in pain, struggling to pull himself upright, but Brasslight flipped him over with ease.

The birdcatcher realized with alarm that he was not as strong as his opponent. Brasslight had been training himself for this moment. As Watborn fought for purchase upon the planks, the pretender pulled him with no effort at all.

Reaching down and opening his hand, he grasped the birdcatcher by the throat, ratcheting his grip.

'I am the catalyst. I am the worm in the bud, the sword of fire. I am change. We will do what Scarabold is too old and scared to do: we will make the world over.'

His grip grew stronger. Watborn felt a bone crack in his throat. With his free hand Brasslight pulled at a stack of stones, cascading them on to his legs.

As pain burst over him, his vision of the chancel began to blister and fade from view. *I should have made a plan*, Watborn thought. *Why did I ever think I could just walk in here?*

Brasslight dropped to his knees and withdrew a dagger, bringing himself close so that he might better enjoy Watborn's death.

With a creak and a groan and a blast of sawdust, the bomb-damaged floorboards split open beneath them, so that they rolled down to the floor below.

They landed on something at once soft and hard. Dazed and torn, Watborn rubbed at his burning throat and peered through the grey haze of falling filth.

They had fallen on top of a great pile of books at the rear of the Cistern Library. As Brasslight began to heave himself up, the volumes slid out beneath his feet. Stones fell from the floor above, one of them punching Brasslight in the back with a sharp crack.

The noise and dust brought another disturbance.

Something shifted in the miasma.

Something uncoiled itself.

More pages slipped away, revealing the iridescent emerald scales of the great adder's tail. Orobus was awake.

Watborn looked up; bricks were still dropping through the hole in the chancel floor, riling the reptile that was now moving all around them.

Brasslight was the first to reach a standing position. He had sighted a pair of great crossed axes upon the chimney breast and tore one down effortlessly as the snake slithered past.

As Watborn tried to find his balance, the reticulated body crushed more books. The diamond head ploughed through a mound of illuminated Bibles. Orobus recoiled from the memory of their effect. The snake slowly rose to study these interlopers, eyes of liquid gold flattening as it moved closer.

Brasslight swung the labrys down. Watborn ducked back, shifting more books and sliding lower as the emerald tail encircled them.

The blade buried itself in a vast leatherbound volume. By throwing his arms around the book, Watborn now anchored the weapon. He was able to wrench it free from the volume, but it was so heavy that he could barely raise it to head height.

Instead, he swung it around and dropped it down on to Brasslight's foot. The blade cut deep into the tin bridge of the shoe, pinning him to the floor. The leather stitches held fast. He lost his balance and toppled to the ground, leaving the foot pinioned beneath the table. The stitches split open the skin of his stump like a ripe pomegranate.

Brasslight frantically grasped at the bindings but could not loosen them in time. Sensing what was about to happen, he pulled the dagger from his belt and braced himself, admirably unafraid.

Orobus rose around him, arching its body so steeply that it seemed to be suspended from the ceiling, then dropping so that its wide red maw sank over Brasslight's head. It slowly, delicately closed its jaws and pulled upwards, tearing Brasslight out of the tin foot like plucking an apricot, lifting him off the ground in an attempt to let gravity aid its digestion.

The majority of Brasslight swung from the great adder's mouth. The snake would have no need to eat again for a month. It lost interest in pursuing a further meal and settled down to consume the pretender at its leisure.

Only the shining tin foot, still pinned to the floor by the labrys, was left behind.

Watborn checked his leg. The inflamed right shin was an exposed white blade rimed in scarlet. Wincing as he tamped the ragged skin over the bone, he tried to stand.

By fighting for the Princess he had chosen a side; there could be no going back now. As he set off to find her, Orobus lay bloated and unmoving, barely bothering to watch him leave.

Brasslight was still fidgeting beneath its scales.

112

The Firing of the Jupiter

Giniva hurtled down steps and along corridors, heading for the outer wall and the nearest gate, knowing exactly where she would find the Great Wound and his Queen. They would be where they needed to be – at the line of battle.

When she reached the great courtyard she found it disordered with bloodied bodies and missiles. Her path was barred by Timmorian's men.

'It's too dangerous,' called one. 'Bullmarsh's troops are against the curtain wall and are climbing corpses to reach over the top. This time they'll get over.'

'Where are your burial details?'

'They are overwhelmed, Your Highness.'

'I must speak to the King,' she said. 'It is a matter of life and death.'

She felt Mater Moribund's cold hand on her shoulder before she saw her. 'It is not safe for you here, child. Let me take you inside.' She turned her around and started to march her away, but Giniva shook her off and ran back. Behind her, the Queen hurried to catch up.

Scarabold was seated in a makeshift bunker built from bricks, cannon-carriages and dead archers. He might have been looming out of a cave at her, he appeared so haunted. 'Daughter, what are you doing? It is unpredictable here. Someone just threw a horse at us. Are you sprouting yet? Has he done his job? Should you not be in confinement?'

'It is very important that we speak.'

'Not now, my little rabbit; it is our most dangerous hour. My spies say there are war machines coming that can knit the mal

446

humours of the air and strike at us with concentrated miasma. And there will be flaming poisoned spears carried aloft by heraldic angels whose voices can shatter glass.'

'Why would you believe such things?'

'It is said they have enough righteousness to split the heavens on their side. We have been marked by the Devil himself.'

'The soldiers appointed by les Sœurs aux Cadeaux Étranges have been wrapping their ammunition in religious warnings blessed with holy water,' Timmorian confided. 'His Majesty has taken the stories to heart. The allies have new armaments and fresh troops, but we have a weapon to combat them. Come and see.'

Moribund barely had time to grab the Princess again when Giniva pulled free and dashed across the courtyard.

'Vitrolio forgot we had it,' said Scarabold, huffing to join her. 'You'll like this. Behold, the Jupiter.'

Behind him was the largest iron cannon she had ever seen. Its sides were decorated with elaborate scrollwork depicting naked youths going into battle. Its iron mouth was fully eight feet across. There was no ammunition in the world that would fill it.

Her curiosity got the better of her. 'Where did you find this?'

'It was always in the armoury – ornamental, I think. It was just a matter of adapting it. We had a few misfires earlier.'

'What does it use for ammunition?'

'Men,' said Scarabold proudly, joining her. 'We're going to blast three or four at a time up into the enemy's midst, just as they're scaling the walls. Instead of waiting for them to land on our soil, we're sending our forces to them. We're about to try it out. Watch.'

Grand-Marshal Timmorian timed his men as they clambered into the mouth of the cannon. The enemy ladders had been adapted to find purchase against the walls and troops were scuttling sky-wards. Time was running out to stop them.

Giniva could hardly bear to look. She did not wish to be show-ered with body parts. Timmorian started the countdown the moment the last man's head disappeared inside the mouth of the Jupiter.

A detonator exploded in a cauldron beneath the carriage with a hollow thump and the men shot upwards in a skein of grey chain-netting.

When the Princess dared to look she saw that the netting had successfully wrapped itself around the furthest ladder. The men had landed so hard upon it that its rungs had shattered, cascading bodies back to earth. One fellow had not completed the flight and now dangled in the net beneath his fellow propulsionists. Unfortunately, hanging there while trying to maintain their balance, the survivors were sitting targets for Bullmarsh's infantrymen, and were speared serially.

'I think we can do better than that,' said Timmorian. 'Reload it.'

Manticore manoeuvred the Princess beneath the stone lip of his shelter. Scarabold continued to stand and watch, oblivious, entranced by the wonder of primitive mechanics. Of Mater Moribund there was no sign.

Several Sheathwings manhandled a bomb over the crenellated wall and released it. Its clay container fell slowly, turning through the air with surprising grace. It hit the centre of the stone courtyard mere yards from the shelter, but did not explode.

'A dud!' Scarabold shouted jubilantly. Even though it had failed to go off, the bomb had managed to fragment the flagstones. Only the King walked towards it. Everyone else was still taking cover.

At that moment, a new threat appeared. While the Great Wound and his Grand-Marshal had been concentrating on firing the Jupiter, Bullmarsh's men had finally succeeded in shooting grappling-hooks into the broken portcullis and were preparing to climb over the last barbican.

After this hurdle they would have the run of the square mile.

'Father, I must speak to you,' Giniva yelled over the din of whizzing hooks, tumbling bricks and screams. 'It is of the utmost importance.'

'Giniva, of all the times you have ever wished to hold conference with me, now is the worst possible moment,' the King shouted back as a fresh troupe prepared to enter the Jupiter. 'We are fighting for your future child.'

'But that is why we must speak.'

'Do you understand that we have already lost this war? Everyone is against us. There is no one left to fight on our side.' The King was known for his suicidal assaults on enemies but this time there was a new fatalism in his tone. 'These skirmishes are but the twitching of a corpse. But we will not leave while our hearts still beat within our bodies. I will not let them take you.'

'Listen to me, Father. Everything has changed.'

A cannonball smashed through a brick arch, filling the air with choking grey dust. Scarabold seized a ladder and dragged it to his men. 'You'll have to speak up. Where have you gone? I can't see a bloody thing. There is a storm coming; rain will restore the view. Go and speak to your mother and I will join you when I can.'

There was nothing she could do. No amount of brave behaviour on her part could drag Scarabold from the smoking heart of the battle and make him listen. She alone had the power to change history and end the war, if only someone heeded her.

How many battles had been lost because a general had failed to listen to his own side? Scarabold's attention was hard enough to seize in times of peace, but now he was fully focused on the battle – not on its tactics or strategies or its possible outcome, but on the minutiae of each advance and retreat. He was a warrior first; it was his great strength and his greatest weakness.

Giniva knew she could easily die before revealing the truth. She felt the weight of history upon her. In despair she returned to the edge of the courtyard and went in search of her remaining stepmother. She had seen Moribund's dark cloak disappearing around a corner.

Someone must be told, and if it couldn't be Scarabold, it had to be the Queen.

113

Cuts

'Be careful with our richesse.'

As the corridor was not wide enough for them to carry it side by side, Spackle and Peut were taking turns dragging the chest along the corridor towards their room. Its metal corners sparked and left wavering lines along the flagstones. The twins had traded more jewels, gold and silver than they could ever use, and had enough promissory notes to provide themselves with everything they would ever need in life.

'The spoils of war,' said Spackle.

'Mother will be pleased with us,' said Peut. 'We should celebrate.'

'We didn't keep any food back for ourselves.' Spackle dropped the chest and pushed open the door to their apartment.

'I wouldn't worry about that,' said Goldhawk, pulling them inside and kicking the door shut. 'I know just what to do.'

The head cook stank. He stood before them, his white uniform entirely blackened with blood. Stuck to it were patches of ram's fur covered in dangling pink shreds of intestine. The beast's shaggy pelt had kept him alive inside the cold-store, but was now crawling with maggots. In one fist he still held the cleaver with which Watborn had skinned the beast.

'You two go everywhere together, don't you?' he said, his voice seeping menace. 'And yet I can never remember which of you is which. Peut, identify yourself.'

Peut raised a tentative hand.

'Peut, I am going to feed you slices of Spackle, and Spackle, I'm going to serve you portions of Peut.'

'We didn't mean it!' screamed Peut. 'We were going to set you free.'

'Please don't feed us to each other,' cried Spackle. 'We'll cut you in on the gold.'

'No, it is I who shall cut you – perhaps afterwards I'll splice you together into one single revolting little creature, then take you to the pike in the moat.'

'There's a war on,' said Spackle. 'Time to make money – it's what you do when there's a war.'

Goldhawk dragged them to the nearest window and looked out. The enemy ladders could be seen above the ramparts, and the men vaulting on to the walkways were now so close that he felt as if he could lean out and touch them. One of them had managed to scramble up the body of the great stone lion and was attempting to raise a flag from its jaw.

'So you would leave me to die and sell off the provisions we intended for all to the higher bidder? That's war, is it?'

Spackle looked at Peut. 'Well, yes.'

Goldhawk remembered that the King himself had first left him and his staff to die, but such were the rules of engagement. Besides, it proved that Scarabold was a strong leader who could make difficult decisions. He liked to think he would have done the same thing.

'We'll give you the largest share,' said Spackle. 'There's enough for all. Fair's fair.'

'Speaking of fairness, I have a better idea,' said Goldhawk. 'It's time you learned what it is like to fight for your King and family.'

Stowing one protesting twin under each arm, he set off for the roiling battleground below.

114

On the Cloud Bridge

On the horizon a tidal wave of black cloud had rolled in and was sweeping towards Watborn with alarming speed.

He could see bolts of lightning passing horizontally through the vapour like bright-blue filaments. The region was always storm-swept, but for once the adverse weather could prove useful.

The storm was touching down. The skies cracked open and the maelstrom descended in a hellish funnel. A hand of air reached out and spun clouds that sucked slates from the roofs and flung topsoil into the courtyard. In the ensuing darkness, all that could be seen above the portcullis was the arcing of fire-arrows.

Avalanches of brick and iron thundered through the floors, transforming them into a maze of blocked-off routes. In order to reach the Princess, Watborn knew he had to climb all the way down to the great courtyard, but he became lost in the upper reaches. When yet another staircase proved a dead-end he was forced to climb up again and pass around, through an arboretum filled with immense ferns.

He had arrived at the Cloud Bridge, the longest unsupported open walkway in the entire house. It was the only way across.

The Cloud Bridge originally comprised the outcrops of two great arches which had been joined a century earlier. It was used by those who had a head for heights, as it was dangerous to cross even in fine weather. The strong winds that blasted over its unshielded sides could snatch a child into the sky. The copper-coloured bricks had a patina of verdigris and were slippery with clumps of loose moss. There were no railings left. At its narrowest point the walkway was three feet wide. There was nothing below except the distant roofs of the kitchens and the grey mists that permanently wreathed the gaseous moat.

It's too late to go back, he told himself, *it's time to face your destiny*. He quickened his pace and headed for the first step on to the Cloud Bridge just as the storm broke.

It seemed a lifetime ago that he had been building hides on the Marshlands of Breornsey, capturing curlews, lapwings and thrushes. He had been drawn to Londinium as if by a magnetic force, taken into an unimaginable war.

He knew that what happened now would decide his fate. He did not care about making a mark upon the world. He would have liked a child to carry on his line but the gods had not granted him one. His life was not something to be thought about in detail. For a brief time he had pulled back the curtain and glimpsed another world, and it had filled him with a quiet choler – that men could be used as ballast and women as chattels to serve the whims of the few.

But it was not why he had come here. He had come to discover who he was. And even now he did not know.

Far below him, nets full of yelling men flew through the air and became entangled with each other. Surrounding them were half a dozen clumsy walking slingshots that had none of the grace of wildfowl. Some were brought spiralling down with flaming spears, some simply stumbled and fell over without being touched. There was no sense of military intelligence at work, none of the beauty of ancient warfare, just men chaotically hurting each other with whatever was at hand.

Watborn had studied the war machines and knew that to prove victorious they needed more than long wooden legs and the guiding hand of a stiff breeze. Men died in mud with their guts fallen out, to be trampled upon by their own allies.

As he watched, another half-dozen souls were blasted from the great cannon below, up through the air and into a tower wall, missing their target by a dozen feet. They fell to the moat and mostly missed that as well.

When a bomb landed on the armoury he threw himself to the stones, but nothing happened. He rose to see it sticking out of the courtyard bricks, undetonated.

And there beyond the far side of the Cloud Bridge was Giniva, leaving her father's shelter, running back into the untouched part of the main building.

He followed her eyeline and saw a familiar crow-like form moving along an open-sided passageway.

Moribund.

115

Whores and Mares

The matriarch was moving between the arches. Whenever she stepped into their shadows she vanished, only to burst back into the light like a dark sea-bird rising from water.

The sight of Scarabold facing his inevitable defeat filled her with horror. She knew he would refuse to acknowledge the outcome and would fall fighting. The Alliance would continue to arrive in waves until all hope was exhausted. They would overrun the castle, and in seeking to right its wrongs would destroy what was left. She loved her husband in her own way and could no longer bear to watch his destruction.

Giniva ran after her, begging her to stop. 'We have to speak of this,' she cried.

Moribund wheeled about, impelled by a tone she had never heard in her daughter's voice before. 'What are you talking about?'

'It was your idea to marry me off. To make sure I would be with child because you could never rule. I was not of your blood.'

'What do you know about blood?' countered Moribund. 'Nothing. This whole war is about blood. The triumph of the bloodline must be assured. Look at you. You think you can transform yourself from a pampered high-born to a woman of the land just by changing your clothes? You are still play-acting, like a character from your storybooks. You have no idea of the meaning of sacrifice.'

Giniva refused to be sidetracked. 'Your signature was not on your scroll of betrothment.'

'What are you talking about? Of course it was – I signed it with my own hand.'

'And I saw it with my own eyes. There is only Scarabold's hand.'

'It bore the signatures of us both,' Moribund insisted, 'and was witnessed by the Bishop.'

'You knew that as the eldest daughter of Perseo and Castilia I came under the First Rule of Exception. I was the true heir. You removed my real mother, but I was beyond your reach. But you didn't know about Dwinoline's plot to take power, and now she is dead.'

'Plots! Plots!' Moribund whirled about and crushed her head between her palms. 'Never unity, never sisterhood, never kindness – this is how we were raised, you foolish girl, forever set against each other while the men pursue their victories. We are a distraction. We're not women; we are either whores or brood mares, whatever our station in life. That is all there is for the females, whoever they may be. Why do you think all your childish whims were indulged? To keep you in your place.'

She advanced on the Princess, eyes blazing. 'And where have you led us? To this very day, when all our enemies unite to swarm over us like insects and we can do nothing but capitulate. Londinium will be dismantled stone by stone. Those creatures out there are not like us. They do not share our values, nor live the way we do. So we plot and contrive and think we will survive – for this. For *this*.'

She threw her arms wide at the arrows raining down, the fires on the battlements, the dying horses, the piled-up corpses, the lines to the portcullis, the storm breaking overhead, the stench of death everywhere.

It was not the reaction Giniva had expected. 'You've always known the throne was mine,' she said. 'You murdered my birth mother. I don't know who or what you are.'

'Spoken like a true princess,' said Mater Moribund mirthlessly. 'I no longer know what I am either. All I know is that I was once a daughter, then a mother, and all the time destined to be a monster. Never a whore. Never a mare. A monster.'

116

We Are All Monsters

Watborn could feel the Cloud Bridge shifting beneath him in the storm-wind. His boots struggled to find purchase on the moss-green bricks. He did not dare to look over the sides, but something drew him to stare down at the battle raging below. He nearly lost his balance. His ragged ebony hair was batting at his eyes, obscuring his vision. The storm was directly overhead. The roiling air reeked of ozone, the clouds crackling with azure fire as angry thermals hit the glistering bridge.

When he was more than halfway across, a powerful blast of rain almost dislodged him. On the far side was the arch that led to the main staircase. Divorcing itself from one of the stone columns was a bizarre figure of blood and bone that loped forward into the sudden downpour.

Brasslight was entirely crimson with snake-blood. The light of madness was in his eyes. In his right hand he still held the dagger. He had refitted the mangled tin foot over the bare stump of his ankle, but now the pieces clanked and scraped.

'Are you surprised to see me?' he called. 'This should be a lesson to you, farmboy. The only way to kill a monster is from the inside.'

There was no way past him. Watborn wanted to turn back but could not bring himself to do so. Every conflict boiled down to this.

Why had Brasslight come for him? Was he reminded too strongly of his own trajectory through the castle? Did he see Watborn in his glass and find himself wanting? The truth was simpler: the birdcatcher would always stand in his path. He would keep on coming.

Watborn had no weapon. As he threw himself at the pretender, his muscles bunched tight. He felt the dagger slip into his shoulder and cut across the arrow wound, searing against bone. He punched low, tipping Brasslight off balance, but a fist remained closed around the knife handle.

They fell slowly together, landing on the lip of the bridge.

Even now, Brasslight's insanity gave him extra strength. Pinned beneath him, Watborn squirmed like a trapped bird. He tried to keep the dagger from pushing deeper but the pain was excruciating. The fishy stink of Orobus enveloped him; having hacked his way out, Brasslight seemed to have become part snake himself.

Above them the sound of war vibrated, shimmering the rainfall.

Brasslight pushed down harder, twisting the dagger. He was remote in his revenge, as if taking it was nothing more than stitching a wound or dismounting a horse. Wild-eyed, he swung around and pushed at Watborn's shoulders, sliding him towards the edge of the bridge until his legs had nothing but air beneath them.

Watborn tried to see through the obscuring rain. He felt his centre of gravity shift as he was moved towards the maelstrom below.

Brasslight bore down on him.

The downpour soaked his face. Pain crushed his chest. His eyes spilled bitter diamonds. The moss tore beneath his grip, detaching itself from the brickwork, and he felt himself sliding off the precipice of the Cloud Bridge.

He made one last futile attempt to grab hold of Brasslight's jacket, but the wet material slipped through his fingers. As the raw stump of the pretender's leg descended upon his face, punching down, he lost his handhold and dropped out into space.

117

The Centre Ceases to Hold

Giniva and Moribund stood opposite each other in the covered arches, shielded from the rain by the half-demolished roof of the cloisters. Beside them, the ivied walls were spattered crimson whenever another of Timmorian's men fell from the sky.

Moribund was detached and frozen. Her bony hands hung at her sides, the fingers curled as if desiring to hold on to something but unable to do so. Her bloodless skin was as grey as the walls. She shivered with cold, a rare sign of feeling.

Giniva felt no hatred for her stepmother, only pity. There was nothing more to be gained by nurturing bitterness. Around them, part-hidden in the shadows, were cleaners, carpenters and maid-servants in ragged brown tunics, clinging to the walls in fear of the fight still raging on the battlements above.

Several of the Sheathwing soldiers were tearing away at a colossal lightning rod that protruded from one of the turrets. Every few minutes there was a crackle of electric fire and another blackened body fell.

'They're idiots,' said Moribund. 'Look at them. They see their fellow men burned alive and can't wait to follow them.'

At the portcullis Scarabold's men were managing to hold off the Alliance. Their regrouped position above the enemy troops on top of the barbican kept the Sheathwing and the F'Arcys bottlenecked between the gates and the moat. At their backs, the cypresses prevented the withdrawal of their supply carriages. Bullmarsh should have ordered the trees cut down. Now it was too late.

The Queen released a long, slow exhalation. 'This is a fine state of things, child,' she said finally. 'Look upon us and learn. It is what happens to families when the centre ceases to hold.'

'If my stepfather had shown any interest, he might have seen who we really were, Leperdandy and I.' Giniva looked out at the soldiers spiralling down into the chain-nets that hung over the walkways. They looked like trapped fish, flopping back and forth until they were speared.

'You still have his ear,' said Moribund. 'He will do anything you say, even though you are not his blood-child. It was vexing to hear that Dwinoline's plot had crossed with my own. I thought I knew everything that went on around here.'

'You taught me to look for secrets within secrets,' said Giniva.

'I suppose I did.' The keystone of an arch landed near them with a bang. Moribund did not flinch. 'You know you are unsaleable now that you are ruptured.'

Giniva decided not to disabuse her of the notion.

'Like my son, quite useless. You may as well leave us. Isn't that what you wanted to do all along?'

'Tell me one thing,' she asked. 'Does the Great Wound believe I am his daughter?'

Moribund's eyebrows rose. 'Of course. Why would he know anything about the bodies of women other than what we choose to tell him? How little did he attend? I shall tell you. I presented you at the age of two and he thought you were newborn. Even peasants make better fathers.'

A fresh squall of rain marred the moat, bubbling and sparkling and flattening the water. Giniva tipped back her head. A narrow arc of red fire passed overhead as another volley of burning arrows was unleashed at the Diableries. It was hard to tell now whether either side was making any progress at all. Close by, a tall section of unsupported battlement lazily divorced itself from its moorings and fell inwards in a tumbling, bristling ball of ladders, soldiers, cannon and spears.

At the moat's surface, a long, twisting flash of greenish-black momentarily lifted the water upwards and was gone. The pike was taking the fallen. Moribund studied the chaotic floundering in the water with an anthropological eye.

'This,' she said, 'is what happens when men rule the world.'

118

The End of the Richesse

Goldhawk strode across the embattled courtyard with a spy under each arm. As soon as he identified a battalion commander, he threw Spackle and Peut down before him. 'These two will undertake your most dangerous mission, whatever it is,' he explained. 'They have volunteered.'

'No, we haven't!' cried Spackle.

'He's trying to make us!' screamed Peut.

'So you don't want to fight for your King and defend the realm?' asked the commander, whose name was Dom. 'That would be treason. Sergeant, put these two in uniform at once.'

'We'll tell our mother,' warned Spackle.

'Our mother has the ear of the King,' said Peut.

'By the end of this day I think someone else will have the ear of the King,' replied Dom. 'And the rest of his head.'

Goldhawk waited and watched as the pair were forced sobbing into helmets, tunics and boots. After checking that they were correctly attired (albeit in absurdly large sizes), Dom thrust a couple of ancient, dull-bladed halberds into their shaking hands. The weapon was a kind of slashing pike, impossible to use without training. Worse, these ones were ornamental and had no edges.

'You have to tackle your enemy at arm's length,' he warned, pointing at the various notched spikes and hooks along the shaft of the pike. Spackle could not lift his.

'I think you're a little too short,' said Dom after consideration. 'Perhaps a fire-lance. These use black gunpowder to propel projectiles.' He handed them a pair of long-stocked weapons with rust flakes peeling from their barrels.

'H-how does this w-work?' asked Peut.

'Pay attention,' said Dom. 'It's light and smooth-bored, and fires from the shoulder. That's your lower sling, that's your upper sling, that's your piling swivel, and there's no safety catch—'

'Why n-n-not?' asked Spackle.

'We always saw off the trigger guard; it saves time,' Dom replied. 'Use the bolt to open the breech, slide it rapidly backwards and forwards like so, ease the spring, don't get your thumb caught or you'll lose it, cock and balance before firing, then reload. Got it?'

'N-n-no!' said Spackle and Peut in unison.

'Don't worry, you'll work it out.'

'We'll share our richesse!' Spackle begged the commander.

'Yes, our richesse!' cried Peut. 'We have silver neckchains and gold brooches and fine jewels!'

'Can they be fired from cannon?' the commander asked.

'No, our richesse is for the adornments,' said Peut forlornly.

'Then you can stick your richesse up your arses. Get up them ladders.' Dom pointed to the makeshift climbing frame attached to the damaged portcullis.

'But what do we do?'

'Kill anyone who tries to come over.'

'We don't know how to fight,' said Spackle, horrified at the thought.

'Don't worry, you'll soon learn,' called Goldhawk, aiming them up the portcullis ladders and prodding them towards the enemy. *Perhaps it'll be the making of them*, he thought as he turned back towards his kitchen. *Or perhaps they'll get kebabbed together on a single lance.*

As he was forced to climb, Spackle made one last appeal. 'We can get you anything you want,' he begged.

'Can you?' said Dom. 'Then get us a bloody victory.'

The twins made it to the top of the wall, clambered over and were suddenly gone. Only a pair of long, terrible shrieks were heard, identical in tone and timbre, and cut off at the exact same moment.

A pair of ears turned up on a soldier's neckchain some days later, but it was impossible to tell if they were Spackle's or Peut's.

119

The Foot on the Crown

Watborn hung in the sky, moving neither up nor down.

He wavered in cloud, his arms and legs outstretched, his hands and boots helplessly caught in a ragged hammock of chainmail mesh that hung from beneath the walkway like the tendrils of a jellyfish.

Below him, two dead men hung in the rigging, flies in a web. They might have been illustrating some ancient church parable about the wages of sin.

An immense lightning rod from the east turret had fallen towards the bridge, only to become entangled in the nets. Twice he saw it crackle with errant fire, but knowing he would be shaken free at any moment, he climbed on to it.

As boys, he and Finmoor had practised tightrope-walking between two high elm trees with a fishing net tied in the lower branches to catch them. He tried not to think how far he could fall.

When he drew level with the bridge once more, he saw that Brasslight was watching him from its centre, waiting for him to fall to his death. Even though his shoulder burned every time he pulled on it, he had no choice but to haul himself along the conductor.

Overhead the sky was ruptured with wild bursts of luminescence. The lightning rods had been dipped in molten silver, the better to draw down fire from the sky. It was the height of insanity to be lying on a structure coated with the most conductive material on earth. He was still several feet from the edge of the Cloud Bridge, and Brasslight was waiting for him. He needed to move.

He arrived at a decision not a moment too soon. As he jumped, an emerald streak crackled down and struck the gleaming gantry, causing it to convulse in a paroxysm of storm-fire.

Brasslight had no time to react. The mast twisted and crashed through the narrowest part of the Cloud Bridge as if it were no more than a cat's cradle. Several gargoyles plummeted to earth like ugly bombs. Down came the gantry again, cascading bricks and stanchions in every direction.

As the clouds lowered, the rod was hit a second time. The surrounding storm-sky had blue and yellow lanthorns flickering inside it.

Watborn looked back and saw that the spot where he had been standing had melted. Overhead, the explosion of clashing atmospheres was strong enough to send a starling from its sycamore perch over a league away.

When the glow had faded and the storm had passed, all that was left was a warped, flimsy structure hanging across the missing brick section of the Cloud Bridge. One day far from now it would be incorporated into the bridge itself, in commemoration of the great conflict.

When Watborn reached the far stump of the bridge, which looked as if a titan had bitten into it, he saw that Brasslight was waiting for him with his dagger arm still raised.

He had no more strength left in him to fight.

There was no movement from the pretender. He remained perfectly still. Watborn realized that he was smouldering.

Brasslight had been connected to the lightning rod by the wet moss that ran across the bridge. He had been fried where he stood. The fault, it seemed, lay with the reticulated tin foot. It had conducted electric fire to him. It sparked and danced about on its own.

The pretender toppled forward on to his face. When legends came to be told, it would be said that he smashed into a thousand pieces, turned to stone, but in truth there was very little of him to be recovered.

The tin foot fell from the Cloud Bridge and bounced on to the crown of the great stone lion, but failed to come to a stop and spiralled off through the floors below. Nobody ever found it. Nothing was excavated, only buried.

120

Tear Out the Root

'Is there a precedent for calling a halt to the hostilities?' asked Drumband.

The captain's boots had vanished in viscous brown mud, so that he could barely move. His heavy woollen greatcoat was so sodden that it felt as if he were carrying a dead animal on his back. A cut above his eye had lowered a veil of blood across his vision, but he could tell that the allies were milling in confusion somewhere near the palisade of pfitzers.

The walls were blackened with fire. Oily smoke belched across the moat, which was filled with cadavers. There was no medical tent; the dying had been left wherever they had fallen.

'Only the King can do that now.' Bullmarsh's eyes were filled with tears. The tangled wreck of gantries and walkways groaned with trapped warriors. Dreams of a glorious victory had been washed away in the downpour. He tried to take stock of the situation.

There was no difference between those within and those without. They had fought each other to a standstill. The losses were appalling on both sides. Scarabold's men were depleted and exhausted, but the gates held. The realm had not been overrun. It had survived, but at what terrible cost?

'Have any men made it inside at all?' asked Bullmarsh.

'A few in small groups, but they can achieve nothing without support. They will be captured through their loyalties.'

'How so?'

'They are wearing the tunics of their factions. They might as well be sporting targets on their backs.'

There was another chink of rubble as a wall toppled. Much of the castle-city had been destroyed, each ruination becoming a part of it, as if it needed to devour itself in order to regenerate.

'Sir?' Drumband ventured. 'The Queen's daughter demands that the conflict be suspended for a brief period so that she may speak with you urgently. She has the permission of her mother to initiate the proceedings in extraordinary circumstances.'

'Tell her she can come to me in the safekeeping of my guards. She has one hour to make her case, no longer,' Bullmarsh said numbly. 'After that time, we regroup and the hostilities resume. That girl may be a blue-blood but she's a pain in the bunghole.'

'A word of caution,' Drumband suggested. 'While the negotiations are in their most delicate stage, it's probably best not to mention what happened to her brother.' Word had reached them that the Sisters had proved more ruthless than the allies, but at least the boy was still alive; he had been seen entering the main gate, although he was almost unrecognizable to the men who saw him pass.

Bullmarsh removed his gloves and wrung them out. 'Perhaps the King is ready to capitulate.'

'Scarabold would rather cut out his own heart.'

'And the allies will never withdraw, so we are left to fight until the munition stocks are gone. That's the trouble with kings. They always know less than everyone else.'

'Then, if we are not to die today, we need a miracle,' said Bullmarsh.

Giniva was admitted to Bullmarsh's tent with her brother. Leperdandy was leaning on an elegant silver-topped cane and had one half of his head swathed in black linen to spare the feelings of others. The officers tried not to look surprised.

The earthen floor was badly flooded, so they picked their way to higher ground and waited for a table to be set before them. With a faint sense of outrage, Giniva noted that it was one of her own dressing tables.

Fitting his massive frame into a small chair, the General waited for his guest to speak. But now that the opportunity had presented itself, Giniva hardly knew where to begin.

'I take it you have never set foot inside our home, General,' she said.

'No, my lady, nor any of my family,' Bullmarsh replied. 'Our fealty to you was long before my time.'

'Within it is a peculiar feature, its purpose lost to all. It can only be seen by members of the royal family, and they have long ceased to recall it. A line picked out in crimson that passes from one roof to the next, down throughout all the known parts of the building.'

'The known parts?'

'There are places where none of us have ever ventured. Old places. Somewhere near the bottom.'

Bullmarsh spread his broad dark hands on the table. 'I fail to see what this has to do with the ceasefire.'

'We had a mage of the sciences, Magister Ambrosius. He was studying the family bloodlines when he was murdered. All his discoveries were destroyed. But he left this.' She opened the Ambrosius Hypothesis and pinned it down, for there was a cold draught blowing through the tent.

Bullmarsh stared at her in puzzlement. 'I am an army man,' he said. 'I never learned to read.'

'Then, if you will permit me. Tell me, General, what do you think this war is about?'

Bullmarsh sucked at his spectacular moustaches. 'Why, it is territory. Also family, and honour and revenge.'

'In a word, blood, wouldn't you say?'

'Yes, ma'am, blood.'

'Ours being the wrong type in your eyes, and yours being wrong in ours? For belief, which informs all the humours, begins in the blood?'

'I suppose that sums it up.'

'Shall I tell you what this says?' She held up the Hypothesis. '"We Are All One."'

Bullmarsh waited. 'Is that all?'

'What do you suppose it means?'

Bullmarsh shook his head impatiently. He was a simple man and growing tired of puzzles.

'I did not know either. None of us knew. What it means is this: we are all of the same blood.'

'The same blood? This is fools' talk.'

'I mean that the Sheathwing, the F'Arcys and all the other dynasties with whom we form alliances or fight against, even les Sœurs aux Cadeaux Étranges, are related. In short, sir, we are one great family. Our blood is no different from one tribe to the next. It is all the same.'

Bullmarsh struggled to take it in. 'What about the peasants?'

'Even them. A mix of all, shared by all.'

The whole time, one thing had puzzled Giniva more than any other. How had Minerva Mentle escaped to the Sisters with a new-born infant in the middle of a hellish thunderstorm? It was not feasible that she had ridden alone through the avenue of cypresses, finding her way through the maze after dark, in lashing rain, with a child at her breast barely an hour into this world.

The simple answer was that she had never left Londinium at all.

Snatching up a much-creased and folded map from Bullmarsh's war-table, Leperdandy turned it before him. 'Attend me, General, I beg you. Using his books, Magister Ambrosius taught me that our family, your family and the people of your allies – we are all of the same blood.'

'That is the stupidest thing I have ever heard,' Bullmarsh snorted. 'The division of the classes by the humours of the blood is an element common to all our families. Blood – the good and bad of it – is the structure that binds us.'

'I suppose you believe the royal blood to be a shade of blue.'

'It is thicker, richer, *different*. How else are we to tell ourselves apart?'

'Perhaps we are not meant to.'

'Then how will we know who governs us?'

'We are all one, General Bullmarsh, under different names. The tribes have been fighting themselves.'

'But the Marshlands, the Under-Bournes, the Hill Forests, the Chalklands,' said Bullmarsh. 'They are so far from each other that we cannot have intermarried.'

'We were all one to begin with. How can it have been otherwise?'

'But this is heresy. Where is the proof?'

'The mage devoted his whole life to proving these four words,' Giniva replied. 'The evidence has been destroyed, so we must have faith.'

'And your father – does he believe we are all one?'

Bullmarsh was at heart a modern-minded man. There were too many gods to worship so he believed in none of them. He had no truck with history either, because even if it had been written down he could not read it. He only trusted what he could see and feel, and now this pair wanted him to accept the impossible. It would mean the end of wars, for a start.

'My father is the only way he can be,' said Giniva sadly. 'He is the sole impediment to peace now.'

The General rose and walked to the sodden flap of the tent, then slowly raised it. Patches of dull crimson fire burned on the moat. Gutted brown bodies hung over the battlements. Rubble smouldered below. The smell of roasting meat revolted even as it made stomachs rumble.

'Could it really be?' he asked. 'All bloodshed meaningless?'

'Bloodshed usually is,' Giniva replied. 'The Beetle Earl had realized the truth. Perhaps everyone knew more than us.'

'But if that is the case and we are one, the ceasefire must be made to hold longer.' He sounded disappointed.

'My thoughts precisely,' said the Princess.

'However, your father cannot be excused,' said Bullmarsh. 'He is the root and the cause. And it is because he outraged the Sisters that your brother is . . . as he is.' He nodded curtly to Leperdandy.

'Then the root must be torn out,' said Giniva.

121

Untouchable

Giniva's heart contained a storm. A fearful rush at the thought of an ending, a terrible sense of loss and waste, the pain of defying the Great Wound. But by allowing her to believe he was her father, he had betrayed her most of all.

Waiting for her were Scarabold – who knew the truth and said nothing, as it would have brought an end to his purpose as a warrior-king – and Moribund, who was lost within a world of intrigue and manoeuvre.

As the Princess left Bullmarsh's tent and crossed the courtyard, her ragged clothes dragging through pools of mud and blood, Leperdandy leaned on her arm for support. Surrounding them were commoners – women, men and children, most of whom she had barely ever noticed. They enjoyed the protection of the monarchy but were without loyalty or understanding. They watched her pass in silence, their heads slowly turning. She could not imagine what they were thinking.

'We have acted according to our conscience,' said the princeling. 'We can do no more than that. Perhaps now there will be an end to the suffering.' He sat on a collapsed section of wall. 'I must rest a minute.'

The Princess had not heard. As she walked ahead, a homely figure stepped into the light on the wet flagstones in front of her.

One side of Dwinoline's face was masked in dried blood. Her right eye was a ruin, her left socket in tatters, but the ball was intact. Giniva recoiled in horror. The former First Wife was still trailing rainbow-coloured tapestry threads from her bodice. She outstretched her arm as if she wished to claw her nemesis from the face of the earth.

The Princess could only turn and run, but her path was blocked by the commoners standing at the edge of the moat.

'I should have known you would be our destroyers,' said Dwinoline blankly, as if accepting the inevitable. 'I preserved our history and you have only ever sought to unravel it.' With a scream of rage, Dwinoline jabbed her tapestry hook through Giniva's shirt and dragged her towards the edge of the moat. Leperdandy attempted to rise but he slipped on the mossy stones.

As the Princess tried to pull her arm free, her shirt tore. Dwinoline punched her in the stomach with surprising force. Giniva fell hard and slid towards the encrusted edge of the moat.

The former First Wife was about to launch another attack on her stepdaughter when, from out of the cloistered shadows, a great brown bear covered in ragged scars loped towards her, twisting its great head back and forth.

During its imprisonment on the rooftop it had had time to reassess its relationship to humans, and had come to the conclusion that they were not to be trusted unless they were dead. One swipe of its immense paw knocked the former First Wife clean out of her pattens. Its jaws seized on her neck and bit out a crescent of pink flesh and red bone.

The commoners quickly parted, anxious to keep out of their way. Dwinoline slithered on to her side, then on to the sloping stones, trying to roll away from the bear. By doing so, she sank into the moat.

It was shallow here, and a moment later her bloody head and shoulders thrust themselves above the level of the water. Arms raised high, she screamed and twisted, but she was stuck in the mire and there was a great bite out of her neck that fountained dark blood each time she turned.

Everyone saw her. Nobody moved. The commonfolk were used to freezing in the presence of royalty. They knew they were not allowed to touch a member of the reigning family. They brushed a hem on pain of death. To them, royal blood was different.

Before Giniva could do anything, a black-green barb rose lazily along the moat's surface like an opening seam, and Dwinoline was snatched. The great pike's spiny teeth clamped her neck in the same ravaged place and swept her from view, pulling her under. The green ripples quickly stilled. Lakeweed closed over the spot. A moment later it was as if she had never been there.

471

Giniva looked around for help, shaking. The commoners stared and stared. The bear shook its matted fur and lumbered away.

'Why didn't you do something?' she cried. But as she ran from one to the next they backed away from her, averting their eyes. She knew they were forbidden from acting in her presence. No neighbour was to be trusted, and certainly not a royal. Such was the way of Londinium.

For the first time she saw the gulf that existed between them all. Although they shared the same hearts, the same flesh, the same blood, they would never believe it in a million years. They would seek out difference and use it to divide themselves.

As she turned from one stony face to another, she looked up. There, standing at the top of the steps under the main arch to the cloisters, was the familar silhouette of the birdcatcher.

PART FIVE:
Rebirth

122

Farewell to the Old Ways

Scarabold would not have it, of course.

He had already warned anyone within earshot that he would take flensing knives to his opponents' naked bodies and peel off their skin in a single continuous strip before committing to a cease-fire, as if he had confused them with oranges. He refused to leave his post at the battlements, so the post left him.

Grand-Marshal Timmorian arranged for the cannon to be withdrawn in accordance with the royal ceasefire. Thus, with nothing to do and no one to fight and the rain falling harder than ever, now being mixed with pieces of hot metal and the occasional limb, the Great Wound took shelter in his council chamber to brood and grow bitter.

The Decrepend was seated in the nearby armoury, surrounded by rolls of rotting parchment taller than himself. He, too, was bereft. There was no map or diagram that could offer him guidance. Without instruction from the King there was only empty ritual.

Becoming aware of the darkened doorway, he looked up and found Watborn standing there. Between them stood a magnificent jointed suit of tempered red steel, topped with a golden helmet plumed with blue and white egret feathers.

'The Great Wound wore that during the Great Siege of Twenty-Eight.'

The Decrepend rose and scratched his numb rump. 'The battle took place in an ice-storm. Our enemy came from the top of the world. Everyone speaks gibberish up there, so the peace parleys were a waste of time. What a battle it was. The troops' hands froze to their swords. The ground was too hard to admit any bodies so they were left where they dropped. No man died in vain, and no man died without glory.'

'And the women?' Watborn enquired.

'Women? They ruled the hearth, not the land. How goes our fight?'

'There appears to be a new ceasefire.'

'I suppose you've come to see how far the once-mighty King has fallen, and to gloat. It says a lot about the times when a commoner can wander into the royal quarters and not have his head smitten off for the presumption of it.'

'Will you tell me where he is?'

'He is in his council chamber and will see no one, least of all an archer. Who are you?'

'I am no one,' said Watborn. Taking his leave of the Decrepend, he went to find the King.

There were no guards posted in the corridor. It appeared that everyone had fled. The door to the council chamber was ajar. The detonations now prevented it from shutting.

'I know who you are.'

The Great Wound sat upright on the couch in his rubble-strewn chamber and studied Watborn through his good eye. There was blood in his beard. He looked as though the guts of him had been scooped out and replaced with ashes. 'Vitrolio says you are his most trusted man. I imagine you are the one I should be most wary of.'

Watborn remained in respectful silence. He was waiting for proof of this dissolute red-faced fellow's greatness.

Scarabold rose stiffly and made his way to the window. He appeared so much older that it seemed as if the years had been waiting for this day to catch up with him. 'The men look as if they have lost the taste for battle.' He turned suddenly. 'Why are you here?'

'I seek an audience with you, Your Majesty. As your subject—'

'Do not say you have the right.' There was iron and gravel in his voice. 'In my experience, those who are most concerned with their rights are the ones who have never had to fight for them.'

'I have a right to revenge.'

'Ah, so that's it. Did you bring a dagger? I don't see a weapon. If you do have one on you, get rid of it or you'll be hanged for treason.'

'I don't.'

'And yet you plan to kill me.' Scarabold had survived seven

assassination attempts and an attack from a farmer armed with a weasel. He looked up now, his interest piqued. 'Explain yourself.'

Watborn took a deep breath. 'When I was twelve years old, your men rode into our village—'

Scarabold held up a scarred hand. 'Don't tell me, they slaughtered your parents with their broadswords. Except I know that they did not, because my men do not kill away from the battlefield. We don't even know who our enemies are any more. So if your heart nurtures a burning fire for vengeance, there must be another reason. Out with it, lad. There are many others awaiting their turn.'

'My parents died because of an order issued to your men.'

'I issue no peacetime orders. Others do that for me.'

'So you bear no responsibility.'

'I should grind your skull beneath my boot for speaking to me without proper respect.'

'Someone commanded your men to cut the heart from our cow.'

'Necromancy. Nobody here would command such a thing – except the seer.'

'There was a girl in our village called Calmora who had visions.'

'Calmora from Breornsey.' The King studied him carefully. 'Did you do her wrong?'

'I had stolen her heart, although I did not know it.'

'And she used her position here to take revenge upon you. Do you see? This is not a matter for the monarch at all. Make your revenge terrible indeed, but strike the one who deserves it.'

Scarabold rose and stepped over a fallen column. The great armoured suit of St Ethelbar Squeam, the First Warrior-Chancellor, lay in pieces, his mummified body smashed to grey powder.

'Londinium and its people are all but destroyed, but not its King. Hell's blood, I need a drink.'

He extracted a flagon of red wine from the rubble and wiped his sleeve across it before biting out the cork with strong yellow teeth. 'Tell me, what is your name?'

'Watborn, Your Majesty. Artur Watborn.'

'Lately, Artur Watborn, everyone is against me. I am feared but no longer respected. It disturbs me to say it, but the old ways don't work any more. I have to ask myself if everyone else is wrong, or I am. I want my daughter back. She is all I have left. Tell me, how can we end this?'

'I know nothing of state affairs, Your Majesty.'

'But you know my daughter, apparently. You see, I'm aware of what goes on *inside* my House, at least.'

'I know her a little.'

'What I want is something she will never give me.'

'You could reconcile with your opponents.'

Scarabold took a great swig from the flagon. 'You mean concede. Tell me, are you sound in limb and head? You won't turn out to be mad like most of the members of my family?'

'I think I am well enough.'

'Then let me give you two bits of advice. Never tell a king what to do. And make yourself useful to the dominion. Be of practical use. Can you do that?'

Watborn chose his next words with care. 'I can make sure all the fires are out. Find out who is still alive and missing no limbs.'

'A good start.'

'Gather all the survivors together. Help everyone who is injured. Ensure that they have water and food.'

'Keep going.'

'We can't shift any of the fallen walls without ropes. Everyone must work together regardless of rank.'

'No rank, eh? Easier for a commoner to say than a king.' He slaked his thirst and passed over the flagon. Blood-red claret dripped from his beard. 'To do such a thing would require casting aside centuries of ritual and protocol.'

Watborn said nothing.

'It's very odd having a conversation with a commoner that doesn't end with me wearing his teeth as a necklace. I suspect you have been sent by Fate to test me.' He took back the flagon and swigged from it. 'When the old ones left, they took their gods with them, but I dare say the Religiouses will be back again. They seem to find ways of getting in through the cracks, like persistent rainfall. What is it you want?'

'What do you mean, sir?'

'People only swear to causes when they want something. Is it gold? We have none. Power? You wouldn't know what to do with it. Do you want to marry my daughter? Is that it?'

'I want a better life for the people of Londinium and for all those who live beyond its walls.'

'A fine aspiration, usually a lie.' The King shook his mane. 'But you see, that's where you let yourself down. Your life is too short for such grand dreams. They are beyond your competence. You can only fail. Try something simpler. Get a hospital up and running, or something. Look after my daughter.'

'That's her decision, not mine.'

'Just do your part. What were you, back in your village?'

'A birdcatcher, sir.'

'Then whatever you do is a step up. I wish you every success. Wait, you are not yet dismissed.' He rose to dig around on his paper-strewn table and produced a scrap of parchment. 'Pen, pen.' He waved his fingers.

Watborn found a pot of ink but no pen. Scarabold broke a splinter of wood from the table and dipped it. He scrawled something, dripped dust and tallow across it and waved the page dry.

'Keep this safe. It was paper before I touched it but now it is a decree. Your royal warrant. I am entrusting you with a responsibility. You shall have the authority to rebuild this House. Well? What are you waiting for?'

'Your Majesty—'

'No speeches. You have the better deal. Being king usually ends badly.' Smacking his lips, he drained the last of the flagon and hurled it against the wall. 'Well, we each have our roles to play. We had both better get started.'

123

A New Kind of Family

It was a family gathering like no other before it.

King Scarabold and his remaining wife, Mater Moribund, sat on one side of the great scarred oaken table in the Tainted Hall, now swept clear of all cloths, candlesticks and platters. On the other side the Princess sat beside her brother. Moribund and Giniva were clothed almost identically, and wore opals at their throats. High above them a chill, lonely wind moaned through the rafters and the edges of tapestries rustled, as if knowing that change had finally come.

Scarabold released a blast of rectal wind and removed a smidgen of cork from his goblet. The ceiling might have fallen in but fine wine was irreplaceable.

'So we grieve for the wounds to our son Leperdandy and for the loss of our wife Dwinoline,' he intoned with solemnity, touching his cup to theirs. 'But new life brings new strength. The Ladies of All Martyrs carried on building a charnel house while they were giving birth, delivering their dead children directly into it. Yours will be a healthy male, my dearling. I know what you're thinking: the brave young Sabine who favoured her independence, shackled to a squalling brat within this crumbled mausoleum. But what is there for you outside? Certainly not the freedom you thought you would find.'

'I am not with child, sir,' said Giniva coolly. 'It was a ploy on behalf of the pretender, nothing more. Now I wish to ask you a question. Why did she not sign your scroll of betrothment?' Mater Moribund glared at the Princess. 'I have seen it for myself. Her signature is not on it. Is she really of different blood?'

'I signed the scroll,' said Moribund through closed teeth. 'The Bishop was our witness. Your impertinence is breathtaking.'

'It's true you have no right to demand anything, Giniva, but we choose to answer.' The Great Wound shook his leonine head. 'There were always stories. I have no time for rumour. The scroll in the Haven of the Afterlife is not the one Meldred signed. I switched them and burned the original.'

Moribund gaped.

'But why?' asked Giniva.

The King fixed her with his working eye. 'Why do you think? I did not wish her to give birth to an heir in the knowledge that she could wield power over him. I needed to put a break-clause in the marriage contract, something which could keep my ambitious wife in check. You think I didn't know who I was marrying? I always knew.' The King slumped in his chair. 'The birdcatcher was right. It's time for a change. There appears to be no other option now, does there?'

Giniva settled her hands on the arms of the chair. 'I plan to remain here and take a consort.'

'After all we've been through?' cried Moribund, astounded.

Scarabold pressed his spatulate fingers on the table and leaned forward. 'Why this new mood?' he asked.

'My brother needs me. I will find someone of my choosing. There is too much work here for one.'

'So all our efforts to find the most useful suitor came to nothing,' said Moribund, her head high, looking away in sharp profile, a raven in seclusion. 'So many lives lost and ruined.'

'Had you forced one of my suitors upon me, you would have committed the same mistake this family has always made,' said Giniva.

'Oh, this is something absurd about *love*,' spat Moribund. 'Bird-song and lute players, sentimental burbling. You are gravely deceived if you think you know what love is. Men will only seek to take advantage of you.'

'Love is a physical movement in the heart – Magister Ambrosius once told me so.' She looked from one step-parent to the other. 'Instead of strategic alliances I will give myself in joy.'

'I will not listen to such blasphemy—!'

'My child will fulfill the royal stipulation. Only male heirs to the throne to be recognized, except for the eldest daughter of the eldest son. A baby will be raised within these walls, not spirited off, drowned or locked away.'

Moribund threw herself back in her chair. 'But this is a mockery of all we have held to be right and decent!'

'A mockery is feeding from the flesh of our own,' said Leper-dandy. 'A mockery is taking all and returning nothing.'

'Silence, both of you,' said Scarabold suddenly. He turned to Giniva. 'What you suggest breaks every convention of decency. You are my brother's daughter. The laws clearly state—'

'If they contravene me, I will change the laws,' said Giniva. 'That is what rulers do. You have all been finding ways to work around them for long enough, so why not alter them to suit your circumstances and have done with it? You are still the monarch, in name at least, and share the blood of my father, your brother. I am not your enemy. I will form a new kind of family for you. I say farewell to the old ways. So long as the intention is to the good, what does it matter that the shape is different?'

'What will the people think?' wondered Moribund.

'They will think whatever you wish them to think,' she replied. 'You are still their rulers until your time is done, or until you choose to share responsibility.'

Scarabold remained even-tempered as he twisted his moustaches. 'And if I do not agree that this is in our best interests?'

'Our enemies are held at bay for the present, but the truce will not last long,' Giniva warned. 'If you know of another means by which the family can still survive and prosper, please tell me.'

'You know I have none.' The Great Wound sighed long and deep. 'By hell's torments, you may not be my daughter but you could well pass for her.'

For once, even Moribund closed her mouth and kept her counsel. There would be ample time, she decided, in which to conspire anew.

124

Our Home Is Not the World

Steadfast and patient, Watborn was waiting outside for them when the meeting concluded.

'So you have the ear of the King now,' said Giniva.

'I have his warrant,' Watborn replied. 'We are to rebuild Londinium.'

'The ceasefire is not yet in full operation.'

'Then it is the perfect time to get started.'

'And how do you intend to achieve this feat?'

'I am making a map. If I may be permitted to show you?'

'This is not the time, archer.'

'Then give him time,' said her brother sharply. 'Or else act as you always have done.'

Stung, she stepped aside. 'Very well. I command you to show me.'

Watborn led the pair down the great circular staircase to one of the lowest floors. On each circuit the light grew fainter. 'I thought to start at the bottom. I made a discovery.'

They took flambeaux from the sconces and continued down in near blackness. The Princess stopped. 'I'm not sure I trust you.'

'I trust him,' said Leperdandy, going ahead.

They reached the base of the stairwell. 'At the edge of my village I found a picture in the ground,' Watborn explained. 'Made of tiny tiles. Men in coloured robes on couches, a white bull and dancing girls in flowers.'

Watborn lowered his flambeau and illuminated the floor: gold and cobalt, silver and vermilion. The mosaic was a grander version, undamaged and complete. Characters arranged in an airy room, surrounded by a blue river.

'The picture in our village is similar but not as skilfully painted as this one,' said Watborn.

'I have seen these people before. The magister showed me others.' Leaning on them, the princeling painfully lowered himself to the edge of the mosaic.

'They don't look like us,' Giniva decided. 'They're the Italians, aren't they? They're more like you, Watborn. Where were they from? Who were they?'

'I hoped you would know.'

'This is the Rushing River, the Tamesis, which we see beneath us when the fog lifts, yes?' Leperdandy pointed out.

'The villagers used to call it Smash-the-Boats,' said Watborn unhelpfully.

The flambeaux revealed the larger scope of the floor-picture. Beyond the villa could be seen colourful towns fancifully arranged upon green hilltops.

'Those are the settlements for which I know only names,' the princeling said. 'Wexerley, Wroxeter, Abingdon, Colchester, Ipswich and Who-Knows-Where. The people who were here before us were from the warm south. Our mothers had their children. The maps in the rotunda are beautiful but they are wrong. We are builded upon a wild island surrounded by a great foaming sea filled with serpents, and the only other bloods come from beyond that sea.'

In the flickering lights of the flambeaux, the dancing girls appeared to move.

Watborn studied the mosaic's elegant depictions. 'So they came here and ruled us. What did they want?'

'What do they ever want? Slaves and precious metal and land.'

'Then why did they leave?'

Leperdandy gave a shrug. 'Perhaps we disappointed them. Too cold, too small, too wet, too backward. Why would they stay?'

'Others stayed,' said Giniva. 'The nuns who came from Gallia, les Sœurs aux Cadeaux Étranges. There are all sorts of unusual names here that we have made easier to fit our mouths. We are as boiled together as the bones in our cooking pots.'

'Not all,' said her brother. 'The mad ones with the big red beards stay behind the Roman Wall far to the north. And long may they remain there.'

'If we accept one,' said Watborn, 'we accept all.'

'*We?*' repeated Giniva.

125

A Witness to History

The F'Arcys, the Sheathwing and the Sisters' Men held a council that lasted for three days amid many raised voices and much heated wrangling, but in truth the matter was decided at the outset.

A state of war could not be sustained. The residents had survived behind their battered walls for over three centuries and were not so easily disposed of. The allies were disorganized and poorly supplied. Their lines of communication had collapsed and their troops were demoralized.

It was in everyone's interests to find a solution.

Finally it was agreed to open the castle-city to trade that would benefit those within and without. The coastal route leading to the basin of the river would be rebuilded and new rules of commerce would be enshrined. Treaties were drawn up and signed, oaths were sworn and property deeds changed hands.

One edict was written in stone: that Londinium would replace its king with an elected council. Royal pageantry would be retained along with certain minor privileges, but it would be controlled along very different lines. Reparations were to be made, debts repaid and old enmities quashed, although they would arise again in the decades that followed.

The Church attempted to wrest control, but without a king of faith it could not establish the roots it needed to flourish. In the absence of the Abbot and his clergy, there could be no written records, and so a great part of history vanished into darkness.

What had been missing from Londinium was a sense of purpose. Now came a drive to present it as a power for good, and the good involved making money. With new-found wealth, the seeds of corruption would be sown, but for now just enough heeded the warnings of the past.

In the days that followed, Watborn found himself a witness to history.

He was there when the gates were opened to the lands beyond. He was promoted and rewarded for his steadfast loyalty, yet his role in the proceedings was a minor one. He was, after all, a bird-catcher, not a landowner, and while some things changed in the land there was much that did not.

The privileged clung to their assets with a corpse-grip, and a new system of executions had to be instigated to ensure fairness. Londinium had no warrior-heroes about whom great myths were written. It became, in truth, a rather dull place, concentrated on accounting and management, solid and dependable but hardly the stuff of legend. No epic poems are sung about balancing the books. No tombs are inscribed with legends extolling the virtues of being on time.

No more blood-soaked battles marked its passage through the centuries. After a while it became hard to recall what had really taken place and what was mere embroidery.

Only Dwinoline's carefully folded tapestry held the true story, but no one could remember where it had been placed. When history happens it rarely feels like history at the time, and people are terribly careless.

This was all in the future, of course.

For now, Londinium and its people lay in smoking ruins. There was much work to be done.

126

All of It Foretold

Giniva made her way to the scented sepulchre of Calmora the Seer. Her mind, so usually made up, had been seeded with doubts.

From the moment poor Leperdandy told me about my first suitor, she thought, *I was sure I would leave this place. I could have made a list of all the things that shamed me and held up each one as a reason for going. But if we are all one blood, there is surely no need to leave.*

As she climbed over spines of fallen brick and tattered tapestries, she thought of the rooms she had played in as a child, of Leperdandy's theatre shows and hiding in the arboretum. She remembered the pale-lemon sunlight shimmering above the battlements and icicle fights on the tourney court. The smell of warm bread in milk, the taste of spiced tea and honeycomb, wet pink petals sticking to the windows in a storm. It was as if everything that had once been pinned down and clearly labelled was now being expunged of all identifying marks.

Truly, she thought, *I know not who I am. It means I must start afresh.*

There was a fall of bricks behind her. She stopped and studied the shadows but saw nothing.

Calmora was clearly not ready for visitors, royal or otherwise. Most of her veils were pinned back with clothes pegs and she was washing her hair in the font.

'A prediction now?' she asked, twisting the water from her dark mane. It was as if she no longer regarded Giniva as a high-up and could consider herself an equal. The survivors were all starting to behave differently.

'The war is over,' said Giniva, 'although I have no idea how long the truce will last.'

'If you're asking me, I can't give you an answer.' The seer wrapped a purple cloth around her head and flicked it back. 'Too big a question. Do you have any food? Anything at all? Everyone's talking about the shining new future that awaits us all but there's no fucking bread.'

'I was not going to ask.' She dug into her pocket and produced a heel of toasted dough, handing it over.

'Then what?'

'The bloodlines set in the floors and ceilings. I always thought they were just decorative.'

'The origin of your family was written into the stones themselves.' Calmora knotted the cloth and dried her face. Without her dark make-up she looked like any other kitchen-girl.

'Then it's true that we're all of one blood?'

'Of course it's true.' She gave a quick, false smile. 'There. A straight answer for once. Happy now? Anything else?'

'Mater Moribund.'

'Oh. So you know about her. Or at least you think you do.'

Giniva regarded the seer doubtfully. She had never put her faith in oracles. There were too many human mysteries to solve without adding fantasies to them. 'How do you know about these things?'

Calmora was untouched by sceptics. She unwrapped her hair and shook it out. 'Over there.' She pointed. 'Bring me the biggest one.'

The Princess lifted the tallest volume from a great stack of leatherbound books. They looked like the ones in the sealed section of the great Cistern Library, the rotunda, but could not have been.

Calmora threw the book wide. 'I stole it ages ago. Back when I was still in the kitchens baking your pastries. See for yourself. Everything is foretold. There's no trick to it.'

She ran a finger down the page on which the tome had fallen open. 'Here, the enemy without and the enemy within. The defeat of the Alliance and the death of Brasslight. Anger and tragic ending of the King. Rejoicing at the transformation of Londinium. Revenge of Moribund. Reduction of population by rats. Defeat of the invaders. Wait, those parts have not yet come to pass.'

'Then they can still be changed. Where does it all end?' asked Giniva.

'End?' Calmora seemed puzzled by the idea. 'It never ends. It's not like one of Lady Dwinoline's romantic tales, which always finish with an embrace.' She slapped the cover. 'This book is your world. It goes on for ever. You are but' – here she riffled through the previous section and held it between thumb and forefinger – 'just this many pages. Actually, less. You think history starts and ends with you? The city will always be here in one form or another.'

'What do you mean, one form or another?'

'It is merely a foundation. It is an idea builded upon other ancient settlements, changed and embellished and emboldened, and new ideas will be raised upon it in turn. It is not a kingdom.'

'Then what is it?'

'Why, just a home, of course. With residents and rulers and walls and gates, standing at the edge of the Rushing River. It must always be fought for, otherwise it will turn to evil ways.'

'And its purpose?' asked Giniva, her old impatience bubbling through.

Calmora threw back her head and released a high, delighted laugh. 'A thing that is made of stones has no purpose, foolish Princess! It is only a container, a melting pot for its ingredients.'

She reached out a slender hand and seized Giniva's arm, pulling her forward. 'The stones can be shaped by you. You no longer have a kingdom. Nor will you be a princess, but a mother.'

Giniva pressed a hand upon her belly. 'How?'

'Why, you will marry him, of course.'

'Who?'

'The man with his foot on the crown.' Laughing, Calmora cast the book aside with such violence that Giniva feared the pages would fly out. 'You're not with child now, silly girl! The boy came to me for an enchantment so I mixed him up some coloured water. There are no such things as enchantments, except in the heart. Now, go and make your preparations for the long and terrible road that lies ahead!'

Giniva ran from the room.

Calmora's peals of laughter followed her out of the chamber and down the hall, through the shattered cloisters, up brick-strewn staircases, over the cracked bridges, until they were lost within the castle-city's damp, dark entrails.

The yellow-eyed seer dropped on to her couch and ceased her laughter. 'I know you are there,' she called. 'You may as well come in and get it over with.'

Watborn stepped into the chamber of lights and shadows. He had been following the Princess through the castle for hours.

'Well, well. I was sure you would come one day,' said Calmora. 'What you seek is on the table over there.'

A short thin-bladed dagger with an intricately carved handle glittered on the polished cedarwood.

'I always wanted what I couldn't have,' she sighed. 'Do you know how long I waited for you in the dusk-light every night?'

'I saw you, Calmora.'

'I cast spells for your attention, all for nothing. You only ever thought of your family and your cow. I kept all the things you touched. They gave me visions. I could see everyone's future but my own. That's the way it is with seers. So, of course, when the Kingsmen offered to take me with them, I left Breornsey. I asked for your cow's heart, so that I could see the future more clearly. My gift is real, you know. Amid all the stories and lies I was the one who told the truth. I perfected my craft. It's not an easy thing to do around here, speaking honestly. You usually end up with your neck on a block. But you – you're moving into a sphere of power now, so take up that dagger and you may finally have your revenge. Do it now and make it quick.'

'I amn't going to kill you,' said Watborn softly. 'You shall stay here for your punishment.'

'That is no punishment at all.'

He removed the dagger from the table. 'I will lock you in this room until the end of your days, and you will answer truthfully whenever I have need of your services. If you lie to me once, I will abandon you in the wilds below.'

'I don't understand.' Calmora sat up and studied his eyes. 'If the situation was reversed, I would take up the dagger and cut out your heart. I am the cause of this. I am why you are here.'

He looked down at his boots and shook his head. 'No. The castle drew me. Once I entered the walls, it made my purpose known.'

'And what is your purpose, Watborn?'

The birdcatcher silently withdrew, taking his leave and locking the door firmly behind him.

127

A Leap into Glory

The armies of the Alliance, especially the over-excitable fringe-dwelling ones, did not take the news of peace very well. The Fraternity of the Green Corpse and the assassins of the Devil's Tongue felt marginalized and angry, but they usually did.

It was all very fine to talk of laying down arms and uniting in brotherly love, but how were they going to divide the spoils? The F'Arcys had done more than their fair share of ransacking silver plate and the Sheathwing were selling stolen horses. Nor could the appointed peacekeepers be trusted. As money, food and weapons changed hands, new fights broke out each day. Huge amounts of food vanished every night. Two soldiers from the Devil's Tongue started carrying out surprised sheep under cover of darkness.

New laws were set. A treaty was drawn up that divided everything and satisfied no one. The invasion may have ended but isolated factions were still battling each other with sword and fire.

King Scarabold was forced to dress himself. Ratchet had been blown to smithereens while washing the royal underwear, not that anyone had noticed until part of him turned up in a laundry basket.

It took the Great Wound the best part of an hour to get the breastplate and chainmail on, and then he could not reach the leather fastenings at the back. Every bone in him ached. He had grown old and stiff without noticing.

He caught sight of himself in the dressing mirror. Dress armour was intended for pageantry, not warfare, but he needed to be remembered in his finery. He hoped the minstrels would be singing about his final moments a thousand years from now, but rather doubted it.

He entertained the idea of wielding a broadsword, but they were buggers to lift. He eventually decided on a medium-sized labrys with a wickedly sharp edge. Carrying it down to the barbican took for ever because he could barely walk. There were pains in his hips, his thighs, his swollen ankles. He had been hoping to create a fine tableau for posterity but feared the overall effect might be one of absurdity. The chainmail functioned like a corset and prevented him from bending. It chafed and pinched.

As he clumped among the warring factions he was surprised how many different types there were. Absurd young men with funny accents dressed in wicker armour with strange hats, a group of men younger than him dressed in laurels and red togas moaning about the good old days, some woad-painted wild-haired women with leather breastplates complaining about men, some mad-looking fellows with bright-green faces and blue tongues, all prepared to attack each other for no reason. He did not recognize such people as true warriors.

Warfare wasn't what it once was.

It took him a while to locate the angriest knot of fighters; they were wearing the purple-and-gold insignia of Cadeaux Étranges. Clambering effortfully on to a small section of wall, he wondered if his ancestors were watching. He rather hoped not. It would have made a grander sight to ride into battle but he had no idea where his prized charger had gone. Eaten, probably.

He stared down into the brawling, bloodied tumult of bodies. These days men just rushed each other on open ground. Outcomes were impossible to predict, soldiers impossible to control. If he gave them broadswords they fought too slowly. Their weapons were so heavy to lift and swing that they might have been walloping one another with lengths of iron pipe. The most common injury among the infantrymen was shoulder dislocation.

Grand-Marshal Timmorian had settled on a combination of long-swords, halberds and short daggers, and look at his men now – broken into small groups and cut off, hacking at their own side.

King Scarabold's world was laid before him. He felt as tired as death. What was life if not one long fight to the finish?

Blood follows blood, he thought. *I cannot keep my grip on the crown by murdering all the claimants*. The irony of those murders being lately committed by his children had not passed him by. *We must never be conquered,* he thought, *but there must be a better way to rule.*

The Great Wound did not really care whether history thought kindly on him or if it erased him from the books. Not for him the slow fading of humours on a goose-feather bed surrounded by wailing relatives. He had been born into strife and would leave the same way.

He threw off his eye-patch, half expecting to see more.

The men stood silently watching him, awed.

Bracing himself on the wall and trying not to fall off, he looked down on the warring sects and slowly, painfully raised the labrys to his left shoulder.

He knew this was the end; he had a short reach and no speed. He was also a very large target. He thought his final words should have some profundity, something for the history books to latch on to. The battle-cry he shouted before he leaped was something he remembered from his childhood. Its language is forgotten now but it translates roughly as, 'All right, which of you bastards wants some?'

It turned out they all did. There was prestige to be had in bringing down a king.

> The stomach tenses.
> The muscles flex.
> The tongue tastes bitter.
> The sinews curl.
> The heart pushes.
> Blood rushes.
> Breath shortens.
> The moment of no return arrives.
> Every life comes to this.
> A step into oblivion.
> It is terrifying.
> It is wonderful.

As the Great Wound dropped upon his enemies and they in turn fell upon him with a roar, he flung an echoing bellow into the sky and was consumed in flesh and metal.

A painting made much, much later by a fey, inferior artist of the Drawing Room School showed the Great Wound in red-and-silver armour sprawling upon the shocked enemy troops, speared with bristling lances like some exotic jungle beast fallen foul of hunters. There is such fury in his terrible visage that those beneath him are quaking with fear even as they run him through. The colours are dazzling, azure and scarlet and emerald, the setting sunlight like fire on the sword blades.

It was precisely how King Archim Scarabold III wanted to be remembered. After the canvas was unveiled it was hung in the council chambers, only to fall from fashion and be stored in a broom cupboard, where it was destroyed by fire four years later. Thus was Scarabold's reign expunged from history.

But those who had been there remembered him for ever.

128

The Lighting of the Way

'You again. Always you.'

She studied the figure standing before her, limned in vermilion light. He was once more dressed in the green wool and brown leather boots of a village birdcatcher. He seemed to ration his movements and words, as if he could not afford to waste them.

'My lady.'

'You are everywhere, Artur Watborn, yet nobody quite knows who you are. You make no sound. You're always at the edge, always around the corner, always where something is about to happen. Why is that, do you suppose?'

Watborn gave a shrug. 'Your safety is entrusted to me.'

He removed the royal warrant from his jerkin and handed it to her.

'My father.' Giniva's hand touched her mouth as she read.

'He spoke only of you.'

Now that the soldiers had all drifted away, there was only the sound of nightingales and dunnocks in the linden branches, and the sluggish lopsided rhythm of the broken water-wheel far below.

She folded the paper as carefully as if she were handling a baby plover.

They stood between the paws of the great rampant stone lion, on the grey battlements beyond the rooftop parade ground. Down in the courtyard the residents were clearing charred debris and dragging stones on to wooden trolleys. Men swore, women carried, babies cried. The population worked without complaint, ceaselessly, as if taking whispered instructions from the great lion itself.

The Alliance had gratefully withdrawn, taking their dead with them like wasps leaving a nest. They had washed the gore from their clothes and were heading south-west, still fighting among themselves about the building of the new coastal route. Around them swarmed merchants, eagerly selling souvenirs from the war: pennants, arrows, bits of wall, keepsakes, teeth.

'My dreams of escape have amounted to nothing,' said Giniva. 'I am once more bounded in a walnut-shell.'

Watborn turned to hold her gaze. 'Those who would have stopped you are gone. You're free to do as you please.'

She turned away from the wide horizon. 'I have to bury my father and tend to my brother. I have lost so much since the last moon that I scarcely know how to go on.'

'But you will.'

'There are so many more changes to be made. I have a lot of work ahead of me.'

'You are not alone, my lady.' He coughed discreetly. 'There are many of us now. The building of the hospital is already half complete.'

She placed her palms on the stone paw and felt the warmth of the late-autumn sun. 'There will be those who secretly work against any change I make. Mater Moribund will not take kindly to being told what to do. You cannot unpick centuries of history and restitch it into your own pattern so easily.'

'My lady, you are young.'

'You are not so very old, Watborn.'

'Time is not on the side of working men.'

'Yet I think I will know you for a very long time. Calmora told me so.'

'I wouldn't take her too seriously.'

She closed her eyes and drew in the deepest breath. When she opened them again, she studied him afresh.

'Well, Artur Watborn, we must transform ourselves. We cannot be called Londinium any longer. If we are to advance, the past must be entirely lost to history. I shall bury Dwinoline's tapestry deep inside the earth.'

Watborn snapped off a small sycamore branch that had pushed its way from beneath the lion's back paw and scratched an inscription in the dirt.

NO-LAND.

He scrubbed at the letters and rearranged them.

LON-DAN.

He changed the 'A' to an 'O'.

LONDON.

Tilting his head on one side, he tried it on his tongue. The Princess studied it too.

'Leperdandy read in the magister's books that we were once called Lud-din and Lun-dom,' she said. 'No one could ever decide which was right. Now we have much more to name. Did you know that many of our people came from places across the channel of water? Fresh arrivals from old and new worlds, with strange speech and disgusting habits. Within a year they became just like us.'

'I'm sure there are many who will help, my lady. I have to find a man named Herne. He did me a great kindness.'

Giniva stretched, standing straight-backed and alert, her hands pressing at the tops of her hips. She looked out across the blasted turrets, her long pale neck extended, her face somehow thinner and stronger, so that he could see the woman emerging from within the girl. The misted wind lifted the ends of her hair, and a thin shaft of sunlight touched the chained heart at her neck.

There is a colourful painting by a Pre-Raphaelite artist of minor renown that shows Artur and Giniva side by side beneath the great stone lion, fighting off the invading barbarian hordes. This heraldic moment never occurred, of course, but it makes an attractive tableau, and the stitching on their clothes is very finely delineated even though the entire scene is wildly romantic and hopelessly inaccurate. It has a title, a fine piece of doggerel indeed:

Naught shall make us rue if England
to itself do rest but true.

Watborn stood beside the stone paw and breathed deep. He could smell fresh-cut hay and wheat, lavender seeds, rosemary and sweating horses.

Giniva looked as if she had finally found her purpose.

Something dug into his side. He was leaning against a broken piece of the lion's golden crown. He pushed at the gilded band with the toe of his leather birdcatcher's boot and wondered if the segment could be made into a sword. The gold was too soft to be honed. Besides, there were plenty of fine weapons belonging to fallen soldiers at the bottom of the moat that could be

raised and restored to glory. Everything could be made into something else.

He stepped forward beside her.

'So, we are to be together,' she said without turning.

He did not answer at first. Finally: 'It seems so.'

'My first kiss was in a moat.'

'If you will allow, our next one will be better.'

She turned and was about to embrace him when there was a
splintering of wood and a yowl as a gatepost landed on a cat. The
Squeam shoved his way out of the damaged roof entrance. He had
a large soiled bandage wrapped around his head like a bloody turban.

'You sent for me, my lady? I'm very busy. There's a bear wandering about the grounds eating people.'

The Squeam had never before been summoned by the King's
daughter, but with Scarabold gone to glory and Moribund taken to
her bedchamber with melancholia, this gossamer-girl was now in
charge. He rose to attention as much as his question-mark spine
would allow.

'I want you to light the castle,' said Giniva. 'Place a lanthorn in
each window and on every battlement, and where the stones have
tumbled down, raise poles to the height of the original walls. Place
a light atop each one so that its shape is once more restored, and
people can see how it will look again.'

'I'll have to use fish-oil for the lamps,' the Squeam complained.
'We ent got any else, but fish-oil stinks, if you don't mind that.'

'Use what you have. We must light the gates and bridges bright
as day, put lamps in the walkways and windows and arches for all
to see. The people know how much work there is to do and they
need a common purpose. Before, they looked to the King. Now,
they must look to us, and this will be a castle no more but a city,
which is to be called the City of London.'

'Oh, I like that,' said the Squeam.

'Can you carry out this task for me?'

'It will be my greatest joy to deliver your desires, my lady.' The
Squeam bowed gravely and complained beneath his breath as he
limped away.

The milk-white sky had died to frayed crimson. The marsh-fog
had lifted for once, revealing an undulating patchwork of green
and brown fields, each one pinned at the corner with a single dwell-
ing. From within the walls of each pulsed the red glow of a hearth.

Small lands, small homes, short lives, a hundred thousand tiny kingdoms bounded by hedgerows.

At the centre of these lands, accumulated in the coils of the river's tail, stood a square mile of stone holding the City of London. Rent asunder now and part demolished, it would defy destruction, raising blasphemous fingers to the dark heavens as if to say, *You cannot destroy me, for all is within that life demands.*

And what of the future? The seer made predictions but almost all of them were wrong or, at the very least, incredibly offensive.

It was expected that Mater Moribund would find the role in black-mantled widowhood that she had been born to play, but she surprised everyone by wasting away from a surfeit of grief, thus revealing her humanity for the first and only time. Of course, it was discovered later that she was still alive, which caused complications.

Dwinoline's work was buried. In threads of gold and purple, amber and olive, the stitched panels unfurled to a length of thirty-seven feet. Kept from water and weevils, its delicate needlepoint survived intact. It is still there, undamaged and unfaded, lying underneath the pavement near Cripplegate, waiting to be found. The tapestry might have proved more important than the Lindisfarne Gospels or the Westminster Abbey Bestiary.

Some written histories from the Rotunda Library were saved, but the scrolls had rotted in places. Worse, the formal language used for the accounts was lost, so that translators trying to uncover their morphology were only able to decipher scraps. *Bá cálendas* – the beginning; *ætforanweallas* – outer walls of a house; *burgstede* – a house; *æðelu* – a noble family. The syntax was corrupted and inconsistent.

In an effort to decipher the early history of London, lexicographers tried a substitute vocabulary. It was little more than guesswork. A word they might have taken to mean a large wolf or snake could be translated as 'creature of ancient extraction' or even 'animal before man'.

Some of what was described in the undamaged pages seemed out of their time, but who knew what the Italians might have left behind? One passage spoke of the settlement's last remaining residents living in the ruins of Roman houses until they were driven out by ghosts. Another went on about underfloor heating. Had the occupiers adjusted to the miserable weather and stayed longer, who knew what they might have builded here?

One era does not simply stop so that another can start. They overlap and blur even when they are opposed. The past soon became unreadable. No one could remember what had been lost from London's earliest days.

We are told that seven centuries before these events, the wolf-lord Bladud was the first monarch to die in an aviation accident when his wings came off somewhere over the settlement of London. Nor was there any proof that Scarabold's ancestor, Pendragon, might have led the country against Saxon invaders. He was the summation of every noble trait embodied in the idea of an English warrior-king. In short, the hero of a fairy tale.

The history of London was a crystal showing colourful versions of many different truths, depending on the light. In the ancient mind there was little difference between fact and fancy, so how could any transcription be trusted? Without the tapestry, all written records proved useless. Four hundred years of history retreated into permanent night.

But in the present day, one treasure was drawn quite by chance from the London soil, although no expert ever associated it with the myths in the scrolls.

The mackerel-skin packet lifted from beneath the site of old Cripplegate contained two small relics.

The first was a finely wrought golden heart with a pair of slender chains crossed over it.

The second was a right foot. No ordinary foot but one of elaborately jointed tin, with iridescent toenails made from mother-of-pearl.

If you believe in the voice of the past, it will show you its face.

The workmen who uncovered the gold heart and the tin foot missed Dwinoline's tapestry by a distance of . . . a foot. It had been preserved because it was wedged under a great slab of slate. If only it had been uncovered, its final image would have proved illuminating.

It showed a slender young woman, her blonde braids sewn with violet clematis petals, her hopeful green eyes looking towards the sky and the sun's rising fire. She is standing beside an unidentified man with a bow. Behind them rises a magnificent city, no longer a castle but a dazzling agglomeration of colour and light.

The Princess looked out at the Hesperian fields and hedgerows.

Watborn tried to see what she saw. He looked up into the dark above his head; the stars were tirelessly spinning above him, and a comet fell, brief fire arcing. He imagined a city in ghostly form, sparkling with lights in the velvet night sky. The contours of the newly restored capital would be marked by lanthorns, but why should it not rise still further into the sky, with impossible buildings reaching up to the heavens? There was no limit to what they might achieve.

They remained like this, lost in their separate thoughts as the sun sank, Artur and Giniva, caught at a golden moment in time. Watborn felt the warmth of her arm against his.

Giniva had inherited her father's sense of occasion. She needed to mark the day of renaming. Raising her head, she spoke loud and clear. Her voice carried far on the cool evening air, so that she was heard by rabbits in the ragged meadows beyond.

'We shall be called a castle keep no more,
But raise a city here for all to see
And wonder at its mighty skill to thrive.
For overcoming first their ancestry,
Were guided to this spot our family,
Who lost their way until once more the stars
Shone forth to shape their purpose to an end,
And should we ever waver in our cause
May find these lights to bring us home again.
As all misfortunes of their days are shorn,
The gilded phoenix London is now born.'

Many years later, Watborn asked her why she had spoken out on that cool violet night, after so much had been lost and so many had suffered.

Giniva told him she had been calling to the people of London, who were no longer hers to command but who held the first place in her heart, for they were her duty.

And he loved her all the more for that.

ભ FINIS ભ

Christopher Fowler was the much-loved author of almost fifty novels and short-story collections, including *Roofworld*, *Spanky*, *The Sand Men*, *Hot Water* and, of course, the celebrated Bryant and May mysteries. He also wrote three acclaimed memoirs – *Paperboy*, *Film Freak* and *Word Monkey* – while his other non-fiction includes *The Book of Forgotten Authors* and *Peculiar London*, Bryant and May's singular and typically eccentric guide to the city. *The Foot on the Crown* – completed just before he died – is his last novel.

The winner of multiple awards, including the Green Carnation Prize, the Last Laugh Award and the Crime Writers Dagger in the Library for his body of work, Chris died in March 2023.